Leaving THE Land

Leaving
THE Land

JOHN L.
MOORE

A JAN DENNIS BOOK

THOMAS NELSON PUBLISHERS
Nashville • Atlanta • London • Vancouver

DEDICATION

To Gary and Wayne,
Wayward minstrels, chariots of fire.
Come home, prodigals, come home.

ACKNOWLEDGMENTS

Sincere thanks to Frank Maguire, Cathy Bastian, Tom and Nan Haygood, and my wife, Debra, for reading and commenting on this manuscript. Thanks also to Mary Lou Wall and Austin Lewis for their limitless generosity.

Published in Nashville, Tennessee, by Jan Dennis Books, an imprint of Thomas Nelson, Inc., Publishers, and distributed in Canada by Word Communications, Ltd., Richmond, British Columbia.

Scripture quotations are from the NEW KING JAMES VERSION of the Bible, Copyright © 1979, 1980, 1982, 1990 Thomas Nelson, Inc., Publishers.

Lyrics from the song "'Til The Circle is Through', by Ian Tyson, © 1993, as they appear on page's 73-74 are used with permission from Slickfork Music—SOCAN.

Library of Congress Cataloging-in-Publication Data

Moore, John L.
    Leaving the land : a novel / John L. Moore.
        p. cm.
    "A Jan Dennis book."
    ISBN 0-7852-8288-2
    I. Title.
PS3563.06214L4   1995
813'.54—dc20   94-46921
                                                        CIP

Printed in the United States of America
2 3 4 5 6 — 00 99 98 97 96

In spite of their friendship they were so far apart, the bowstring so taut between them; a seeing man and a blind man, they walked side by side; the blind man's unawareness of his own blindness was a consolation only to himself.

Narcissus and Goldmund
Herman Hesse

CHAPTER ONE

1972

For miles and miles and miles there was nothing but the sand, sagebrush, and the distant mountains of the northern Nevada desert. Intersecting the vastness was a narrow two-lane blacktop highway. At a wide spot in the road sat a ramshackle bar with a set of aged gas pumps, an attached post office and living quarters. Across the road from the buildings, Ezra Riley sat on his well-traveled aluminum-framed Coleman backpack watching the last rays of sunset reflect orange and crimson in the oil-black windows of the bar. As if on cue, the moment the sun slipped beneath the horizon the neon bar light flashed on spelling *Gambling and Spirits* in red and white.

The bar did not tempt Ezra and he was not concerned about a night in the desert. Darkness and wildness were home to him. His only worry were three cowboys whose '64 Ford pickup sat in front of the bar. Ezra's eleven months on the road had taught him that a hippie in the West was second to field mice at the bottom of the food chain.

The Ford had arrived two hours earlier with the cowboys pointing and laughing as they spilled out. One had yelled something at Ezra. They wore big floppy black hats, white shirts with leather vests, and pants tucked into cowboy boots. Ezra guessed they were too young to drink legally. He ran a hand down his shoulder-length hair and stared at his hightop moccasins. Suddenly he wanted very bad to be out of Nevada, or at least away from this location. He stared west. Walking the highway would do little good. If the cowboys were bent on mischief they would pursue him, baying at the moon like hounds, enjoying the hunt as much as the capture. Another part of him, honed to hardness by three months of rigorous training in the mountains to the north, wished to be found, desired to test his new skills. His dual natures, passive and aggressive, sparred for supremacy. It was better to avoid trouble, he decided finally, and was preparing to find a hiding place for the night when he heard a noise behind him.

He turned to see an old car emerging from the eastern dusk as humped and slow as a desert tortoise. It was an ancient sedan with bashed-in fenders, a cracked windshield, and an old man with a dirty gray beard behind the wheel. It stopped with its rusted nose pointed north on a gravel road. A shadowed figure moved from the passenger seat and Ezra heard a cheerful good-bye acknowledged by a following grunt. The door opened and a person got out. The car rattled away. It was another hitch-hiker. He stood assessing the situation like a young prince surveying a country claimed in his name. He saw Ezra and called out to him happily: "Hey, brother, what's happenin'?"

"Not much," Ezra said. He had mixed feelings about the stranger's arrival. Another hiker made rides harder to get, but the odds were now one better if the cowboys started a fight. But the newcomer did not look like a fighter. His denim pants were decorated with loud-colored patches neatly sewn as if by a mother or girlfriend, and his brightly dyed tee shirt was crisp and clean. A twelve-string guitar was slung over his back, the strap passing under black hair shorter than Ezra's but so curly it jumped from his head like millions of little springs. He had sideburns and a wispy Fu Manchu mustache. He was Ezra's size, perhaps shorter, and about the same age: nineteen or twenty. His backpack and sleeping bag were new. He crossed the highway and offered Ezra his hand with the bent-fingered shake of the counterculture. "My name's Walker," he said.

"Ezra."

"Whoa. No jive, man? Ezra, really?" He had the large brown eyes and long lashes of a cocker spaniel puppy. A pampered spaniel. Ezra had the lean, haunted look of a coyote on the run. "Ezra? For real?" he said laughingly.

"Yes," Ezra said with a knife-edge to his voice. His name had brought endless ridicule from his bachelor uncles but he was not about to take the same from a hippie-wannabe.

"Wow. That's heavy," Walker said. "Heavy duty Bible name. I've never met an Ezra before. That's righteous, dude."

Not only was he not a fighter, Ezra decided, but he seemed in need of a babysitter.

"Got any dope?" Walker asked hopefully.

Ezra didn't answer. He was a road veteran who had escaped several busts by exercising caution.

Walker saw Ezra's suspicious stare. "Whoa, man. It's cool. I'm no narc," he said, offended that such an idea would even be considered.

Ezra shook his head. "I'm not carrying," he said.

"How about a beer then?" Walker asked, nodding at the bar. "I'll buy ya a cold beer."

"I don't drink beer."

"That's cool," the newcomer said. "Do you drink wine?"

"I drink wine."

"I'll go over to that bar and get us a bottle," Walker offered.

Ezra was deliberately cool. He sensed the stranger was latching on, wanting a traveling partner. Ezra did not want the responsibility. "I wouldn't go in the bar," he warned.

"Why not?" Walker asked with an innocence so pure it bordered on arrogance.

"There's three young cowboys drinking in there, and they are looking for trouble."

"Well," Walker laughed, "they will have to look somewhere else."

"They already are," Ezra said. He nodded toward the bar.

The three cowboys staggered from the bar with six packs and whiskey bottles in each hand. They piled into the pickup, the headlights popped on, and the driver spurred the Ford to life. It roared from the bar in a spray of gravel and braked to a jolting stop beside the hitchhikers.

"Whoa, you goat-ropers," Walker said. "Slow your beast down."

"What's it to you, you hippie-faggot?" the closest one asked. He was lean and tanned with a lump of tobacco in his lip. The small one in the middle was almost invisible under his hat. The largest and drunkest one was driving. None of them could shave regularly. Ezra guessed them to be high school seniors.

"Got an extra beer?" Walker asked.

"I'll give you a beer shampoo," the big one said. The others laughed and watched Walker for a reaction.

"No, just a regular beer would be fine," Walker said innocently.

Ezra prepared for war. The little one was of no concern. Walker could handle him.

Warfare was not on Walker's mind. He stepped up to the truck and rested his folded arms on the windowsill. He was face-to-face with the lean cowboy. "So, what's the reason for the party?" he smiled.

"We just joined the marines," the lean one drawled.

Walker raised his eyebrows. "Oh, I'm impressed. Real killers, huh?"

"We volunteered for Nam," the small one chirped.

"And we don't like longhaired hippie-types," the big one said. "I think we ought to give you guys a haircut."

"Oh, I wouldn't do that," Walker said.

"Who's gonna stop us, you hippie-faggots?" said the lean one.

Ezra took a deep, slow breath, widened his stance and bent his hands into karate fists. He stood about six feet behind Walker. He would use him for a shield if he had to.

"Well, I don't suppose there is anyone to stop you," Walker said.

"But it just isn't a good idea." He nodded toward Ezra. "You know who that is?" he asked.

They shook their heads.

"Ever hear of David Cassidy?"

"David who?" the lean one asked.

"David Cassidy. You know, from 'The Partridge Family.'"

"I don't watch TV much," the lean one said, spitting tobacco down on Walker's canvas tennis shoes. The big one grunted in agreement.

"I do," said the little one.

"Then you know who that guy is, don't you?" Walker said. Ezra took a step back into the darkness.

"It does look like him," the little one said.

"Who cares?" said the lean one. "Let's cut their hair anyway."

"I'll tell you who cares," Walker said. "He's under contract with a big studio. You know who owns those big studios, don't you?"

"Who?" the lean one asked mockingly.

Walker eased closer to the truck. "The Mob," he whispered.

"The Mob!" said the small one. Nevada boys knew about the Mob.

"That's right," Walker said softly. "But don't go spreading it around."

"Ah, this is bull," the lean one said. "He ain't no TV star."

Walker stepped back and waved toward Ezra. "Then go ahead, cut his hair. Take your chances. You'll soon be in Nam anyway."

"If he's this David Cassidy fellow, what's he doing out here in the middle of nowhere anyways?" the lean one asked.

"Man, you don't know what it's like being a star," Walker said. Confidence rose in his voice. He had control of the story. "He's surrounded by fans constantly. It drives David nuts. Every once in a while he just has to sneak off and pretend he's someone else. I tag along to keep an eye on him. He even tried to ditch me in Salt Lake City but I caught up."

"Prove he's Cassidy," said the lean one. "Have him play us a song."

"Tell you what," Walker said. "David has to save his voice. It's so sore now he can hardly talk. I'm just his equipment manager. He sings much better than I do, but I'll give you a little taste and you judge for yourselves." He picked his guitar up. "What do you guys want to hear?"

"Merle Haggard," the big one muttered.

"I don't know any country western," Walker said. "Except for a little Kristofferson." He pulled a harmonica from his pocket and played the chorus of "Me and Bobby McGee." Then he pocketed the mouthharp and finished the song with his guitar, singing a clear but soulful alto.

The power and clarity of Walker's skill drew Ezra forward into the headlights to better hear and see him.

"Gosh, he's good," the little one said. "I know I've seen him on that TV show before."

"I've been on the show, but I'm an amateur compared to David. Like I said, I'm only his equipment manager."

Ezra eased back into the darkness. A star should act reclusive, snobbish.

"Where you guys headed?" the driver asked.

"Back to L.A.," Walker said. "The studio bosses have a couple of goons out looking for us. You guys haven't seen a couple of characters that look like hit men?"

"Yeah, I did," said the small one. "We passed them on the highway coming here." Walker had captured the three within the story, and they were now capable of creating their own characters.

Walker shook his head. "We have to get back to L.A. before they find us. Those boys have no sense of humor."

"Heck, we'll take ya," said the big one. "It's only forty miles. Go ahead and climb in the back."

Ezra gave Walker a cautious glance. Twice before cowboys had given him a ride only to dump him on a dusty country road in the middle of nowhere.

"Well, thanks guys," Walker said. "But that night air just wouldn't be good for David's voice. He might catch a bad cold back there."

"He can drive," said the big one. "And you can ride with us and play your guitar." He got out of the truck and began loading the backpacks. "Wait until I tell the girls that I let David Cassidy drive my pickup." He handed Walker and Ezra each a bottle of beer. Ezra took his reluctantly.

Ezra drove slowly through the cool May night serenaded by the muffled music of Bob Dylan, Kris Kristofferson, and Crosby, Stills, Nash, and Young. He had never met anyone like this stranger. He was devious, but absent of guile, and his confidence was contagious.

In the back of the pickup the cowboys shivered and switched to whiskey. Walker matched them drink for drink, but he sipped while they gulped. After thirty miles they demanded cowboy songs.

"I don't know any," Walker said. "But if you guys want to do the singing I can pick the melody."

The three began a raspy version of "Cool Water."

The cowboys sang in rough, drunken disharmony. Walker tapped on the back window. Ezra looked in the rearview mirror and saw the white flash of a smile and a silhouetted finger pointing at the singing cowboys. Ezra knew what Walker was thinking: *Their minds are mine,* he was saying. *I can make them do anything I want.*

The cowboys sang, Walker played, and Ezra drove all the way to Reno.

CHAPTER TWO

Outside Reno Ezra stopped on an exit ramp and pulled his backpack from the back of the truck. A neon forest of casinos cast an unearthly glow in the distance. The cowboys stared at him through a haze of alcohol.

Walker reached over and grabbed Ezra's arm. "What are you doing?" he asked. "Aren't we going into town, to a motel or something?" He was half-drunk and primed for action.

"I'm crashing by the side of the road," Ezra said and began walking down the dark highway embankment. Walker watched in surprise.

The lean cowboy climbed from the back of the truck, his face reddened from the cool night air. "We'll take ya to Reno," he said, putting his arm around Walker. "Let's go to Reno, Mr. Singer-man. We joined the marines today. We're going to Veee-ett-nom."

Walker looked up at a face flushed with youth and enthusiasm and lit by the glow of Reno's artificial light. The lean cowboy was America: proud, young, and spoiling for action. Walker saw a death in his eyes, a death the lean cowboy never imagined possible. He stepped out from the cowboy's arm and stared at the city. Reno offered everything Walker was pursuing: music, drink, drugs, and women. But his new friend, Ezra Riley, was stalking the dark and he offered something else, something mysterious. Walker stared at the retreating shadow of the hitchhiker hunting his den. Ezra was a veteran of the road. Walker knew he was someone to learn from. "You guys take care," Walker told the cowboys. "Stay alive, you hear?" Then he ran to catch up with Ezra Riley.

Ezra trudged on, feeling with his feet for an area free of rocks, cactus, and broken bottles. He could hear Walker hustling after him.

"Why we crashing here?" Walker asked.

"I travel on a dollar a day," Ezra said. "I can't afford motel rooms."

"A dollar a day! How do you eat?" Walker looked up at the Interstate thinking he might have made a mistake, but the Ford pickup was already weaving its way to Reno.

"How do I eat?" Ezra said. "Sparingly." He found a sandy area and rolled out his sleeping bag, took off his boots and jeans, and crawled in.

Walker stood quietly in the dark for a few moments. "I need to brush my teeth," he confessed.

"So brush 'em," Ezra said.

"What do I use for water?"

"Use your canteen."

"I don't have a canteen."

Ezra reached into his pack and threw his at the voice. He heard Walker catch it. "How long have you been on the road?" Ezra asked.

"Three days."

"I thought so. Where are you coming from?"

"Indiana. But I took a bus to Kansas City. I started hitchhiking there."

Ezra's suspicions were confirmed and his curiosity settled. The guy was interesting but he was a total rookie. His bravado had worked on the cowboys but the next time it might get them both killed.

"I'm going to San Francisco," Walker said. "I'm going to get into a band. How about you?"

"I'm just traveling," Ezra said. "Going no place in particular."

"Where are you from, man?" Walker spat out a stream of toothpaste suds then gargled with water and spit.

"Montana. The eastern part."

"Montana. Whoa, heavy-duty, man. Montana. I want to go to Montana someday. I was born in Florida but my folks travel a lot. I've lived in Nebraska, Kansas, Colorado, and Missouri. Small towns mostly. I've been going to school in Indiana. It kept me out of the draft. What's your lottery number, man?"

"Two-seventy-six," Ezra mumbled.

"Mine's four," Walker said. "Can you believe it? Four. I have always been lucky. I even get a high number in the draft lottery. But I ain't goin', man. No way."

"You better get some sleep if you think you're traveling with me," Ezra said. "I'll be on the highway at dawn." He lay quietly gazing at the stars that shone like a million diamonds in the clear desert air.

Walker was still standing, staring at the distant crimson glow of Reno. "You know, you really do look like David Cassidy," he said.

"I'm not particularly proud of that," Ezra said. "But I have to admit you kept us out of a fight."

"For the intelligent, fighting is a last resort." Walker fumbled in the dark with his sleeping bag. He cussed when the zipper stuck but managed to climb in. He swore again—his cursing was an experiment with vulgarities—when he realized the ground was hard and bumpy, then sighed as if expelling a deep thought. "Do you believe in fate?" he asked Ezra. "I think it's fate that we met," he said.

"Why is that?" Ezra asked.

"Because my first name is Jubal." Jubal was the first musician listed in the Bible. My middle name is Lee. Jubal Lee. Get it? Jubilee. That's another Bible name. So you see, I have two odd Bible names and out in the middle of nowhere I run into a fellow hitchhiker with an odd Bible name. Don't you think that's fate?"

"Karma, maybe," Ezra said. "Or coincidence. So what do people call you?"

"I like Jay. But then you have jaywalker, right? I get tired of the jokes. So, man, call me what you want," he said. "Call me hungry for good dope, fine wine, and hot women." He waited for Ezra to laugh. Ezra didn't.

There was a short silence, then Walker asked, "So, do you want to go to San Francisco with me?"

"No," Ezra said.

"How about if I go with you, then? Where are you going?"

"I don't know."

"Let's go to Frisco, man."

"What's your old man do for a living?" Ezra asked.

"He's a preacher," Walker admitted reluctantly.

"That's what I thought."

"How come? Why did you think I was a preacher's kid?"

"I don't know. Maybe because you are overly rebellious."

"Aw, man," Walker said. "That's how PKs are. We're all so repressed we're about to bust at the seams."

"So why are you on the road? What are you running from?" Ezra asked.

"Man, I ain't running *away* from anything. I am running *to* things. I want to taste some life."

"And that's a rock 'n roll band in San Francisco?" Ezra asked.

"You got it, baby. And where are you going?"

"I just drift," Ezra said. "The last few months I was helping build a martial arts monastery in the mountains north of here."

"Far out. Karate. I can dig that. So why did you leave?"

"The sensei was weird. He was just using his students for slave labor."

"Storm?"

"So you booked. I can dig it. So what do you do, man?"

" I do music. What do you do?"

"I write."

"I knew it!" Walker shouted. "I knew it! It's destiny. We are meant to be together. You write. I play. You gotta come to Frisco with me."

Ezra didn't answer for several minutes. He did not like commitments or big cities, but he wanted out of Nevada. "I'm going to sleep," he said, and as he drifted off he could hear Walker softly whistling to himself, happy as a rain-soaked frog.

The first sound he heard was terrifying. It seemed to drift in like a gale of wind and shook Ezra in his bag. It was a high-pitched, blood curdling scream, something like that of a child or a mountain lion, but it was neither of those. It was something he knew. Something close to his heart. It was a horse. The scream of a horse in pain. It lasted but an instant, then it was gone. Ezra had been shaken from his slumber and rolled to the edge of wakefulness, then left to drop, shaking, back to an exhausted sleep. The scream lingered hauntingly on the front porch of his memory.

Later, perhaps a few minutes, maybe an hour, Ezra was awakened again, this time by someone calling his name. He opened his eyes, remembered where he was and that he was not alone. He listened intently. Walker was snoring softly. He was childlike even in slumber. Ezra went back to sleep and moments later it happened again.

"Ezra."

He heard it plain and simple, and it rolled him gently from the depths leaving him awash on the edge of consciousness. Someone was calling him. It did not come from the darkness around him, but from somewhere deep within himself. He rolled on his side and could barely see the darkened outline of Walker huddled fetuslike in his bag. Walker had not called him. Not audibly. The voice had come from Ezra's own soul. That did not bother him. He was no stranger to the subconscious, to the terrain of dreams, visions, and visitations. He considered briefly that Walker was right. Their meeting was one of destiny. Fate. Karma. Then he put himself to a practiced sleep, riding deep breaths to relaxation.

But in his troubled depths, stored for future reference, the sound of Jay Walker calling his name became fingers that entwined in the mane of the screaming horse and the two sounds became one.

CHAPTER THREE

The rumble of diesel trucks awakened Ezra to a sun rising in a red haze. He rubbed his eyes and stared at a yellow cocoon—Walker huddled in his mummy sleeping bag. Ezra rose, pulled on his pants and boots, and splashed canteen water on his face. "Time to rise and shine," he said to the cocoon.

A head of dark, curly hair emerged through the yellow drawstring followed by a squinting face shadowed by three-day stubble. "Man, it's too early and too cold," Walker said. He sat up with the bag pulled to his neck and his knees drawn to his chest and rocked there until his eyes opened sufficiently to see Ezra shouldering his pack, then he jumped out of his bag and quickly began dressing. His body was slender with long muscles and thick dark hair on his chest and legs. Ezra had never felt attracted to boys or men. He loathed the idea of homosexuality. Yet, in that fleeting glimpse of his unclothed companion, there was a stirring within him that was not sexual, but artistic. From his curly hair and oversized eyes to the flowing lines of his limbs and torso, Walker was a model of physical excellence.

"You slept naked?" Ezra said. "Didn't you get cold?"

"I froze to death," Walker said.

"I sleep clothed," Ezra said. "You never know what might happen in the night."

"I hate clothes," Walker said. He dressed quickly and followed Ezra up the embankment. The morning was cool and clear with just a thin film of dusty haze on the horizon. Some of the passing trucks still had their lights on. Ezra stuck out his thumb.

"Man, what's for breakfast?" Walker asked.

"Don't you have any food?"

"Naw, man. That's what restaurants are for. They feed people."

"Look in the top left pocket of my pack," Ezra said. "You will find some granola bars."

Walker lifted Ezra's pack. "Whoa, man, what do you have in this thing? Rocks? What does it weigh anyhow?"

"Ninety pounds." Ezra stood facing traffic, his arm out and thumb hooking west.

"Books," Walker said, unzipping the top pocket. "Let's see what you got. *Siddartha, Narcissus and Goldmund, Demian, The Glass Bead Game.* Man, all these books are by the same guy. Who's Hermann Hesse?"

"A German writer."

"Heavy, man, heavy. And I mean real heavy. And you have note-books, and a camera. And more books. Ayn Rand, Lopsang Rampa, Alan Watts. Man, you got books by people I've never heard of."

Ezra stared at him incredulously. His travels had taken him thousands of miles, and he had stayed with countless young people in com-munes, farms, and apartments. Everyone was reading Hesse and Watts.

"Naw, man, it's true," Walker said. "I've never heard of these peo-ple."

"What were you reading in school?" Ezra asked.

"The Bible mostly," he said. "It was a Bible school. But I was a music major. I only took the required religion classes."

Ezra rolled his eyes. He had a Jesus Freak on his hands. A Jesus Freak who wanted to get stoned and play rock 'n roll.

"Don't bad-vibe me, man," Walker said. "I'm a drop-out, remem-ber? I went to school to please my father and avoid the draft, that's all."

"Read one of those books if you want," Ezra said.

"Which one?"

"*Narcissus and Goldmund.*"

"Far out." Walker pocketed the book. "So what do you write, man?"

"Poetry, mostly. Blank verse."

"Far out, man. That's our destiny. I knew it. I knew it was fate, man. You are going to write the lyrics, and I will set them to music and do the performing. Beautiful." He rubbed his hands and his eyes shone like little candles. "We're going to do great things, man."

Ezra could not help but be amused. It was nice to hear someone, any-one, be supportive and enthusiastic, even if it was Walker, whose naive curiosity reminded Ezra of a puppy playing in traffic. "I'm going to call you Jay," Ezra told him. "Because you are a jaywalker. You're lost in traffic."

"That's cool," Jay said. "I like that. I like the word *jay*, it's short for joint and I sure could use a hit of good dope." He began eating a third granola bar. "So, man, was the martial arts training tough?"

"We were taught how to inflict pain and how to endure pain."

"Bummer. I want to inflict pleasure and endure pleasure." Jay tossed the granola wrapper on the ground. Ezra picked it up, folded it neatly, and put it in his hind pocket.

"So, who's your idol?" Jay asked. "What writer do you want to be like?"

"Bob Dylan," Ezra said.

"That's cool. I like Dylan. What do you like about him?"

"His lyrics. He's America's greatest poet."

"Show me some of your stuff, man."

Ezra looked at him blankly.

"Your poetry, man. Show me some of your stuff."

Ezra reluctantly dug into his pack and brought out a worn notebook. He handed it to Walker.

Walker skimmed through several poems quickly then read several more slowly. Finally, he read a couple out loud to himself. He looked up at Ezra with a look of conviction and awe. "You are the real thing, man."

"Thanks," Ezra said. Ezra knew he was the real thing, but no one else had ever told him so.

Jay smiled and handed the notebook back. "Destiny. It's destiny, man," he said. He ran a plastic comb through his kinky hair. "And the next car is going to stop."

The next vehicle was a bright orange ten-year-old Volkswagen van with a bushy-haired, bearded driver and a big yellow Labrador. The brake lights flashed red after it had passed, then the back-up lights flashed white.

"Whoa, I told you so," Jay shouted. "Man, a freak, too. Righteous. He'll have some dope."

"Play it cool," Ezra warned him. "Longhairs aren't all mellow anymore."

The man was in his early thirties. He had a Harley-Davidson emblem tattooed on his left bicep. His eyes were dilated and red. "Where ya headed, brothers?" he asked.

"San Francisco," Jay said.

"Hop in," said the man. He slapped the big hound on the side. "Get in the back, Farley." Ezra and Jay loaded their backpacks and Jay climbed in the front and Ezra sat in the back with the dog. The man was an auto worker from Detroit moving to San Francisco to become a Scientologist. "I got some good weed," he said. "And I won't be needin' it anymore." He tossed it in Jay's lap. "Here man, it's all yours. You can keep it. Need papers?" He reached into his shirt pocket and brought out a handful of rolling papers. Zig-Zag, American Flag, licorice, and strawberry. "Take your choice, man."

Jay's eyes glistened like a child with an overflowing Christmas stocking. He turned in his seat, held up the baggie and papers, and flashed Ezra a bright smile. But Jay could not roll a joint. After ruining several papers and spilling much of the weed on his lap, he handed the baggie and papers back to Ezra. Ezra peeled off one Zig-Zag paper, licked it, and pressed it against another. He curled the paper, ground in a line of grass, then rolled a tight joint one-handed. He handed it up to Jay.

"Wow, righteous, man," Jay said. "One-handed. Where did you learn to roll joints like that?"

"By watching cowboys roll Bull Durham."

Jay lit the joint and inhaled deeply. His eyes widened then he coughed out a cloud of blue smoke. "Heavy, man," he said, and handed the joint to the driver. The driver puffed long and hard and handed the joint back to Ezra. Ezra took a light toke before returning it to Jay. Jay sucked in greedily.

"What's your names?" the driver asked. "You can call me Coon Dog."

"I'm The Jay Walker," Jay said, coughing out smoke. "And my partner is The Montana Kid."

Coon Dog reached under his seat and pulled out a package of Oreo cookies. They ate cookies, smoked dope, and listened to The Grateful Dead all the way to the Bay. They got lost several times because Jay let the map fly out the window and the trip took them all day. No one cared.

CHAPTER FOUR

They crossed the Oakland Bay Bridge, a steel spiderweb strung across deep blue waters, bordered by green bushy hills and a distant mountain range of concrete skyscrapers. Coon Dog drove slowly, gripped by drug-induced caution and the suddenness of an arrival that was all day in coming. Jay was wide-eyed with wonder. He had arrived in the Promised Land. Ezra was claustrophobic and sought solace in petting Farley who all but laid on him. Ezra hated big cities.

They wandered through narrow streets bustling with traffic, up and down steep hills, drifting with the flow of the city, waiting to be washed up to their destination as fateful as a bottle on a beach. But it did not happen. Coon Dog was lost.

"Man, I don't have a clue," he whispered as he found himself again on the freeway. He took the first exit he could reach and stopped at a service station. "You guys do what you have to do," he said. "I'm going to call the church and have someone come get me."

Ezra and Jay shook hands with Coon Dog, shouldered their packs, and started down the street. The neighborhood was like any small town with little brick buildings on a central street except for the winos lying passed out on the pavement, the doors and windows of stores secured by iron bars and behind them, the growlings of Dobermans and German shepherds. Jay smiled and nodded at the passing people who were all black.

"We're in a ghetto," Ezra said.

"Yeah, man," Jay said cheerfully. "Righteous, ain't it?"

In the center of a street a lanky man was bent under the hood of a television repair van, his sharp elbows sticking out like swords. He looked up as Ezra and Jay passed, then ran after them. "Boys," he yelled. "Boys."

Ezra and Jay stopped and turned around.

Beneath his bushy Afro the eyes were serious and intent. "Man, I don't know where you guys are from, but it's gonna get dark around here

in 'bout an hour and if you're still in this 'hood you are as good as dead."
He pointed to a freeway overpass rising above a railyard. "There's your
closest exit to get back downtown," he said. They thanked him word-
lessly and steered silently toward the freeway.

"Don't look anyone in the eye," Ezra warned. "Just put your head
down and walk."

"Man, my dad trained me to look people in the eye," Jay laughed.

"Mine did, too. And both our dads would be dead if they hung out
around here."

When darkness fell drivers turned on headlights and zipped by like
fireflies. Ezra kept his thumb out and watched nervously for signs of
trouble. Old black railroad hobos, wrinkled as raisins, walked by and
nodded a hello. Jay strummed his guitar and softly sang a Woody Guthrie
tune. He was unconcerned. Destiny was on his side.

With eyes trained in the badlands of Montana, Ezra detected a gang
of teenaged boys walking up the railroad tracks. Darkness was descending and there was nowhere to run. He was about to warn Jay when a small
foreign car screeched to a stop. They piled in. The driver said they were
crazy for being there and dropped them downtown on Market Street
where the heart of the city was quiet. A few late-working businesspeople
walked the streets to cars or hailed passing cabs. "We need to find a place
to crash," Ezra said. They turned down a sidestreet where the businesses
slowly gave way to narrow apartment buildings and weathered houses. A
big-bellied, bald-headed man in a dirty sleeveless tee shirt appeared in a
doorway. His thick, pasty arms were mottled by faded tattoos of anchors,
palm trees, and American eagles. He watched them with watery, hungry
eyes. "Where you boys from?" he asked.

"Montana and Indiana," Jay said.

"Well, Montana and Indiana," the man said. "Do you need a place
for the night?" Jay nodded. Ezra hesitated.

"Follow me," the big man said.

Ezra looked at Jay and shook his head. "I don't think so," he whispered.

"Ah, c'mon man, do you wanna sleep out on the street?" Jay said.

Ezra paused at the door but the man already had Jay in tow. "Be
quiet," the man warned. "My landlord frowns on overnight guests." He
led them up a dark narrow stairway to a faded blue door, its paint crack-
ing and falling to the floor in little flakes. He unlocked it and ushered
them into a small, crowded apartment. String-tied boxes were piled in
stacks that reached the ceiling in the apartment's one large room. A
couch, chair, and bed fought for the little remaining space. Off to the side
were a tiny bathroom and a kitchen with yellowing linoleum. A lone win-

dow looked down on the city, and curled up on the sill like a large cat was a lanky young man with neatly groomed hair and mustache. He glowered at them with feline eyes.

"My name is Lieutenant Patterson," the bald-headed man said. "And this is my roommate Sam. Sam's from South Dakota." Jay and Ezra said hello. Sam did not return the greeting. "This is Indiana and Montana," Lt. Patterson said. "They need a place to stay tonight."

Sam stood up, glared jealously at Ezra and Jay, then stretched his long frame. "I'm going to a party," he snarled as he pushed past them and out the door.

"Sam's moody," Lt. Patterson said. "Would you boys like something to drink? How about some wine?"

"That would be great," Jay said. He had already found a place for his backpack and guitar.

The lieutenant checked his refrigerator. "Sam drank it all," he said. "Well, why don't you boys come with me. There's a little store down the block. I'll get us some wine and cheese."

"I think I will stay here," Ezra said.

Jay laughed at him. "Come on, man, this is San Francisco. Let's go see some of the city."

The lieutenant gave Ezra an impatient, measuring stare, then smiled and rubbed Jay's shoulders. "Montana must be tired," he said. "You and I will go." Patterson's face was smug with pleasure. He had trapped fresh young meat, luscious young men glowing with youth. *Montana* was handsome in a dark, forbidding way, but *Indiana* was beautiful. In fact, *Indiana* was the most beautiful creature he had ever seen—he was like a god—and Patterson knew he could be reeled in easily if played correctly. Putting an arm around Jay's shoulders, he ushered him from the room.

The moment they were gone Ezra began inspecting the apartment. The ashtrays were filled with cigarette butts. Old issues of *The San Francisco Examiner* were piled in corners. A wooden plaque reading "Lt. Commander L. J. Patterson USN" hung on the wall above the mountains of boxes. Ezra reached for a box from the stacks, untied the string, removed the lid, and looked inside: magazines depicting men having sex with boys. He retied the string and carefully put the box back as he had found it.

Half an hour later the lieutenant and Jay returned with bottles of Spanada and Bali Hai.

"It's Saturday night and the town is poppin'," Patterson said. He poured wine into tall glasses for Jay and Ezra. He poured himself a smaller one, and said, "Drink and be merry, boys. The life of the road must be a hard one." Ezra took his glass and moved to the windowsill. Jay sat on the couch. The lieutenant sat beside him. "I have lots of movies," he said. "Would you boys care to watch a movie?"

"What do you have?" Jay asked.

The lieutenant smiled lustily through yellow teeth. "Illegal movies," he said. The hair rose on the back of Ezra's neck. He took his glass to the kitchen sink, poured the wine out and washed his mouth with water. When he came back Patterson was refilling Jay's glass. He had one hand on Jay's knee.

"Do you want to see a movie?" Patterson asked Jay.

"Might as well," Jay said. "It's too crowded in here to dance."

Patterson laughed heartily at Jay's little joke.

Ezra took a step toward Jay. Patterson glowered at him. Ezra met the eyes without emotion. "I think we should move on," Ezra told Jay. "There's not enough room in here for us."

"Oh, it's no problem," the Lieutenant said. "You can sleep on the couch, Montana, and Indiana can sleep with me. Sam won't be back. Not tonight."

"Hey, man," Jay said innocently. "I can sleep on the floor. It's no big deal."

"I wouldn't hear of it," Lt. Patterson said.

"Do those stairs we came up lead to a roof?" Ezra asked.

"Yeah, why?" Patterson asked suspiciously.

"I'm sleeping on the roof," Ezra said. "I am used to sleeping outside."

"Oh, that might not be safe," Patterson said.

Ezra grabbed his pack. "I'm used to the outdoors," he said. He looked at Jay to see if he was going to follow. Jay flashed an ivory smile, held up his glass, and swirled the amber fluid. "You should stay where the wine is," he said.

Ezra felt protective of his new friend, but the claustrophobia was choking him. He had to escape. Jay would learn the hard way, he decided. As he was closing the door he heard Jay say: "He's a cowboy, man. A real cowboy. He loves sleeping outside."

Pigeons cooed at him as Ezra rolled out his bag on the tarred roof between heater vents. The stars were not visible because of the streetlights below. Ezra wanted out of the city. He wanted to sleep but sleep came slowly, and when it finally came, it was light and troubled. In the middle of the night he awakened. He felt a presence coming toward him. He slowly reached into the hightops of his moccasins and grabbed an open pocketknife, then feigned sleep, but every muscle in his body was coiled for action. Someone nudged his foot. "Hey, man, wake up." It was Jay.

"What's going on?" Ezra asked. He sat up but kept the knife in his hand.

Jay sounded desperate. "Man, come on, we gotta get outta here."

Ezra scrambled to his feet, pulled on his boots and rolled his sleeping bag. "What happened?" he asked.

"That guy's a pervert," Jay said. "Come on. He might be after us." They snuck quietly down seven floors of steep, narrow steps.

"So what went down?" Ezra asked.

"I cut him, man," Jay said.

"You cut him?" Ezra said. "How bad? With what?"

"I didn't mean to. I hit him with my glass. The glass broke. There was blood everywhere." Jay was nearly running down the street.

"Hold up," Ezra said. "It's two in the morning. Where are we going to crash now?"

"I don't care if we walk all night," Jay said. "I want outta here." He walked quickly, his steps fueled with anger. His mind was troubled. After several blocks he began to talk. "When we went for the wine, I saw a really good looking chick and it made Patterson mad and he told her to buzz off. The girl yelled at him with a voice deeper than mine. It was a drag queen. Can you believe that?"

"Yeah, I can believe that," Ezra said. "I've been in Frisco before."

"You knew all along, didn't you? Why didn't you drag me out of there?"

"You're the one that wanted to enjoy the city."

Jay became quiet. He did not want to admit that Sundays in his father's church and a year in an Indiana Bible school had not prepared him for the world. In tight situations he was dependent on Ezra, and it made him uncomfortable. He wanted to be Ezra's equal.

For an hour they passed through quiet streets frequented only by an occasional car or pedestrian. They were both very tired when they approached a longhair sitting on the streetcurb. His stringy, tangled hair hung to his waist. He wore no shirt, only torn blue jeans, sandals, and beads. "Hey, man," Jay said. "Do you know where we can crash for the night?"

The junkie looked up with dull, glazed eyes and pointed with a thin arm to a tall dark building. "Basement," he said, then his head rolled down.

Ezra and Jay moved through shrubs to the back of the large building. A dim light radiated from the basement windows. They found a door in the back and descended to one large room lit by blacklights, psychedelic posters, and colored strobes. The air was thick with the smoke of incense, marijuana, and hashish, and the room was packed with people; many were sitting or lying on the floor. A naked woman covered with body paint danced slowly to the music of The Doors. No one paid Ezra and Jay any attention. Stepping over bodies, Ezra led the way to a back corner where he spied a few feet of floor space. He leaned his backpack against the wall, then reclined against it.

"Man, this is heavy," Jay whispered. "We've got everything in here. There's a guy over there shooting up."

"Play it real cool," Ezra warned him. "You would be best off getting some sleep."

"Man, this is like a county fair. The carnival is in town. Who can sleep, man?"

A pretty young girl with flowing brown hair and a paisley patterned granny dress walked by. She looked at Jay and smiled. "Keep an eye on my guitar, man," Jay said, and he rose and followed her.

The blacklights and strobing color lights broke everything into disjointed shapes and movements. People were visible, then gone in an instant. As Ezra's eyes adjusted, he inspected the surroundings. The younger freaks were passed out on the floor. A couple of grizzled older hippies were crumbling opium into a hash pipe. One young girl was exploring a man's face with her fingers. Occasionally he heard a laugh, but there was little noise except for the blaring music. Joints were lit and passed around. Then Ezra's wandering eyes fell on eyes staring back at him: an older biker with greasy black hair and beard sitting by himself. He wore a sleeveless Levi jacket showing arms covered with tattoos of snakes and goat heads. He radiated hatred and Ezra quickly looked away. When he snuck a glance back, the biker was staring somewhere else and a changing strobe light bathed him in an unearthly orange. A pearl-handled hunting knife was sheathed on his belt. The biker turned and stared into the light causing his eyes to glow red like the eyes of an animal caught in headlight beams. The light rotated away and the biker was coated with darkness. Ezra looked for Jay and discovered him in a huddle of bodies smoking from a water pipe. The girl with the long hair was leaning on his shoulder. Jay took a long toke from the pipe and turned and kissed the girl. They shared the smoke as he blew lightly into her mouth.

Ezra looked back at the biker. From the shape of the man's silhouette he appeared to be staring at Jay. Ezra took his knife from his pocket and kept it unopened in his fist. With his other hand he drug Jay's backpack and guitar over him, like blankets, then settled deeper onto his own pack to rest. The minutes crawled by. Ezra drifted to the edge of sleep. He thought about his hometown—his parents, his cowboy neighbors Austin and Cody Arbuckle—what a different world from theirs was he in now. He drifted to a light sleep and dreamed of open prairie, dust raising behind a trail herd, and cowboys shouting at cattle. He saw his father's face, strong, tanned, and lined with conviction. He saw the laughing face of Austin Arbuckle taunting the world, his blue eyes dancing with recklessness. Ezra stared deep into his face. Then he was shook awake. Instinctively, Ezra struck out.

Jay caught his arm. "Man, we gotta split," he said. His eyes were wide with fear.

"What now?" Ezra asked.

Jay looked about nervously. "There's demons, man. There's demons."

"What are you talking about?" Ezra pulled himself up and looked around the room. He had dozed for an hour and the mood of the party was now somber, the people asleep or drugged into a passive oblivion.

"I can see demons, man. I mean, I can *see* them. They are in people and around people. They take over people's faces and they laugh at me and mock me.

Ezra grabbed Jay by the shirt. "You're speed-rappin' man. What are you on? What did you take?"

Jay shook his head. "I dunno, man, but there are demons here. Everywhere. There's one that was near you. He was big and black. He talked to me and said his name was Death. When he moved away, I came over. We gotta leave, man. Quick."

"Okay, okay," Ezra said. "Grab your stuff."

"Man, that's where it is," Jay said. "There's the death demon," and he pointed at the biker who sat by himself in an opposite corner. He was awake and alert.

Ezra forced his arm down. "Don't point," he whispered. "Don't draw his attention."

"Man, he has the big black one, man. He has the death demon."

Ezra took Jay by the arm. "Follow me, try not to step on anyone." They moved through a minefield of bodies. Ezra stepped over the girl in the granny dress. She was asleep. The blacklights coated people's hair as if they were outlined by an electric current and the pulsating strobe lights alternately bathed the walls in colors of blue, orange, red, and yellow. As they stepped to the door a face suddenly appeared before them as if floating disembodied in the darkness. The greasy black hair hung in tangles around a callow, yellowed face. It was the biker, and he and Ezra were only inches apart.

Neither of them moved. Ezra could see nothing but the face. He could not see the man's body—he could not see his own body—but he felt the biker's posture as surely as if he were in his skin with him. There was something near Ezra's neck. He could not see it, either, and it was not touching him so he could not feel it, but he knew it was there. Jay bumped into Ezra's back, and he sensed Jay's panic as he looked over Ezra's shoulder into the face of a killer.

Something ill and ancient had arisen in the biker and controlled his eyes and instantly Ezra imagined a slashing of stainless steel erupting a geyser from his neck. He pushed the thought back to where it had come, from the eyes of the man in front of him. Willpower met willpower and for several endless seconds neither person wavered. Ezra prepared himself to die and the fearlessness that came over him weakened the biker's resolve. The biker moved one step to the side as if excusing himself. Ezra moved cautiously past him, ready for any sudden change in the man's intent. Jay followed, clinging to Ezra's shirttail.

They passed the man and ran upstairs to the backyard. A faint glow of dawn was rising on the city. Jay staggered to a bushy hedge, fell to his knees, and his twisted stomach tried vomiting his fear, but he could only manage the painful coughing of dry heaves.

Ezra watched the door, his backpack in one arm as a shield, his other hand formed into a karate fist, until Jay rose shakily to his feet.

"He had a knife on your throat, man," Jay said. "I could see it. The blade was yellow and purple and orange and he stuck it in your throat and the blood shot out onto the wall and wrote your name in letters . . . "

"You're trippin', man," Ezra said. "Let's get out of here." They ran down the street, past the curb where the junkie had been, into the great unknown of the neighborhood. Ezra moved at a quick jog, carrying both backpacks. Jay followed with his guitar.

"He's followin' us, man," Jay said. "The demon is followin' us. Satan wants to kill you, man. Satan wants to kill us both." Jay ran frantically through a hedge and down an alley until Ezra overtook him and grabbed him from the back. Jay continued to rattle words. "There's demons everywhere, man. You got one. He's going to try to kill you someday. But the biker's got the big one, man. He's the chief of demons, man."

Ezra was breathless from the run and his arms ached. He dropped the packs. "What did you take, Jay?" Ezra asked. "What was it?" He needed to know what he was dealing with.

"I dunno man, but it's heavy. Like, man, I didn't even know where I was or who I was for a while. The girl called it an odd name, like T. L. Green or something like that. Man, I'm ripped, man. I am really, really ripped." In his mind he saw himself as a small child in Sunday school with colored pictures of Jesus and the apostles on the walls, and the apostles were smiling at him and turning into wolves, bats, and spiders.

"You're tripping on acid," Ezra said. "Timothy Leary Green. Did you take a full hit, or did you split it with the girl?"

"We each took one," Jay said. He was now in the front row of his father's church, his mother was at the piano and his brothers and sisters sat beside him. The congregation had no faces. He looked at his brothers and sisters and they had no faces, he looked at his mother and father—

"Man, you're going to be tripping for a long time," Ezra said. "Another six or eight hours at least. And when you crash you are going to crash hard."

"Man, why does anyone take this stuff? It's gonna kill me, man."

"You'll be all right."

"What am I going to do, man? What am I going to do?" Jay sobbed. "It's Sunday. I should be in church. Man, we have to find a church. We have to go where the death demon can't get us. I gotta find a church, man."

"No," Ezra said. "You don't want to go to a strange church tripping on acid."

"I gotta get to church, man. It's Sunday. I have to go to church. My father wants me in church. It's the Last Days, man, and evil is being turned loose on the world." His speech was rapid and desperate, the words spitting out like bullets from a machine gun.

Ezra wanted to tell him that his father was not there, his father did not know Jay was tripping on LSD. But Ezra knew nothing could be explained to Jay while he was still peaking on the acid. He had to humor him until he came down. As dawn strayed golden fingers upon the streets of San Francisco, they walked in search of a church. Jay constantly looked over his shoulder for the stalking demon. He could not see him, but he could hear his footsteps.

CHAPTER FIVE

They were haunted pilgrims on a quest. A claustrophobic country boy and a stoned preacher's kid. Ezra felt cut off and surrounded. To the west was the Pacific Ocean, to the north and east was the bay, to the south miles and miles of city. He had no hills to escape to. Jay was on a psychedelic roller-coaster ride of terror. The streets heaved and breathed, rising to the sun then descending to the portals of hell where Jay could hear the anguished cries of souls reverberate through the grilled gates. Every passing automobile was an ogre of iron and steel that snarled, hissed, and showed its teeth. "My father's preparing his sermon," Jay said. "He's about to preach. My mother is sitting at the piano. I can hear the music, man."

"We'll find a church," Ezra said. Ezra was a veteran of bad trips. He knew the routes to sanity.

"Satan wants to kill you and me, man. We were born for the End Times. We have a destiny and he wants to kill us just like he wanted to kill the baby Jesus. We should be in my father's church, man."

"We will find a church," Ezra repeated. He spoke with the confidence of a wagon boss, of someone experienced at leading people through danger.

"Man, the trees are talkin' to me man, the trees are talkin'," Jay whispered softly; he did not want the trees to hear him. "The leaves are rustling with music. I don't think I'm ever gonna come down, man."

"Think good thoughts," Ezra said. "Feel the sun on your skin and look at the flowers in the gardens. You will come down before you know it."

Jay stopped and stared at a flower garden. He watched the flowers sprout, grow, bud, wither, then sprout again. Ezra took him by the arm and led him down the street. "Remember what you have been telling me. You have destiny on your side," Ezra said.

"Man, I broke the link," Jay said. "I broke the link to destiny. I'm afloat. I'm lost in the cosmos, man. I broke the chain, man, I broke the chain. I've sinned big time, man. How can I ever face my father? Find me a church, man. Find me a church."

It appeared on the end of a downhill street, lit by the sun breaking through vaporous clouds. It was white with a high steeple, surrounded by cars and a crowd of people filtering in. "There's your church," Ezra said.

"Oh, God, oh, God, thank you, God," Jay moaned.

They joined the flow of worshipers entering the lower level of the building, a basement beneath the sanctuary. The crowd was all colors and kinds of people: blacks with Afros, blacks with shaved heads, Orientals, Hispanics, white people in suits and dresses, white people looking homeless and lost, older white men with gray hair tied back in long ponytails, and Indian men in turbans. Even with their backpacks and Jay's guitar the two hitchhikers blended in and no one paid them any particular attention "Man, this is like roll call in heaven," Jay said. "All nations and tongues."

They went down a hallway wing looking for a safe place to stash their packs. They passed a series of offices, the door windows painted with the nature of the ministry: Gray Panthers of the Bay Area; Black Panther Party; United Farmworkers; Gay and Lesbian Alliance; Students for a Democratic Society; Young Communists League; Soldiers to Save Our Planet; Tarot, Palmistry, and Astrology; Man-Child Love Association; Witches and Warlocks of the Bay.

Jay dropped his pack and stood trembling in the hall. His wide eyes scanned the office doors. He heard guttural moanings resonate from deep within the cavernous hallway and the offices glowed with an unearthly light that smelled of sulfur. "Man, this place is death," he said. "The demons are here, man. The death demons. Just like the one that settled on the biker, man. Man, we gotta get outta here, man. This is hell, man. We are in hell." His paranoia had been ignited by panic. Above them the sanctuary began to shake with music and people began clapping their hands. Jay dropped to his knees, cowered, and trembled like a pup in a thunderstorm. "Oh, Jesus, forgive me," he pleaded. "Save me, Lord."

He jumped to his feet and ran down the hallway and out the door. Ezra grabbed Jay's backpack and followed. He found him a block away, hanging onto a telephone pole, sweat dripping from his face. "Oh, Jesus," he was crying. "Oh, Jesus, forgive me."

Ezra took him softly by the arm. "Follow me," he said and while carrying both packs, led Jay to a park and laid him down in the cool grass. "Just stare at the sky," he told him. "Watch the clouds until you come down."

"There are witches and demons, man," Jay said. "I'm in hell, man."

"What would your father do if he was here?" Ezra asked. He knew it was a long shot, and potentially a dangerous one, but he decided to evoke an image of authority in Jay's mind. It worked.

"I'm sorry, Daddy," Jay sobbed. "I'm sorry."

"What would he do?" Ezra insisted.

"He would call on the blood of Jesus," Jay cried.

"Then do it," Ezra demanded.

Jay prayed a long and mournful prayer, then afterward he lay motionless on his back for three hours, staring up until the swirling, speeding kaleidoscope of clouds slowed to pale cirrus-stratus. Ezra stayed close by like a watchdog. Joggers and Sunday strollers gave them a wide berth. One freak started to approach to panhandle food or money but the look in Ezra's eyes discouraged him. It was early afternoon when Jay finally sat up. "Man," he said. "That was heavy. Heavy as in terrible, man. What time is it? I sure am hungry, but my guts are twisted in knots."

"You will be able to eat in an hour or two," Ezra said.

"Man, you must have done a lot of tripping," Jay said. "Have you ever seen trips like this?"

"More than once," Ezra said.

"Man, I saw demons," Jay said. "I know I saw demons. Especially that one on the biker dude. That was one big black demon, man." He held his hand out and watched it shake. "Man, I need a cigarette. You got a cigarette?"

"No," Ezra said. "What you need is food and sleep."

"I can't sleep, man. I'm still too wired. My stomach is tied in knots. I feel like I've been up all night drinking Drano. What are we going to do now, man? Where are we going to crash?"

"We will have to find a hostel or something," Ezra said.

"I know a place," Jay said. "It's another trip, man. You might weird-out, but it's safe, man. We'll be safe there."

"What is it?" Ezra asked suspiciously.

"It's called Teen Dare, man. It's like a Christian reform center for drug users. Former addicts run it. One of them spoke at our church once. His name was Bob and he was from here."

"I don't know," Ezra said. He wanted nothing to do with Jesus Freaks.

"Man, it's safe. They will give us food and a place to sleep. But I need to come down a little more first. I can't walk in like this."

"I don't want anything to do with Christian cults," Ezra said.

"It's not a cult, man. It's just young people helping other young people."

"I don't want to be around Christians."

"So where do you want to be, man? Back in Patterson's apartment? Back in the drug den?"

Ezra thought for a minute. "Okay," he said. "We wait an hour for your mind to clear some more. Then if you want you can give them a call."

CHAPTER SIX

They walked fourteen blocks to the Teen Dare Mission, a large, white building on a busy hillside street. Jay knocked and a tall, prematurely bald young man answered. "Yes?" he said, regarding them suspiciously.

"Hi, Bob," Jay said, "I'm Jubal Walker and this is my friend, Ezra. I called you a little while ago. You spoke in my father's church in Kansas."

"Oh, yes," said the man. "Pastor Walker. And how is your father?"

"He's fine," Jay said with a forced cheerfulness.

The Teen Dare director ushered them into the living room. There were religious plaques and paints on the wall. A wall had been removed and a big kitchen with a large homemade table extended the living room. Between the table and a semicircle of well-worn sofas, a staircase led to a single upstairs room the size of a barracks. Ezra saw five or six young men reclining on beds and he could see only half the room.

"We had a rough night," Jay said, excusing their appearance. "We had to flee homosexuals and bikers . . ."

"Are you both Christians?" Bob asked.

Ezra bristled and challenged the question with a glare. The question was obviously meant for him. Jay interceded. "I am, of course," he said. "Ezra will be, but right now he is more of a pilgrim."

Bob shook his head. "That presents a problem." He frowned thoughtfully and furrowed wrinkles rippled up his forehead before meeting the placid baldness of his skull.

"Man, we've got no place else to go," Jay said.

"Well, neither of you use drugs, do you?" His stare was as bright as a spotlight.

Jay lied and shook his head.

"I guess it's okay for a night or two," Bob said. "I know I don't sound very Christian but we have ten desperate young men upstairs, each one of them born again after years of drug use. We have to be careful for them. It just so happens there are two empty beds upstairs, so perhaps this is all in the Lord's plan after all."

"I would just as soon sleep outside," Ezra said.

"No, we can't allow that. You two will have to sleep upstairs but you will be on your own. You won't have to follow the program, except for meals."

"The program?" Ezra asked.

"Each young man upstairs rises to pray for an hour every night. So there is someone praying continually from eight P.M. until six A.M. Then there is group Bible study for two hours in the morning followed by an hour of discussion. Right now they are resting and meditating on the afternoon Bible study which ended an hour ago. I will now take them to a church gym for an hour of recreation and exercise. This will be a good time for the two of you to get settled, take showers, and rest up. Dinner is at seven, followed by an hour of group encounter."

Ezra gave Jay a doubtful stare. He would rather have stayed in the drug den and taken his chances.

"Man, it sounds great," Jay said. "We've been in a black ghetto and in some strange occultic church . . . "

"This can be a dangerous city," Bob said. "Just last night, not too far from here, some biker went nuts at a drug party and slashed up ten people."

Ezra and Jay exchanged glances. "Was anyone hurt bad?" Jay asked.

"Five people are hospitalized. Two are critical."

"What happened to the biker?" Ezra asked.

"He cut his wrists but the paramedics saved him. It's just a case of demons on the loose, guys. You are in a spiritual war zone when you walk this city." He paused. "By the way, what exactly are you two doing, are you going anywhere in particular?"

"We just wanted to see the country," Jay said. "But we are on our way home now."

After Bob and the ten young men left, Ezra and Jay showered then stretched out on the beds. Jay was ecstatic. He had survived the acid trip, had a shower, was on a bed, and food was next. All of his creature comforts were being met, and he quickly forgot the earlier torments. "This is great," he said. "I love San Francisco."

"I'm leaving here tomorrow," Ezra said.

Jay stared at the ceiling. He did not want to hear that. Wherever Ezra went he would have to follow, and he did not want to leave. "Where ya going, man?" he asked.

"I don't know. Out of the city. Maybe New Mexico. What are you going to do—stay and try to hook up with a band?"

Jay rolled over onto his side and stared at Ezra. "Man, you can't leave. We have a destiny to fulfill. We gotta stick together, man."

"If it's destiny we won't be able to stop it. But I'm bookin', Jay. What are you going to do?"

Jay rolled over again and stared at the ceiling for several minutes. He was sullen when he spoke. "I don't know, man. I don't want to stick around here either. Maybe I'll go south and check out the Jesus Movement around L.A."

"You're into this Jesus stuff, aren't you?" Ezra asked.

"Yeah, man, Jesus is cool. Churches aren't all that hot, and being a preacher's kid is definitely a bummer. Bad trip, man. But Jesus is all right."

"I don't want anything to do with churches," Ezra said.

"Man, you don't have to have churches to be a Christian. That's what it's all about around L.A. The people are meeting in homes and on the beach, just like the early Christians did."

"That sounds cool," Ezra admitted. "But wouldn't that type of Christianity put your father out of a job?"

"Yeah, well, there're other things he could do, man."

"What's your old man like?" Ezra asked.

Jay folded his arms behind his head and grinned. "He's a foot-stomper, man. A hellfire-and-brimstone, don't-take-any-prisoners type. As a preacher, he's a two-shirter."

"A two-shirter?"

"Yeah. He preaches so hard during his sermon that he sweats right through one shirt. So before he greets people at the door he runs into his study where my mother always has a clean shirt hanging for him and he changes real quick."

"He sounds a little radical."

Jay laughed. "'Sold out for God' is what he calls it. But he can preach the heathen to the altar of repentance. What about you? What's your old man like?"

"Last of the old-time cowboys," Ezra said. "He ran wild horses during the Depression and was a fighter and drinker when he was young. Sort of a local legend, I guess."

"Far out. Man, you really live on a ranch? In the country? With horses?"

Ezra nodded. He did not like thinking about the hills, his horses, the sunsets spilling color over the badlands.

"Man, I never would have left that," Jay said. "What a life."

"It's not everything you imagine," Ezra said.

"Oh, your old man, right? He wanted you to be like him. I know that tune, man."

"Yeah," Ezra sighed. "My dad wanted an all-around cowboy. He was raised by a real old-timer named Charley Arbuckle, and I was raised with Charley's two grandsons. They're both cowboys." Ezra smiled and stared down at his pack on the floor. "But they wouldn't last a week on the road."

"Man, I think cowboying would be cool," Jay said. "I used to watch those Saturday matinees. That would be great. Just me, a horse, a guitar, and a pretty lady."

"That's not ranching," Ezra said. "Ranching is digging postholes in the heat and throwing hay bales when it's thirty below zero."

"I could dig that, too, man."

"If you want to know what it's really like you should be in my home-town next weekend," Ezra said. "It's time for their annual Bucking Horse Sale. It's a real redneck revival."

"Wow, what is it, man? Tell me more."

"It's like a rodeo except there are three or four hundred bucking horses bucked out of the chutes. It's pretty wild."

Jay turned and leaned on one elbow. "Let's go," he said. His dark eyes were as shiny as a squirrel's.

"What?"

"Let's go to this bucking horse sale. I'll make you a deal. I'll visit your hometown and you visit mine. Or the one where my folks are now. Then we will compare notes to see who has the most radically weird father."

"You're talking over two thousand miles of hitching."

"So? That's nothing for you, right? Besides, what else do we have to do?"

"I thought you were heading for the Jesus People scene."

"That can wait," he chirped. "It will be there later. Let's go to this redneck revival you're talking about."

Ezra shook his head. "No way, man. I left all that. That's why I'm on the road. I don't want anything to do with it."

"The deal is," Jay continued, "we have to do it without being seen by anyone. I can meet your dad and you can meet mine, but we can't let our fathers see us." His eyes flickered with excitement. "It will be a trip, man, don't you see? You can meet my dad and say that you know me, that you met me on the road, and I'll do the same."

"What's the point?" Ezra asked. He was amazed at Jay's fortitude. He had been stoned on LSD all night and still had the energy to plan a new adventure.

"That's it," Jay shouted. "There isn't any."

"I like reasons," Ezra said. "The romance of the road left me about six months ago."

"What's wrong, man?" Jay challenged. "Are you afraid of your hometown?"

It was Ezra's turn to stare at the ceiling. He was in a strange house with people who were stranger. The dangers of the city had been nipping at his heels for twenty-four hours. He would go anywhere as long as there were hills and fields, rivers and streams. The thought of returning to Yellow Rock terrified him. But he would not be going back alone, and the large crowd in town for the bucking horse sale would help hide him.

"It's like a mission," Jay said. "Sons of destiny returning to the homeland. Me confronting the father of The Montana Kid. You inspecting the sire of The Jay Walker. It's poetry, man. You've been gone almost a year. Aren't you curious about things?"

"Okay," Ezra said. "We'll do it." He didn't think it was poetry, and he wasn't that curious about Yellow Rock, but Jay was laying down a challenge. Besides, this would get him out of San Francisco.

"Far out, man. Far out. Destiny, here we come."

That night the prayer vigils kept Ezra awake. It was an odd sensation to be roused by someone muttering to God. He had the feeling they were praying for him and he resented it, and several of the young men must have been aliens because he could not understand their languages. Jay stayed up late talking to Bob. Ezra caught fragments of their conversation. Bob was urging Jay to return to Bible school in Indiana. "If you won't do it for the Lord, do it for your father, do it for your music," he heard Bob say.

"Man, I will do it when I am doing it for me," Jay answered, and though half-asleep, Ezra sensed the anger in his friend's tone.

The following morning did not dawn crisp and clean for Ezra. It was only a pale white extension of the night before. His mind was burnt and fuzzy and he longed for the solitude of open spaces.

Jay talked Bob into giving them a ride to Highway One north of Sausalito. Bob continued preaching to Jay as he drove, imploring him to return to school, return to his father, return to Jesus. "I will," Jay kept promising him.

Ezra rested his head against the window. They had spent thirty-eight whirlwind hours in San Francisco and, like it or not, the fierce intensity of the experience had forged a bond between him and Jay Walker.

When Bob let them out, he shook Jay's hand first and told him he would be praying for him. Then he turned to Ezra. "Brother," he said. "You are a seeker. If you will seek God, He will be found by you. But He is found only in His son Jesus." Bob's deep, green eyes radiated with a warm intensity.

Ezra was polite but distant. "Thanks for the bed and shower," he said. He was disinterested in Bob's spiritual path. Christianity was too narrow, too urban, too domesticated, and reminded him of his mother's legalistic moralizings. He would find God, every fiber of his body was poised and pointed to that intent, but he would do so by bypassing the pitiful pilgrims of organized religion. But after Bob had driven away, Ezra felt a longing, as if his resistance to Bob had been too strong and he had allowed something valuable to pass by. But to woo it back suggested the city, robots sleeping in barracks, rising on the hour for perfunctory prayers and marching like machines to organized recreation and introspection. It was not discipline that Ezra feared—he was actually in search of it—it was the communal responsibility, the denial of independence. Christianity demanded a corporateness and all that Ezra had ever learned, whether through life or books, put the importance only on the individual. The teachings of Jesus asked for death to self, but Ezra could not offer on the altar of sacrifice that which he did not know. He did not yet know who he was.

Jay stood on the edge of a cliff overlooking the ocean. The breakers of Stinson Beach slapped the rocks beneath him. A sea breeze billowed his curly hair, and he spread his arms as to take flight. He had talked Ezra into taking the slower, scenic route up Highway One, and he was delighted with his first good view of the Pacific Ocean. "On the road again, man," Jay shouted into the westerly breeze. "We are on the road again."

Ezra smiled at his arrogance. Jay Walker knew nothing of the road. Ezra looked down the long stretch of blacktop. The road was a different lover when she was the only lover you had. She was jealous and demanding. She could reward you with pleasure and heightened awareness or leave you dirty, disgusted, and wounded. She was as moody as a woman, as strong-willed as a horse, as dangerous as a pet lion.

"The road," Jay shouted into the wind, his wonderfully resonate voice drowning in the crashing of the breakers. "I am a child of the road!"

"You promised Bob you would return to Bible school," Ezra reminded him.

Jay stomped on the blacktopped highway. "This is it, man," he laughed. "The road is my Bible school, and I'm going to graduate with honors."

"But will your father attend your graduation?" Ezra asked.

For the first time, Walker looked at Ezra angrily. "Let me tell you something," he said. "All my life I have been told what is good for me, what I should be doing, what a good Christian is. Man, I've got time for all of that later. I want to learn about life for myself, man. I want to touch the stove and see if it is hot instead of always being told not to touch."

Ezra shrugged, leaned his pack against the guardrail, and rested against it. "Then stick out your thumb and get us a ride," he said.

Ezra dozed in the morning sun for an hour, finally awakened by passing cars spitting gravel against his legs. He rubbed his eyes, stood up, and looked up and down the highway for Jay but couldn't see him. For a moment he thought Jay had caught a ride and left him and Ezra had mixed emotions. Jay was a bother, but he was endlessly interesting. Then he caught a flash of yellow and looked over the guardrail. On a wide, grassy shoulder of the road Jay had rolled out his sleeping bag, curled up like a baby on top of it, and was sound asleep. He had one hand close to his mouth, almost as if he were sucking his thumb, and with his curly hair and vulnerable innocence, he looked like a small lost child.

Ezra took a light jacket from Jay's pack and spread it over him. Then Ezra made a den in the underbrush for himself.

Ezra and Jay slept until noon. When they awakened Jay was ravenous. "Food," he said. "I have to have real food. No more granola bars. No more peanut butter and honey sandwiches. I want food." He walked half a mile to a roadside store and returned with cold cuts, cheese, rye bread, mayonnaise, mustard, and a bottle of wine. They ate on the rocks above the breaking waves of the Pacific.

"This is a little extravagant," Ezra said. "How much did it cost you?"

"All I had," Jay said. "I am now officially broke."

Later, at Ezra's urging they returned to the highway, and Ezra thumbed for rides while Jay looked through Ezra's books.

"I thought you were going to read *Narcissus and Goldmund*," Ezra said.

"Aw, man, that book is about a monastery."

"It just begins in a monastery."

Jay held up books by Lobsang Rampa, Sri Aurobindo, and Madam Blavatsky. "You got some bad stuff here, man. Why do you read this junk?"

"Truth takes many paths up the mountain," Ezra said.

"Jesus is the truth, man," Jay answered solidly.

"The truth is relative," Ezra countered.

"The truth is absolute, or it is not the truth."

"If truth is absolute in your life, how can you justify drugs?"

Jay winced as if the question were a low blow, as if drugs were not real to his life, he was only walking in someone else's dream. "I can't justify drugs," he said solemnly. "But I have forgiveness for my actions."

"It is ironic," Ezra said, "that you, as a Christian, seek the broad path of the sensual, and me, an animistic pagan, seeks the narrow way of austerity and discipline. Don't we have our lifestyles confused?"

The discussion was ended by a Triumph TR5 convertible sports car skidding to a stop beside them. Behind the wheel was an attractive blonde. She lifted her sunglasses and looked at them. "Where are you going?" she asked.

Jay jumped up quickly. "Wherever you're going," he said.

"My trunk is full," she said, getting out of the car. "But I have some straps. We can fasten your packs to the luggage rack." Her straight hair fell below her shoulders, and her eyes were an emerald green. She wore hip-hugging denim bell bottoms, sandals, and was braless under a Mexican peasant's shirt. They helped her strap the packs down.

"My name is Melanie," she said. "Hop in." The Triumph had small bucket seats with a stick shift between them. "It might be a little tight," she said.

"No problem," Jay said and he took the middle, his left arm around the back of her seat, the stick shift between his legs.

She looked at him and smiled. "Maybe you better shift," she said, and they roared onto the highway, the little sports car hugging the curves and the girl shouting questions. "Where are you guys going?" she asked.

"Up the road," Jay said. "Until we get to Montana."

"Far out. You guys can crash at my place tonight if you want."

"Great," Jay said. "Where do you live?"

"We have a beach house in Mendocino, but it's empty except for me. My parents are in Europe for a year."

They followed the curves of Highway One for hours. The wind whipped Jay's curly hair and the sun tanned his face. When he and the girl spoke to each other, the wind carried their words away from Ezra. Jay was posturing and competing with him for the blonde's affections but Ezra was unconcerned. He was attracted to very certain types of women: ones with deep, thoughtful eyes, irregular beauty, and adventurous natures. Their driver was physically beautiful but had the spoiled, pampered look of a greenhouse flower.

They finally pulled up to a large house on a cliff overlooking the ocean. The girl braked in front of a three-car garage. "This is it," she said. "This is our summer cabin."

The indoors revealed a sunken living room, loft, recreation room, a cedar-paneled den, and a two-story wall of windows on the west side that showed a large deck on stilts, a bricked patio with a hot tub, a putting green with hole and flag, and an elongated staircase that descended to the beach.

"There're four bedrooms," Melanie said. "You can put your stuff anywhere you want. Are you guys hungry? We can barbecue some steaks. How about a beer? There's a bathtub downstairs and a shower upstairs if you want to clean up."

Jay nudged Ezra. "This is heaven, man. Can you believe it?"

Ezra showered and Jay took a bath, and they both put on clean clothes while Melanie put their soiled clothing in the wash. Ezra pulled his wet hair into a tight ponytail. He wore a loose-fitting tee-shirt, his Karate gi pants, and was barefoot. Months of carrying a ninety-pound pack had built and defined his arms, shoulders, and chest.

Jay hovered like a housefly around the girl as she put steaks on the grill but she did not seem to mind the attention. "What do your parents do?" he asked.

"My father's an attorney and my mother's an interior designer," she said. "And me? I'm a junior at USF majoring in art history. Am I an artist? Not at all. I can't even color with crayons."

"Then why pursue art history?" Jay asked.

She shrugged and smiled. Her teeth were so clean and white they sparkled like light. "I will probably marry someone rich," she said. "We will have a big house and entertain a lot. I will have to have something to talk about. So I took art history. We will collect art and I will talk about it."

"There's other things to talk about," Jay said. "Like philosophy, religion, poetry, music, architecture."

"I want to talk about things I can put on my wall," she said.

After dinner Ezra did the dishes while Melanie gave Jay a tour of the house. When they returned, Jay had his guitar slung on his back. "We are going down to the beach," he announced. "Do you want to come?"

The invitation was feeble because Jay wanted the girl alone. "I'll stay here and rest," Ezra said. He watched them descend a long wooden staircase to the beach. A deep loneliness fell upon him but it was not his. It belonged to the house and the people that lived there. Their lives were shallow and pretentious, and the house spoke of acquisition and possession.

As the sun set he lay on the putting green reading Alan Watts in the fading light, his head propped up on his rolled sleeping bag, when the girl came up the steps. "Hi," she said meekly. "I came up for blankets and pillows. We are going to sleep on the beach."

Ezra nodded.

She sat down beside him. "You are very good-looking," she told him.

"Thank you," he said.

"I don't want you to feel left out." She ran her hand lightly over his forearm. "It's not like I chose Jay over you. He just sort of claimed me."

"It's okay," Ezra said.

"I have friends. I could call someone. They would be glad to come."

Ezra smiled softly. "Thank you," he said. "But I am very tired. I will be happy to get a good night's sleep."

She looked at him for a long time. He mystified her. There was a depth and seriousness in him she had never seen in a young man before. He was gentle, but dangerous at the same time, as if he walked on a raw edge of life she had never experienced. Impulsively, she leaned over and kissed him lightly on the cheek.

Ezra looked at her with dark, questioning eyes. She was pretty and intelligent, but shallow. When Ezra looked in her eyes, he could see all the way to the bottom. There was no depth or mystery.

She felt his eyes search her and was confused by it. She pulled back, rose to her feet, and moved quickly to the house for blankets and pillows. Minutes later he heard her footsteps on the staircase and saw the glow of a small fire Jay had built on the beach.

CHAPTER SEVEN

Ezra was up early the next morning, pulled on his running shoes, and ran two miles down the highway and back. The house seemed large and empty when he returned. He showered then had cereal and fruit alone on the patio as the sun climbed over the western hills. He could see the crumpled pile of blankets on the beach, the forms of Jay and Melanie indistinguishable beneath the folds. He wondered what it was that drew him to someone he did not particularly care for. *Was it fate?* He liked Jay and, yet, was repulsed by him as well, and he wondered if Jay felt the same about him. *What traits did he have that Jay abhorred?* At his worst, Ezra found Jay vain, manipulative, and short-sighted. At his best, he was intelligent, deep, and caring, and in any case, was immensely talented. *How did Jay see him?* Jay sensed depth, Ezra knew. And he respected talent, but what traits of character did Jay like or not like? He wondered about it as he washed his few dishes and was still wondering about it while packing, and Jay came in.

"Wow," Jay said. "What a night." His hair was uncombed and his clothes rumpled.

"Where's Melanie?" Ezra asked. The question was half-rhetorical, he wanted Jay to give an account for himself, and half-symbolic, for while he was not attracted to their beautiful guest he liked her and felt a debt of loyalty for her kindness.

"She's still sleeping," Jay said and he went to the refrigerator and took a long drink of milk from the carton.

"Let's hit the road," Ezra said. His voice was purposeful and brimmed with conviction. Ezra knew the soft seductions of the situation would hurt someone if they stayed.

"Hit the road?" Jay turned around, his dark eyes sparkling with surprise. "We can stay here all summer, man. Longer than that if we want."

Ezra smiled. "What about your big plan to visit our fathers?"

"Who cares, man? We've got it all here. She's beautiful, man, and she's rich, and she's got lots of friends." He turned back to the refrigerator to search for food.

"It's not my scene," Ezra said. "I want to earn my own way."

Jay troweled a slab of jelly onto a bagel. "She has lots of friends with horses. You could be a horse trainer. You can pay rent if you want or move in with someone else." It all seemed so natural to him. Here was luxury, comfort, and convenience. What more could anyone want?

Ezra swept the room with his hand. "Look around you, Jay. Is this what you want? Million-dollar beach homes with no soul or spirit?"

"I can live with it, man," Jay said.

"Well, I can't," Ezra said. "It's too soft. It's not who I am." He started for the door.

Jay ran after him and grabbed him by the arm. "Wait, man, wait." He looked at Ezra, then at the floor. He rubbed his Fu Manchu mustache and stared out the spacious windows to the beach. His eyes became vague and vacant like rooms without furniture lit by a sterile light. Ezra had seen those eyes before in himself while in the hills, horseback with his father and uncles, being laughed at, cursed, being made the butt of jokes. Jay had his own dark cellar where bull snakes moved like slow freight trains between the rafters and the wounds of remarks scurried like frightened mice. Ezra did not know the details of Jay's woundings, but he saw the evidence of the scars.

"Okay, okay," Jay said. "I'm coming with you. Let me grab my pack. It's out on the patio."

"You don't have to come," Ezra said.

"No, man, you're right. It's destiny. It's you and me, man. Not me and her."

"Aren't you even going to tell her good-bye," Ezra said.

"I can't," he confessed. "I have a weakness for beautiful things. If I even look at her, I know I will stay."

When they reached the highway Ezra continued to walk, his left arm extended, the palm up and thumb out. He wanted to put distance between them and the house. Jay followed half-heartedly. A farmer gave them the short ride to Fort Bragg and an insurance agent took them to Highway 101 where the Interstate ramp was crowded with hitchhikers; most had obviously spent the night there. They looked at Ezra and Jay disdainfully as the car let them out.

"Man, we'll never get a ride out of here," Jay said.

"Follow me," Ezra said. They walked a mile to a large truck stop. Ezra leaned his pack against a pole at the edge of the parking lot where eighteen-wheelers were parked in rows like long metallic beasts, their diesel engines purring while the drivers walked back and forth to the restaurant, service station, and gift shop with log books and shower kits in their hands.

"What do we do now?" Jay asked.

"We wait," Ezra said.

The trucks came and went for an hour until a burly man in his fifties approached them. He wore a clean short-sleeved shirt, Levis, and a leather belt with a Kenworth buckle. His forearms were knotted with muscle and his hair was cropped short. "Are you boys afraid of work?" he asked.

"I'm not," Ezra said.

"I'll give you a ride to Eureka and a job when you get there." His voice was gruff but the lines in his face were friendly.

"We'll take it," Ezra said and he shouldered his pack.

"What do we have to do?" Jay asked.

"Unload half a trailer-load of potatoes," the man said, and he led them to a powder blue tractor cab outlined with red trim. *Merlin Anderson, Boise, Idaho* was scripted on the doors above an American flag. Jay and the backpacks were fitted into the sleeper while Ezra rode shotgun.

"What's your names, and where are you boys from?" the trucker asked as he scrawled in his log book.

Ezra told him.

"My name's Merlin." He offered them a meaty hand. "I haul spuds to California and all kinds of fruit and vegetables back to Idaho."

"Man, you have a beautiful truck," Jay said. "I've always wanted to drive a truck like this."

"It breaks your back and keeps you away from your family," Merlin said.

"Well, I didn't want to do it for a living," Jay said. "I just want to do it for fun sometime."

"You don't drive these for fun," Merlin said. "We'll be in Eureka in a few hours. There's a strike going on there at the warehouse. We'll go in by the back gate but we'll probably still get pelted with a few eggs and tomatoes. The strikers burned up the forklifts so the trailer will have to be unloaded by hand. The pay is thirty dollars a piece." He stuck a stick of gum in his mouth and chewed aggressively, like someone who had recently given up cigarettes, while he maneuvered the huge rig slowly and smoothly to the Interstate. "How old are you boys?" he asked.

"Nineteen," Ezra said.

"That's what I thought," he said. "My boy Scotty was nineteen when he got killed in Vietnam. Either of you planning on going into the service?"

"Not me," Jay laughed.

"I don't know," Ezra said.

"Take my advice," he said, "and don't go in until the war is over, and it will be over soon. Those are the words of a man who spent eight years in the marines and served in World War Two and Korea."

"If I get drafted, I'm going to Canada," Jay said.

"Well, you do what you have to do," the man said. He adjusted the squelch on his citizens band radio and popped another piece of gum in his mouth. "I used to think that all you hippie types were cowards and bums. But that was before Scotty died. He was a real good kid. He could have had a heckuva career in electronics. But he joined the Corps to please me. Then they sent him back to me in a box."

They did not talk again for a long time and Jay shot Ezra worried glances, but Ezra was not concerned. Merlin was not dangerous. He was simply a man in pain, and Ezra's and Jay's youth had reopened the wounds. But then, that is why he picked them up, Ezra knew. Merlin was looking for his son by befriending those who were his age when he died.

When they got to the warehouse in Eureka, the strikers were at the front gate, walking and carrying placards or sitting in their cars smoking cigarettes and drinking coffee. Most of them looked Hispanic. They glared angrily at the truck as it roared by.

The few strikers at the back gate rained rocks and eggs on the truck as it sped into the yard, and blue-shirted security guards had to restrain the strikers from entering the grounds. Merlin backed the truck expertly to the dock, set his brakes, and hopped out, his paperwork in hand. He opened the trailer's back door, and Ezra and Jay stared in at a small mountain of potato sacks.

"The sacks weigh seventy pounds," Merlin said. "You will have to pack them to the dock, stack them on a cart, roll the cart into the warehouse, and stack them again. You might as well get to work, boys, and I'll take care of business." He walked off in search of the warehouse foreman.

"Geeze," Jay said, staring at the hundreds of burlap sacks. "This will take us forever."

"Only if we stare at them," Ezra said, and he walked into the trailer and grabbed his first sack, packed it to the dock, and laid it on the cart. He looked at Jay who shook his head sadly. Ezra went back for another.

"This will take forever," Jay repeated. "Forever for thirty dollars."

Ezra returned with another sack. "If we work hard, it will take four, maybe five hours, that's six or seven dollars an hour. Those are good wages."

"I bet I could make that in two hours by panhandlin' and singing songs for quarters."

"So start singing," Ezra said. He packed the third sack out with the bag lifted over his head.

Jay grunted and stepped into the trailer. "I should have stayed with Melanie," he said.

It was dark when they finished. Ezra had done more than his share of the labor. Jay was strong enough, but disinterested. "I hate work," he kept saying, as if somehow the mantra would magically release him.

They collapsed on a pile of potato sacks when they finally finished. Every muscle in Ezra's body ached but he said nothing. He let Jay do the complaining. Merlin showed up with sacks of hamburgers, French fries, and Cokes from a Burger King. "If you boys want, you can sleep here in the warehouse tonight," he said. "There are some clean, empty sacks stacked in the back. They'd make a good bed. In the morning you can ride with me to Portland."

"Great," Jay said sarcastically. "More potatoes to unload?"

"Nope, cherries and apples, but there's no strike in Portland. I'm afraid I can't offer you any work there."

"What a shame," Jay said.

"If you want, I can take you all the way to Boise," Merlin told Ezra as he pulled off the exit ramp into Portland. They had left Eureka long before morning light. Both boys were tired and sore, and Jay quickly climbed into the sleeper and went back to sleep. He was still asleep when they arrived in Portland.

"I have a three-hour layover here," Merlin continued. "There's a bus line not far from the docks that will take you downtown if you want to look around."

It had rained for two days but the sun was shining brightly on the glistening Oregon river port. Ezra jostled Jay awake. He squinted, rubbed his eyes, and stared out the windshield. "I thought Portland was on the ocean," he said.

"It's on a river. You're looking at the Columbia," Merlin explained.

In a bold sign of trust, Ezra and Jay left their backpacks in the truck, but Jay took his guitar and they caught a bus that took them past flower gardens and city parks to the business district. "This is a beautiful city," Jay said. "I could live here." Jay insisted on a lunch of fresh fish and shrimp washed down by espressos. After lunch they sunned themselves on a park bench and Jay played his guitar and sang. After a few minutes a young businessman tossed a dollar bill in Ezra's lap. Jay began singing louder and soon a small interchanging crowd had gathered. People stopped, listened, and moved on, their places taken by others. Ezra sat on the ground forming a hollow bowl by spreading his jacket open between his crossed legs. It embarrassed him, but people continued to toss quarters and dollar bills until Ezra reminded Jay they needed to get back to the truck.

"How much did we score?" Jay asked. They quickly counted the money. "Twenty-eight dollars and forty cents," Jay laughed. "Now you tell me this doesn't beat packing potato sacks."

"It's an eight-hour drive to Boise," Merlin told them. "More than that if I obey the speed limit." They started east on I-84, the Columbia River on their left shoulders. Ezra's and Jay's packs were with the fruit in the "reefer," the refrigerated trailer, so Jay had room to lay back, pick his guitar, and sing.

"You're real good," Merlin told him. "You should do that for a living."

"I plan on it," Jay said.

"You boys packin' any dope?" Merlin blurted.

"Why do you ask?" Ezra said suspiciously.

The driver chuckled. "A lot of drivers take drugs," he said. "Speed, mostly. It keeps them awake on the long hauls. Me, I never have. I was just curious. I figure Scotty probably smoked pot a time or two. I was just wondering what it was like."

"I've got some," Jay said. "You wanna get stoned?"

"You're carrying?" Ezra said angrily. "You should have told me. You could have gotten us busted."

"Don't sweat it, man. Melanie had some righteous stuff. Premo hash and some great Hawaiian weed. She gave me half a baggie."

"We'll wait until we get close to Boise," Merlin said. "There's a truck stop on the edge of town."

It was midnight when they hit Boise but the service station and 24-hour cafe were busy. Merlin pulled his rig to the back of the lot. Jay was asleep.

"Are you sure you want to do this?" Ezra asked. "You can just let us out here."

"I want to do it," Merlin said. "I don't plan on becoming a user or anything, I just want to know what it's like."

Ezra shook Jay's foot. "Hey, wake up," he said. "We're in Boise and Merlin wants to get stoned."

"Far out," Jay said sleepily, and he rummaged in his jacket pocket for the baggie and papers. He handed them to Ezra. "I'm too sleepy to roll," he said.

"You can't roll anyway," Ezra said. He licked two papers together and rolled a large, tight joint. He lit it and passed it to Merlin. The truck driver looked at it warily, smelled the smoke rising from the tip, then put it to his lips.

"You have to suck it in and hold it down," Ezra said.

Merlin took a long toke, held the smoke for several seconds, then coughed it out. "I gave up smoking years ago," he said.

Jay took the joint and sucked long and hard. He passed it to Ezra.

Ezra shook his head. "Whatsamatter?" Jay asked. "Ain't you gonna smoke?"

"One of us better stay straight," Ezra said. "Just in case."

"Ah, c'mon, man, you can't drive this rig, anyway," Jay said.

Ezra shrugged and took a hit.

"Man, you act like you're goin' on the wagon," Jay said.

Ezra passed the joint to Merlin, then blew the smoke out. "I am," he said. "Someday I'm going to be straight. All the time."

"Bummer," Jay said, taking the joint. "I've tried that route."

They smoked two joints. Merlin became relaxed and quiet. Jay was talkative through fits of giggles.

"So whadya think, man," Jay asked the trucker. "Are you high or what?"

"I don't know," he answered slowly. "I think I'm hungry. Let's go eat."

"He's got the munchies, man," Jay laughed.

They went to the restaurant and took a booth in the back. Their waitress knew Merlin by name. They ordered breakfasts. Ezra was stiff and a little paranoid, Jay laughed too loud at things that were not funny to anyone else. Merlin became transfixed by the neon lights reflecting in the window beside him. When their meals came, Jay ate hungrily, Merlin ate slowly, but Ezra ate little at all. He watched the crowd for truckers who might be friends of Merlin's and the parking lot for patrol cars. He felt guilty for helping get Merlin stoned.

"So?" Jay whispered. "What's it like, man? Do you like getting high?"

"I don't feel any different," Merlin said.

"Right," Jay giggled. "You always stare at lights for five minutes at a time."

"Maybe a little different," Merlin admitted.

Merlin paid for the meal, and they walked back to the truck. It was a clear, starry night, and the three sat in the grass on an embankment near the Interstate. Jay rolled another joint. He and Merlin smoked it.

"You know," Merlin said thoughtfully. "I lied to you boys."

"About what?" Ezra asked.

"About those potato sacks. They weighed ninety pounds. Not seventy." He paused and the silence was short but long in their world. "I just thought I would tell you," he said.

"You miss your son a lot, don't you?" Jay said. They both felt the agony in the truck driver's soul, but Jay was the one who could approach him with words.

"With all my heart," Merlin said. "With all my heart."

"What was he like? Did he look like you?" Jay asked.

"No, like his mother. He had sandy brown hair and was a very good high school wrestler. Third at state at 165."

"I wrestled for two years," Jay said. "I was good but I didn't like it."

"Do you boys miss your fathers?" Merlin asked.

The question rolled out like a hand grenade that landed between their feet. Neither one answered for a moment, then Jay said: "We are on our way back to see them."

"I bet they miss you even if they don't know how to show it," Merlin said. "Tell me about them. What are your fathers like?"

"Like I told you, man," Jay said. "Mine is a preacher. We never lived anywhere for more than a couple years. I went to eight different schools in eight different towns. It's hard to make friends when you're moving around like that."

Eight schools in eight towns, Ezra thought. That explained a lot.

"We never had any money," Jay continued. "I didn't get my first bike until I was fifteen. By then all the other kids were getting cars."

"Money isn't everything," Merlin said. "I have made good money driving this ol' truck. If I had it all to do over again, I would have spent more time with my kids, especially Scotty."

The writer in Ezra was imagining scenes and characters. He saw Jay as a skinny, self-conscious, curly-haired kid in a new school where everyone knew him only as the kid of that shouting preacher in the little church on the wrong side of the tracks. He saw Merlin's son, Scotty, alone on a wrestling mat searching the stands, looking through the faces of parents, trying to find the father that was many miles away driving a lonely stretch of California highway.

"What about you, Ezra?" Merlin asked. "What's your father like?"

"I guess I really don't know," Ezra said. "He has a bad temper, I know that."

"He's a rancher," Jay said. "Man, if my father had a ranch—"

"He's a cowboy," Ezra said, cutting off Jay's monologue. "He quit school after the fifth grade and put a ranch together by running wild horses and trapping coyotes," Ezra said.

"He sounds like an interesting man," Merlin said.

"I suppose he is," Ezra answered.

"I bet they are both real good men," Merlin said. "Fathers aren't perfect, boys. Most of them work too hard to make a living. Life isn't fair, boys. Life sure as heck isn't fair."

A silence surrounded them that was bigger than their efforts to break it. Each was in his own smoky, vaporous world, communing with the ghosts in his mind. When the spell finally broke and the marijuana began to wear off, Merlin said, "I think I better get home now. Irene will be expecting me."

They followed him to the back of the trailer where he unlocked the door and retrieved their packs. The night was suddenly darker, and the world bigger for Jay and Ezra. He shook their hands. "You are both good boys," he said. "It was a pleasure to meet you."

They watched his long silver trailer pull away. Then Jay followed Ezra to the grassy knoll. They rolled out their sleeping bags and stared up at the night sky.

"Wanna smoke another joint?" Jay asked.

"Man, you smoke dope like there's no tomorrow. The revolution is over, Jay. This is the seventies, not the sixties."

"Hey, so I have to make up for lost time."

Ezra rolled over onto his side and rested his weary head on his arm. Ten minutes later Ezra was on the edge of sleep.

"Whadya thinkin' about, man?" Jay said.

"I was thinking about sleeping," Ezra growled.

"No, seriously, man."

"I was thinking about the badlands on our ranch," Ezra said sleepily. "It was winter and the air was clear and crisp, but the sun was warm. I was in the sandstone buttes of the badlands coaxing bobcats out of the rocks by making little squeaks on a predator call. The cats stood against the blue sky, their coats glistening in the sun, their ears poised to hear the sound of my call."

"Then you shoot them?"

"No. I just watch."

"Hmmm." Jay stared at the stars and crossed his hands on his chest. "That's the difference between you and me, man."

"What, that you would shoot them?"

"No. That you go to sleep dreaming about badlands and bobcats and I go to sleep dreaming about Melanie."

Ezra rolled onto his side and zipped his sleeping bag tight to his chin. "That's the difference," he said. But he went to sleep thinking about Melanie, too. Thinking that he should write her a note thanking her for her hospitality, and in his own way, apologizing for Jay.

CHAPTER EIGHT

It rained during the night and the boys scurried to an unhooked semi trailer and slept under it. They were awakened early by the noise of trucks and quickly climbed from their wet sleeping bags.

"Motels, man," Jay said. "That's why there are motels: so people don't have to sleep in wet sleeping bags."

Ezra nodded at the truck stop. "Let's get some coffee then get on the road." They ate a large breakfast in a corner booth while Ezra scanned the restaurant for truckers that might give them a ride. There were no prospects so they went to the highway. An hour later an office supplies salesman stopped. He took them as far as Twin Falls.

Two hours later they were still waiting. Ezra wrote Melanie a note and penned a poem about Merlin. Jay read *Narcissus und Goldmund*. Cars with clean-cut people drove by, most swerved to the other lane to avoid them, the drivers staring straight ahead, the young children pressing their faces to the windows and gawking at them as if they were animals in a zoo. Jay made faces back at them.

"It's Mormon country," Ezra explained. "Hitching is always tough in Mormon country."

At noon a battered Ford Galaxie rattled to a stop and a pot-bellied young man in a dirty tee-shirt climbed out and yelled. "Come on, freaks, let's go." He had unkempt brown hair and a three-day stubble growing around fuzzy muttonchop sideburns. Jay and Ezra threw their packs in the back and climbed in. The Galaxie roared off in a cloud of blue smoke.

"I'm Wally," the driver said. "You guys want a beer?" A cooler in the backseat was half-filled with warm water and cans of Pabst.

Jay took one. "Nice car," he said sarcastically.

"Thanks," Wally said. "I stole it a week ago." He looked at them and his round face split with a grin that display stained, broken teeth. "Ha, ha," he shouted and tromped on the gas pedal. The old Ford gathered speed until it was rumbling down the highway at 120 miles per hour.

"What's the rush?" Jay asked.

Wally finished his beer and tossed the can out the window. "Cops are after me," he laughed and nodded at the cooler. "Get me another brew."

Jay handed him a warm beer. "So what did you do?"

"Shot a hippie," he said and stared at the two of them for several seconds while the car drifted into the other lane. He nonchalantly corrected his course, gulped his new beer, and stared vacantly ahead. The accelerator was still floor-boarded and the engine temperature gauge moved steadily toward the H.

"Shooting a hippie. That was probably a good idea," Jay said. Ezra winced. He sat next to the door and was quickly thinking of how to escape.

"I thought so," Wally said seriously. The car sped on, past Burley and Rupert, toward American Falls. Ezra could not believe there were no highway patrolmen on the road. He was often harassed by the law but now prayed to see a patrol car.

"Don't you think it would be a good idea to slow down?" Jay asked.

"You tellin' me how to drive?" Wally exploded as the car veered toward the ditch. Jay reached up and eased the steering wheel back. The man did not even notice.

"You're drivin' fine," Jay said.

Ezra watched the telephone poles fly by. He had to do something before they all died in a car wreck, but their driver was too drunk, too unpredictable to second-guess. *He's possibly armed,* Ezra thought, *and capable of wrecking on purpose if provoked. Had he shot a hippie?* Ezra didn't know, but he guessed him capable of it. They soared through a flat area with farms bordering both sides of the highway. The fields were a deep brown from the rain the night before and streams of water flashed like white rays between the rows of crops.

Suddenly Wally's head dropped heavily onto the steering wheel. The car drifted into the left lane.

"Grab the wheel," Ezra shouted.

As Jay reached up and took the steering wheel Wally slumped onto Jay's shoulder but his foot remained pressed against the gas pedal.

"What do I do, man? What do I do?" Jay screamed.

Ezra bent down and pushed the driver's big foot off the pedal. Wally stirred and mumbled as if he were waking up.

"He's comin' to," Jay whispered.

Ezra rose back up. "Let the car slow to forty then steer it off the road and into the fields. Watch out for the fence. Don't hit a post. Hit wire, nothing but wire."

"You're crazy," Jay said. Wally was slowly shaking his head as if to clear it. His foul, beer-soaked breath blasted Jay's face. The car's inertia had decreased to sixty miles an hour.

"There's a car ahead of us," Ezra warned Jay. "We better not try and pass. Steer now. Do it."

Jay pulled the car to the right, it rumbled off the Interstate embankment, leveled with a crash and bounced toward a four-stranded barbed wire fence.

"Between the posts," Ezra shouted.

Jay aimed the Galaxie and it crashed through the fence, breaking the wires like they were hair strands, bounced over a small ditch and belly-flopped into a large mud puddle where it became instantly stuck, the rear wheels spinning helplessly. The concussion threw all three of them into the dashboard, awakening Wally. "What's happenin'," he mumbled.

Ezra threw his door open and jumped out. Jay scrambled out behind him. They grabbed their packs while Wally struggled to get out of the car and onto his feet. "Where you goin'?" he muttered. "I'll shoot the both of ya . . . "

Jay and Ezra ran through the muddy field and up the embankment. "Is he shootin', man?" Jay asked. Ezra didn't answer. As they reached the top, a car skidded to a stop and a man stepped out. He looked at the boys then down into the field where Wally was staggering around in the mud, a pistol in his hand. "Get in the car," he said. They crowded their packs into the back and jumped into the front seat. Both were breathless.

"What in the world is going on?" the man asked as he shifted into gear and sped away. He was in his early thirties with stylishly long hair and a trimmed mustache.

"We got picked up by a crazy drunk," Jay stammered. "He fell asleep with the car going a hundred-and-twenty."

"You guys are lucky to be alive," the man said.

"Thanks to you," Ezra said.

"Yeah, thanks," Jay said. "Can we stop soon? I think I'm going to wet my pants."

The driver stopped at a rest area near Pocatello. His name was Dave, and he said he was a salesman from Salt Lake City.

"What do you sell?" Jay asked.

"Pharmaceuticals," he said.

"Man, I just can't believe this past week," Jay said, addressing himself to the driver. Having relieved his bladder, Jay was eager to relieve his emotions. "Last Friday we got picked up by some drunk cowboys in Nevada, then by a Scientologist who gave us his dope and let us off in a ghetto in San Francisco. We got picked up by a homosexual, and I cut him with a glass. We fled to a drug den where I dropped acid, and a biker knifed some people. Then we went to a strange church and from there to a Teen Dare center. Then a gorgeous blonde picked us up and took us to her beach house. After we left her, we were picked up by a truck driver who took us from Eureka to Portland to Boise, and we got him stoned, and that crazy drunk. I was sure he was gonna kill us, man." Jay rattled his story off like it was a wild but normal week in the itinerary of a foot-loose wanderer.

"Now you have been picked up by Mister Normal," their driver, Dave, said.

"Normal is okay for a while," Jay answered.

"Most hitchhiking can be real boring," Ezra said. "A lot of long waits and rides with lonely businessmen or freaks too stoned to talk." He was embarrassed by Jay's vivacity and wanted to balance his travelogue with an expression of his own veteran reasonableness.

Ezra's heart fluttered when they crossed into Montana late that after-noon and approached the small tourist town of West Yellowstone, the west entrance to Yellowstone National Park. The farm fields and pas-tures of Idaho were behind them and the landscape had turned to blue-green forests and snowcapped mountain peaks. Dave pulled into a quiet picnic area and turned off the car. "Have you guys ever seen Old Faith-ful?" he asked.

They shook their heads.

"Let's stretch our legs," he said, and he got out of the car with the keys in his hand and walked around back to the trunk. Inside was an expensive metal ice chest and a stainless steel carrying case. As Jay and Ezra watched he opened the case. It was filled with scores of small vials filled with a light blue liquid.

"My pharmaceuticals," he explained, handing each of them a vial, then taking two for himself. "I'm not as normal as I look. This is psilocy-bin distilled into liquid form. The cooler is filled with magic mushrooms and peyote. I deal in organics, gentlemen, nothing but the purest, most natural hallucinogens. Let's do these vials then we will go watch Old Faithful." He drank his two vials, Jay drank his, and Ezra followed. Dave closed the trunk and started back to his seat.

Jay grabbed Ezra by the arm. "What's psilocybin?" he whispered.

Ezra looked at him incredulously. "It's the drug in magic mush-rooms," he said. "Its like acid only natural."

"Far out," Jay said. "We're tripping again."

Dave drove twenty miles out of his way to get to Old Faithful. The tourist season had not started and the inn and parking lot by the geyser were relatively quiet. Since taking the drug Dave had changed. He seemed older and harder as if a mask had melted away, and his true persona, that of a longtime drug dealer, had emerged. The effects of the psilocybin snuck up on them gradually. Their pupils slowly dilated, colors became more intense, and the air sparkled with tracers when disturbed by the slightest movement. The three of them became quiet as they were pulled into their own consciousness, like three spelunkers entering separate caves. With a handful of tourists they watched the geyser's timely eruption, the sulfuric spray exploding into the evening air with a sunset in the background, the droplets of water taking forever to fall in slow, dancing rainbows of colors. They leaned quietly against a railing, still absorbing normally imperceptible motions and colors, long after the other spectators had left.

"Far out," Jay said finally.

Dave walked quietly to the car and the boys followed. They drove away like the other tourists, each of them quietly riding the coaster of their own trip, the car pointed north toward Gardiner, Paradise Valley, and Livingston. At Mammoth Hot Springs Dave stopped again, pulling into another quiet picnic grounds.

"Man, I'm on a nature trip," he said. "I can't take being cooped up in this car." They got out, locked the car, and he walked off on his own following a small babbling mountain stream. Jay and Ezra wandered into the forest. Jay began touching and picking at the moss that grew on the north side of the Ponderosa pine. The night was dark but moonlight filtering through the trees illuminated the moss. Ezra heard Jay think to himself: *Man, this mushroom stuff is great, man. I could do this stuff every day.*

"You would get burnt to a crisp," Ezra said.

Jay looked at him strangely. Only Ezra's voice had actually spoken. Jay had said nothing, yet Ezra had heard him.

Ezra turned and walked back to the clearing where the picnic tables sat next to the mountain stream. The water glowed in the starlight like molten silver. Ezra sat first on a picnic bench, but it felt artificial, man-made. He moved to the side of the stream where he could feel the hard, dark earth, the sharp rocks, and the cool moisture radiating up from the ground. Forests made him claustrophobic, reminding him of a dark, dank earth-cellar at home, the one his sister Diane had often locked him in. He needed the prairie, the unending sea of grass with sagebrush whitecaps, the endless horizon beneath a sheer sky.

"Where're you at, man?" a voice said softly. Dave had approached him from the back.

"I'm on the prairie, riding my good horse, Gusto, watching the grasses blow in the wind."

"You're not a mountain person," Dave said. "Where's your partner?"

"Lost in the moss."

Dave melted down into a cross-legged sitting position. The flesh on his face seemed to slowly crawl with life, his eyes were deep and hollow with tiny pinpricks of light, like flashlights shining from deep within a cavern. "You two are an odd team," he said.

Ezra nodded. *It isn't by my choice,* he thought to himself and he felt Dave receive the transmission as their minds linked. There was something wise and ancient about Dave, but it pulsated with darkness, like a wary old troll guarding the road to a mysterious castle.

"I deal peyote to the Indians," Dave explained. "I sell mescaline and mushrooms to the back-to-earth types including some professors up in Missoula." The words came out slow and streamlined as if they could lay on an eastern Montana horizon and barely be visible.

Ezra nodded, but he really did not want to know.

"Your friend scares me," Dave said. "He could get a guy busted. Too immature, too plastic. I'd be careful, man."

Ezra nodded again.

"You don't scare me," Dave said. "You've been down the road. But you have something in you that's scary. You are fighting your own anger. You have a temper that you are desperate to control. And it's got you all bottled up."

"Are you a psychologist?" Ezra asked.

"I was," Dave chuckled. "Got my masters at Michigan State. Almost had my doctorate when I bagged it all. Good organics give you remarkable insight into people, don't they?"

"Sometimes."

"Yeah, and sometimes the insight is all wrong, too. Everything is a mind trip. Everything in this whole world is just a mind trip. You would think something was real, wouldn't you?"

Jay stumbled out of the forest. His body was drawn and tight and his eyes wide. "Ezra," he whispered desperately. "Ezra."

Ezra got up and walked over to him.

Jay was hugging himself. "It's turning bad, man," he said in a ghostly whisper. "I'm bad-trippin' again, man."

"Be cool," Ezra warned. "Everything's okay."

"Pharmacia," Jay whispered, the word came out clear, like the tone of a silver bell on a cold winter morning.

"What?"

"Pharmacia. The Bible says it's witchcraft, man. It's black magic. God spoke against it and commanded the wizards to be slain."

Ezra put his arm around him. "Cool down," he said softly. Jay aggravated him. One moment he was zealous about drugs, the next moment he was in a sweaty state of panic.

"Man, I gotta tell you something, man. I never had sex with Melanie."

"It doesn't make any difference," Ezra said.

"Yeah, man, yeah it does. It makes all the difference. I didn't have sex with her. I am sure I didn't."

You are "sure" you didn't, Ezra thought. *Don't you "know"?*

Jay gave him a look of sheer terror as if he had read his mind, knew the question Ezra wanted to ask, and stood on the edge of a psychic precipice begging him not to ask it.

Ezra didn't. "We better get over to the car," he said.

Dave was at the car. It was time to drive on. Ezra led Jay to the vehicle and positioned his pack on the rear window ledge so Jay could lie down in the back. He covered him with his jacket.

Dave took Ezra aside. "Is he okay, man? I know it sounds cruel, but we could leave him here. We could drive on without him."

"No," Ezra said. "He needs me." He was surprised by his own words. He had never defined his relationship with Jay like that before.

"Be careful of people who need you," Dave warned. "They always take more than they give back."

"This is all new to him," Ezra explained. "He comes from a real religious background, and when he trips he gets real high and free, then he crashes down into paranoia." The effects of the psilocybin were wearing off Dave and Ezra, but Jay was wandering aimlessly within a maze of his own mind.

"Man, he's bad news," Dave said. "He's got to be one or the other, either straight or a freak. He can't be the two things he's trying to be or he's going to end up being psychotic."

"Yeah," Ezra said. "I know."

They drove on quietly through the dark night, the meadows thick and lush in starlit grass, the jagged teeth of mountain peaks biting at the sky. Jay pulled Ezra's jacket up over his face and stayed enshrouded until Dave dropped them off in Livingston. They were bound east, he was going west to Bozeman.

They rolled their sleeping bags out in the barrowpit of the highway. Jay broke out of his silence. "Man, I'm never doing drugs again, man. Never."

"Do you have any dope on you?" Ezra asked.

Jay nodded and took Melanie's baggie out of his pocket. There was enough pot in it for one joint. He handed it to Ezra.

"That's enough to get us busted," Ezra said, and he took it into a pasture and emptied the bag to the wind, scrunched the baggie up and put it under a heavy rock.

"That wild man in the car this morning," Jay said. "He was sent from Satan to kill us. You and I have a destiny, we are meant to be a team from God, but if we keep doing drugs, God is going to punish us. He's going to deliver us to Satan and let our bodies be destroyed that our souls might be delivered."

"God doesn't want to punish us," Ezra said.

"We must all face judgment," Jay answered.

Ezra tried to change the subject but Jay talked long into the night, telling stories about church camps and revival services; he preached sermons and quoted from the Bible and recited hymns he had memorized. He talked long after Ezra went to sleep, the words coming out like a tape recorder disgorging yards of entangled tape.

It was Friday, and Ezra could feel the call of home and the slow, hard chilling of his heart. Jay awakened hungry and filled with energy. His strength of flesh was remarkable, and his memory was selective. After a night of drug use, he remembered only the good things and was eager for new adventures. He talked about Yellowstone Park like it had all been a delightful experience. Jay and Ezra in Wonderland.

A series of short rides took them to Big Timber, Columbus, then Billings. The hometown was getting closer and Ezra grew more quiet. Jay, on the other hand, became animated with excitement. "This is great country," he kept saying. "I can't believe you left a ranch, man. Get me on a ranch and I'd never leave."

I never left, Ezra wanted to say. *The land is with me at all times. I did not leave the land, I was forced into exile, thrust into the world to define the difference between myself and the father who sired me.*

In mid-afternoon they caught a ride in a banged-up '59 Chevy with three drunk cowboys on their way to the Bucking Horse Sale in Yellow Rock. Ezra feigned sleep, sharing the back seat with the cowboy who had already passed out. Jay sat in front, playing his harmonica, sipping whiskey, and hearing stories about calving heifers in the Pryor Mountains.

They arrived at Yellow Rock early Friday evening. Ezra could not resist the pull of the familiar. He saw the sun setting on the prairie and badlands and knew that nighthawks were taking flight and deer were stepping tentatively into creek bottoms, their ears raised like radar dishes. He was in the landscape of his soul but was torn between accepting its embrace or fleeing. The cowboys dropped them off on the edge of town.

Jay went downtown to visit the bars. Ezra rolled his sleeping bag out in the city park and watched the cars, crowd, and lights from a distance. His father, mother, and younger sister were just a few miles away. He wondered if his dog and horse could sense his presence as substantially as he could feel theirs. He knew his father would be talking with old rodeo friends and bartering prospective bucking horses. His mother was probably standing slim and nervous at the kitchen window, coffee in one hand, cigarette in the other, wondering where her only son was. Ezra seldom wrote. Just a postcard now and then, every few weeks. A drunk Indian wandered by with a bottle of wine, and he and Ezra drank and talked until midnight. Ezra told him he always wanted to have been born Indian. The Indian told him he was crazy. Ezra said he meant an Indian in the early 1800s, before white men. The Indian agreed. When the wine was gone, the Indian left, and Ezra climbed in his bag. He did not sleep well. He dreamed he was shirtless in the summer hills of his youth, riding his paint horse through chalky, rose-colored badlands. The sun was hours old when Jay returned and Ezra was packed and waiting.

"Man, what a night," Jay said. "I didn't get one moment of sleep. I met a lot of people who know you, man. I told them you were studying karate at a remote monastery. They thought that was cool."

Ezra said nothing.

"I met Lacey," Jay said.

"What?" Ezra asked. "You saw her? Did you tell her I was here?"

"Hey, man, I know our deal. I told her what I told everyone else. Only she didn't seem too impressed."

"She's too young to be in the bars," Ezra said. "She's only sixteen."

"Maybe, but she kisses like she's older."

"She what—"

Jay laughed at his protectiveness. "Relax, she was with Austin and Cody Arbuckle and your other sister, Diane."

"Diane's in town?"

"She's home showing the ranch to her new Jewish husband. He doesn't seem too crazy about Yellow Rock."

Ezra glanced west toward the Interstate. The hometown was starting to strangle him. He felt confined as if he were a child again and Diane had trapped him in the cellar. His self-esteem toppled around him and relived the terror of brandings when his bachelor uncles mocked him and called him names. He wanted the open road. Jay saw the highway stripes flashing in Ezra's eyes. "Whoa, man," he said. "Hold your horses. We're going to the Bucking Horse Sale, remember?"

"Let's just hit the road," Ezra said. "Let's forget this whole thing."

"No, man. We made a deal. It will be a gas. I will meet your father, then we will go to Kansas and you'll meet mine. We're going to the sale."

"It will cost us ten dollars each to get in," Ezra said.

"No, man," Jay laughed. "We're sneaking in. That's part of the fun."

"I hate it here."

"Man, it's ghosts, man. You're fighting ghosts in your mind. Vapors. Mind trips. There's nothing here to be afraid of, man."

"You haven't met Charley Arbuckle. Or my father."

"I will."

"Did you know I once had six bachelor uncles that all lived in the same house?"

"You're jivin' me, man."

"No, it's true. Four of them are dead but two still live there."

"You never told me that, man."

"My bloodline doesn't scream for publicity."

"Man, everyone has strange relatives," Jay said. "My father's sister was committed to an institution. She's still there. My mother's father ran off with a bearded lady from the circus when she was four years old."

"You're kidding?"

"Yeah, I'm kidding, but it sounded good. It's true about my dad's sister though. Some people think mental illness runs in our family."

"I know it runs in mine," Ezra said.

Jay became forceful. "Grab your pack, man. We are going to the sale. You gave your word, and I'm holding you to it."

They stashed their packs in the brush on the riverbank then climbed over the fence of the Yellow Rock Fairgrounds while two girls distracted the ticket-taker. Jay insisted on going behind the chutes where the horses were penned and the contesting cowboys waited, stretching nervously in an atmosphere reeking of adrenaline and testosterone. Ezra tried to hold him back. "Let's just get a seat in the side bleachers," he said. But Jay would have no part in being a mere spectator. He saw it as a wild and colorful cowboy circus with dust rising in the air, horses clamoring in the chutes, and buckle-bunny cowboy groupies sitting the fence like railbirds, soaking up sun and sipping beer. He wanted to drink it in like a hearty glass of beer.

Ezra followed part way to the chutes then hung in the shadows of the arena fence. He did not want to chance a meeting with his father and Charley Arbuckle—both of whom would be in the area as consignors of horses—or Austin and Cody, who as bronc riders would be behind the chutes. He also knew that a drunk cowboy at any instant might sucker punch him from behind then cut his ponytail off for a trophy. He squatted near the fence and watched the furious, dusty action as saddle bronc and bareback riders exploded from the chutes on wild and spoiled horses.

From a distance he could distinguish the tall, long-armed frame of his father and the wiry, gnarled old cowboy beside him. His father seemed as strong and proud as ever. Charley Arbuckle looked as hard and crooked as a cedar post. Ezra felt drawn and repulsed simultaneously by the sight of them and the world—their world—around them. It was in this arena that Ezra had been thrown from a bull and chastised by Charley for having "quit the critter." Now, with eleven months of adventure under his belt, he felt half-ready to challenge the world that had beaten him. But half-ready was not ready enough, and he sunk into a depression mired in a cold, repressed fury.

He watched in stone silence for an hour but the smell and sounds brought back tortured memories of cattle drives, of an ornery blue roan horse named Ribbon Tail, of uncles screaming and cursing him. He retreated to the banks of the river where he sat in the cool shade of a willow and watched the slow, blue-green water roll lazily eastward. The sounds of the announcer, auctioneer, and buzzers were distant echoes, like the cawing of crows in a faraway field. After several hours he returned to the rodeo arena, determined to locate Jay and catch a ride to the highway.

The selling had slowed. Much of the crowd had dispersed. There were still horses to be bucked but a shortage of cowboys to ride.

"We are now paying mount money for cowboys," the announcer stated. "Ten dollars per head for every horse you ride." Ezra watched impatiently as a few cowboys lined up to earn their pay. He kept a wary eye on his father and Charley Arbuckle. They still stood in the arena as resolute as statues. Ezra watched Austin ride one out and could sense the pride radiating from old Charley. Then Cody came out on a little paint mare and bucked-off on the third jump. Ezra was unprepared for the next announcement. It dropped from the heavens with the authority of God. "Our next mount money cowboy, from Manhattan, Kansas, is J. L. Walker."

A surprised Ezra pressed his face against the arena's woven-wire fence. The chute opened and there was Jay, astride a thin sorrel horse, his hand plunged deep into a bareback rigging. He wore boots and spurs but no hat. He tried to lay back and spur as if he had been coached but the momentum brought him up and over the horse's head. He rolled once in the dirt and jumped up smiling. Jay had been afraid when he climbed down on the horse, but he had found fear to be as stimulating as drugs. His senses sharpened. He could smell the horse, the dust, the wood and paint of the chute, the sweat on the cowboys around him; he could see the tanned, leathery face of Johnny Riley who stood yards distant in the arena. Jay knew he was doing what Ezra Riley would not do and he felt enlarged for it. And though he was afraid, he was not stricken by fear because he was ignorant and innocent. No horse had ever kicked him, bitten him, or thrown and drug him through the dirt. When the chute gate opened the entire universe seemed to suddenly break in a golden dawn, he was God's special child, a chosen vessel. Getting hurt was not his destiny. He rose loose and fell loose. He walked back to the chute smiling, imagining a deep roar of approval from the small crowd that remained.

Austin watched Jay's cocky strut with a vengeful stare. He would not be outdone by a dude. He pushed another cowboy aside and put his own rigging on the cowboy's horse. He rode the horse with a cruel fury, his lean body laying back, his legs whipping the spurs into the horse's shoulders and raking them back, the rowel marks leaving little trails of blood on the animal's hide.

Jay bounced happily to the chute gangplank and dropped his borrowed rigging on a second horse. His name was announced and he came out on a high-leaping sorrel bronc. Jay was whipped from the horse's butt to his shoulders, flopping like a coon tail on a car antenna, until bucking off over the right shoulder on the fifth jump. He landed hard but got up, brushed himself off, and walked back to the chutes.

Ezra could not believe what he was seeing. He had been bucked off many times. He knew the pain. And even more, he knew the terror of crawling down into the narrow chute and strapping yourself to a thousand pounds of fury.

Austin rode a third horse to the buzzer and the crowd cheered. He was a handsome sight. Lean, dark, and dashing with perfect teeth that flashed in a sly, conceited smile.

No sooner had Austin set foot to the ground than the chutes opened and Jay came out on a palomino mare. The audience sensed a contest had developed between the flashy local cowboy and the hatless rookie, and they cheered when Jay gamely rode to the whistle.

Austin followed on a squealing paint that pitched itself backward, lost its footing, and rolled over Austin. The crowd emitted a loud collective gasp, then applauded wildly as Austin rolled unscathed through a frenzy of striking hooves and jumped to his feet.

Jay followed on a little black mare that ran and hopped and he rode her easily, even pretending to fan her with his imaginary hat as he has seen cowboys on television do.

Ezra was astounded and jealous. Jay was not only recklessly brave, but naturally athletic. He was learning to get in rhythm with the individual styles of the horses, and he rode for the pure joy of riding, not for the competition with Austin or the money. If respect was the one thing lacking in Ezra's attitude toward the preacher's kid, Jay now had it. And in spades. But Ezra was also envious. He knew if he could be as daring as Jay

Walker, his father, uncles, and Charley Arbuckle would accept him. His father would talk proudly about him to his friends. The ranch would be his, a kingdom for an heir, and his uncles would step aside when he entered a corral, not daring to utter a word of criticism or ridicule. Or this is how he imagined it would be.

The unannounced rivalry between Austin, Yellow Rock's favorite son, and Jay, the interloper, grew in intensity. Cody backed away and did not ride any more horses. The other cowboys, too, backed from the chutes to watch the personal duel.

Every horse that came in was now either Austin's or Jay's. When Austin rode his fourth, Jay did, too. He was lasting longer with each ride and learning to lean back against the horse's rump and rake his spurs on its shoulders.

Austin rode five. Jay rode five. The pickup men gave him pointers when they grabbed him from the bronc and fans in the stands shouted encouragement.

Austin rode his sixth. Jay followed. Austin climbed on number seven. Jay bucked off his seventh horse. He was tiring and his riding arm was getting sore. Austin bucked off hard from his eighth horse and got up slowly. He was hoping the supply of horses would end, but he would ride until he died before he gave in to the curly haired kid from Kansas.

Jay rode his eighth horse to the whistle but walked more slowly and stiffly back to the chute. Austin rode his ninth but he didn't spur. He just hung on until the whistle. Jay's ninth horse did not buck, it only ran wildly around the arena before crashing into the wire fence. Jay rolled free. The announcer encouraged everyone to give the two cowboys a big hand because the day's sale was over. There was no more bucking stock.

When the announcement rattled over the tinny speakers, Austin was behind the chutes stuffing his rigging into his warbag but Jay was in the arena, having just rolled free from his last horse. He stood and waved to the crowd, then walked across the dusty, hard-packed ground, straddling the shadows that leaned long and black toward the east, and approached the two older men who still stood ominously against the fence like guardians of the past. Hours before he had recognized them instantly from Ezra's descriptions. Charlie was a slight, tight-faced old man with fancy boots and a big hat. John Riley was tall and broad-shouldered with arms the length of well ropes and hands as big as buckets. The setting sun made his clean-shaven, weathered face shine. He had strong features, rugged like the badlands, but sharp as a cold northern wind. His black hair was gray at the temples.

"Mr. Riley?" Jay said.

John Riley looked up. "Yes?" he said.

Jay extended his hand. "My name is J. L. Walker," he said. John Riley's handshake made Jay think he had stuck his hand in the jaws of a massive trap.

"You got salt, boy," Charley Arbuckle spoke up. "You rode those critters with a lot of try."

Jay thanked Charley and shook his hand, but his eyes stayed on John Riley who quietly appraised the friendly, curly haired kid.

"I just wanted to tell you," Jay said, "that I met your son, Ezra, last week in California."

An almost indiscernible light of concern lit John Riley's eyes. "How is he?" the father asked.

"He's doing fine. He's been studying karate in the mountains of Nevada," Jay said.

Charley grunted and looked away.

"How did you run into him?" John Riley asked.

Jay lied. "I met him at a rodeo. He was there covering it and taking pictures for a paper. I was just passing through and had never been to a rodeo before. Ezra and I got to talking, and he said I should come to the Bucking Horse Sale, and if I did, to say hello to his father."

John Riley's strong Irish face softened, his brows furrowed and he stared at the ground. Jay thought John Riley might choke or stutter. But he didn't. Instead he looked back at Jay. "You've never rode broncs before?" he asked.

"No, this was my first time." He nodded at Charley. "I borrowed the boots and spurs from your grandson, Cody."

"You rode good," John Riley said. "For your first time."

"I loved it," Jay said. "It's sort of like dancing. It takes a few turns to learn the steps." Both men nodded. They understood.

Jay paused, waiting for John or Charley's next step. After a long minute, John Riley nodded at the concession stand. "Buy ya a beer?" he said.

Jay thought for a minute. He was tempted. Ezra's father intrigued him. He was a man with a powerful physical presence and an unwavering aura of confidence. Jay wondered what tales lay in the core of the man's soul and was enticed by the lure of drinking with a cowboy who had swept the Montana plains of wild horses. But Jay had not seen Ezra for hours and was haunted by the fear that he had left. He could not bear that. As interesting as John Riley seemed, his stories were of the past while Ezra's stories were the future. He reached out and shook the man's huge hand again. "I sure wish I could," he said. "But I have to catch a ride home to Kansas."

John Riley's lips quivered in forming words that Jay guessed had to do with Ezra, but Johnny swallowed them, gulping them down with effort, like a coyote gorging himself on meat, then he nodded at Jay, the motion lowering the brim of his silver Stetson without cutting off eye contact. The cowboy's hazel eyes swirled with a mixture of fire and loneliness, friendliness and challenge, then John Riley and Charley Arbuckle turned and walked away.

It was dark when Jay met Ezra at the fairground's rear entrance. Jay was counting his money and humming as he walked up. "Ninety bucks," he said, flashing the bills at Ezra.

"So what did he say?" Ezra asked.

"He wanted to know how you were doing." Jay said. He had been paid with a check but had talked the sale's secretary into giving him cash.

"And?" Ezra said. "Anything else?"

"So, how did I ride, man?" Jay said, ignoring Ezra's question.

"Fine. What else did my father say?"

"He wanted to know what you were doing. I told him you were studying the martial arts in Nevada."

"You are such a persuasive liar," Ezra said. There was an underlying bitterness to his tone.

"It's not really a lie. Time means nothing to God. In a cosmic way you are still studying karate in Nevada."

"So? What did you think of him?" Ezra asked as they walked to the river to retrieve their packs.

"Nice guy. Good-looking. Wouldn't want to fight him, but he seems good-natured."

"That's it?" Ezra was shocked. He had never thought of his father as being handsome or friendly.

"Yeah. I liked him. But he seems lonely. I think life has kinda caught up with him. He's a man with some regrets."

Ezra was feeling the pull. He had been home too long. The hills north of Yellow Rock with their scorio-tipped ridges and magpie nests were calling him. His worried mother was calling him. His paint horse on Sunday Creek was nickering softly in the breeze. The nicker became louder in his mind, and louder still until Gusto seemed to be screaming and the imagined sound of a horse screaming terrorized Ezra. "This was a stupid idea," he snapped at Jay.

"Why? I had a great time."

"You could have gotten killed out there. What made you get on all those horses?"

"Why not, man? I loved it. It's one big dance." The two of them walked quietly in the darkness, the sound of Main Street traffic grew louder with each step. Ezra was brooding in his jealousy and in the guilt of knowing he could not so much as walk up to his father or make a phone call to his mother. He felt weak and emasculated. He felt like he had as a child at brandings when his uncles mocked his every attempt to rope or wrestle calves until he ran and hid and watched the commotion from a distance. He was that same small, shamed child today, hiding from the sale while Jay basked in the spotlight.

"You know what?" Jay said finally. "I think you are crazy for leaving all of this. This is heaven, man. A ranch. Horses. I'd stay in a minute and ride bucking horses every day. If my dad had a ranch here in Yellow Rock, I would never leave."

"What do you know about it?" Ezra said angrily. "You think every day is like this? You think it's all fun and romance, cowboys riding into sunsets, and strumming guitars? You were lucky today, man. That's all. Just lucky."

"Whoa, man. I'm lucky every day. Besides, it's nothing to get sore about."

"You'll think sore in the morning."

"Naw, man, I won't be sore. Now, chill out a little, man. We're getting back on the road. I dig where you're coming from. A prophet is without honor in his own town."

"What's that got to do with anything?"

"That," Jay said, "has precisely to do with everything. That is why you cannot live in Yellow Rock. You have a call of God on your life, a destiny intertwined with mine. We are partners in The Last Days."

"You're nuts," Ezra said.

Ezra was too sullen to say anything more. They humped their packs to the Interstate. The fourth car by was a salesman on his way to Rapid City. He was mesmerized by the charm and stories of the curly haired one. But the mysterious young man with the ponytail said nothing. He was in a war within himself.

CHAPTER NINE

Sunday morning found them in an expensive motel room paid for with Jay's winnings. Jay was so stiff Ezra helped him dress. They ate a large breakfast at a truck stop then stepped out on the highway.

"Does your father's church have a Sunday night service?" he asked.

"Of course," Jay answered.

"Let's try to make it."

"No way," Jay laughed. "That's only twelve hours from now and we have seven hundred miles to go. No way, man. My father will be in the city park there tomorrow morning at 10:30, if we are lucky we might make that." Ezra knew Jay did not want to go near his father's church any more than Ezra had wanted to go to the Bucking Horse Sale. But Jay's run of phenomenal luck suddenly turned in Ezra's favor. A lime green Torino with spoiler, racing slicks, and a jacked-up rear-end skidded to a stop beside them. A young man with short hair got out. "Can you guys drive?" he asked.

"You bet," Ezra answered.

"I have to be in Kansas City tonight or I'm AWOL," he said. "I'm bushed. I've been driving from Seattle nonstop. You guys drive while I catch some sleep in the back."

They stashed their packs in the trunk and roared off down the highway with Ezra at the wheel. Jay liked fast cars, and Ezra expected him to drive, but Jay was becoming increasingly withdrawn. He blew softly on his harmonica, complained about his soreness and stiffness, and stared vacantly out the window. The farm fields and pastures zipped by in a fluid blur and the telephone poles passed like a picket fence. The closer they got to Kansas the more quiet Jay became.

"Hey, man," Ezra finally said. "I acted like a jerk yesterday. Sorry about that."

Jay shrugged. "No big deal," he said and he buried himself in *Narcissus and Goldmund*. The soldier awakened in Nebraska and rolled a joint. Ezra took a couple of tokes but for the first time, Jay declined.

"Aren't you guys heads?" the soldier asked.

"My partner has to stay straight for a change," Ezra explained.

When they crossed the Kansas state line Jay said, "I don't see why it's so important that we get there in time for the service."

"You saw my father in his church," Ezra told him. "I'm going to see your father in his."

Pastor Walker's church in Manhattan was a simple frame building with unpainted windows and a steeple that barely rose above the neighborhood trees. The melody of traditional hymns drifted through the walls and onto the mild evening air as Ezra hesitated at the door. Now that he was there Ezra was afraid to enter. Jay spoke to him from the bushes. "Man, we're here now. You might as well go in. Take a seat in a back pew. When the sermon's over, you can get away quick enough."

"I just remembered how much I don't like churches," Ezra said.

"Go on in, man."

Ezra cracked the door, slid in sideways, and quickly took a seat in the back. The pews were of a blonde wood and as hard as iron. Several people in the congregation of twenty or thirty glanced back at him. Ezra kept his head down and stared at the hymnals racked on the back of the pew.

Jay's father was pacing the dais like a leopard in a cage. The resemblance between father and son was remarkable, except Jay's hair was curlier. There was a large wooden cross on the wall behind the dais. Carved on its horizontal crossbeam was: *Ye Must Be Born Again.*

"Brothers and sisters," Pastor Walker began. "You know I consider Sunday nights to be the nights for the faithful." He was a slim, compact man in his late forties. His forehead was high and his shiny black hair was slicked back. A placid, staid woman Ezra guessed to be the pastor's wife sat in the front pew with five stair-step children, ranging from about four to sixteen. She had played the piano during the hymns.

"Sunday mornings are a blessing," the pastor continued, raising his arms and pacing as he talked. He had a very physical presence, Ezra noted. His footwork and arm movements suggested he might once have been a boxer and he had a pugilistic style of preaching. "But Sunday mornings can often be the service for the merely religious, for those whose service to God is all style and no substance. They talk the things of God, but then deny His power." The preacher's hawklike eyes observed the young stranger in the back.

"On Sunday nights," he shouted, his voice rising in a glorious crescendo of fine-tuned articulation, "I am free to preach the truth. I am unfettered, liberated from the warm-water demands of Laodecians. I am Lazarus, called from the tomb." He rolled his *r*'s wonderfully, and Ezra knew from whom Jay had inherited his powerful voice. The man walked as he talked, stalking his own message as if it were a mouse in the grass and he a hungry cat. "And I can tell you," he shouted, and pointed to the back pew, "that if you do not know Jesus as your personal Lord and Saviour your soul is bound, condemned to an eternity wandering the dry and waterless regions of hell, moaning and mourning for your poor decisions, pitying your state and hating yourself, for this very night, from these lips, YOU KNEW BETTER!"

Ezra felt riveted to the pew by the man's piercing eyes, but he met the contact. He had faced down a biker with a knife near his jugular. He could handle Jay's hellfire-and-brimstone father.

"Do you know Jesus?" the preacher shouted. "That is the question, the one question, the only question of eternal importance."

Ezra squirmed in his pew. He was outnumbered. Everyone there was different from him, therefore, against him.

The preacher turned and faced the large wooden cross at the front of the church. "God will not turn his back on you," he said. "You must not turn your back on God." He whirled around, his face flushed with blood, sweat beading on his brow, his arm and eyes pointing at the pew in the back. But it was empty. Ezra had left.

The next morning they spied on Jay's father from behind a children's merry-go round. They were in Manhattan's main city park and in its center was a grassy knoll with one lone park bench. A single figure sat there, his legs crossed, one arm stretched out on the back of the bench, his head tilted back as if gazing at clouds.

"Today is his day off," Jay said. "He comes here every Monday, no matter what the weather, and spends an hour or two alone on that bench. He says it is his best escape from phone calls."

"I hate to disturb him," Ezra said.

"You are not disturbing him," Jay reprimanded. "You are bringing him news of his son."

Ezra advanced across the green. He wore clean clothes and his hair was tied back in a tight ponytail, which—when it was not visible—made his hair appear styled as the preacher's. He felt the pastor's eyes—or so he thought—even though the man's head did not move. He sat beside him on the bench. Jay's father slowly lowered his head and looked calmly at Ezra. "Good morning," the preacher said. He did not seem surprised at all.

"Good morning," Ezra answered. He was well scrubbed and his clothes had been washed by two girls who had let the odd traveling pair spend the night in their apartment. The girls wanted to party, but Jay was moody and argumentative. He left and walked the streets alone while

Ezra told stories about life on the road. Now, sitting next to Jay's father, Ezra felt suddenly guilty for his influence on Jay, and for his own life of drugs, eastern religions, and occasional lovers.

"You were at my church last night," the pastor noted.

"My name is Ezra Riley." "I met your son Jay last week in California." The statement was sort of true, but the spirit behind it was a lie and Ezra knew it. And he knew the pastor knew it, too.

Pastor Walker's eyes became direct and sharp. "California," he said. "I might have known. Is he okay?"

"He's fine."

Pastor Walker folded his arms across his chest as if containing his frustration. "What was he doing?" he asked.

It was hard for Ezra to lie. "He was hitchhiking, like me. We traveled together for a while. We went to an amateur rodeo and he got on some bucking horses."

"So," the father sighed. "My son is now thinking of becoming a rodeo cowboy."

"No, I think he is trying to join some Jesus Movement in southern California and hook up with a Christian band."

"Hmmm. I wonder if that is good or if that is bad." The pastor's brow furrowed and he crossed his arms on his chest.

"He told me to stop by if I was in the area and say hello and tell you that he was okay."

The preacher's dark eyes scrutinized Ezra. "You have quite a story yourself, don't you, young man? How long have you been on the road?"

"Almost a year."

"I hope you taught my son something about street smarts."

"I tried." Ezra said. "He doesn't learn very easily."

"You don't have to tell me that." There was a weary frustration in his polished voice when the father talked of his son.

"Jay can be very bold," Ezra said.

"Reckless is the word. Utterly reckless."

"Yes," Ezra said. "That is the word."

"And gifted. Reckless and gifted. That is a dangerous combination."

Ezra thought about it. He didn't know what the pastor meant. They each looked up and watched a cloud float by, their own thoughts going with it.

Then the preacher turned the focus back on Ezra.

"And what is your impression of my son, Jubal, Mr. Riley?"

"I've never met anyone quite like him. Extremely talented musically, of course. And reckless like you say, but also innocent at the same time."

"Innocent?"

"Yes. Innocent."

"Hmmm." The preacher folded his hands behind his head and tilted his head back, his eyes again on the clouds. "I must admit that my son is often a disappointment to me," he said softly. "The problem is everything comes too easily for Jubal. He is, as you know, bright, charming, and of course, a musical prodigy. The charm will be his downfall. I have tried to deny him things hoping he would learn discipline, but it hasn't worked. It has only frustrated him. Did he tell you about Bible school? Of course, he did. Did he tell you he left or that he was kicked out?"

"He said he left."

"Jubal defines everything by his terms. He was kicked out. Some rather serious trouble, I'm afraid."

"Mr. Walker, uh, *Pastor* Walker, have you ever heard of a book called *Narcissus and Goldmund?*" Ezra asked.

"No. I don't think so," he said thoughtfully.

"A German wrote it. Hermann Hesse. He won the Nobel Prize."

"And what is the significance of this book?" the preacher asked.

"It had a great impact on me when I first read it a year ago," Ezra said. "It helped launch me on the road. It is about two men who meet in a monastery. One, Narcissus, is a brilliant young scholar, teacher, and monk. The other, Goldmund, is a handsome young student who leaves the monastery in search of art and sensual pleasures. When I first read the book, I thought I was a Goldmund. But then I met Jay, uh, Jubal. Compared to him I am Narcissus. I am the monk."

"Is it a Christian book?" the preacher asked.

"What do you mean?" Ezra was still uncertain about religious terms and polarizations.

"I mean, is it the type of book one would find in a Christian bookstore? Like where one would find C. S. Lewis or John Bunyan?"

Ezra shook his head. "No. I don't think so." He had never been in a Christian bookstore.

"Then I doubt that I will read it," Pastor Walker said. "But I understand your point. I understand it perfectly. Jubal is this, uh—"

"Goldmund."

"Goldmund. An odd name. What does it mean?"

"It is German for Gold Mouth."

Pastor Walker sighed deeply. "Ah, that is Jubal. A golden mouth and a silver tongue. I believe 'Golden Mouth' is also the meaning of the name of a famous man of God, a Catholic saint named Chrysostom. Do you suppose Jubal is a saint?"

"I don't know," Ezra said. "I haven't known any saints."

The preacher smiled at the answer, and the two continued watching puffy cumulus clouds float across the blue Kansas sky. Ezra remembered Jay in the park in San Francisco, transfixed on clouds as he descended from LSD. His father seemed equally riveted.

"Do you know what the anointing is?" the preacher asked finally.

Ezra did not like admitting ignorance. "No. Not really," he said.

"It is when the power of God descends upon you, or rises up from within you, whatever the case may be. I have never done drugs, Mr. Riley. I have never so much as touched a beer in my life. But I can tell you this, the anointing is the most wonderful thing that can be experienced. But we must not try to manipulate it. It must choose its own vessel."

"Why are you telling me this?" Ezra asked.

The pastor's dark eyes were soft but intense. "You will know about the anointing some day," he said.

"I am not even a Christian," Ezra protested. "Isn't your prediction better suited for your son?"

"I wish it were," he said sadly, then the preacher smiled with a sense of abandon, glanced at his wristwatch, and tilted his head back again to view the sky. The clouds were gone. The sky was a pale ashen-blue. "You will likely see Jubal again," he said. "Maybe soon. Maybe a long time from now. You will be able to see for yourself which character he is in this favorite little book of yours. Is he the man devoted to God or is he the one given to pleasures? But as for you, I have no doubt which one you will be, Mr. Riley."

Ezra felt the conflicting duality of the rodeo arena at Yellow Rock. Part of him wanted to run, part of him wanted to stay. The preacher's spirituality seemed as narrow as a railroad track but as deep as a canyon. Ezra was intrigued by the man, and challenged, but chattering voices in his mind demanded he leave. He fidgeted on the bench hoping the preacher would say something else, anything that would lean further into predictions of his destiny. But Pastor Walker said nothing. It was Monday, the pastor's day off, the park bench was his—he had owned it for years, and the sky itself had been claimed by him.

Ezra felt like a trespasser, a pagan on holy ground. "I have to be going," Ezra said awkwardly.

The preacher came down from the atmosphere, met Ezra's eyes, and took his hand in a fierce grip. Walker had the hands of a man who had toiled outside, not the soft, limp, smooth hands that only caressed the onion skin pages of Bibles. "God go with you," he said. "And take care of my son."

Ezra nodded and walked away, down the green knoll, toward the merry-go-round, swing sets, and sandbox.

"Tell Jubal hello," the preacher said quietly from behind him.

Ezra shouldered his pack and began striding down the street. Jay followed like a poodle, nipping at his heels with questions.

"So what did he say? What did you think?" he asked. Jay seemed younger and smaller in the limits of his father's town and Ezra knew that was how he had felt in Yellow Rock. Always the child, never a man.

"I like your father. He's strong, intense, and direct. His religion is too narrow for me, but he believes it deeply. He is worried about you. He thinks you are gifted but too easily seduced by your own talent."

Jay laughed. "Man, that's all I've heard my whole life. I can't help it if most things are easy for me. What does he want me to be, a nuclear physicist or a brain surgeon?"

"No, he wants you to be humble," Ezra said.

"Humble?" Jay said. "Man, I'm young. I'll be humble when I'm older."

"What happened at the Bible school?" Ezra asked.

"What do you mean?" Jay asked defensively.

"You know what I mean. What happened? Why did you get kicked out?"

"It's not important, man."

"Did you get a girl pregnant?" Ezra asked.

"I dunno, man, maybe." Jay turned inward to a bitter silence. A black cloud of anger enveloped him.

Ezra walked briskly, directly, as someone who knew where he was going. Where, Jay finally asked, *were* they going?

"I don't know," Ezra said. "New Mexico, maybe."

Jay stopped in front of a Main Street business and read a flyer taped to the window. It announced antiwar demonstrations at the University of Kansas in Lawrence. "We are going there," he said, pointing to the poster. He was suddenly buoyant and adventurous again as if Ezra's encounter with his father had never happened.

"The University? How come?" Ezra asked.

"Because Nixon is bombing Hanoi and escalating the war in Cambodia. Because that is where the action is."

"I'm not into politics," Ezra said.

"But you're a writer, man," Jay insisted. "It will be material. You have to be more involved with life, man. What are you ever going to write about if you spend all your time in solitude?"

"I've been in campus demonstrations before," Ezra said.

"But I haven't," Jay said emphatically, determined to have his way.

"Okay," Ezra said. "We'll go to Lawrence."

CHAPTER TEN

It was a pleasant evening on the streets of Lawrence and the crowd of marchers slowly grew as it wove through the neighborhoods of old Victorian homes and boulevard trees. "Join us," the crowd shouted to onlookers, and gradually more protesters were absorbed into the unit.

Minutes after reaching the town Jay and Ezra had found a place to crash in a house rented to a group of longhaired art students. Their leader had aspirations of being a guru. Ezra tried to discuss Eastern philosophy with him, but he was too stoned. He simply sat in a lotus position on the living room floor while he counted the revolutions of the ceiling fan and ate corn flakes out of the box.

Three girls lived in the house. One was a dancer, one a painter, and the third one was a radical feminist. The painter asked Jay to pose nude for sketches. Jay didn't mind.

"When's the demonstration going to happen?" Jay asked her as he sat naked on a stool.

"Oh, there will probably be one tonight," said.

"I have a low draft number," Jay explained.

"Everyone here is against the war," the girl said.

"I sure am," Jay said. "Now my friend, Ezra, he's different. He's not against war. He's just against losing wars."

The girl stared intently at her work. It was the best she had ever done, but the magic wasn't hers. It was the subject. He seemed to have a way of crawling from the stool, through her, and onto the canvas. She had sketched many nudes but she had never seen anyone so natural with his clothes off. She would have left school and traveled with Jay had he asked her.

The dancer was interested in Ezra, and he spent time showing her karate movements that could be choreographed into a dance routine. Once, while they were close, she ran her fingers across his chest and nodded toward her room upstairs. He shook his head. She was too rich and pampered to interest him, and he was above being one of her toys.

That evening Jay and Ezra sat shirtless and barefoot on the roof of the house. The inhabitants had gone their separate ways to different parties. Jay did not want to party. He wanted to be involved in a demonstration. The artist told him to wait on the roof. The demonstration would come to him. They could hear it in the distance and felt it grow in numbers and move to them in the rising volume of the voices. It suddenly appeared like a large snake, rounding a boulevard with the leaders in the front holding large placards. There were several hundred young people marching. They saw Ezra and Jay on the roof. "Join us," the crowd shouted at them.

"Here we go," Ezra said, and he walked to the edge of the roof and dropped lightly to the lawn below. Jay followed.

The crowd grew like a simple life-form that moved by absorbing other single cells. Voices called out for an end to the war in short, cadent slogans. Jay's eyes twinkled and his voice was exuberant. Ezra moved along quietly, scanning the crowd and the onlookers for anyone that seemed suspicious. There were plants in with the marchers, he knew that. Longhaired FBI agents. He had seen them before. The crowd moved from the neighborhoods to the entrance of the university where they were met by the state attorney general and eighty state policemen, four rows of twenty, in full riot gear of flak jackets and helmets with face shields and riot batons held to their chests. The student leaders went forward to talk to the state's supreme lawman, and Ezra pushed his way through the crowd to follow them. He wanted to stay aware. Jay did not follow. His attention was on a braless redhead with earrings shaped like marijuana leaves.

The tension was building between the demonstration leaders and the police. "We are going in. It's our university," Ezra heard a student say to the attorney general as he made it to the front.

The attorney general was a short, impatient man in a three-piece suit. "You disperse in five minutes, or I turn the police loose," he warned them.

"We aren't leaving," the student said.

The attorney general turned to his troops: "One, two, three, four, five," he said and raised his hand and dropped it. The eighty policemen advanced at a stiff jog, their riot sticks raised and ready in a two-handed grip. The student leaders broke rank and ran igniting a ripple of panic that moved through the crowd and turned it like a large snake down the sidestreets of Lawrence. Ezra, though barefooted, was fleet and conditioned by the road. He darted quickly through the running students. He saw a girl fall and heard her screams as others trampled her. He scanned the fleeing students for Jay but could not see him. Ezra wasn't worried. Jay was too slippery to be caught. The crowd spilled down a side street like a school of frightened fish, then turned and entered the campus through a back entrance fronted by small stores, shops, and faculty residences. Campus security and local police rushed to cut them off. The crowd hesitated for a moment which allowed the state police to approach from behind. The troopers swung their batons at random. Ezra saw a curious young professor step from his apartment doorway and take a blow to the side of the head. He crumbled like a wad of paper.

"Kent State! Kent State!" some in the crowd began to yell. Other students and bystanders were felled by the batons, girls were screaming, and the students scattered wildly to escape. Ezra resumed searching for Jay. He did not want him to do something reckless. As he looked he saw a tall, blonde girl step from a store with a stack of books. A passing trooper swung his baton. The girl raised the books to protect herself, and the riot stick struck them, sending her backward against the store window. Her books fell to the street. The policeman raised his baton again. Ezra came running. As the baton descended he jumped in the air, rotated his body and sent a stiff right leg into the policeman's chest. The flak jacket absorbed the impact but the officer was knocked backwards through the store's plate glass window. The girl had fallen and Ezra reached down to help her up. He saw anger and alarm in her blue eyes and her mouth seemed to form a slow-motion scream. He never saw the baton blow that dropped him to the pavement.

He awakened on the iron grid of a jail cell bunk. His head throbbed and his vision was blurred. There were others in the cell, young people like himself, and more in other cells. A bearded fellow with rainbow-colored suspenders was wiping Ezra's forehead with a damp handkerchief. "You okay, man?" he asked. Ezra tried to rise, but flashing, white-hot pain dropped him to the bunk and he was awash again in unconsciousness. He came to several hours later and was alone in the cell. He lay quietly for almost an hour before a jailer came by and noticed he was awake. "Hey, you," the jailer said. "You got any identification?" Ezra shook his head, an action he regretted because the pain sliced his skull in segments. "Your name Riley?" the jailer asked. Ezra grunted a yes. "There's people here to see you."

Jay looked both nervously amused and concerned as he entered the cell block. "You okay, man?" he asked, pressing up against the bars. He was followed by a young woman with sandy blonde hair. Ezra did not say anything. His eyes were still trying to distinguish between light and shadow.

"I brought you these, man," Jay said, and he passed a shirt and Ezra's moccasins through the bars. Ezra reached for them but the moccasins dropped to the floor. "Man, they should have taken you to the hospital," Jay said. His tenderness embarrassed Ezra.

Ezra struggled to put the shirt on. Every motion produced explosions of pain in his head. "What time is it?" he asked weakly.

"Eleven o'clock," Jay said.

"Monday night?"

"No, man. Tuesday morning."

Ezra's eyes finally focused on the two of them. The girl was about his age and an inch taller than Jay. She held the bars with long, delicate fingers. Her eyes were deep and stratified with layers of emotion, knowledge, and character. She was the girl of the books.

"Thank you for helping me," she said.

Jay stood protectively beside her but she paid no attention to him. "I brought her," he explained. "She was wandering around the station trying to find you." His charm was working, but he was the only one feeling its radiance. The girl ignored him, and Ezra was repulsed by his affected, almost effeminate, manner.

"You were hit from behind," the girl said.

"What's the deal?" Ezra asked. "When do I get out?" He was alert enough to feel trapped and claustrophobic. He could not stand confinement. He needed the hills or a long expanse of highway.

"Man, you kicked a cop." Jay said. "That's assaulting a police officer, man."

"He was defending me," the girl said. "There were witnesses."

"Did you see it?" Ezra asked Jay.

Jay shook his curly haired head and glanced at the floor. "No, man, I didn't see it." He did not admit he had escaped down an alley when the batons began swinging.

"There's a Student Legal Defense Office," the girl said. "I will get you a lawyer."

Ezra nodded. "What about my stuff?" he asked.

"I brought your pack, man." Jay said. "It's back at the sergeant's desk." A peculiar tension laced his voice. He was attracted to the blonde, but she showed no interest in him. He was possessive of his friendship with Ezra and jealous of the girl. The blonde and the jail bars were conspirators that could keep Ezra and Jay from the road life. They stood in the way of destiny. He fidgeted nervously and stared at Ezra with wide, childlike eyes, his mouth half-open to form words he could not mutter.

"My name is Anne," the girl said. She offered her hand through the bars. Ezra held it lightly. Her grip and her eyes were firm and direct. "I owe you," she said. "I will get you out of here." Ezra smiled weakly. He would have bargained with the devil for his release and was more than pleased to have Anne as his advocate.

"Man, they're going to hang you," Jay said. "You're not even a student and you kicked a cop. They'll paint you as a traveling agitator."

Ezra sighed and leaned against the bars. He knew Jay was right. Ezra had been in other demonstrations and had seen other people arrested. He looked up at Jay. "You don't need to stick around Lawrence," Ezra told him.

Jay feigned a disagreeing shake of his head, but he could not portend loyalty. He wanted to avoid the serious matters of life and jails were definitely serious. He drummed up a smile and a hopeful sparkle. "I thought I would hitch out to southern Cal," he said. "You could join me there."

Ezra nodded softly. His head hurt and he was behind bars. He didn't have any immediate plans. He looked away from Jay to the tall blonde. "What's your last name?" he asked.

"Cavanaugh," she said. Ezra felt pulled into the sanctuary of her eyes. Somehow she was his future and his confinement was necessary for realizing it.

"I'll get Anne's address," Jay said. "When I find a place for us in southern California, I will write you and let you know where I am."

Ezra nodded again but he did not look at Jay.

"We got songs to write, man. We'll make all of this a song." He turned to Anne. "I'm a music student," he said.

"So am I," she answered matter-of-factly, but her eyes were locked on Ezra's.

Jay was hurt and insulted. He felt rejected and shut out by both of them. "Well, I'll be going," he said.

"Good luck, man," Ezra said. He heard Jay's steps on the cold corridor floor. He heard the steps halt at the hallway door and knew he was looking back down the shadows and bars of the cellblock. "We'll meet up again," he heard him say. "It's destiny, man."

Ezra did not answer. He did not believe it. Jay Walker had been an interesting part of his life, a page or two in a long book, but he did not expect to ever see him again. There was no malice in Ezra's consideration. He simply did not believe Jay could be responsible enough to make his dream of destiny come true.

Jay was leaving. As he opened the door a gentle breeze rolled across the concrete floor and caused a rippling sound at Ezra's feet. Ezra looked down. Jay had left *Narcissus and Goldmund* on the floor just inside the cell. He looked up. Jay Walker was gone.

CHAPTER ELEVEN

1989

As iron sharpens iron,
So a man sharpens the countenance of
his friend.
Proverbs 27:17

In the soft rustling of the ivory grasses he did not hear the voice of God but he might well have. Ezra Riley lay with his face turned to a pale canopy of September sky. The shadow of a single cumulus cloud lit upon him briefly, then whispered by, wavering over the land like a large butterfly wing. If its passing was ominous, he did not notice. It only cooled him momentarily as he relaxed in the lap of the soil. Ezra felt nourished by the earth, rooted to origin and destiny by having his flesh upon its brown skin. He was a lover of the land and felt loved in return. He was not pantheistic in his passion, he was simply an earth person, as others are people of other elements, of sky or water. Perhaps even fire. He wondered who fire people were. Rock stars? Satanists? Arsonists?

His other love, a horse, stood nearby, its head low and ears splayed, one hind leg bent in the posture of repose. Split leather reins trailed from the bridle's grazing bit across the blue gamma and slender wheatgrass to Ezra's hand. He held them loosely. Horses also represented the soil to Ezra. They walked the earth, slept on the earth, ate from the earth, fertilized the earth. He had heard the theories that some men born of the prairie became wonderful sea captains, the waves of rolling grasses and endless sky graduating to waves of salt water and limitless horizons. He did not feel that way. The sea scared him. He needed something to put his feet on. He liked foundations, the feel of something substantial in a world increasingly turbulent.

At his side, the pages of three small books ruffled in the breeze. They were a small journal of his own writings, a pocket-sized collection of the Gospels for meditation, and an official notebook for compiling information on the detailed lives of cattle. This last one being for his job. For three years Ezra had been a part-time government cowboy. He tended cattle March through November on the 100 square miles of ranching and farming land known as the Fort Kellogg U.S. Range and Livestock Experiment Station—or simply, as locals called it, " he Fort." His supervisors were scientists, intense, distant, brainy men with doctorates in reproductive physiology, genetics, and biology. Men with good natures but large egos who labored like maniac dwarfs over experiments the staff cowboys often laughed at as being wastes of time and the taxpayers' money. Ezra did not laugh. He did not want to fall into the cynicism common to federal and state workers. He wanted one day to quit his job and walk away unmarked, unbranded from the experience.

Ezra glanced at his watch. He did not like being bound by time and hated even more the dictates of a labor union, but according to the rules he had to take two coffee breaks a day. With his mandatory fifteen-minute break coming to an end, he sat up, encircled his arms about his knees, and stared at a red-tailed hawk riding an updraft above him, its wings stretched out rigidly for lift.

"My view is almost the equal of yours," he told the bird. "Probably better. You look only for mice and rabbits." From his hilltop vantage he looked down and across Prairie Dog Creek to a small, bucolic herd of ruminating cattle, their tail switches flicking at flies. Beyond them The Fort's fields of ripening corn glowed bluish-green, capped by thousands of scarlet tassels waving in the breeze like handkerchiefs. Past the corn, the patchwork was the yellow acreage of newly harvested grain, the stubble standing headless in the sun. Farther away, past a grove of cottonwood trees and upriver from the huge feedlot, the sunlight reflected off the roofs of the barns, offices, laboratories, and residences of The Fort's headquarters.

The spurs on Ezra's boot heels tinkled liked miniature bells when he rose to his feet. His horse, Shiloh, raised his head dutifully and cocked both ears forward like pointed index fingers. Ezra put the books in his saddle bags, tightened the girth, grabbed the saddle horn with both hands—the sorrel braced itself—and pulled himself into the seat. It was two o'clock and his government day was an hour from ending. He worked ten-day shifts beginning at six in the morning, then returned to the Riley ranch and did the same chores—minus the experiments and the scientists—until dark. He did not really have a ranch of his own, he owned one in common with his two sisters, Diane and Lacey. And he had few cattle. He did have the responsibility of caring for his uncle, Solomon, his ranch, and what remained of Solomon's beef herd after nearly a decade of drought on the Montana plains. Working for Solomon, he decided, *was* like working for a scientist. A mad scientist.

Ezra reined Shiloh to the south toward the muted sound of highway traffic. He rode back following the fence line that bordered the Interstate. The cattle sometimes tested the fence, stretching their necks through the tight woven wire to reach the greener grasses of the barrow pit. Ezra repaired the breaches by finding the dislodged staples and tacking them back with the fencing tool he kept sheathed on the skirt of his saddle. He liked the contrast of riding next to the highway, which stretched above him like a concrete ribbon.

Amid the roar of passing trucks he heard a car brake then shift to reverse. He looked up at a luxury sedan—it might have been a Lexus or a Bonneville, Ezra did not know the different models. A man and a woman got out. "Can we talk to you?" the man shouted. Their car was stopped illegally on the shoulder of the road, its warning lights flashing. A subtle twinge on the reins brought Shiloh to a stop.

They descended the steep embankment carefully. The man wore khaki shorts and a knit pullover and the woman a blouse, slacks, and sandals. They were in their fifties.

"Would you mind if we took your picture?" the man asked.

"Where are you from?" Ezra replied.

"New Yawk," the woman said.

Ezra smiled thinking of Uncle Joe. "Go ahead," he said. Uncle Joe had always had a thing about New York City. Ezra, as a small child, would be riding drag behind a herd of slow-moving cows and Uncle Joe would say: "Ain'tcha glad you ain't in New York City?"

They snapped one of him alone. Shiloh turned his head and stared at them as if on cue. Then the woman stood beside the fence, its bottom woven wires and top three barbed wires separating her from the man and rider like a Berlin Wall of cultures. Her white, fragile arm rested daintily on the post as if the barbs below her were sharks that might jump off the wire and bite her. The man placed them within the framework of badland hills and beneath the famous Montana sky. The camera clicked.

"Have you been a cowboy all your life?" the woman asked. Her brown eyes were quick and curious. She was an intellectual, Ezra guessed. They looked like interesting people.

"Pretty much," Ezra said. What else could he say? He had been born to the land and separated from it only by a temporary exile. "What do you folks do?" he asked.

"We are book editors," she said. "We live outside Greenwich but work in the city. I do some riding myself. Hunter-jumpers. May I ask you, why is your saddle so big and heavy? Wouldn't it be easier on the horse if you rode English?"

Ezra looked down at his A-Fork custom-made saddle with a rubber-wrapped dally horn, nylon lariat wrapped in an Oregon strap, and aluminum horn loop, fencing pliers, and saddle bags held by saddle strings. Fully rigged, the saddle was light at forty-seven pounds. "This is my office, ma'am," he explained.

The man waved his hand at thousands of acres of dry prairie and eroded hills as if trying to grasp the enormity of what he was seeing. "Is this your ranch?" he asked.

"No," Ezra deadpanned. "It's yours."

They looked at him curiously and smiled. "I don't understand," the man said.

"Do you pay taxes?" Ezra asked.

The couple nodded.

"Then I guess it's your ranch," Ezra said and he bid them good-bye and nudged Shiloh into a trot. He was accustomed to tourists waving when he rode the fence line beside the Interstate, and he always waved back. He knew he appeared slow, historic, and mysterious; an icon of the west. In reality, he was but another union employee leaving his shift. Now a car had stopped, and he was an image on a slice of Kodak paper. Better an image, he decided, than the overworked tangle of muscles and nerves that he knew himself as.

Ezra suffered from a deep tiredness of soul and bones. He was thirty-seven years old. Besides some weathered creases in his tanned face he had changed little physically through the years. His hips would have fit in his high school jeans because his ten added pounds were padded onto his arms, chest and shoulders, the reward of labor. He worked two jobs. His wife, Anne, worked one. His twelve-year-old son, Dylan, was involved in school music and sports activities that Ezra rarely attended. They were steady members of a church that demanded their attendance, if not their participation, and through it all he had to keep Diane, Lacey, and Solomon happy—an impossible task. Ezra Riley was desperate for a change.

He looked up the embankment to the roofs of speeding cars shining in the sunlight. The road. Sometimes he wished he were young again and living the free life of the highway. Not that it was ever free, he reminded himself. Everything had its price.

Pastor Tom Jablonski backed his truck out of his driveway. It was a yellow '79 Dodge with a Pittsburgh Steelers bumper sticker. He drove down the tree-lined Yellow Rock streets to Main Street where one-hundred-year-old brick buildings stood two and three stories tall. He turned right at The Buffalo Bar. He needed to see Ezra Riley and had called all day but got only an answering machine. The pastor could never keep track of Ezra's odd hours and rotating shifts. Then, too, Ezra did not work year-round. *Was he off in September?* The pastor didn't know. His wife, Darlene, did not like Ezra Riley. She thought him independent, arrogant, and secretive. Pastor Tom paid little attention to Darlene's discernment; she had not been herself since the accident. *How long was the normal grieving process?* He had counseled other parents that it was approximately two years. Their tragedy had occurred two years and three months ago. He drove down the highway ignoring the rolling hills, gumbo buttes, and twisted little creeks. Eastern Montana had not met his and Darlene's expectations. No mountains. No trout streams. And most of all, very few trees. He realized the plains and badlands had a stark, seductive beauty, but he resisted acknowledging it. He did not want to like eastern Montana.

His truck almost bounced into the ditch because of the washboard corrugation as he drove down the Riley lane. Jablonski had visited only once before in the new preacher's obligatory first visit. It had been an awkward evening. He had informed Anne she was no longer worship leader because Darlene always led worship. Anne had been gracious, but he knew she had been hurt. Ezra—seeing his wife's pain—was obviously angered.

Ezra's dark side was the temperament of an artist, Jablonski reasoned. *Wasn't Ezra a writer? Wasn't that why he was calling?* He needed help publishing a church newsletter, a tool to augment his detailed sermon notes, a resource for the shut-ins and backsliders that missed his messages, and heaven only knew, there were more and more of those every week.

Like Ezra, the pastor was a private and independent man. It was humbling for him to ask for help, but with no church secretary and an outdated computer system, he simply could not produce sermons, sermon outlines, radio programs, *and* a newsletter. What Jablonski would not admit to himself was that Ezra was a challenge, and he urgently needed a challenge.

A blonde dog growled at him as he got out, and he hesitated, wondering if it would bite. The dog gave him a sideways look and shuffled away on old, tired legs. A few years earlier Blondie would have taken his leg off, but viciousness was no longer worth the bother. She ambled to the bunkhouse where she could lay in the shade and watch the stranger from a distance.

Pastor Tom knocked on the door repeatedly, but there was no answer. He looked around the well-maintained ranch yard. There was a paint horse in the corral, but no sign of human activity. Pastor Jablonski knew nothing about ranching. He had been raised in Pennsylvania, the son of a mill worker, and he missed his home state. Especially the Steelers. It galled him that the one television station reaching eastern Montana broadcast only Denver Bronco football games. He missed the Steelers, and Darlene missed the loving support of her elderly parents and two older sisters. But of course, it was more than that. They both missed what could not be returned, what had been stolen from them on a dark, rainy night on a slick asphalt road outside Beaver Falls.

Ezra wasn't home. Well, that was okay, the pastor decided. He and Anne would be in church the following evening. He would talk to him then. He was about a mile from the Riley ranch on his way back to town when he met an older Ford pickup pulling a horse trailer. The driver wearing the black cowboy hat was Ezra Riley, but the pastor did not recognize him.

Ezra recognized the pastor and wondered what brought him north of Yellow Rock. It wasn't a social call, he was sure of that. Pastor Tom did not make social calls. His idea of communicating was handing out copious sermon outlines at the church door and recording daily radio broadcasts on a station few people listened to. Ezra unsaddled his horse and threw him some hay, then walked to the house, checked the answering machine—the only message was for Anne—and grabbed an apple from the refrigerator. He went through the morning mail. No letters from Diane or Lacey—that was good. The family ranch situation was strained, and no news was good news. It was only 2:45 in the afternoon. He could fence for a few hours before Anne and Dylan got home. He could saddle another horse and ride on his cattle. Or he could work on the book he had been writing the past few years. Writing was the one thing that, when he was doing it, he never thought he should be doing something else. But it was so hard to start. He pulled off his cowboy boots and laced on a pair of packers. He would fix fence. He would stab the dry, alkaline soil with steel posts.

Ezra was back in the house when Anne and Dylan came home about six. He greeted his wife at the door with a kiss.

"My, you are cheerful tonight," Anne noted. She showed some wear from the day's work at the rest home, but still looked poised and peaceful.

Ezra had never regretted marrying her. She was a woman of substance, and if her soul could be seen she would appear bathed in the colors of Montana sunsets.

"Some tourists took my picture today," Ezra said.

"That made you happy?" Anne asked.

Ezra tousled Dylan's hair as he walked by. The boy was five-six and growing like a weed. "No," Ezra said. "I'm happy because I rode alone all day and didn't have any scientists, bureaucrats, or union stewards bugging me."

"That's what I thought," Anne said. She knew Ezra was happiest when left alone by the mediocrity imposed by standardization. He was unique and fitting him into a mold was impossible.

Ezra packed in a bag of groceries and set them on the kitchen table. The phone rang and Dylan raced to get it. He was at the age where girls were noticing him and he was beginning to acknowledge their attention. They were low on his list, though, behind books, music, sports, and fishing. "Dad, it's for you," he called.

Ezra took the receiver. "Hello," he said.

"Ezra, this is Pastor Jablonski. Will you be in church tomorrow night?"

Ezra rolled his eyes. Anne caught his grimace from the kitchen and knew it was either the pastor or Uncle Solomon on the phone. "I don't know," Ezra said. "It depends on my day." People in the congregation had been pressuring Ezra to run for the church board and the pastor insisted that board members be present at all services whenever possible. The election of the board and the vote on the pastor were but weeks away.

"Well, there are a couple of things I need to talk to you about," Jablonski said. "Would you mind if I came out for a minute?"

"Right now?"

"It will only take a second."

"Okay."

The groceries were put away, and Anne was beginning supper when Jablonski drove up in his truck. Ezra called to him from the bunkhouse, a remodeled old railroad building. It was one large room with an antique wooden desk, an old western couch and bookcases built from corral plank. The walls were decorated with buffalo skulls and Ezra's framed color photographs of the badlands. He invited the pastor in. Jablonski did not comment on Ezra's office, he just looked around for a chair, and finding none—other than the one in front of the desk, the one Ezra was sitting in—he sat on the couch.

A lunchbox-style Kaypro computer sat on the desk, its green cursor flashing on its little dark screen.

Pastor Tom was uncomfortable. He was used to dealing with board members. He could tell them what he wanted, but Ezra owed him no allegiances or debts. He was a thickset man, barrel-chested and wide-hipped. "I, uh, I've been mighty busy lately," he said. "Producing sermons and radio programs, and well, I have a desire to have a newsletter. Something for shut-ins and the like. I was wondering if you might have time to give me a little hand with it?"

Ezra was amazed but not touched. "I'm sorry, pastor, but I can't do that," he said. "I'm working at The Fort, taking care of two ranches, and trying to finish a book in my spare time."

"Oh," said Jablonski. "Well, if you are too busy, you are too busy." He sat on the edge of the couch staring down at the red indoor-outdoor carpeting.

"Is there something else?" Ezra asked. He did want to be polite but knew dinner was waiting.

Jablonski looked up. His hands hung unclasped between his thick thighs. "I got a call the other night," he said. "It was from an evangelist who planned on passing through and wanted to speak in our church. I'm usually not interested in that sort of thing, but it turns out that I once knew this man's father, and, well, I sort of owe the father a favor so I agreed he could speak Sunday night."

Ezra nodded to encourage the man to get to the point.

"This evangelist," Jablonski continued, "says he knows you."

"Knows me?" All the evangelists Ezra knew could stand on the point of a horse-shoeing nail.

"His name is Walker. Do you know anyone by that name?"

It made no connection at first and Ezra shook his head.

"Odd first name. Jubal Lee Walker."

Ezra's head jolted. *Jay Walker?*

"You do know him?" the pastor asked.

Ezra smiled and looked past the pastor, through a window that opened to Sunday Creek where the evening was settling a dark blanket on the yellowing leaves of the cottonwood trees. "I knew him once," he said. "A long, long time ago."

At 5:30 the following morning The Fort's crew of six cowboys met in the main barn, a massive structure made of hand-hewn pine during the Indian Wars. They had no orders yet so the cowboys used the idle time to sweep the wooden floor and clean the stalls. The rising sun shot shafts of golden light through a row of narrow, rectangular windows. Illuminated dust particles shimmered in the light and Hercules, the barn cat and official Fort mascot, paraded through the beams, strutting from one cowboy to another to have his black-and-white back rubbed. Ezra worked quietly, still intrigued by the idea of Jay Walker coming to town. It was not Jay himself that captured Ezra's imagination, it was the memories of the road, of a bygone era and a lost, idealistic youth. He chuckled softly to himself realizing he had become what he had rebelled against then and that his earlier identity was a secret to most who knew him now. He was long removed from having hair below his shoulders and rolling dope with Zig-Zag papers.

He was sweeping the rough wooden floor when a cowboy's curse broke the reflection of his morning. One cowboy looked at another. Both looked out the window. "It's Der Fuehrer," one said, and more vulgarities broke the air.

Ezra leaned on his broom and rolled his eyes. He was afraid of this. Alex Frankforter was a high ranking GS employee, a crop scientist raised on a small farm in Arkansas. His plant research was so singularly average that he was relegated primarily to administrative and public relations responsibilities. He was a paper-shuffler and glad-hander. Every few months when the blackboard in the main office hallway showed all the scientists were busy and the cowhands idle, Frankforter excused himself from the office to play trail boss. He dug out his boots, belt buckle, and straw hat, and invented a ridiculous project for the cowboy crow.

He was a big man and the sunlight faded when his shadow filled the barn. "Saddle up, gentlemen," he shouted. "We're weighing calves on the Schottenfeld project."

The cowboys shook their heads in disgust but started for their horses. They were not scheduled to weigh calves today because the project's head, Mark Schottenfeld, along with the station director, were giving lectures at the Meat Animal Research Center in Nebraska. Their absence had left Frankforter in charge, and he had intruded into another scientist's domain.

Pete Royce walked by leading his bay saddle horse. "Someone should shoot this fuehrer, too," he whispered to Ezra. Royce was sixty-two years old and a month from retirement. He had worked at The Fort for sixteen years after losing his ranch in the cattle crash of 1973.

The six cowboys loaded their horses in two four-horse trailers and followed Frankforter's new government pickup to the back side of the experiment station. Frankforter pulled a trailer that contained a portable scale and thirty steel panels that would be constructed into a temporary corral.

Ezra rode in a truck with Royce and Frank Henry, another older cowboy. The mood was dark. Henry smoked and flicked ashes on the floor of the weathered truck.

"The way I figure it," Royce said, "Der Fuehrer will be after me or you, Ezra."

"Why do you say that?" Ezra asked. He knew Frankforter liked to pick out one man to ride and ridicule, but that man was usually Henry, a government-hating libertarian whose parents had lost the family ranch when the WPA dammed the Missouri River in the 1930s.

"My time here is about done," Royce said. "He will want to give me a parting shot. Or he will be after you because you're the youngest, and you've always managed to avoid him."

"Ezra turns the other cheek," Henry laughed. "He's a man of the Word. If I had the chance, I would turn Der Fuehrer's other cheek with the hot end of a branding iron."

Frankforter pulled his shiny GSA-issued four-wheel drive up to the largest windmill on The Fort's one hundred sections.

"What's he up to?" Henry said. "The dang fool isn't going to have us set up the panels here, is he?"

The windmill and its forty-foot steel water tank sat on the grassy crown of a hill. The only level spot was the ground beneath the water tank.

"Riley, Royce," Frankforter shouted. "You men start setting up panels. The rest of you get the cows gathered."

The older cowboy winked at Ezra. "See what I told you? Riley and Royce. You and me. We're his special pupils today."

The steel panels were ten feet long and weighed seventy pounds. They were fitted together by placing the hooked male ends of one into the circular female ends of another.

"Build a long wing out here," Der Fuehrer said, pointing to the south. "Then circle the corral out to the west, then narrow it up as you go up the hill to the east. The alley will curve around the water tank and up to the scale." Frankforter disappeared after giving the orders. He did not plan on packing any panels himself.

"This is not going to work," Ezra said. "Cows and calves are not going to work uphill into the sun. They won't be able to see a thing. They'll think they're stepping off a cliff."

"He doesn't want it to work," Royce said.

"You men could talk less and work a little more," Frankforter yelled from the comfortable seat of his truck.

When the other cowboys brought in the sixty pairs of experiment cattle, they could not believe the facilities that had been constructed.

"Ain't no way," Henry said. "Ain't no way under God's heaven that this is ever going to work."

Frankforter picked two cowboys to help him at the scale, one to push calves down the alley, and left Ezra, Royce, and Henry to try and crowd the animals uphill into the blinding sun.

"I don't want you chousin' these cattle horseback," Frankforter told them. "Do it on foot. Now, bring me cattle."

The men tried sorting off a dozen head and easing them toward the alley. As they neared the entrance a wily old lead cow turned and bolted down the hill, the others followed her. Ezra, Royce, and Henry waded back into the stirring cattle and sorted off another draft. A handful of bold, curious calves took the lead and were entering the alley when the pumpjack kicked into life, the windmill blades whined and the calves spooked and roared down the hill, glancing off the men and spinning Royce into the dirt.

"We don't have any cattle up here yet," Frankforter yelled.

"We're going to have to do this horseback," Ezra said. Henry and Royce agreed, and the three mounted their ponies. They sorted off a tamer cow for the lead and started her and three calves into the alleyway.

"You men get off those horses," the Fuehrer screamed. "I don't want you jamming these cattle horseback. You get back on foot."

They led their horses back to the trailer and tied them. "He's just trying to make it as hard on us as he can," Royce said.

They sorted another small draft off and had to run uphill to keep with them. Royce and Henry were too old, their knees too arthritic to keep up. The cattle turned back at the gate and spilled around them.

Frankforter came storming back to the pen, shouting at the three men from the other side of the panels. "What's wrong back here?" he demanded. "I've got three know-it-alls back here, and you can't bring me any cattle? I might as well have trained monkeys from the Billings Zoo."

"You set the panels up wrong," Henry said.

"Listen, old-timer," Frankforter said. "I'm the one that's got the long letters after my name. P-H-D. Got it? If you had those letters after your name, all they would stand for is Post Hole Digger. That's all you're good for is digging postholes out here in the gumbo. Now you are a cowhand, and I am a cow boss and I want some cattle in this alley in five minutes or I am putting the three of you on report."

"You're going to get someone hurt," Ezra said. "We're climbing a hill in cowboy boots, and the cattle are turning back and running over the top of us."

The panels shook as Frankforter climbed over them. He approached Ezra angrily, towering over him by four inches and outweighing him by fifty pounds, and he came at him from uphill, increasing his advantage. He poked Ezra stiffly in the sternum. "Listen to me, Riley, I make the calls around here, not you."

Instinctively, Ezra took a deep breath and settled into a wide, balanced stance. His eyes blazed with a cool fury, but his face and body appeared passive. "I would not do that again," he said calmly. Training from nearly two decades ago rolled up from his subconscious like information called from a computer file. In an instant, a variety of options, an assortments of kicks, punches, holds, and gouges flashed through his mind then stopped instantly on the appropriate reaction. *Tomoe nage.* *Block the arm, grab both lapels, insert right foot in notch between groin and leg, pull forward, roll backward, propel opponent overhead. Let loose or remain with opponent. Distribute the punishment according to the situation.* He knew what he could do, and he waited to do it.

Frankforter puffed himself up, moving his balance into his chest, making him top-heavy and ideal for the movement Ezra had selected. His eyes were smug and condescending. He underestimated his opponent. "Don't do it again, you say," Frankforter smirked. "And just why not?"

"Because I will roll you to the bottom of this hill," Ezra said matter-of-factly. There was neither malice nor braggadocio in his tone; he could have been talking about the weather.

Frankforter laughed, raised a pointed finger, pointed it at Ezra's chest, then stopped abruptly as if he had seen a ghost. For the first time in Frankforter's shallow, academic life he was staring into the eyes of a man who was one step into the future. There was no pride, no meanness in Ezra, just the calm intensity of someone who knew the outcome of a storm before the winds blew. The brown eyes were lit by an unusual light, like the sun reflecting off sharkskin from the depth of the sea, and Frankforter could feel Ezra in his head, searching for weakness and finding plenty.

"Go ahead," Henry laughed. "Give ol' Ez a poke."

Frankforter withdrew his hand. He was a disgraced man, caught in his bluff, but he still yielded power and was desperate to save face. "You will work the cattle as I tell you," he said angrily. "Or you walk."

"If you fire me," Ezra said, "are you going to continue to work cattle this way?"

"The cattle will be worked my way," Frankforter insisted.

"Fair enough," Ezra said. Three brisk steps took him past the bureaucrat to the panels by the water tank. He grabbed one by its vertical crossbars, lifted it from its attachments, and hoisted it over his head. He pivoted and heaved the panel into the water tank where it landed with a flat splash and sank to the bottom. Frankforter's mouth dropped. No one said a word. Fueled by the raw fury he had inherited from his father, Ezra grabbed another panel, raised it high, walked to the tank and dropped it in. The resulting splash soaked his shirt. He walked more slowly to a third panel, looked at Frankforter for a long second, then pressed it above his head and threw it in the tank, too. The muscles of his arms, shoulders, and back flared with blood and strained against his wet shirt. He stepped back from the hole in the corral and stared at the herd.

The smart old lead cow saw daylight and stepped forward, testing Ezra to see if he would allow her to pass. He took another step back and the cow trotted single-mindedly toward the gap in the corral with her calf following. The rest of the herd began moving after them.

"Stop them, stop them!" Frankforter shouted at the crew, but no one moved. Der Fuehrer took one step forward, but Ezra was between him and the cattle. Frankforter stopped. The adrenaline necessary to lift the panels was surging in Ezra, rising to his eyes with a reckless energy. He looked hungry for combat. Frankforter took a step back and glared at the cowboy with the hatred of a man whose only power was wrapped in policies, procedures, and politics.

When the dust settled half of the panels had collapsed, and all the cattle were gone. Frankforter took a notepad from his shirt pocket, made some notations, then turned and looked at Ezra. "I hope you realize that you are officially terminated from government employment as of this minute."

"You can't do that," Henry said. "I'm the union steward, remember? There's got to be a filed grievance and a formal hearing. Besides, you ain't the station director. You can't fire anybody."

Blind pride had Frankforter in a corner. He had to assert his authority. "As acting station director, you are suspended," he told Ezra. "You are on official report for insubordination and the destruction of government property."

"He didn't destroy nothin' but your ego," Royce said. Frankforter gave him an angry glare and scribbled in his notebook.

"It's okay, boys," Ezra said. "I was getting tired of paying union dues anyway."

"You are suspended," Frankforter repeated.

Ezra ignored him and tightened Shiloh's cinch.

"Don't you dare load that horse in a government trailer," Der Fuehrer said. "You can just ride him home."

Ezra swung into the saddle. His personal pickup and trailer was across the river and miles away at The Fort. "I was planning on it," he said. "Will one of you guys drop my outfit off at my place?" he asked. All of them nodded.

"You have a problem with authority, Riley," was Frankforter's parting blow as Ezra loped away. "You definitely have a problem with authority."

CHAPTER TWELVE

It was eight miles cross-country from the experiment station to home and Ezra rode it hard, the adrenaline and anger burning a hole in his stomach. He was on Shorty Wilson's land most of the way and he half-hoped that Wilson would see him and accuse him of trespassing. Frankforter had stirred something in Ezra that he would have been only to happy to finish with Wilson. He crossed a high flat north of Yellow Rock where the Sioux had camped before surrendering to the U.S. Cavalry. After defeating Custer, the Sioux and Cheyenne had raided ranches and mining camps then crossed the border into Canada. When they finally came south to accept defeat, it was rumored they buried stolen gold north of town. *If there is treasure in these hills*, Ezra thought, *it is all intrinsic.* Later, the same flat was a campground for destitute ranchers during the Depression. They bedded their herds there before trailing them to The Fort where the animals were slaughtered. But Ezra rode the opposite way across the flat. He was not going south in defeat or depression, but north to the familiar solitude of the Riley Ranch badlands.

When he got home he rubbed Shiloh down, watered him lightly, and apologized for the hard ride with an extra portion of grain. The calmness he had felt when facing Frankforter had dissipated once the danger was past, and he walked to the house seething with unreleased anger. Ezra checked the answering machine and the mail. He thought he might get a call or letter from Jay Walker but there was nothing.

What would he tell Anne? She would understand why he had lost his job, but how could he replace the lost wages? Jobs in Yellow Rock were hard to come by. Even if they offered him the job back, he didn't want it. Dues. Labor meetings. Forced coffee breaks. It made no sense for cowboying to be union. He paced the house nervously, still burning adrenaline. He needed something to do and remembered it was Wednesday and Solomon was expecting him. He always took Solomon grocery shopping on Wednesday afternoons.

Solomon had not driven since a car accident fifty years earlier—when

Solomon held a grudge, even against a machine, it lasted forever—and with his brothers all deceased, Ezra and Anne were his only tickets to town. Solomon's chosen life of solitude had turned ugly in its loneliness, and he looked forward to his weekly shopping trips.

Ezra got in his truck and drove up the road to his uncle's house. Solomon was watching from a window, waiting for his ride. When Ezra pulled up to the house, he tottered out to the pickup wearing his cleanest pair of bib coveralls and a faded denim cap.

"So, what did you do today?" Solomon asked as he got in the truck. "Waste some of the taxpayers' money?"

Ezra did not answer because he had not heard. He had other things on his mind.

"I said, what did you do at The Fort?" Solomon asked gruffly. He wasn't interested in Ezra's day, he was simply hungry for information, news of any kind.

Ezra snapped to attention. The raised voice of an uncle had always done that to him. "I got fired," Ezra said.

Solomon's interest picked up immediately. This was news. Local tabloid family news. "Got caught goldbrickin', uh?" His teasing of Ezra had not ceased when Ezra became an adult and had grown when Ezra went to work for The Fort.

Ezra shook his head. "No, nothing like that."

"Butted heads with a scientist, didn'tchya?"

"No, a bureaucrat."

"They can't just fire you, can they? Ain't you union?"

"I'm union," Ezra said. "But I just flat don't care."

The old man nodded his head. It was as he thought. Solomon was a cynic. He had not expected Ezra to last this long. His nephew was a good enough hand but he was too independent. Men who had owned their own land and cattle could not easily conform to being bossed by federal employees. "So whadya do? Hit 'im?" Solomon liked fights and was hoping for a blow-by-blow description.

"No, I just tore down the corral panels and tossed them in the water tank."

Solomon frowned. This certainly wasn't a fight, but as he thought about it, a little smile twisted his lips. He appreciated a sense of the dramatic and could always count on Ezra for theatrics. "They just fire ya," he asked, "or can they do more than that?"

"There was a threat of jail tossed out."

"Ha. Jail. I don't think you'd like jail."

"I know I wouldn't like jail." He had been in one, in Kansas, but had only told his close friend Rick Benjamin.

"So, whadya gonna do now? No more easy government money rollin' in."

"I thought you and I would rob a bank," Ezra said. "Do you want to be the stick-up man or the driver?"

Solomon snorted. "Can't drive and can't shoot," he said. "And I wouldn't like jail, either." Ezra pulled up to County Market. The old man got out in front of the store and shuffled in on sore, tired feet. He had gained weight, and his legs were weak because he had sold his sheep and had no reason to walk anymore. He spent his days in the house watching satellite television programs he mispronounced as "CBC World Wide of Sports" and "Fifty Minutes." He was seventy-eight years old. His hair was white as snow, but Solomon's face was free of wrinkles, and his mind was sharper than a castrator's knife.

Ezra stayed in the pickup while his uncle shopped. He drew the line at pushing Solomon's grocery cart for him. It was different when Anne took him shopping, and Solomon preferred having her as his chauffeur. She not only pushed his cart, she took him somewhere to eat when they were done. Not Ezra. He just wanted to get home. He had things to do. Solomon had nothing to do.

After an hour Solomon walked out trailing a teenaged grocery bagger. The kid put the sacks in the back of the pickup while Solomon watched. The kid said, "Thank you, sir," because he had to. Solomon grunted and got in the truck. "Buy ya a milk shake through the drive-thru," he said, nodding across the street at a McDonalds.

"Okay," Ezra said. A milk shake did not take much time. It was a treat for Solomon, and it was the old man's way of saying he was sorry about him losing his job.

They sipped their milk shakes quietly on the way to the ranch. Solomon tried once to pump Ezra for more information but Ezra didn't answer. Solomon knew better than to push too hard. Even Ezra had his limits. Ezra packed in the groceries.

"Where ya goin' now?" Solomon asked.

"Up above," Ezra said. He should be going to church, he knew, but he was in no mood for a verbal harangue from the wordy Reverend Jablonski.

Up above. That said it all. Up above meant the big pasture up Sunday Creek, up Dead Man Creek, up all the creeks to where the drainages began on the back of the ranch. Up above meant the back side, the far side, the high point above all problems.

Ezra drove to the crest of the high divide where prairie rolled like carpet to the top then badlands broke violently towards the Yellow Rock River Valley. It was the remotest spot on the ranch. He went there to be alone and because he liked the significance of divides. They were decisive. They spilled water in two separate directions that meandered in trickles through little pools, or rushed in torrents before eventually coming together again. It was not the divides' fault that things divided reunited. The divides made their decisions; it was the leveling of the terrain and the pull of gravity that muddled everything again. Ezra liked decisiveness. He saw things as black or white, north or south, right or wrong.

But things were not always that simple. He had been right in taking action to keep his friends from getting hurt. But he had been wrong to throw the panels in the tank. Now he was out of a job and, if Frankforter followed through on his threat, possibly in trouble with the law. He could not afford the loss of the job, not now that Lacey was pressing for the ranch to be sold, and he owed Diane money for his share of the probate expenses on his mother's estate.

He was twelve miles from the ranch house as the magpie flies, and everything between belonged to Solomon or to Ezra and his sisters. Mostly to Solomon, but even his domain was a fiefdom compared to Shorty Wilson's, whose vast kingdom surrounded the Riley's on three sides. He had the old Benjamin place—Ezra's friend Rick was still in Houston, he called once a year at Christmas; Ezra called on the Fourth of July—and the old Arbuckle place—after a decade of bitter withering, old Charley had finally left the rest home: Ezra and Solomon packed him out in a box.

Ezra needed a friend. The ranch had become a lonely place surrounded by enemies instead of allies. He missed Rick and the joyful comraderie of two men horseback together, neighboring, doing the work each loved. He missed Uncle Sam and his sassy, irreverent humor; and he missed Jim Mendenhall, who had fallen deeper into the bottle since Sam's death. He even missed his wife and son because he did not see them enough, and now, on a night he could be with them, he was alone with his first and most jealous lover: the badlands.

Ezra stared across four strands of barbed-wire fence, the demarcation line between Riley and Wilson property. Wilson represented to Ezra everything that was wrong with the world. A man ruled by greed, rather than a love for the land, for art, or for people.

Wilson not only owned the old Arbuckle and Benjamin ranches that bordered Riley land on three sides, he had also acquired two other ranches and two irrigated farms making him the largest landowner in the county next to the state and federal governments. Everywhere Ezra went he heard it was just a matter of time before Wilson got the Riley place. Fortunately, Ezra did not go many places.

He sat on the divide and watched the sun set over the badlands, being

amazed again how low light produced colors in gumbo soils that were
bland during the day. A box of sixty-four Crayola crayons was in his lap,
and he held the sticks up one at a time to match the colors of the western
sunset. The tips on all of the crayons were perfect, he never used them for
writing or drawing. He used them to define the colors of the sky. Some
thought it odd when they saw crayons in his truck but Ezra didn't mind.
It was the professional thing for him, as a writer, to do. Sunset colors were
an integral part of the book he was writing. The book was nearly finished,
but was untitled. Ezra wasn't worried. The title would come in its own
due time.

"Carnation pink," he said out loud. It was okay to talk to yourself in
the badlands. He rotated the crayon against the sky as if drawing on a
huge canvas. Yes, the dark underlining of the cirrus clouds was carnation
pink.

"Red violet." Red as in the crimson stain of blood. The clouds themselves were red violet.

Then for the background, the subtle color that stretched across the
horizon, the shade of the canvas that pink carnation and red violet had
been splashed upon. "Peach." No, not quite. "Apricot."

Yes, it was apricot. A soft, peaceful, almost apathetic color. The color
of normality. The normality of having a job, getting up, going to work,
coming home, being paid.

The little canyons and deep arroyos around him pulsated with the
red-pink of shale, the yellow and white of sandstone, the blues, grays, and
reds of the clay, and the black of shadows. Creatures began to stir: deer,
rabbits, coyotes, badgers, bobcats. The world was theirs at night.

In the fading light Ezra wrote in his journal:

*September 11. I got fired today. It is an odd feeling to be fired. I feel
both a vacancy and a sense of satisfaction. The colors this evening were
carnation pink, red violet, and apricot. Jay Walker is coming to town.
What brings him? And what will he bring?*

The sunset faded as the colors were sucked into darkness. Ezra got in
his pickup and pointed it homeward; the headlights bounced in the rutted
pasture road like giant fireflies dancing in syncopation.

It was after ten when Ezra came in the house. Anne was already
asleep, exhausted from a day's work followed by the lengthy Wednesday
night church service. Ezra wanted to leave the church but Yellow Rock
did not offer many options, and Anne felt a loyalty to a church she had
once cherished. It was the town's only independent nondenominational
assembly.

He checked the kitchen table to see if there were any notes—any messages from Anne. Maybe from Jay, or from someone at The Fort. The only note was his: *Anne, I took Solomon to town for groceries then went to fix fence on the back side against Shorty Wilson. Love* . . .

Ezra disrobed and slipped into bed. Anne's breathing changed when she felt his weight on the mattress. Subconsciously she had been waiting for him. He knew he should wake her and tell her about the firing, but she had had a long day. He rolled onto his side and placed his hand on the hollow between her hip and her ribs. Just touching her helped center him and after a while he was able to sleep.

Ezra's mental alarm clock rang at 4:15 A.M., and he swung his feet onto the floor in a state of forgetfulness. Then it hit him like a shotgun blast to the stomach: he had no job to go to. But he was awake so he got up, dressed, and went outside. He skipped making himself breakfast; he wasn't hungry. Out of habit he saddled Shiloh and loaded him in the trailer. He couldn't go to The Fort but he could go up on Dead Man Creek and ride on Solomon's cows. Shorty Wilson's cows were always getting in, and he could keep busy putting them out. He was not trying to deceive Anne in not waking her, or in taking the pickup and trailer as if he had gone to The Fort—it just worked out that way.

At 6:10 Anne awakened. Her arm reached over to Ezra's side and her palm and fingers felt the sheet for any warmth from his presence. The sheet was cool. She swung her legs onto the floor and sat up, her sandy blonde hair hanging in her face. She brushed it back with one hand and rose to her feet. Another day: wake Dylan, make breakfast, do dishes, drop Dylan at school, go to work, pick Dylan up, come home. She pulled a housecoat on and stepped into the hallway. She hesitated there for a moment, like a doe sniffing the air before coming to water. Something was not right. There was a vague static in the air that unsettled her. She did not enter the bathroom, she went to the kitchen first. There were no dirty dishes in the sink. That was not uncommon. Often Ezra did his own dishes and put them away. Or had he eaten at all? She ran her hand over the counter. No crumbs. She felt the dishrag. It was dry. He had not eaten. Her slight shrug barely lifted her thin housecoat. Perhaps he had overslept. He refused to use an alarm clock.

She washed her face and hands then had a piece of whole wheat toast and half a grapefruit while doing her morning Bible reading. This morning: Ezekiel, chapter two, the duties of a watchman.

Her makeup did not take long. Anne was not one to loiter in front of a mirror. Her defined, angular face formed a unique beauty, and she was attractive without effort yet pleasantly devoid of vanity. She did not see her uniqueness as any great asset.

She packed a small lunch for herself and another for Dylan. It was a beautiful day. She would eat her lunch outside on the rest home lawn while reading.

She went to one of the bookshelves. There were books everywhere in the Riley home. There were bookcases in the bedrooms, living room, and in Ezra's writing room. Other books were neatly piled in stacks in corners until they could be cased. Books were their one indulgence; even Dylan was an avid reader.

She went to the bookcase in the living room. She had just finished a Mary Higgins Clark. She considered another, but no, Ezra wanted her to read something more literary. It helped his writing when they could both read and discuss the same book. *Not that they had any time lately to discuss anything,* she thought. *So, all the more reason to read something literary.* She plucked two from the shelf. Anne Tyler's *Saint Maybe* and Joyce Carol Oates' *Black Water.* The first was the story of the simple life of a good man, the second the deadly, suctioning pull of a wrong decision. She preferred Tyler but chose Oates. There was something in the air.

She called for Dylan. He was an early riser, often awakening before his mother but staying in bed to read. With his dark hair and brown eyes he was the spitting image of his father, but he was bigger boned and destined to be a larger man. Anne and Ezra had wanted a second child but with the droughts, the family problems with the ranch, and the basic lack of money, it was an idea perpetually forestalled.

Anne enjoyed the drive to work. September was one of her favorite months. The mornings were cool but the days were warm. She had learned to like eastern Montana. The winters were bitter and the summers torrid, but the people were down-to-earth.

Anne dropped Dylan off at school and drove to the rest home. She never got used to the contrast between the fresh outdoor air and the acrid, sterile odors of the home. She enjoyed old people, but she longed for the day when she would not have to work. Her house was never as clean as she wanted, little projects never got done, friends were seldom invited out, and her music was suffering. She needed more time.

As she was hanging her jacket in the employees' closet the staff nurse, Sally Johnson, came in. "Too bad about Ezra," she said.

"What about Ezra?" Anne asked. There was an uncharacteristic edge to Anne's voice, a jealousy not directed at the nurse but at another woman's knowledge of her husband.

The nurse looked at her suspiciously. She was a slender, tight-muscled, fortyish Canadian who wore her hard living in the contours of her face. "About him losing his job," she said.

Anne's mouth dropped. "He what?"

"You don't know?" she declared it slowly, with empathy. "He got fired after a fight with some scientist or something."

Anne was numb. It disturbed her to hear that Ezra had lost his job, but it hurt her more that he had not told her. "How do you know this?" she asked.

"It's a small town, dear," the nurse said. "Especially when you are downtown after midnight like I was."

"It must be another small-town rumor," Anne said. Ezra had been the subject of many unfounded fables in his life. This, she thought, was certainly another, otherwise, he would have told her.

Sally Johnson looked at her with the sad, strong eyes that told her she was wrong.

Sheriff Bill Butler stared at the calendar on the wall. Four days until the opening of the back country elk season and ten days until he and three of his buddies packed into the Bob Marshall Wilderness for two weeks of bugling bulls. He was more than ready for "The Bob" and disappointed about missing opening day, but there was business to take care of.

Butler was a sheriff cut from the old cloth. His lanky frame was more suited to a saddle than an office chair and he despised the mundane routine of domestic disputes, dogs running at large, paperwork, and country club judges that tossed good cases out of court because of silly technicalities. He had three years to go until retirement. He was ready for that, too.

He looked out the window and saw Ezra Riley getting out of his truck. *He got my message,* the sheriff thought.

Butler did not know Ezra except as the son of his late friend, Johnny Riley. He and Johnny had traded many a horse in their day. He heard Ezra was a hard worker, talented writer, and a former hippie who had found religion. As to the rumors that Ezra and Rick Benjamin had turned the heifers loose in Shorty Wilson's store a few years back, Butler only wished he had been there to see it.

Ezra didn't take his hat off when he walked into the office. The sheriff still had his on. "You left a message on my machine that you wanted to see me?" Ezra asked.

"I did." Butler's face was leathery brown and lined with deep smile wrinkles. His gray hair and silver-belly Stetson made his blue eyes seem bluer.

"If it's about the incident yesterday at The Fort, I plead guilty to losing my temper, but no one got hurt."

Butler tipped his hat back with his right index finger. "Why don't you tell me what happened," he said.

Ezra conveyed the story and explained how Frankforter had endangered the crew with his stubborn insistence on following a plan any cowman knew to be foolish. He admitted to throwing three panels into the water tank.

"You probably should have tossed Frankforter in while you were at it," the sheriff noted.

"I thought about it," Ezra said.

"It doesn't sound like you did much real damage."

"The panels aren't ruined," Ezra said. "They just have to be drug out of the stock tank."

"I bet you can get your job back if you want it," Butler said.

"I'm still coming down from the adrenaline," Ezra said. "I don't know if I want the job back. Besides, Frankforter thinks he can have me put in jail."

"Frankforter has no control over that," the sheriff said. "That's up to lawyers, judges, and juries. Once the station director gets back from Nebraska I expect things will take on a different light. I thank you for telling the little tale though, because I knew nothing about it."

"You knew nothing about it?" Ezra said. "But you called and said you wanted to see me."

Butler smiled. "That's right. Let me run a couple names past you."

"Okay."

"Austin Arbuckle."

"What about him?" Ezra said.

"He gets released from the state pen tomorrow," the sheriff said.

"So?"

"Shorty Wilson helped arrange it. Arbuckle will be going to work for him."

Ezra's eyebrows raised just slightly, but enough for the sheriff to notice.

"A few years back when Arbuckle got sent up I seem to remember him tossing some threats your way."

"That was five years ago," Ezra said.

"Some cons forget, some cons magnify their memories," Butler said. "It all depends on how they serve their time. The other Arbuckle, he's connected to your kid sister, isn't he?"

"Cody," Ezra said. "Yeah, he and Lacey are still on the rodeo trail."

"Isn't he a little old to still be riding bulls?"

"He doesn't ride. He drives the pickup for her. She's still chasing cans." It was a western term, slightly derogatory, meaning Lacey was a barrel racer.

"How do you and your sister get along?" the sheriff asked.

"I believe that is a personal matter," Ezra said. "My kid sister is not the one being released from prison."

Butler nodded. "You're right," he said. "I'm an old friend of your dad's. I thought the world of Johnny. I hate to see any turmoil in the family."

"The Rileys were born for turmoil," Ezra said. "Is that it? All you wanted was to warn me about Austin?"

"Austin is one name," the sheriff said. "I have another."

"Who's that?"

"Jubal Lee Walker."

Ezra's eyebrows furrowed. "I heard he was coming to town," he said. "But he's just a name out of the past. What interest do you have in him?"

"Nothing," the sheriff said. "No trouble. We just need to clear up a little paperwork, that's all. Brand inspections, things like that."

Ezra got up to leave. "Anything else?" Ezra asked. He did not dislike the sheriff, but he disliked the imposition of authority. Something about this meeting was very unusual.

"You might want to watch your backside a little more than normal."

"I'm watching it now," Ezra said.

The sheriff studied Ezra as he walked back to his truck. *A nice young man*, he thought. *A nice young man having a difficult week.* He smiled thinking of Ezra's father. Hard riding, hard fighting Johnny Riley. When things got tough, he was the man to have watching your backside. His old friend would have been proud of his son, Butler decided. Then Butler rubbed his chin thoughtfully. As a lawman he thought himself a good judge of character, and while he was not religious, a lifetime of dealing with criminals had made him philosophical. The common denominator he saw in troubled males was a lack of imprinting from their fathers. Some men branded their sons with values, others tossed their sons to the world. Ezra Riley was a good man, but he had a rough edge, which made him no different than most western men. A man's final outcome, the sheriff had decided, depended as much on his innate character as it did on his upbringing. When pricked, all men bled, but there was a considerable difference in what was mapped within the blood.

CHAPTER THIRTEEN

At noon Anne sat beneath a big cottonwood tree on the grounds of the rest home. She was not reading Joyce Carol Oates because she did not want to discuss fine literature with Ezra—she wanted to read a book about communication between husbands and wives and discuss *that* with Ezra—instead, she skimmed through her pocket Bible at random, but the Scriptures were not speaking to her today.

"Hey, can I sit down?" a voice said from above her.

She looked up to see the staff nurse. "Sure," Anne said.

The nurse sat, leaned against the tree, and lit a cigarette. Anne could never fathom why a nurse would smoke. "Look," Sally said, "I'm sorry about running my mouth. I didn't know you didn't know."

"It's okay," Anne said. "Ezra was busy and I was asleep by the time he got home."

"That's nice, honey, but it's no excuse." She took a long pull of her cigarette. "Men!" she exclaimed and blew a cloud of smoke up at the leaves as if to flush out tiny men hiding in the branches. "I've been married three times, you know."

"Yes, I know," Anne said. Johnson was a competent nurse and a nice enough person, but she wore her three failed marriages on her sleeve like a sergeant's chevron.

"Have you tried counseling?" the nurse asked. "Don't you go to church where that nice pastor Stephens is? Maybe you and Ezra should go in for counseling."

"Pastor Stephens left two years ago," Anne said. She had hated to see Pastor Stephens go. He had nurtured her music with the responsibility of leading worship and had befriended Ezra and pulled him into the congregation. Everyone missed Pastor Stephens.

"Well, where did he go?" the nurse said indignantly. "The people ran him out, didn't they? That's what they do to the good ones." She aimed another blast of smoke at the tree leaves, this time to flush out mean-spir-ited churchgoers. "Well, you must have a new pastor; what's he like?"

"He's, uh, the studious type," Anne said discreetly.

"Oh, dry as a bone, eh?" She shook her head, took a long drag from the cigarette, and tapped the ashes off into the grass. "One of those who couldn't find water if he lived in a boat."

Anne laughed. "How come you know so much about churches? You told me you never go."

"Honey, when you've been married three times you learn a thing or two about churches. So what's with this new guy? Does he fit in with this country? Is he the type Ezra could sit down with and really talk to?"

Anne sighed and shook her head. She only wished that he was. "He means well," she said, "but he and his wife came here from Pennsylvania after losing their two teenaged daughters in a car accident."

"Oh, mercy," the nurse said. "They're hurting units."

"Yes, they are," Anne said.

"And the hurtin' unit is here," the nurse said.

"What?"

"Your pastor," the nurse said. "I bet you anything that's him getting out of that lemon colored pickup. I can spot a preacher a mile away. They don't act like normal people."

Anne looked across the parking lot. Sure enough. It was Pastor Jablonski.

"Ugly pickup," Sally said, getting to her feet. "Well, I'm outta here, honey. The next time I keep company with a preacher I am going to be flat on my back listening to the kind things being said at my funeral." She crushed her cigarette out against the bark of the tree. "Take your time, Anne, I'll cover your station."

Pastor Tom advanced across the lawn in tentative steps. He was not an unattractive man. In junior college his thick legs and barrel chest had anchored an undersized offensive line, and he maintained his condition except for a thickening of his waist. His dark hair had thinned and his brows had bushed making him look like a young Ed Asner. He made no attempt at sitting down, so Anne stood up. "I meant to talk to you in church last night," he said. He was perturbed when people left the service quickly, avoiding contact with him, but was growing used to it. Everyone had been doing it for months.

"I sort of rushed home," Anne admitted.

"Actually I was wanting to talk with Ezra."

"I think Ezra had a hard day yesterday," Anne said. "He lost his job."

"Oh? What happened, a government cutback, I suppose." The pas-

tor hoped it was something minor, not a major situation that would add
to the distractions already facing his life. He wanted the best for Ezra
Riley, but he secretively wished it would not include counseling or disci-
pling him. Ezra was too difficult.

"No, not a government cutback," Anne said. "From what I hear it
was more like a Riley reaction." Her eyes politely asked the pastor to step
in, to do his job, to shepherd the flock. "Ezra spent last evening out in the
hills by himself," she said.

The pastor was not dense. He realized that during a time of trouble a
member of his congregation—even if it was Ezra Riley—had purposely
avoided him. Ezra had missed church to deal with his problem in his own
proud, independent way. Much of that was Ezra's problem, of course,
but the fact remained that the sheep were avoiding the shepherd. This
realization pained Jablonski but he felt powerless to come to terms with
it. "Well," he said, "maybe I can talk to him Sunday."

"I'm sure you can," Anne said. "And I'm sure you can catch him at
home the next few days." *Visit him,* was her intended message. *Talk to
my husband.*

Jablonski fidgeted for a moment and ran his hand through his thinning hair as if to release a thought gripping his mind. "What do you know
about this Jubal Lee Walker?" he blurted. The question jumped out like a
rabbit spooked from a woodpile.

Anne could sense Jablonski's insecurity. Something about Jay
Walker threatened him. It was beneath her to be coy, but she was mad at
Ezra for not communicating and at the pastor for his defensive selfish-
ness, so she played with Jablonski's fears. "I only met Jay Walker once,"
she said. "That was seventeen years ago in a jail in Kansas."

"Walker was in jail?" The thought of having a jailbird behind his
pulpit alarmed Pastor Tom as much as Anne had expected.

"No," Anne said innocently. "Ezra was in jail. Walker and I were just
visiting." She waited to see his reaction. He did not seem relieved, just
confused. She glanced at her watch. It was three minutes after one. Sally
would spare her more time but she decided to leave the pastor dangling at
the edge of thought. "I have to go," she said.

Ezra was in jail, the pastor said to himself. And Jubal Lee had visited
him. None of it made sense, and if anything, he was more confused and
concerned than ever

Ezra squatted in a corner of the corral, a bridle dangling from his
hands, the rowels of his spurs pressing lightly on his rump. The three
horses looked at him nervously. Shiloh had been ridden two days in a row
and seemed to be begging for a reprieve; Cheyenne, the young red dun,

kept moving behind the other two thinking he might successfully hide; and Gusto, the sole deliverer of Ezra's youth, stood with his head lowered and weary but with alertness in his eyes. Gusto was twenty-four years old, and the thousands of miles he had covered in ranch service showed in his arthritic shoulders, rough, dull-haired coat, and the display of rib lines. He had not been ridden for two years.

Rick Benjamin had once asked Ezra: "What are you going to do when Gusto dies, sell the ranch?"

It was an appropriate question. Gusto *was* the ranch in Ezra's eyes. When his father had stubbornly insisted Ezra break an ornery blue roan named Ribbon Tail, he soured Ezra on both fathers and horses. It was Gusto that later initiated Ezra's partial healing. The paint's kind but spirited heart reached into Ezra's chest and strengthened him—one heart, beating for two—until Ezra reached an age of independence and flung himself onto the highway. The hardest thing for him to leave had been that horse.

When Ezra returned to the ranch years later, he had to reclaim the paint back from Lacey. Then Gusto reintroduced him to the hills and the ways of cattle. Anne and Dylan, in turn, learned to ride on his back. But now he was old, tired, and crippled. He often lay for hours in the corral, then unhinged himself slowly to get up, and totter—like Uncle Solomon on his way to the store—from the corral. Younger horses pushed him around, mocking him as street kids on roller blades might taunt an old man with a cane. Gusto was still an animal of pride and dignity, but to preserve that, Ezra knew he would have to put him to sleep before winter. The thought of it weighed heavy, like an iron saddle, on Ezra's heart.

He rose and walked to the paint's side and scratched him behind the ears. "How's the old trooper?" he asked. Gusto closed his eyes in relaxation. Ezra patted him on the neck, then eased toward the red dun who tried to escape by running in circles around the corral. The commotion awakened Gusto who looked around nervously, knowing he did not have the agility to escape conflict. The young dun colt tried hiding behind Gusto and Shiloh, but finally he stood still and Ezra bridled him, led him to the barn, and saddled him. As Ezra was closing the tack room door he noticed his father's old .30-.30 rifle in its worn leather scabbard hanging from a nail. With the sheriff's warning fresh in his mind Ezra fitted the scabbard between the stirrup leathers and saddle fenders. It wouldn't hurt, he decided, to pack a little protection.

He planned a short ride because an aching feeling inside told him he better be around when Anne got home from work. Somehow he knew she had learned of his firing from someone else. Probably from the staff nurse, Sally Johnson. He often saw her old Lincoln Town Car parked downtown in front of The Buffalo Bar, where several of his crewmates from The Fort stopped after work. But his plans for a short ride evaporated when he crested a grassy hill and saw a hundred head of Wilson cattle grazing Riley land in the sagebrush-studded valley below him. Ezra swore, knowing he had several hours of work ahead of him. Wilson's cows were sour. They had been gathered and put from Riley grass so often they ran and hid at the sight of a rider. Ezra couldn't blame them. Uncle Solomon had grass to burn while Wilson had grazed everything down to the roots.

It was dusk when Ezra had the cattle gathered and put through a gate, then he propped up the fifty yards of fence they had torn down to get in. He knew that when he got back in the morning to fix it, the Wilson cows would have poked new holes and be streaming through like wartime refugees.

He rode home under skies of silver, gray, cadet blue, and violet by following the fence beside Wilson's CRP land. It was hardpan gumbo soil Wilson had farmed for three years then put in the Conservation Reserve Program. After seeding it back to grass, Wilson was getting paid thirty-five dollars an acre a year for ten years for three thousand acres for keeping the land idle. During that time it could not be grazed or hayed. Until the grass reestablished itself the land grew Russian thistle, or tumble-weed, which collected against the fence and collapsed it, and Canadian thistle, a noxious weed that spread down coulees and onto Riley ground like cancer, choking out native grass in its path.

Ezra hated weeds. They reminded him of the curse in the Garden of Eden and he considered all weeds the stepchildren of Satan. It was only the majestic Montana sky, the shrill call of nighthawks, and the layers of warm air rising up from creek bottoms that kept him from a bout of depression and anger. He labored hard for the sake of land, but with each passing day he was further from ownership while men like Wilson juggled paperwork and milked government programs to create prairie kingdoms that they abused for every penny, nickel, and dime they could wrest from the soil. It made Ezra wish that Montana was still a land ruled by vigilantes and that Shorty Wilson was stretching rope from a cottonwood limb.

He unsaddled the dun under electric light and opened the gate to the horse pasture. The dun rolled twice in the dust of the corral to dry and scratch his back, then leaped up, nickered, and thundered down the creek searching for Shiloh and Gusto. Ezra stood for a moment and listened. There was nothing as pretty to his ears as a horse's nicker and the pounding of racing hooves.

He walked to the house knowing Anne would be waiting for him. She was. He pulled off his boots and hung his spurs on a nail under her watchful gaze. He saw a thousand pages of rebuke in her eyes, but she didn't say a word, she just quietly followed as he entered the bathroom and began running water in the tub. They were both quiet until the tub was full and he was in the hot foamy water. "I didn't mean to keep anything from you," he said.

She sat on the lidded commode. "Ezra, you lost your job yesterday, and I don't find out about it until today? I feel like a fool. The staff nurse knew about it before I did."

"I'm sorry," he said. "I really am. Like I said, I wasn't trying to keep anything from you. It was late when I got home. I should have woke you up, but I knew you would be tired. I thought I'd sleep in this morning but when I didn't, I just got up and did some riding I needed to do."

"Those aren't very good excuses," she said.

"I know, but that's the way it happened." His voice had intensified.

"Okay, but at least tell me about it now. Tell me what happened."

He explained the situation to her.

"You threw some panels in a water tank? Do you really think they will fire you for that?" she asked.

"They might, they might not. I talked to the sheriff today. He thinks I will get my job back when the director gets back from Nebraska next week."

"The sheriff? Why did you talk to him?"

"He called me in. I thought it was about Frankforter's charge that I had destroyed government property. But it wasn't."

"What was it?"

"He just wanted to let me know that Austin is getting out of jail tomorrow."

"That's all?" Anne said. In the past five years so much had happened that Austin was just a dim memory, a thin black vapor that had drifted off to shadowland.

Ezra saw the confusion in Anne's eyes. Sometimes she was too innocent, too unsuspecting of people. "Austin is going to work for Shorty Wilson," he explained. "He will be our new neighbor."

A slight tremor went through Anne's body. She had had one encounter with Austin Arbuckle that Ezra did not know about. If he did, he might still do something they would both regret. "Why is the sheriff so concerned?" she asked.

"He isn't," Ezra said. "It's probably just procedure on parolees."

Anne's countenance softened, and she moved to sit on the floor, her arms on the side of the bathtub. Ezra's past few days had been tougher than she had realized. "If you don't get your job back, do you have any plans?" she asked.

"None at all," he said. "None at all."

* * *

In Yellow Rock Pastor Tom worked in his study until midnight. It was either that, or depend on chemicals like Darlene did. If he did not work himself to exhaustion, he relived the experience of being called to the scene of a rainy night accident on a winding road and finding Darlene's car wrapped around a large pine tree, the two bumpers inches from meeting. If he did not fill his mind with quotes, dates, and Scripture, he saw again his two beautiful daughters being placed on gurneys with sheets over their faces and Darlene lying in the leaves and pine needles, her crushed arm under her, screaming the girls' names. All the while, the other driver, a drunken carpenter, was staggering down the highway, trying to walk home with a rookie policeman chasing him and the rain falling in huge drops that exploded like grenades against the asphalt. He swore that night he would move where it seldom rained. Yellow Rock, Montana, was a logical choice.

At 12:17 A.M. Pastor Tom entered their bedroom, turned on the lamp by his bed, shuffled papers and books on his nightstand, and laid tomorrow's clothes across the back of a chair. Darlene was wrapped in the blankets, curled up like a fetus in a womb. Pastor Tom was not quiet. He did not need to be. Held in the embrace of her chemical cocoon, Darlene could not have been awakened by a high school marching band.

He did not sleep but it was not a Pennsylvania rain that kept him awake. It was the vision of his podium standing stark beneath a shaft of light and a darkness moving from the shadows to assume his place and authority. The form behind his dais was not that of Jubal Walker—whom he had never met—but was the drunken Pennsylvania carpenter, his long blonde hair plastered to his head as if he had just stepped out of the shower, the water dripping and pooling into little puddles on the floor.

"I forgive you," he whispered to the form, his exhausted mind retreating to the recesses of sleep. "I forgive you." But he was not speaking to the alcoholic laborer, but to the dark side of his own inner nature, to the man who lusted to strike and kill in a demand for blood vengeance. Tom Jablonski was a man filled with a bitter red anger, one that sloshed as he moved and thickened like drying paint as he slept. The anger was wrong, but there seemed no release for it, no safety valve he could find, just the constant repressing of its ugly head.

He slept fitfully and awakened at 5:15 with no zeal or expectation for the day. His conscience demanded prayer so he walked to the church, sat in a front pew, and forced an hour of petitioning from his soul. It came out with difficulty, like a housewife wringing the last drop of dirty water from a dishcloth.

CHAPTER FOURTEEN

Ezra imagined himself digging postholes by hand on a sun-baked hardpan flat. He saw his fists, thumbs up, gripped around posthole digger handles, felt his hands separate, and his deltoid and latissimus muscles strain as he raised another bite of hard earth from the hole. Then he pivoted on the washboarded abdominals and obliques, brought the pinchers down hard, and opened their steel jaws, letting the dry, powdery soil fall in a mound. He swung back again, bringing his hands together to open the jaws of the tool, and stabbed downward into the hole. Sweat trickled from his brow and perspiration, dirt, and barbed-wire scratches marred the leathery brown tan of his shirtless chest and arms. His pectoral muscles flexed like piano wires under his skin until they swelled and knotted together in tight, hard bulbs.

Listening to Tom Jablonski teach was like digging postholes in gumbo under a hot sun. Digging postholes with a gun to your head.

"Now then," he heard the pastor say, "point seven, under subheading B, which is the time-renowned truth of a dog returning to its own vomit, I quote from a recent article in *Christianity Today*, by the noted theologian and scholar . . . "

Holy dog vomit, Ezra thought, *this is the second Sunday devoted to Second Peter, a book of three chapters, and he is only to point seven under subheading B!* The pastor's limitless masonry skills used words as bricks to build a fortress around his own heart. He was a lonely, pain-stricken man, but rather than allow people to get close he beat them back with an assault of printed and spoken words.

Every few minutes Ezra looked to see if Jay Walker had arrived. Jay was not scheduled to speak until that evening, but Ezra guessed he would either come early or not come at all. He knew he might not recognize him—after all the years he could be fat and bald—but there were few men in the sanctuary and Ezra knew them all. Jay was not among them, and of those he knew, he could count none as close personal friends. They were nice guys, someone to talk to at church picnics and potlucks, but they seemed vacant and weak as if the last time they had felt a fire in the belly someone had smothered it with wet blankets. He couldn't imagine enduring the road with them, as he had done with Jay, sleeping side by side under the stars, each watching the other's back.

The pastor droned on so Ezra shifted gears and cruised into the dream world of books. His conversion to Christ five years before had made him a churchgoer, but the ordeal leading to it, the hours caught both in the steel jaws of a Newhouse predator trap and in painful self-inspection, had forced his priorities to the surface. They were God, family, land, and writing. He could not deny any without doing injury to all. He had forsaken his writing when first courting the land and learning the skills of a cowman, but during the past two years he had returned to it with a disciplined passion, like he used to have for running before injuries forced him to hang up his Nikes. His collection of essays was complete, polished and awaiting submission. All he needed was a title.

A sudden thought hit him—actually a phrase—and he dictated it on the back of the church bulletin. The thought had not so much struck him as it had surfaced, like a flat leaf rising up from murky water. It was the title. He wrote it again, more legibly, and pronounced it silently to himself, letting the words roll around on his tongue. Yes, it would probably do. It was a good title, an inspired title. And he had Pastor Tom to thank for it. Being held hostage by boredom was liberating to the imagination. He felt Anne shift her weight to see what he had written but he subtly blocked her view. It was not time. It needed curing, like a pepper hanging in the sun, before it could be shared or the spice would be lost.

Out of habit he looked at the back wall where the clock used to be. The pastor had taken it down two months ago saying he was tired of people breaking his concentration by turning and staring at the clock. Now they stared at where the clock used to be. Ezra checked his watch. It was 12:16. The message had started at 11:00. Ezra looked about him. The fifty or sixty other members were equally drained. A couple of the older men had dropped their chins to their chests and were sleeping. Ezra looked outside. It was a beautiful day and there were a hundred things he could be doing at home, things he never had time for, things his sisters or his uncle would notice if left undone. Beside him Anne was feigning attentiveness. The morning message had exhausted her kind intentions and she was adrift in a daydream. Dylan was scribbling on the back of the three pages of notes and outline that the pastor had handed out as an addendum to his sermon. Ezra was concerned for both Anne and Dylan. Darlene's uninspired piano playing and worship leadership had set the tone for a particularly flat Sunday service. Mundane music services depressed Anne, and Ezra had no idea how Dylan could ever learn to love God or pursue a life of Christian service if boring, two-hour sermons were his training ground. He was a spiritual child being provoked to wrath. It might be better, Ezra thought, to let Dylan stay home on Sunday mornings.

Jablonski preached like a lineman creating a protective pocket for his quarterback. He was rooted, immovable, his tree-trunk legs glued to the sanctuary floor. He was a blue-collar man and a Steelers fan. His father had been a concrete worker and Pastor Tom built his spiritual messages the same way: as firm, slow, and heavy as wet cement. Fortresses of stone, Ezra thought again, with the messenger walled within his messages.

Ezra chuckled softly to himself. Anne looked at him curiously. From the deep recesses of his memory came a vision of Jubal Lee's father, strutting, shouting, sweating through two shirts, rushing to change clothes in his study and saluting the people with a firm handshake at the door. What a comparison. The pugilistic Reverend Walker, the banty rooster of preachers, and the wooden Pastor Jablonski, the redwood of reverends. Ezra craned his neck forward to watch Darlene. It amazed him how she could sit so perfectly and dutifully still for so long. She had to be stoned—legally so, of course—but stoned just the same.

He returned to scribbling essay ideas on the bulletin. Anne had frowned at this originally but now she looked forward to getting home and reading Ezra's notes. Should he ever become famous it would make for an interesting anecdote, he told her: the first book written in longhand on the back of a church bulletin.

No, he corrected himself, *it probably wasn't the first*. Ironically, Pastor Tom had thought for months that Ezra was a serious scholar and loyal student and had considered taking him to lunch to reward him. Then one Sunday Ezra's bulletin dropped from his Bible and Darlene picked it up. Ezra's "sermon notes" described the raised hackles of coyotes backlit by painted sunsets, the concentric ripples of dragonflies doing "touch-and-goes" on placid reservoir surfaces, and one man's Druid-like love for the land.

Ezra looked at his watch again: 12:22. *And our preacher wonders why this church is never growing*, he thought. For amusement he looked over at Betty Lou Barber, who was elbowing her husband, Armon, awake. Ezra smiled. Betty Lou had fought to get rid of Pastor Stephens and was now leading the charge to dump Pastor Jablonski. Her family had been in the church for so long you would have thought they had carved the pews themselves. He smiled at the thought of her with a chain saw, barkshave, and sandpaper. She probably could have done the job— Betty Lou was a broad-shouldered, big boned woman in her sixties—

carving the pews one-handed while stirring trouble with the other and barking orders to her husband, the church's main deacon.

"I have a special announcement," Pastor Tom said. His sermon had ended and much of the congregation had not even noticed. A few sleepy heads looked up. "For this evening's service we will have a special speaker." A few more heads lifted. Efforts from the congregation to have special speakers had been rebuffed repeatedly. Pastor Tom had had a stranglehold on all services.

"I would like to introduce tonight's guest at this time," Pastor Jablonski gestured graciously to the back. He expected the man to merely stand and doff a humble salute to the people, but instead he rose and started for the pulpit. Necks twisted for a look at the surprising stranger. He was young and handsome with a toothy smile, tailor-made three-piece western suit, and a forceful, bouncing energy as if blowing in on his own wind.

When did Jay come in? Ezra wondered. Suddenly he was there, an apparition. As he approached, Ezra saw a stretch of highway, a wide blue western sky, a guitar, and two backpacks. He smelled diesel fuel from passing trucks and tasted granola bars and honey. He saw crudely rolled joints and heard America travailing in war and the shouts of demonstrators. He saw a curly haired boy throw back his head and laughingly challenge life. Jay had hardly changed at all. His suit was overdone, reminiscent of his hippie clothes of their first meeting, but he still breathed an air of self-assurance and disarming innocence. Jay the puppy dog, only a little older and more polished with a speckling of gray hairs in his neatly trimmed beard suggesting that forty was his next divide.

"This is Jubal Lee Walker," the pastor said. "I knew his father years ago. He will be our special speaker tonight." Jubal whispered something, and Jablonski dutifully added, "Oh, yes, he's a musician, too."

Jubal Lee took the microphone from Pastor Tom. It seemed to fly to his hand like a dove to the outstretched fingers of Saint Francis. "It's great to be here," he proclaimed. "And praise God!" He was undaunted by the congregation's lack of response. "It has been a long time since I was in Yellow Rock. You may not believe it, but the last time I was here I climbed on twelve head of bucking horses." He paused to let his statement settle. "I ride for a different brand now," he added. "I ride herd on souls and Jesus is my wagon boss."

Still a master of charm, Ezra thought.

"Come back tonight," Jubal invited. "I guarantee you fire. The Lord is good, and He is going to move in a very special and powerful way." He made it sound like a warranty. God moves or you get your money back. He handed the microphone back to Jablonski who took it sheepishly. He turned to a stunned and curious congregation and waved them toward the exit. "Uh, you are all excused," Pastor Tom said. For once he seemed eager to rid the place of people and he did not second Jubal Lee's invitation to the evening service.

The pastor hopes no one comes tonight, Ezra realized.

In the front pew Darlene wrung her hands nervously as she tapped the floor with one shoe. Her auburn hair was bobbed at the sides and her bangs were long. It was not a style for a woman her age, it was a fashion designed to shelter her. She stared out through her bangs like a small child peering through the limbs of a dark and dangerous forest.

The relieved congregation did not race for the doors as usual but hesitated for a better look at the brash young man that Pastor Tom was allowing to fill the pulpit. Jubal graciously shook a few hands and conferred blessings as he strode toward Ezra. Little old ladies tried to detain him. Men looked at him sideways but warmed with smiles as he stopped to exchange names. Jubal glanced at Ezra and winked as if to say: *I will be there as soon as the people let me.*

Dylan nudged his father. "Is this the guy who was your friend, Dad?" he asked.

"This is him," Ezra said. It certainly was. This was the one who talked drunk cowboys into being chauffeurs and sang on street corners for quarters and dimes so they could sleep between clean sheets.

When Jubal finally shook loose from the investigators, he spread his arms and swooped toward Ezra for a hug. "How are ya, brother?" he said, and wrapped himself about Ezra, who stood as stiff as a post. Jubal Lee pulled back, and the two were face-to-face. Jubal's eyes twinkled. Neither had aged noticeably, though Ezra wore the strain of the past five days. Jubal's hair was still dark and curly but groomed to perfection. Ezra's hair was growing out from his summer cropping and was flecked with gray at the temples.

"Brother, it is wonderful to see you," Jubal Lee said. "How are you doing?"

"I'm doing all right," Ezra said. It was a perfunctory answer. The one most men give even if they are stumbling through life gut-shot and bleeding, following a long trail of sorrows. *I'm all right. I'm all right.*

Jubal read Ezra's eyes, saw the depth reflecting behind layers of walls, felt the stiffness in his upper body, the padding of muscle added to what was once a light and wiry frame. "You look good," he said, then let loose of Ezra and turned to Anne. "Good to see you, sister," he said, and he gave her a hug. Anne politely and discreetly hugged him back. She was warm but not familiar. She believed in the scriptural admonition of not laying hands on anyone hastily. Then Jubal turned to Dylan. "And you, young man," he said. "What a spitting image of your father. You must be Dylan Riley." He shook Dylan's hand in a pronounced and grown-up manner.

"Nice to meet you," Dylan said shyly, his large brown eyes twinkling with interest.

"Dylan, Dylan, Dylan." Jubal rolled the name off his tongue. "What memories. You were named for a folk singer of a different generation," Jubal told the boy. "Did you know that?"

Dylan nodded again. He knew he was named for Bob Dylan the singer, but his grandmother had thought he was named for Matt Dillon, the fictional television marshall.

"Marshal Dillon is big and strong and rides such a good buckskin horse, but didn't you know you spell the name with an i and two l's not with a y?"

Jubal Lee turned to Ezra. "Do you still listen to Dylan?" he asked, smiling.

Ezra shook his head. He hadn't heard Dylan in years. His current music collection—the one that collected dust on the dashboard of his pickup—consisted of one Integrity praise cassette and a worn Ian Tyson tape.

"You're not missing anything. I met him once, you know." Jubal Lee turned back to the boy. "Dylan, my man, I brought you something."

"You did?" Dylan asked.

"I have recorded three compact discs, little brother, and you get a copy of each of them."

"We don't have a disc player," Dylan confessed.

"Oh, well," Jubal smiled. "I'll see about getting you one of those too. A Sony Walkman. But, you will earn it, okay?"

Dylan nodded enthusiastically.

Ezra noticed the rest of the church watching with interest, casually looking over their shoulder as they ambled toward the doors. Pastor Tom and Darlene were behind them like sheepdogs nipping at their heels, shooing them to the door. Betty Lee Barber was so curious about the handsome stranger she walked head-on into a pillar.

Who is this guy, the church was wondering, *and what is his connection to the Rileys?*

"Come on," Jubal Lee said, putting one arm around Ezra and the other around Anne. "Allow me to buy you lunch."

They stepped outside. Parked in front of the church was a brand-new blue and silver Chevy Suburban with personalized Colorado plates that read: *PRAISE.* Attached to the Suburban was a matching, all-enclosed four-horse aluminum trailer with a dressing room. *JUBAL LEE MINIS-*

TRIES was painted across the doors of the Suburban and sides of the trailer in bold script. Walker watched Ezra's eyebrows raise and threw back his head and laughed. "Nice wheels, huh?" he said. "We never had anything like this when we were on the road together, did we, brother?"

No, thought Ezra, *and that was the whole point of being on the road. Freedom from materialism.*

Jubal got behind the wheel like a captain in charge of a ship and drove them to the nicest restaurant in Yellow Rock. The Rileys' usual Sunday outing consisted of take-out chicken from Hardees eaten at home on paper plates.

"I don't think we can get a table," Ezra said as they walked from the Suburban. "This place is always packed after church."

"No problem," Jubal said. He opened the door for them. A waitress greeted Jubal cheerfully and led them to a back table, already set for a party of five. Well-dressed diners—accountants, bankers, and insurance agents and wives—watched as they walked by. "Will this be good enough, Reverend Walker?" the waitress asked, showing them to a table in the back.

"It's fine," he said as if bestowing a papal blessing.

"You made reservations?" Ezra asked. There was a presumption in Jay's actions that bothered him, yet it was not out of character for the brash, confident person he remembered from the road.

"One must plan ahead, brother," Jubal answered. "If you had not been able to come, I would have asked Pastor Jablonski and his wife." He turned to Dylan and encouraged him to order anything he liked. "Shrimp, steak, crab. Or all three for that matter."

"This is very nice," Anne said. "But you didn't have to do it. I could have made lunch for us at home."

"My treat," Jubal said. "It has been a long time. Let's celebrate that the Lord has brought us all back together."

"So, what name do you go by now?" Ezra asked.

"Call me Jubal Lee," he said. "It sounds like a party, doesn't it? I hated the name growing up, but I thank God and my father for it now."

"How is your father?" Ezra asked.

Jubal's face stiffened, like a child repeating a memorized poem in front of a first grade class. "He tried to retire last year," he said. "But it didn't last. He has a church in Minnesota." His answer was brisk and final, like a door slamming shut in the wind.

"I see you are wearing a wedding ring," Anne said.

Jubal reached into his inside suit pocket and brought out a laminated 5-by-7 color photograph of a beautiful woman with raven black hair, olive skin, and dark green eyes. On each side of her were small miniatures of herself: dark-haired, smiling girls in red dresses. "My wife's name is Shelley," he said. "That's Shannon on the left, she's ten. And Sarah on the right, she's seven."

"They are beautiful," Anne said.

"Shelley was a model," Jubal said proudly. "Actually, both of the girls have done a little modeling already, too."

"So," Ezra asked, "are you an evangelist now, or what?"

"Or what?" Jubal Lee laughed. "That sounds appropriate. I am an 'or what.' Actually, I fulfill all of the offices of Ephesians four," Jubal said. "I plant churches, I pastor, I teach, and I evangelize."

"You left out the office of the prophet," Anne said.

"First and foremost a prophet."

"What brings you back to Yellow Rock?" Ezra asked.

"In due time, brother," Jubal said. "I will tell you all about it in due time." His eyes twinkled mischievously as if dangling keys to a treasure chest before their faces.

The smiling waitress returned. Ezra and Anne ordered conservatively, accustomed to dining on their Hardees budget. Dylan ordered shrimp. Jubal Lee asked the waitress questions about each entree and the specialties before deciding on prime rib. Ezra noticed the other diners watched him curiously. People were drawn to Jay—no, Jubal Lee—or else he had a way of drawing their attention to him as if he basked in his own light

"And you, Ezra," Jubal Lee asked. "You are on the family ranch?"

The ranch. Ezra thought of several dry and witty remarks. The idea of a "family" ranch produced a few more. "Yes," he said. "Sort of. Does that surprise you?"

"No, not at all. I always thought you would return to ranching. It's in your blood. It was either that, or you were going to be a full time karate instructor."

"I left the martial arts when I left the road," Ezra said. He did not like talking about his former interest in karate and aikido. It seemed a world away from stirrup leathers and latigos.

"I found the martial arts when I left the road," Jubal countered. There was a shade of bravado in his voice, a slight coloration of words that only Anne noticed.

"You?" Ezra said, surprised. To him the martial arts had meant rigid discipline, pain, and sacrifice.

"Yes. I'm a black belt in tae kwon do, a sport karate. Too tame for you, I know." He staged a whisper to Dylan. "Did you know your dad was trained to kill people?" he asked.

"He was?" Dylan said.

"Not exactly," Ezra countermanded.

"Jukado, wasn't it? And Gojo-Ryu? Hardly tame disciplines, Ezra."

"How did you meet your wife, Jubal?" Anne interrupted. She was bothered by an undertone in the conversation, not by the subject itself.

Jubal Lee nodded toward Dylan. "Does he know where the three of us were the last time we were together?" he asked Ezra.

"You can tell him," Ezra said. "I have no secrets from my son."

"The last time I saw your dad," Jubal Lee explained to Dylan, "your father was in jail. But he was in jail for a good reason."

"Cool. What did you do, Dad?" Dylan asked.

"He protected your mother in Lawrence, Kansas," Jubal answered. "He kicked a cop through a plate glass window."

"It's not a pastime I would recommend," Ezra said to his son.

Jubal then turned his attention back to Anne. "Getting back to your question, Anne. After leaving you and Ezra, I had planned on hitching to southern California to become involved with the Jesus Movement, but Shelley picked me up outside of Colorado Springs. She had been doing a shoot in Denver, modeling for the nation's largest wholesaler of western wear, and she was driving home to her daddy's ranch near Trinidad. I went along. Her dad and I hit it off. And needless to say, she and I hit it off."

"What does her dad do?" Anne asked.

"He owns the western wear company," Jubal smiled. "And he dabbles in horses. Expensive horses. He has polo ponies, race horses, cutting horses. They are old Colorado money," he explained. "His grandfather had a gold claim."

"And your wife and girls could not make the trip," Anne concluded.

The slight veil of darkness that covered Jubal's face at the mention of his family was not noticed because his eyes shined brighter. "Uh, no, the girls are in school, of course," he said. "But, enough about me. How about the two of you? How are things going for you?"

"We've been through almost a decade of drought," Ezra said. "I'm in partnership with my two sisters, which is less than ideal."

"Your parents are gone?"

"My dad passed away in '78, my mother in '82."

"I'm sorry to hear that," Jubal said. "You know, I called up here twice looking for you. The first time was in '74, things were a little wild for me then. I talked to your mother. She didn't know where you were for sure. Then I called again in '76. Talked to your dad that time. It was great talking to him again, but you still weren't around."

"We got married in '74," Anne explained. "In '76 we were living in Redlands, California."

"When did you get into the ministry, Jay?" Ezra asked.

"Jubal Lee," he corrected. "Shelley and I were on the fast track for years. Showing horses, she was modeling, I was singing in western clubs. We were making a lot of money and putting most of it up our noses. One night I was hauling some cutting horses back from Reno and stopped at a little place by the side of the road for gas. I thought to myself, this place sure looks familiar, and then I realized it was where I had met you, Ezra. I went in the bar and ordered a bottle of wine in your memory and got to thinking about my life and the wrong directions I had taken. That Sunday I took Shelley to church and rededicated my life to the Lord."

"I'm glad you're not playing your music in nightclubs anymore," Ezra said.

"No, I play for God now. Which reminds me, are you still writing, Ezra?" There was a subtle challenge in Jubal's tone, the soul of one artist beckoning the soul of another.

Ezra held Jubal's questioning eyes for several moments. He never talked about his writing casually. He believed discussion drained the reservoir his talent was stored in. "Yes," he said finally. "I went through a long dry spell, sort of like the drought, but I am seriously writing again."

"Getting published, brother?"

"Not yet."

"We'll change that," Jubal announced.

"You have three albums out?" Anne asked, changing the subject again. It was the writer in Ezra Riley that had first attracted her, not the chivalry of a longhaired demonstrator, and it was the writer she was most protective of.

"Yes, and a fourth on the way."

"That's wonderful," she said politely.

His eyes lit up with a sudden realization. "That's right," he remembered. "You are a musician, too, aren't you, sister?"

"I play a little," she said. It was a tender spot with her, and Ezra stiffened to shield Anne from her woundedness. Every time he thought about his wife and music he wanted to strangle Tom Jablonski.

"Well, my first three recordings were with a small company," Jubal said. "Just stuff I threw together. I worked with a number of big ministries. Never really had time to pursue my music like I wanted to. But I'm flying to Nashville next month to sign with a new label."

Anne saw the waitress coming with their order. Now was the time, she decided, to settle one question on her mind. "Where are you staying, Jubal? You are more than welcome to stay with us."

"Thank you," he said graciously. "But when I minister, it is really better if I just get a room in a motel. That way I can separate myself and concentrate on the things of God."

"We have a bunkhouse," Ezra offered. "You are welcome to it." That was a rare invitation from him. His writing office was considered off limits to visitors.

"No, no, but thank you anyway, brother. Oh, the food is here. By the way, brother, I did leave two horses in your corrals this morning. I hope that was okay. I didn't want to leave them in the trailer all day, and if Dylan can care for them for a while I will be glad to buy him a Walkman in return."

"That's not really necessary," Ezra said, diverting his eyes from Dylan's disappointment. "We'll be glad to keep the horses. Are you delivering them to someone?"

"They are going to a buyer in Canada," Jubal said. "But if we have time, let's exercise them tomorrow. Show me the ranch. The horses can be our toys for a few days."

"You will be spending some time here?" Anne asked.

"If Ezra has the time."

"I should have time," Ezra said. "I got fired from my part-time job a couple days ago."

Jubal Lee raised his brows. "Really? My, how perfect the timing is when you are in the will of God."

Ezra and Anne exchanged glances. It seemed like an odd remark.

The food was set before them. Dylan was ravenous after the long church service and he stared at his shrimp hungrily.

"May I have the honor of blessing it?" Jubal asked.

Ezra nodded. *Certainly,* he thought. *You're the preacher, and you are paying for the meal.*

"Before I pray, I'm curious about one thing. How did you finally come to the Lord, Ezra? I would like to give proper thanks for your salvation."

Ezra thought for a moment. "I guess you could say I was trapped," he said. Dylan smiled. As God's provision for the release of his father, he appreciated the irony of the statement.

"Trapped?" Jubal Lee asked.

"Literally," Anne said.

"How interesting, brother. You must tell me your testimony."

Anne smiled wryly. It was her to turn to play the card of mystery. "In due time," she said. "We will tell you in due time."

CHAPTER FIFTEEN

Sunday night was usually the service for the faithful few at the Yellow Rock Community Believers' Church. Sometimes only eight or ten people showed up.

This evening Pastor Jablonski could not help but count. There were eighty-one people in the church, not counting Jubal Lee Walker, who had yet to show.

"What are you going to do if he just blew out of town?" Darlene whispered. Pastor Tom did not answer because he did not know. Besides, Walker was a performer and he had a good audience. He expected him to appear.

Ezra stood alone on the dais. Jubal had asked Ezra to introduce him. He looked at his watch. 7:04 and still no sign of Jay. He glanced at Anne. She shrugged a smile. Jay—Jubal—had said to introduce him at 7:05.

"Good evening," Ezra said into the microphone. "I know some of you are curious about my relationship with Jubal Lee Walker. Seventeen years ago we were two young men who met on the highway, each of us searching for God in our own way. Now, after all these years, we are reunited under the banner of Jesus Christ.

"I have not seen Jubal in the intervening years, nor have I heard from him, until this morning. In some ways, he is as much a stranger to me as he is to you. But, the one thing I can say is he is singularly blessed with musical ability." His eyes scanned the room. Still no sign of the special guest. Ezra's introduction was over but he did not know what to do. He was about to send Dylan looking for Jubal when low, wafting music sounded from the back of the church. It rose to a tenor peak, trickled down to a bass, then rose again. It was ghostly in its low range, as if coming from a cemetery at night, then it climbed a ladder of resurrection becoming uplifting and etheric until you thought you were eavesdropping on an angelic trumpeter. A door opened and Jubal Lee stepped through playing a tenor saxophone. He bent into the horn and whirled slowly to the music as if the horn were playing him, sashaying down the aisle, the notes to "When the Saints Go Marching In" swirling about him like a cloud. Ezra stood transfixed, watching him approach. Jubal Lee was a Pied Piper, and he had all of the church in his spell.

Betty Lou Barber stood and began clapping to the music. Three or four others joined her. Then ten, twelve, fifteen. Ezra stepped down and took his place beside Anne and Dylan. They were standing and clapping. Soon all the congregation was standing except for the Reverend and Mrs. Jablonski. After a minute, the pastor realized everyone behind him was on their feet and he stood as well, but it took a pleading look to coax Darlene to join him. Jubal Lee slowly whirled to the dais. He wore a sequinned white western shirt, silver bolo tie, black slacks, and ostrich-skin cowboy boots. He pulled the clapping of the congregation with him to the microphone, let his horn hang from his neck, and sang loudly, clearly, resonantly into the mike, his hands clapping over his head, his polished teeth breaking against his smile like whitecaps:

> *Oh, when the Saints,*
> *Go marching in,*
> *Oh, when the Saints go marching in,*
> *Oh, Lord, I want to be in that number*
> *When the Saints go marching in . . .*

He returned to the horn and played it harder, deeper, and louder than before. He squeezed every ounce of life from each note like his soul was rising from his shoes and up through his legs, belly, and chest and funnelling through the horn in a celebration of melody. He whirled slowly again, now across the raised platform to the grand piano. Without missing a beat the saxophone was down and Jubal was on the piano bench pounding all the heart from the song as if this was Sunday in Cajun country and they were all black children at play in the gardens of God. The piano and his voice became a duet and the exhilaration had the people gently swaying, even rocking, as they clapped, and he sang:

> *Oh, when the sons*
> *of God arise,*
> *Oh, when the sons of God arise,*
> *Oh, Lord, I want to be in that number,*
> *When the sons of God arise . . .*

Ezra was surprised to discover his face hurt from smiling. He looked at Anne. Her head was lifted back, her eyes were closed, and tears were streaming down her face, like liquid prayers of thankfulness washing through the dry regions of her soul. The caged bird within her musician's heart had taken wing. The others still swayed and sang like willows in the wind, as if Jubal was a weather wizard, a holy chinook melting the frozen hearts of the white people of the northern plains. His music was singularly pure and powerful, beyond description, as if it came from the throne of God, delivered by an escort of cherubs.

Ezra remembered Jubal's father:

"Do you know what the anointing is, Mr. Riley? It is the power of God falling upon you, or rising up from within you. I have never done drugs—I've never so much as touched a beer in my life—but I can't imagine anything as wonderful as God's anointing. You will know the anointing some day."

Without a falter, Jubal Lee launched into the modern choruses of "Our God is an Awesome God" and "I Exalt Thee." Many in the congregation did not know these songs but it made no difference. They mouthed the words or rocked silently as they stood. Several sat down and placed their heads on the pew in front of them in silent prayer. Only several older men, and Darlene, seemed untouched. They stood rigidly, their arms at their side. But even Pastor Tom was touched by the spirit of the evening. He stood silently, his hands clasped together in prayer, his chin on the fist they formed. Jubal Lee's fingers raced and danced across the piano keys as if they were two children loose on a playground. His eyes sparkled so brightly he stabbed even the back pews with piercing daggers of white light. He ended with a slow, soulful, worshipful rendition of "Holy Ground." A visiting couple, pulled from a nearby motel, sank to their knees in the aisle. Anne did also.

When the song was finished, Jubal let the silence settle on the people, allowing time for the spirit to minister, then, with the timing of a thunderbolt, he strolled to the microphone, removed it from its stand, coiled its cord like a lariat, and spoke slowly and softly: "We have come into the presence of an awesome living God. He is here with us. Turn your hearts, your minds, your very selves to Him tonight. Release your doubts, your fears, your limitations. Pack them now to the foot of the cross and unburden yourself. The Lord brought us naked into this world, and to dust we will return should He not soon return, so let us stand naked before Him tonight. Let down your walls. He will not hurt you. You can only hurt yourself by denying His presence."

He moved to the edge of the platform. He did not step down and move among the people. These were not his sheep, they were Pastor Tom's, and he kept a respectful distance. His voice continued softly. "I have come this evening to bring you a word from God. I have ministered all across this great nation of ours. I have stood on podiums with famous men of God, names you would know in an instant. I have seen stadiums and auditoriums filled with thousands upon thousands of people, but I will tell you this: it is harder to bring true revival to the small town than to the great city. Jesus said that prophets were without honor in their hometown. But this is not my hometown, and I am not a respecter of men. I did not come here to please or entertain you. I came to glorify God and deliver His word. Should he please Himself to display me as a fool, then so be it. Let us all be willing to be fools for Christ."

He paced the dais edge like a mountain lion on a rock ledge prowling with controlled aggression. "If you are weary and tired of standing," he whispered into the microphone, "please feel free to sit." Slowly, but as one, the people seated themselves.

"Brothers and sisters," Jubal Lee said. "Let me assure you, we are living in the Last Days."

"Amen," said Betty Lou Barber.

"And the Word of God says that in the Last Days perilous times will come, that men will become lovers of self, lovers of money, boastful, proud, blasphemers. Children will be disobedient to parents, unthankful, unholy. We are in those times."

"Amen," Betty Lou said again. Pastor Tom turned to Second Timothy, chapter three, the verse Jubal Lee was quoting. Darlene just stared at the floor, wincing with each Betty Lou amen as if someone was shooting her with a pellet gun.

"We are in those times," Jubal Lee repeated himself. "Look about you. We are a lawless generation. Filth and perversion are the norm, decency and morality have been driven from the gates of our country and wander in the wilderness of our collective soul. We are a society that has rejected God, that has tossed prayer from the classroom and made it legal, even fashionable, to kill babies in the womb. We are a society where young people are one, maybe two generations removed from the Church. Thousands, tens of thousands, hundreds of thousands of people, yes, even millions of people walk the streets and they do not know who Jesus is. He is just a cuss word. Or some historical figure. But they do not know He is the Son of God . . . because they have not been told!"

His voice gradually grew louder, more forceful. "We can weep for this country, but do not point at the sinfulness of the unsaved and say there is the problem. No, brothers and sisters," he softened his voice, "for you and I are the problem."

Some people leaned forward in their pews, others lowered their heads, but almost to a person they hungered for the verbal whipping Jubal Lee was delivering. Ezra sat upright, watching his old acquaintance with awe. His talent on the road had been small calibre compared to the guns he was firing now.

"What is our problem?" the preacher asked. "Our problem is that we have allowed our churches to have a form of godliness while denying its power. We tell the unsaved you must go to church then we drag them to an overpriced building, force them to sing a few songs, put a dollar in the collection plate, and listen to morality tales from a man who is quite possibly cheating on his own wife. They want God, we give them religion."

Someone said, "Amen."

"The people want to see the God of Abraham, Moses, and Jacob. They want to see the God of miracles and deliverance. We give them systems, programs, and formulas. We give them mountain after mountain of man's plans, and say, 'Scale these, they will get you to the top,' and all the while we are always learning and never able to come to the knowledge of the truth."

"Amen."

"Amen!"

Pastor Tom shifted uneasily, rested his chin on a fist, and watched his congregation from the corner of one eye. The dam had burst. There was no way now for him to contain what Jubal Lee had already done. The excitement of the people flowed around him like water rising to his knees. Unconsciously, Pastor Tom moved his legs as if searching for dry ground. If he had only known, if he had had a clue that this was the type of preacher Jubal Lee was, he never would have allowed him in the church. But Tom Jablonski had been so removed from the brethren and the brotherhood that he had begun to imagine that everyone was like himself.

"Judgment comes first to the house of God," Jubal Lee suddenly shouted, awakening no one for everyone was already hooked on his words like catfish strung on a setline. "We are guilty of being a defensive church. We hide in these buildings," he swept the perimeter of the sanctuary with his hands, "as if they were forts and the land is full of savages." He slammed a fist into a cupped hand. "We are meant to be an aggressive, forceful, militant church. But we are a church of wimps!"

Betty Lou Barber stood up. An overhead light casting down on her tinted red hair made her glow like a Christmas bulb. "Preach it, Brother Walker," she shouted.

Darlene shot her a lasered stare that could have blown the doors off a dairy barn. Pastor Tom reached down and took Darlene's hand as if defusing a bomb.

Jubal Lee did not miss a beat. "I am a watchman on the wall. I did not come here to comfort the afflicted, but to afflict the comfortable. I am the fire-bearer, the firebrand of a living God who is Himself a consuming fire. All the dead words and dead works preached by hirelings are being gathered like tinder, and in these Last Days fire shall fall from heaven, not on the world like the naysayers and prophets of doom predict, but upon the Church first to burn the chaff from our dry, polluted souls. We must be forged in the blazing oven of the Holy Spirit. Justified. Sanctified. Glorified. Consecrated unto Him for His holy works, dead to our selves, our selfish ambitions and our weak, timid fears."

Ezra could see the shirt glisten, not just from the sequins, but from the sweat soaking through. Jubal Lee, too, was a two-shirter.

"I call on you like a blast from a trumpet. I call on those of you who want fresh fire in your lives. Come forward now. Come stand at this altar and raise your hands to the living God and break the old vessel that the new one might be filled with new wine. Come. All of you who are thirsty, come."

Anne stood up, drawn not by the messenger but by the message, and slid quietly past Ezra. The strangers from the motel followed her to the altar. Betty Lou Barber followed them, and then, as if the dike had collapsed, thirty or forty more formed a semi-circle around Jubal Lee Walker.

"I am calling to men and women of destiny," Jubal Lee said. "I am calling to those who know in their hearts that they were born for this day, for this hour, that they are in the plan of God for the final days."

Ezra's hands were knotted together and his head was down. Destiny. The plan of God. Slowly, others rose to come forward. Ezra felt someone brush by. It was Dylan. His son was making a stand.

"For if you would try to save your life," Jubal Lee said, "you will lose it. But if you will tonight lose your life, you will save it."

Ezra rose from the pew, stepped softly between those who were kneeling and stood beside his wife and son. Anne reached out and took his hand. The pews were all but empty. Three people had left. Only four people had not come forward. Pastor Tom and Darlene were two of them.

Jubal Lee pulled a small vial from his pocket. "I am going to anoint each of you," he said, "as a sign of your new commitment. But don't let it stop here. You must step out in faith. If the Spirit moves in wondrous ways, do not let it startle or worry you. It is not uncommon for people to be overcome by the Spirit when He is pouring out fresh fire. If someone falls, or should you fall, do not worry. The Spirit is the One who knocks down and the Spirit is well able to catch. If there is weeping and wailing, if there is joyous laughter, just let it flow. It is God at work." He slowly worked his way through the throng of people dabbing each with a spot of oil on their foreheads.

Pastor Tom's face turned to flint. Those were his sheep Jubal was anointing, and what was all this silliness about being knocked down, or wailing and laughing? He wanted to stop him but what could he do that would not appear disruptive or defensive? He would have to wait and hope Jubal—like a bad headache—simply went away with time.

Jubal continued down the prayer line. Ezra's eyes were closed but he could hear Jubal's approach, It was as if they were standing above the breakers of the ocean near Stinson Beach all over again. The waves were coming in. He heard the muffled collapse of someone hitting the floor. He heard someone drop to the altar and cry. He heard others begin to sing and another to laugh. He felt Jubal's presence as he came to Anne. Jubal prayed a short, powerful prayer, he called for the caged bird to fly and sing, and Ezra felt Anne crumple to the floor.

The next moment Ezra felt a warmth on his forehead and a lightness flooding his being followed by a sudden heaviness of the heart. He collapsed forward onto the dais, his forehead pressed against the grainy carpet. Jubal Lee hovered over him for several minutes, his hands on Ezra's shoulders. The heart of heaviness moved slowly into Ezra's throat before escaping in deep, mournful moanings as if his soul was being wrung by the hand of God. The moans came more deeply when he realized Dylan was on the floor beside him.

The three Rileys lay there for a long time, long after others had moved back to the pews or gone home. Anne was on her back bathing in bliss, Dylan was crouched beside his father, his eager young heart showing both duty and innocent abandon. Ezra labored effortlessly in shedding his burdens. He was cognizant of voices and activity around him. He heard Jubal praying for others. And he heard Betty Lou Barber when she told Jubal: "Mr. Walker, we would like it very much if you could stay and hold a whole week of revival meetings."

And Jubal said: "That's very nice of you, Mrs. Barber, but that would be a decision for this church, for the pastor, and his board."

And Betty Lou answered: "Well, all five board members are right here, and I am sure I can get an answer for you in just a few minutes. And if you are concerned about finances we can take an offering each night."

"Money is not a concern to me," he heard Jubal say.

"It's destiny, man. You are a writer and I am a musician. We both have unusual Bible names. It's destiny. We are meant to do great things together. Do you believe in fate, Ezra?"

Ezra contemplated the stars that sparkled in the clear Nevada night. "I don't know," he said. "Karma," maybe.

CHAPTER SIXTEEN

There are dreams that men do not remember. They come softly, like a beautiful woman in a silk gown and velvet slippers. They lay warm hands on troubled brows and whisper encouragement to the ear. Their words float like feathers in stillness, turning over and over in the air of the subconscious, reflecting a light from deep within, then fall softly to the floor of the soul and gather like leaves beneath stately trees. Their nature disqualifies memory. They do not jar, rattle, or shock. They cover the sleeper with a sheet of peace and bless him with restfulness.

On Monday morning the fifteenth of September Ezra Riley awakened at 4:15 feeling strong and hopeful. He turned and watched Anne, asleep on her pillow, her sandy blonde hair spread like a spray of water. Quietly he tiptoed from the room then dropped to the floor and knocked off fifty quick push-ups. He examined his face in the bathroom mirror and saw a sparkling, energetic shine in his eye. He washed in cold water, dressed, and went to the kitchen. He did not make coffee. He had been wanting to quit caffeine and decided today was the day for new beginnings.

He picked up his bonded leather Bible to read the psalm and proverb that corresponded to the date. He became so engrossed in Psalm 15, short as it was, that he never got around to the proverb. He prayed for his wife and son, for Jubal Lee and his week of revival. That was easy. Then he prayed for Lacey, Solomon, Diane, and Austin Arbuckle. That was not as easy.

At 5:15 he stepped outside to the cool, cloaked darkness preceding dawn and took his first close look at Jubal Lee's horses. They were registered Jockey Club Thoroughbreds and they moved with the fluid smoothness of ghosts in the murky blue-grayness of the morning. One was a classic bay standing about 16 hands. The other a dark brown standing a finger less, or 15.3. Both had well-sculpted heads, large, kind eyes, and plenty of leg. They were simply as fine of horseflesh as he had ever seen.

His own horses had heart, brains, and cow sense, but these were in another league, the type of horse far beyond Ezra's budget.

He heard Shiloh, Cheyenne, and Gusto come into the corral for their morning feeding. From the sound of their hooves he knew their excitement of discovering strange horses in the corral and felt their raw energy radiating like heat from a stove. They stuck their heads over the top corral plank for a meeting of noses. Shiloh and Cheyenne sniffed, snorted, and squealed. Gusto got to the fence late but he stretched his neck out to make contact with the brown Thoroughbred while Shiloh and Cheyenne argued dominance and territorial claims with the bay.

Ezra smiled. "You're slummin', boys," he told the Thoroughbreds.

At 5:45 Ezra went into his bunkhouse office and typed the title cover for his manuscript. He liked the title and thanked the Lord for it. It was strong, yet ironic. The manuscript was ready for mailing, but he decided to polish the last chapters again before submitting the book to publishers. It was a scary idea: putting one's writing in the mail, addressed to critical eyes, was like abandoning your firstborn on gang-ridden streets.

He thumbed through the pages at random. The words leaped and danced; they shimmered in sunlight and shadow, glowed with a raw, masculine energy, yet were restrained by a gentle, peaceful rein. He read the sentences, paragraphs, and pages as if they were someone else's words, someone much more skilled than he. Then gradually the conclusion came to him: after years of doubting his abilities and arguing with his calling, Ezra saw for the first time the brilliance of his gift. He was good. He was actually very, very good. And rather than drink from the cup of hubris, he felt instead a terrible reckoning with humility. He felt smaller than his work. He felt the presence of the true Author, the true Creator, and his petty concerns about Lacey, Austin, Solomon, and everything else, vanished like vapor before a scorching light. The seduction of the hills, of horses, wildlife, and cowboy living paled, dried and curled like the brittle gumbo flakes that tiled the beds of dry badland creeks. He backed slowly away from his desk and to the door. He would tell no one, he decided. It could all be an illusion. He would mail the manuscript as soon as he decided on a publisher. Then he would wait to see what he would see.

At 6:20 he returned to the house. Anne was dressing. He slipped up behind and gave her a strong hug and a kiss on the neck.

"Hmmm, what was that for?" she said.

"Just because."

"Do it again."

"No, actually I want to start having devotions with you in the morning."

Her eyes became blue candles of joy.

At a quarter after seven Anne left for work, and Dylan left with her for school. As they were leaving, Jubal Lee pulled into the yard. He walked from the Suburban carrying a new saddle, silver inlaid bit with horsehair bridle and reins, and a pair of new buckskin-colored chinks. "Glory to God, brother," he exclaimed. "What a beautiful morning."

"Yes it is," Ezra agreed. He was still wary of Jubal's religious exuberances but an excitement was swelling in his own heart, and if pricked, he might have burst with a hallelujah himself.

"Pick the horse of your choice, brother," Jubal Lee said.

Ezra put his bridle on the brown.

"I knew you would pick him," Jubal Lee said. "We got him off the track in a claiming race. I trained him for cowboy polo. Have you ever played polo?"

Ezra shook his head. He hadn't played at anything for a long time.

Jubal whistled praise songs as he saddled the bay. Ezra saw that he had a good touch with horses. Jubal knew what he was doing, and the horses were at ease around him though he lacked the friendliness that Ezra bestowed on his own animals.

They led the saddled Thoroughbreds through the gate to the creek, tightened the girths, and mounted. The moment he settled himself in his saddle Ezra knew he was on something special.

"A magic carpet ride," Jubal Lee said. "A magical mystery tour, that's what that brown is. He's the smoothest horse I have ever ridden."

"He feels like he's flying when he's just standing still," Ezra said with a smile.

Jubal laughed merrily.

"What's so funny?" Ezra asked.

"That's the first smile I have seen on your face," he said.

"He's a smile-maker," Ezra said. "But I see he has a bad quarter-crack on that front hoof."

"He was crippled when I got him," Jubal said. "But I do corrective shoeing. He's sound as a dollar now."

They headed for the hills, men on horseback, partners. It made Ezra think of Rick Benjamin and Jim Mendenhall; of his father riding with Charley Arbuckle; of the exclusive fraternity of the mounted man, the man superior to others. He smiled as he caught himself sounding like old Charley. He did not think about The Fort and cowboys working for the government and belonging to unions. He thought of his father and the thousands of horses that Johnny Riley had ridden, and Ezra wished that his father could come back for one day and fork his legs around this wonderful brown while Ezra rode the bay.

"You're deep in thought," Jubal said as the horses trotted a narrow trail. They worked their ears like joysticks—the ear always determined the focus of the eye, as they scanned the unfamiliar country.

"I was thinking about my father," Ezra said. "I wished he was here to ride this brown."

"He would have liked him," Jubal said.

There are dreams that men do not remember because they are too familiar. Dreams that unlock bolted doors and smash in windows. Dreams that clank through hallways with leaden feet hobbled by rattling chains. Dreams that scream. Dreams that twist the mind and leave the dreamer dried, dull, and defenseless in the morning.

Pastor Tom awakened at 4 A.M. with a headache. He rose, took two aspirin, and tried to go back to sleep. He couldn't. He rose again, dressed, walked the four blocks to the Yellow Rock Community Believers' Church, and entered his study. He got his books out but could not concentrate.

Jubal Lee Walker was a disruption. Pastor Tom's plans for finishing his study on Second Peter were stalled because of Jubal Lee's weeklong revival service. Tom Jablonski was angry. He defined himself within the borders of his studies and his control over the church. For the first time ever his board had gone against his wishes. He had Betty Lou Barber to thank for that. *Betty Lou the Battle-Ax.* She had prompted the quick meeting of the board then hovered nearby like an eagle with a bomb in her talons. They would do her bidding or face her manipulative wrath.

He asked the Lord to forgive him. It was not kind to call Mrs. Barber a battle-ax. Accurate, but not kind.

His eyes refused to focus on the reading material which was as dry and tasteless as stale potato chips. He got up, walked around his office and sat down again. It didn't help. His eyes strayed from his books and locked onto the picture frame on his desk. The young, fresh faces of his two daughters came into sharp clarity. He had captured them, smiling, wet, and lively, at a church picnic a week before the accident. They were victors in a youth group water balloon fight and were exulting in their victory, laughing and smiling victoriously at the camera. Their shirts were wet, their hair glistened, their smiles were pure and white, and their eyes danced with teenaged joy. Judith, the elder, had her arm around Caroline's shoulders whose right fingers were raised in a V for victory.

Has it come to this? he asked them. *Will I lose this church because of*

a handsome, charismatic musician and his overwrought emotionalism?
The thought sickened Jablonski. The election results were a foregone conclusion to Darlene—one she looked forward to—but he had hoped the
people would endure sound doctrine. That hope was now gone. Their
response to Jubal Lee Walker proved the people of Yellow Rock had itch-
ing ears. They wanted flash, flare, and strange fire. Tom Jablonski offered
only the cement foundation of fundamental truth.

He had a dark foreboding within him of five torturous nights seeing
his pulpit claimed by a person of suspicious force. If the first night was a
disaster, each succeeding night would be worse. Evangelists always
worked toward a feverd pitch. He knew, he had tried being one and had
Walker's father to thank for showing him it was not his call. And now, in
paying back Reverend Walker's magnanimity, he had been cursed with
his son.

But try as he might, Jablonski could not deny that the hand of the
Lord had touched people the previous night. Men who slept through his
sermons were at the altar on their knees. Jablonski loved these people and
did not want them hurt when Jubal Lee Walker blew out of town taking
his lofty promises of perpetual kingdom living with him. When Walker
was gone and the people came like refugees begging for titillating food,
who would fill their plates?

Fear drove Jablonski from his desk to the sanctuary. He sat in a front
pew to pray, the photo in his hand. He traced the outline of the gold-
plated frame as if it were a rectangular rosary.

"God," he said out loud, his own voice scaring him. "You know that
as much as I teach on prayer, I am really a hypocrite. I don't pray well, and
I don't pray very often." His prayer life had consisted mostly of silent
meditation while poring over his study materials. "Oh, God, what would
you have me do?"

He stopped as if to hear an audible answer. Instead, he felt an internal
unction to move to the dais and recline at the altar. How would he do it?
He was not one to offer himself boldly to God, like a bride with arms
outstretched to her groom; nor was he the warrior, able to pray down
heaven with the weight of his petitionings.

He did it the only way he knew. He got up and knelt on the floor. His
first revelation was how stiff and sore his joints were. Kneeling hurt his
knees and ankles. He bent forward onto his elbows, resting his head on
his unclasped hands. That position hurt his lower back, and he also felt a
twinge in his shoulder. He was tempted to return to the pew, rationalizing
that it was guilt and not the voice of God commanding him. But he
couldn't. He felt glued to the carpet. The burden in his heart had weighted

and tipped him toward the altar. He determined to endure the pain of his old football injuries by looking at the photo of his girls.

He imagined them talking to him. Caroline, the younger one, was always jubilant and outgoing. She had the gift of smiles. *Don't worry, Daddy,* he heard her saying, *we are in heaven now and soon you and Mommy will be with us. Everything here is beautiful. There is no pain.* Judith was more serious and contemplative. *Dad,* he heard her say, *don't worry about this gadfly, Jubal Lee Walker. Your way is correct. Your doctrines will prove to be right in the end.*

Gadfly. Pastor Tom smiled. How did a fifteen-year-old girl come up with a name like gadfly? Then it dawned cruelly on him that she had not. It was his word. He was imagining his daughters talking to him.

The mind plays tricks on you when you are tired, he told himself. He tried to resume praying, but the words came out like a mantra woven from a wool blanket that surrounded him, covered him, and lulled him to sleep. When he awakened two hours later, he was so stiff he could hardly move.

Ezra and Jubal rode at a trot for a mile, slowly letting the horses warm their muscles and acquaint themselves with their new surroundings. The brown gelding was so fluid and light of foot that Ezra did not have to post the trot, he could sit back in the saddle and enjoy the ride. As they crested a grassy plateau the brown eased into the bit and graduated to a long-strided lope. The bay pulled beside him and Ezra could feel the competitiveness between the two horses. Each animal stretched a little more in the neck, the stride lengthened and the breathing came deeper and quicker, their nostrils flaring from pink to red. Both riders fed their mounts some rein and the race was on.

They sailed across the prickly pear and through the needle grasses and sage. The Thoroughbreds matched each other, and the riders rode joyfully, throwing smiles at one another. There was no desperation, no lounging in the animals, and no determined competitiveness from the riders. It was a race run for the sake of running.

A mile melted beneath them before the brown and bay were slowly reined-in at the edge of a cliff. They stopped there on the edge of space, nervous but controlled, their necks and chests soaked in lather. Townships of countryside stretched out before them, a tapestry of badlands, rolling prairie, buttes, wheat fields, and summer fallow.

"Where are we?" Jubal Lee asked.

"The northern edge of Solomon's property," Ezra said. "Everything beyond us belongs to my neighbor Shorty Wilson, the richest man in the county."

"Who's he?" Jubal asked.

The anger and resentment in Ezra rose from his depths in black, roily waves. It pushed against the hope and optimism secured the evening before and left his heart feeling dark and polluted. If he had said nothing at all, the intensity radiating from Ezra would have told the story. He burned with generational anger, with the clannish hatred he had been taught as a child through the example of his forebears and lodged in the genetic code of his bloodline. He tried to subdue his reaction, but the bitterness laced his voice like strychnine: "Wilson's a coyote," Ezra said. "He bought out our neighbors and plowed up the land. During the dry years he got disaster payments, now he is making a fortune on government conservation payments. He's a nightmare of a neighbor."

"How so, brother?"

"His noxious weeds invade our grasslands; he leases his land out for deer and antelope hunting then trespasses on us to kill the game, and he lets the fence down to steal our grass."

"He's just another man who needs to know the Lord," Jubal said. "But I get the feeling there is something personal at stake here."

Ezra sighed deeply. He respected Jubal's spirituality and knew his own heart was transparent before Jubal's insights. "He's made no secret of wanting to own this ranch," Ezra said.

"Maybe he will," Jubal said. "It is only land and all land belongs to God, not men."

No, thought Ezra, *it is not only land. It has never been only land. It has always been more.*

"There is more than land involved in this," Jubal said again.

"I was in on a practical joke once that he wants to pay me back for," Ezra said. "But I was never caught."

"You, a practical joker?" Jubal laughed. "I find that hard to believe."

"I was coerced by sorrow, alcohol, and friendship. Me and a couple friends turned a trailer-load of heifers loose in a dress store Wilson owns. He was in the store at the time."

Jubal Lee laughed louder. "Now a few years back I would have done something like that, but I just can't imagine you doing it."

"It was during my uncle Sam's wake," Ezra said. "Our prank was our own type of memorial service." He reached back to a saddlebag, brought out his binoculars, and focused westward on a small trailer house. Its metal shell glinted in the morning sun like a discarded beer can. "Do you remember Austin Arbuckle?" he asked.

"Of course," Jubal said. "I rode against him."

"He was released from prison a few days ago and moved into that trailer. He's working for Wilson."

"What was he in prison for?"

"Fraud and grand larceny. He was a crooked cattle buyer that got caught."

"You seem to be spying on him," Jubal noted.

"I am," Ezra said.

Jubal nodded at the scabbarded rifle on Ezra's saddle. "Is that why you are packing the carbine?"

"Just insurance," Ezra said.

"The weapons of our warfare are not carnal, brother. I don't think the Lord would have you put your trust in rifles."

Ezra stared at Walker. Jubal's gaze was riveted on the distance as if his soul had taken wing and slipped through the horizon's crack between the sky and hills. He sat motionless in the saddle for a minute before his lips parted. "I want Anne to play the piano for me," he said.

"Hoo, boy," Ezra said. "Nothing like drawing a line in the sand."

"Anne's a psalmist and a minstrel," Jubal pronounced.

"That may be true," Ezra said. "But that piano is Darlene's. She would kill before relinquishing it."

"She will let Anne play, brother," Jubal said confidently.

"How do you know?"

"I will explain to Pastor Tom and his wife that it is part of their ministry to her." He sat poised in the saddle as if posing for a portrait. Everything about him, the new basket weave stamped saddle, the elkhide chinks, the silver inlaid bit and spurs, the meticulously trimmed beard, the expensive Stetson with the Cutter crease, was perfect. He was a poster boy for the corps of affluent, fashionable horsemen.

"Anne may not want to play," Ezra said.

"She wants to play."

Ezra shrugged. "It could be the straw that breaks the pastor's back. I would imagine he's having conniptions about last night's service anyway."

"Let him," Jubal said harshly. Then his tone softened. "Your pastor is a good man," he said. "But he has a controlling spirit. He needs to be set free."

"Oh, he's going to be set free," Ezra said. "Set free to go on down the road. The church elections are coming up."

Jubal was suddenly defensive of Jablonski. "Elections aren't scriptural," he said. "If a man of God doesn't know where he belongs, then he isn't a man of God." His eyes flashed with a fire as silver as the underlining of clouds that masked a burning sun. He turned again to the vista and one could almost see his soul leave his body as if he was claiming everything within his vision as Joshua had claimed the Promised Land.

Ezra watched Jubal's transformation and wondered if he was seeing the courage of a visionary or the rootlessness of a tumbleweed. "And where do you belong?" Ezra asked.

Jubal leaned over his saddle horn to allow the long muscles of his back to stretch. "I belong where the Spirit moves," he said. "Cody, Jackson Hole, Sheridan, Fort Collins, Denver."

"I guess that is wherever you are," Ezra teased.

Jubal looked down at him and smiled as if to say: *You have that right, brother.*

"It must be hard on Shelley and the girls," Ezra said.

Jubal stared again at the hills. A shade of darkness fell across his face and he breathed in deeply, as if swallowing it. "It is," he said.

"What's your purpose in Yellow Rock?" Ezra asked.

The air around Jubal seemed to crackle, the darkness lifted, and he looked down at Ezra and flashed a scintillating smile; his oversized brown eyes twinkled with mischief. He raised his right hand from the saddle horn and pointed. "You," he said.

"Me?" Ezra pivoted in the saddle and stared into the black shade beneath the brim of the silver-belly Stetson where slivers of silver light flashed in Jubal's pupils.

"That's right," Jubal said. "It's destiny time, brother."

Ezra turned and looked back at the rolling vista. The day was quickly warming. He could feel the sun on the back of his neck. He did not say anything for several minutes and in the silence a pronghorn antelope buck walked innocently up from a coulee and stood on the ridge not forty feet from the riders. Its buckskin and white hide glistened in the morning sun and the curved horns shined blacker than patent leather. Both men saw the antelope immediately but it did not see them.

"That buck would go sixteen inches," Jubal whispered.

"Sixteen and a quarter," Ezra said softly. "With a six-inch base and an inch of ivory tips."

"That's a Boone and Crockett buck."

"Yes. He would make the book."

Then the buck suddenly caught their wind, turned, and pricked his ears. In one isometric bounce he was up and running, speeding across the plateau at fifty miles an hour, little puffs of dust exploding under his hooves.

"Whoo-wee," Jubal whistled. "Look at him go. I know guys in Colorado who would pay a thousand dollars to shoot that buck."

"Yeah, I suppose you do," Ezra said.

"Does outfitting interest you?" Jubal asked.

"Not in the least," Ezra said. "Anne's talked to me about it because so many ranchers are doing it. But making money off wildlife isn't my thing."

"Well, let's trot on back," Jubal said. "I'll take you to town for coffee. I have a proposition that might interest you, brother."

Ezra felt the eyes from the coffee crowd as he and Jubal walked into The Cattleman's Cafe. It was 10:00 and the lawyers, store owners, and clerks were tanking up on caffeine. He was interested in his townspeople's reaction to Jubal, but most just glanced as if they were accustomed to seeing him, a couple looked at him curiously, many did not look at them at all, and several seemed to have contempt on their faces. *What did they see that caused them to appear disdainful of Jubal Lee Walker?* Ezra wondered.

A girl in a blue smock greeted them as they slid into a corner booth. She was no bigger than a bug and looked too young to be a waitress. "Another pot of coffee, Reverend Walker?" she asked.

Jubal flashed a smile. "You read my mind, sister."

She turned on her heels for the kitchen where the smell of frying bacon, sausage, and hash browns was as thick in the air as branding smoke.

"You've already been in here?" Ezra said.

"Six o'clock this morning. Bacon and eggs and a tall stack." They slid into a booth with blue vinyl upholstery beneath a large, tinted photograph of cattle grazing green prairie.

"*Reverend* Walker." Ezra said. "Does it seem odd to be called that? Doesn't it sound like someone is talking about your father?"

"Yeah, sometimes it does," Jubal said. The young waitress brought cups and a coffee pot. She was eager to please Jubal, and Ezra guessed he left large tips, the greenbacks shedding from his silver money clip like leaves off a tree in a windstorm. When she turned to Ezra, her eyes were friendly but their glow had dimmed. Her shine was only for Jubal. She started to pour his coffee.

"None for me, thanks," Ezra said.

"What can I bring you then? Tea? Coke?" she asked.

"I'll just have water," Ezra said.

"Don't worry," Jubal told the girl. "I'll drink enough coffee for both of us."

"I bet you will," the girl laughed, and she walked away, her hips rolling with the verve of youth.

"It's my one vice," Jubal said.

"Young waitresses?"

"No," Jubal laughed. "Coffee. I drink lots of coffee."

Ezra leaned back in the booth and stretched out his legs. "So, what's the deal, Jay? What's on your mind?"

"Jubal, not Jay."

"Sorry."

"Look around at these people," Jubal said. "They are all living in the flesh. They worry about food, sex, money, and work. They worry about the *whats* in life."

"Yes?"

"And then there is you. You live in the soul. You are concerned with dreams, visions, art, culture, philosophy. You are concerned about the *whys* in life. Not what people do, but why they do it."

"Okay," Ezra said, in a general acceptance of Jubal's observation.

"Then there is me. I live in the spirit. I know the *whats* and I know the *whys*. I am in a position of leadership, so I must determine the answers to the other questions, the *wheres, whens,* and *hows.*"

"What do you mean?"

"Take you for example. Most of the people in this cafe are only interested in what you are doing. But you, yourself, you analyze your motives. You want to know why you do things. I know what you are doing and why you are doing it. So my concern now is whether change is necessary and what is the timing and method to implement that change."

"And how is it," Ezra asked, "that you have managed to get to this level of questioning?"

Jubal brushed the question aside. "We will talk about that later," he said. "First tell me about you. How did you come to make a decision for Christ? You mentioned something about a trap."

"I got my hand caught in a coyote trap with a winter storm blowing in," Ezra said. "It was a freak situation. I absolutely could not get out by myself. About the time I thought I was going to freeze to death the Lord did a miracle. Dylan found me by following our dog."

"Oh, my. Now there is a testimony. You can tell me more about that later. What is going on with you in the present tense? You've just got fired from your job at the experiment station."

"Suspended. It's a union job so there will have to be a hearing."

"And what is the status of the ranch?"

Ezra sighed and pulled the brim of his hat down. "Not good," he said. "Lacey wants me out. She either wants to be on the ranch, or she wants the ranch sold."

"Can she force the issue?" Jubal asked, pouring himself a fresh cup of coffee.

"Yeah. We are still an undivided estate. Under Montana law she can either force the ranch to be split in three pieces or she can have the whole thing sold on the courthouse steps, which would please Shorty Wilson to no end. He'd buy it cheap, plow it up, and kill off all the game."

"Why not split it?"

"It's too small now for one family to make a living from it. Split it three ways and you have ranchettes."

"But doesn't this affect Solomon? Would any of his land be sold or would he be interested in buying the estate land?" Jubal asked.

"Solomon couldn't care less as far as I know. But who knows what goes on in that crafty old mind?"

"Ever thought about just getting out; sell the place, and let someone else have the headaches?"

"What would I do?" Ezra said. "I've been ranching for the past ten years. I've given this ranch the prime of my life."

"Come to work for me," Jubal said.

Ezra smiled. "Sure. Doing what? I don't play any instruments."

"There's other things, brother. After a year of training I could see that you got your credentials—"

"My what?"

"Credentials. Papers. You would be licensed to pastor."

"Me? A pastor? You've been drinking too much coffee." Ezra had sometimes thought of preaching or teaching Bible studies, but he had no desire to be a "professional Christian," someone whose wages were dependent upon selling a gospel he believed should be given freely.

"I'll start you at two thousand dollars a month," Jubal said. "You would help supervise the churches I am starting. Plus you would handle some of the administrative duties and communications, like newsletters and flyers before I do a revival in a new town."

"A PR man?" Ezra asked cynically.

"Sort of. But it's the Lord's work, remember that. Also, I would commission you to write songs."

"I can't write songs."

"You can write poetry. I will put your words to music. You throw me the good pitches, brother, and I will hit them out of the park. I will guarantee you that."

"Oh, I don't know—"

"We could be talking some serious money as a songwriting team, Ezra. Plus, you can pick where you want to live. I'm on the road all the time anyway. Cody, Sheridan, Jackson Hole . . . "

"Those are high rent districts."

"We can swing it. I'll loan you the down payment you need to buy a house wherever you want."

"Well, that's mighty generous, Jubal, but—"

"No buts. Just pray about it. You have nothing going for you here. You may have lost your job. Your sisters are giving you a hard time. Solomon isn't opening any doors for you."

"Well, I sort of like it here. I like the people in Yellow Rock."

"Live here then. Get a little place on the edge of town, or stay at the ranch if you want. There could be something for me in the works here, who knows?"

"What do you mean?" Ezra asked.

"I shouldn't say too much," Jubal said. "Besides, you know better than I do about the condition of your church."

Ezra began to push Jubal for an explanation but stopped as he noticed two men enter the cafe. They walked in the door, stood for a moment, and looked around as if they held The Cattleman's mortgage. One was dressed like a desert buckaroo with an oversized black hat, western shirt, and tight Wranglers pushed down into colorful boots that reached to his knees. His blonde hair hung straight from under his hat and his brown eyes glowed like hot agates. He looked to be in his early thirties. The other man was smaller, older, and pot-bellied with thinning hair. He had a splotchy red complexion—the face of a serious drinker—and a flap of loose skin hanging from his chin like the brisket on a Brahma cow. He wore a camouflage khaki shirt, camouflage utility pants, and lace-up hiking boots. They walked down the aisle staring through people as if they did not exist as they looked for a particular place to sit. Someplace where they could keep an eye on both doors and everyone who came or left.

Ezra brought his water glass to his lips and watched them from between his cupped hand and the brim of his black hat. The blonde cowboy stared at him as he walked by, measuring Ezra like he was a post, then glanced at Jubal. The man had a flat nose, a rugged, rawboned build, and a diamond stud in his right ear. Ezra thought he saw a spark of recognition light his marble eyes when he looked at Jubal. They took a booth across the room.

The conversation and clatter in the busy cafe either dimmed, Ezra reasoned, or his senses had heightened. Suddenly nobody else seemed to exist in the cafe except he and Jubal and the two strangers. He watched them warily for a moment, then nodded discreetly in their direction. "Did you check those guys out?" he whispered to Jubal.

Jubal shook his head. His face was turned from them as he spooned sugar into his coffee.

"Take a look at them," Ezra said. "The young one acted like he knew you."

"He probably just saw me preach somewhere."

"It wasn't that kind of look." From the corner of his eye Ezra saw the cowboy nod in their direction. He seemed to be discussing them with the older man.

Jubal glanced quickly at the men then returned his gaze to his porcelain coffee cup. He stared down at the black coffee like it was a rabbit hole and he was a rabbit. "The young one is a player in Vegas," he said quietly.

"A player? You mean a card dealer?" Ezra asked. He had his right hand over his lips to muffle his voice and shield his lips from being read.

Jubal smiled. "Well, he does a little of that, too, but he's a different type of player. A different type of dealer."

"Oh. So how does he know you?"

"Shelley and I used to deal coke. There's a blizzard of snow blowing on the horse circuits. We dealt with him a couple times."

"Do you know the older man?"

"No."

"What do you suppose they are doing here?" Ezra asked.

"Is bow season open?" Jubal asked. "I would guess the old guy is either a bow hunter or he reads too many *Soldier of Fortune* magazines."

"Bow season opened yesterday."

"That's it then, brother. They're up here hunting."

"The young guy looks like trouble." Ezra said. His eyes were almost drawn to him, like a cobra to a mongoose. The man's presence seemed to fill the cafe, and Ezra saw that others, including the young waitress, were giving the table a wide berth.

"He is trouble," Jubal said. "And in case you ever need to know, he's left-handed and carries a knife in his boot top."

"Odd remembrance for a preacher," Ezra said.

"Our weapons aren't carnal," Jubal said. "But his are." He finished his coffee and jangled a generous tip onto the table. "I have to get back to my room," he said. "Think about my offer, Ezra. Pray about it with Anne."

As they rose to leave, Ezra could feel two sets of eyes drilling him in the back like the hot slugs of a pistol. Jubal walked ahead of him, and Ezra could not tell if the ballistic appraisal was for himself or if he was merely the shield in front of the real target.

CHAPTER SEVENTEEN

Darlene Jablonski sat beside her husband in a front side pew with a hymnal in her hand. She knew a hymnal would not be used and that is why she held one. It was her security and a display of rebellion. She hoped *Reverend* Walker saw it. She hoped he understood that she saw through him and everything he stood for. She could not look at the piano. It would not seem right to see someone else sitting there. "It will be a ministry to Anne," Jubal had told her husband. What could Tom do? Of course he had to say yes or appear little and selfish. Darlene had been playing the piano in church since she was fourteen years old. The piano had become her identity, and more than that, it had become her anchor since losing her daughters. And now the anchor was gone. She held no ill feelings toward Anne, nor was she competitive; she simply felt adrift, cut loose from her moorings by a man she neither respected nor trusted. Darlene Jablonski did not care if she and her husband were voted out of the church; life itself meant little to her anymore, but she detested the idea of being ushered out by a glib, handsome charlatan in a three-piece western suit. And somehow she blamed Ezra Riley—no matter that Jubal Lee had come to Yellow Rock because of her husband's past connections to Jubal Lee's father—her feminine instinct told her that Walker was in Yellow Rock because of Ezra Riley. And she hated him—Ezra—for being the magnet.

Pastor Tom looked down at the hymnal in his wife's hand. He did not say anything. It could just as easily have been a gun she was holding. But he was not worried. He knew of no one murdered by a songbook.

The sanctuary of the Yellow Rock Community Believers' Church held one hundred twenty people. This night it was ten or fifteen short of being full. As Ezra looked around he saw numerous guests from other churches as well as several people he had never met. He looked up at the dais and smiled at the sight of Anne on the piano bench. She looked beautiful but was obviously uncomfortable. She had insisted on praying with Pastor Tom—not Jubal—before playing. Jablonski had been embarrassed and confused but uttered a quick blessing, a head sprinkling of a baptism when Anne would have liked to have been dunked.

At 7:08 Jubal Lee bounced from the pastor's study at the left of the sanctuary as if freshly lit with flaming oil. He became armed when he strapped on his guitar, as a soldier with his weapon, then he nodded at Anne. She began a soft chorus. Her fingers were light and tentative on the keys. Jubal smiled at the people. It was Monday night, let the revival begin.

"Body of Christ arise," he commanded into the microphone. The congregation stood. "We are in the presence of the King," he said. "Let us offer him our sacrifice of praise." Then he began to sing. The song was a call for repentance. Immediately the night had a different flavor from the previous one. It was gentler, more subdued. Ezra could feel the Spirit quietly massaging the hearts of the people while he basked in Anne's beauty. She became a different person at the piano as the music lifted her and carried her to high places.

Numerous people began raising their hands. Ezra had never raised his hands in worship and felt awkward simply thinking about it, then he looked beside him and saw Dylan with both hands above his head. There was a purity and innocence on his son's young face that convicted Ezra of his own masculine hangups. He tried moving his right arm but it remained stationary as if tied to his belt.

"Sing to the King," Jubal exhorted, and the people moved heartily into the second song, except Darlene who stood because she had to but stared angrily at the floor.

During the third song Jubal invited the people to the altar to pray. They filtered slowly from the pews. Dylan was first. Ezra swayed uncomfortably as others passed by in the aisle, then slipped out and joined his son. The room was bursting with music as Anne regained her confidence on the piano and Jubal—who had been rousing the night before on saxophone and keyboard—was at his best on guitar and vocals. His command of the songs was absolute, yet effortless. The praise grew in waves, ascending to mountainous heights then splashing down on the worshipers, where it was collected and released in yet another wave. Some people knelt, some lay prostrate, one staggered as if she were drunk.

"Pray with someone if you feel the leading," Jubal encouraged, then the music continued. Ezra stood protectively above his son who knelt on the dais, his head on his hands.

The music came to a soft halt after the seventh song. "Please stay in an attitude of praise," Jubal said. "Remain at the altar if you wish." Ezra seated himself beside his son.

Jubal picked up his large, leather Bible. "The word tonight," he said, "is from the fourth chapter of Ephesians, verses eleven through thirteen."

He cleared his throat, then spoke eloquently without the benefit of the microphone: "'And He Himself gave some to be apostles, some prophets, some evangelists, and some pastors and teachers, for the equipping of the saints for the work of ministry, for the edifying of the body of Christ, till we all come to the unity of the faith and the knowledge of the Son of God, to a perfect man, to the measure of the stature of the fullness of Christ.'"

Jubal stood silently, his head down as if keening his ears to the voice of God. He resembled his father in size and eloquence, but the son was not as combative. Where the elder Walker was pugilistic, throwing his sentences out like flicking left jabs, then thundering home right hands of rhetoric, Jubal Lee was a dancer. He took the congregation by the hand, led them from their well-worn seats, and whisked them to places they had never been before. When he needed to accent a point, he did it with a teasing challenge that bordered on flirtation.

"Look around you," he invited. "We call this a church. It is only a building. You are the Church. The Church is people. The Church is the body of Christ. The Lord has given us five offices in the Church so that each of you might be equipped to minister. You are to come together, each one with a psalm or spiritual song, that you might edify and equip one another." His eyes flashed with white fire and the gentle voice rumbled like distant thunder. He seemed harnessed with authority.

"You go to the barn or the garage to get tools," he said. "That is where you are equipped. But the work is done in the fields. You do not go in a barn, grab a rake and a hoe, and sit there all day holding them. You take the rake and the hoe out into the field, and you prepare the field for harvest."

The people at the altar and the few left in the pews watched and listened intently. They could relate to his symbols. They were rural people. They understood rakes and hoes. Pastor Tom talked about Hebrew verbs and Greek nouns. The people did not understand Hebrew verbs and Greek nouns.

"All across America, the Church of today is hiding in the barn. People come to church and are taught, and preached at, but they are not equipped and turned loose to do the work of the ministry. You sit holding your rakes and hoes and admiring your neighbor's rakes and hoes, but you hang them on the back wall when you leave this building, and Monday morning in the workplace, you have no tools.

"It is not your fault," Jubal Lee continued. "We have inherited a patriarchal system where one man, the pastor, tries to rule over a church consisting mainly of women. There are few men in the churches of America today. Women are the real power because they are the majority. They are the foot soldiers. They are the prayer warriors. The men of the church—the few there are—have been told they are only good for menial tasks: building maintenance, serving on the board—which usually means being a 'yes man' to the pastor—administrative duties, ushering, passing the collection plate around."

He knows this church, Ezra thought. From where he sat he looked around heads to check on Pastor Tom and Darlene. His head was down as if embarrassed. Darlene was smoldering, you could almost see the smoke rise from the back of her neck.

Jubal paced the dais; he took a microphone from the stand and whipped the cord out in front of him. It rippled in little black convulsions like a long, skinny snake. "People, this is not what Jesus intended," he whispered in the mike. His voice resonated in the sanctuary. "Jesus came and died so that the Holy Spirit might empower His people. We have a crisis in the Church that can be solved when we empower the laity. That means you. Are you prepared to do the work of the ministry?"

A raw aggression began building in Jubal's belly. It bubbled like a volcano and he struggled to contain it. Ezra even saw flashes of Jubal's father's features illuminate his face. Jubal paused and coiled the microphone cord. He was beating the monster down, reminding himself to stay gentle.

His face was soft again in seconds. "Are you ready to follow Jesus?" he begged sweetly. "Do you desire to be equipped that you might minister? If so, I want you to stand around this altar. Stand if you want a ministry."

The short silence that followed was horrible in its revealing power.

People all around Ezra were rising to their feet. Anne watched quietly from the piano. Dylan stood with his eyes closed, arms raised, and his head tilted backward. Ezra studied him with amazement. *This was the same boy who listened to Milli Vanilli, dreamed of Lamborghinis, and wanted a phone in his bedroom?* Ezra rose to stand beside him.

"If you desire the deeper things of God," Jubal continued, "stand now as a candidate. Stand and say: 'Lord, equip me, give me the tools I need that I might do your will.' Stand and I will come, anoint you with oil, and pray for you." He walked to Anne, whispered to her, and she began playing softly.

Five people left the altar and returned to the pews, joining the half dozen that had not come forward, including the Jablonskis. Jubal Lee began at the east side of the long line of people. He touched each with oil and prayed for them individually. It was to be a slow process, but the people at the end of the line—with Ezra and Dylan—did not seem to care. After Jubal's touch one woman fell forward on her knees and wailed deeply, another fell straight over backward. A couple of astonished men moved to catch her but were too late. She bounced heavily off a pew and onto the floor but lay quietly, as if she had landed on pillows.

"Don't worry," Jubal told the two men who stared at him in helpless confusion. "The Spirit knocks them down, and the Spirit will catch them. I've never seen anyone hurt yet."

For the first ten minutes Ezra watched as if he were at the county fair, walking through the carnival, taking in the sights and sounds of a mysterious and forbidding world. But there were no more sideshows. The people were prayed for, and in turn, most knelt and continued in prayer. The effect was contagious, and he realized his own needs and questions and slowly raised one heavy, uncooperative hand and closed his eyes. He prayed for his family, his writing, the ranch, and Jubal's offer—which he hadn't told Anne about, so he prayed to be more communicative.

In due time Jubal worked his way to the Rileys, coming to Dylan first. Jubal anointed him with oil. "Young man," he said, speaking as if Dylan were a stranger, "I believe you are called to full time service in the ministry. May the Lord confirm this in His good time." He put his hand on Dylan's forehead. Ezra watched in quiet awe as his son took two staggering steps backward then collapsed to the floor.

Jubal looked at Ezra and smiled. "Your son is called," Jubal said, his large brown eyes swirling with darkness and light like ship beacons on an oily sea.

Ezra closed his eyes and held his hands together below his belt. He consciously leaned forward a little into Jubal Lee's touch. He did not want to fall over backward. He widened his stance to maintain his balance. Jubal dabbed oil on his brow and prayed softly for several minutes, then he embraced Ezra in a powerful hug. Ezra stood like a cottonwood tree, his strong, stiff limbs not yielding in return. He was not comfortable in the embrace of a man, and he thought the hug would last forever. Finally Jubal stepped back, tears running down his face.

"I have a word from God for you," he said. "I realize in light of what I asked you this morning that this word might appear manipulative, but believe me, I have no ulterior motives. I can only say what the Lord has spoken to my spirit."

Ezra nodded. He didn't believe a word was going to hurt him one way or another. He had never had a "word from God" before, at least, not as far as he knew. He expected a generic, well-known Scripture.

"It is only three words," Jubal said. "And I don't know if I totally understand what they mean." He looked at Ezra long and hard.

Ezra nodded again giving Jubal permission to continue.

Jubal laid his hand on Ezra's forehead. "The Spirit would say unto you these three words: *Leaving the land.*"

Ezra was wrong. You could be hurt—or at least, impacted—by words. Witnesses saw him stagger backward twice, as Dylan had, as if struck by hard blows to the chest, then he crumpled to the floor. When he opened his eyes several minutes later, he did not know how he had come to be there. He did not remember falling. He tried to get up but couldn't.

From above him he heard Jubal Lee laugh. "Just lay there for a while and enjoy it, brother," he said. "The Lord isn't done with you yet."

It was too much for Darlene. Ezra's dramatic fall was proof to her of fabrication and evidence of Ezra being Jubal's co-conspirator. Pastor Tom put a hand out to restrain her, but she jumped to her feet and stormed from the building.

Ezra was on his back for twenty minutes. When he finally got to his feet, half of the people had gone home, others were praying for one another. Betty Lou Barber had Jubal in a corner talking to him, and Pastor Tom was watching from the back foyer. He stood in the hallway that led to the rest rooms. He was backlit and all Ezra could see was his silhouette, thick and black like the shadow of a cedar tree.

Anne had continued playing background music. She felt obligated to be at the piano as long as anyone was being ministered to. It had been a rollercoaster night for Anne. She had been nervous about playing and sensitive to hurting Darlene, then excited by the Lord touching both her son and husband. But when Darlene fled the building Anne almost went after her. She ached for her pastor's wife. Darlene's wound was so deep and festered, and Anne wanted to tell her that she understood about the piano and to reassure her about her and Ezra's intentions. But, the main threat to Darlene Jablonski was Jubal Lee and Anne could not reassure her there. She did not know Jubal and had some reservations about him herself. But she did know the signs and wonders were real. They were not staged, nor were they the product of emotionalism or the devil. God was doing something very real in Yellow Rock, Montana, and she was glad to be a part of it. Anne swayed slowly back and forth, her head rocking gently as she played. Every few moments she looked around. Pastor Tom had left his pew and was standing at the back of the darkened sanctuary. He was motionless for several minutes as if deciding what to do. Finally he moved to an exit, and when he opened the door light flooded in from the porch. It fell in a long yellow rectangle across the foyer carpet and onto the back row of pews. For a second it illuminated the lean, hard features of a man sitting there by himself. Then Pastor Tom went out the door, closed it, and the figure in the pew was again in darkness. She strained to see him better but she didn't have to. The profile was forever frozen in her memory from a bitterly cold day eight years before when she and Dylan were alone in the trailer house. The man sat for several minutes without moving. She wondered if he was staring at her, if he could feel her staring at him? Her fingers hit the wrong keys and her eyes bounced back to the sheet music. When she looked back a few moments later the man was gone as if he had never been there at all. But he had been there and she knew who it was. It was Austin Arbuckle.

The Rileys were quiet on the drive home. They were tired and Anne had to work in the morning, and Dylan had school. Finally Anne broke the silence. "What did Jubal say to you?" she asked Ezra.

Ezra hesitated. "I don't want to say just yet."

"You don't want to tell me?"

"Of course, I do. But I want to test it. I don't want to give it any more power than it is supposed to have. He just told me three little words, nothing real important."

"When are you going to tell me?" she asked. Dylan watched with interest. He had heard Jubal's message to his father.

"Soon. I just have a lot on my mind, okay? There's something I haven't had time to tell you."

"What?"

"Jubal offered me a job this morning?"

"A job? What kind of job?" Anne asked.

"I guess it would mean being his right-hand man. I would oversee his ministry, help him write songs."

"Where would we live?"

"Anyplace we want between here and Denver."

"I don't want to move," Anne said. "How about you, Dylan?"

Dylan shrugged. "I don't care," he said.

"He said he could help us buy a house in Cody or Sheridan, or wherever, or we could stay here in Yellow Rock if we wanted."

"Oh? Did he mention wages?" Anne did not want to move and she knew ministries were usually thinly financed.

"He promised to start me at two thousand a month."

"Two thousand?" Anne asked incredulously. "Where does he get that kind of money?"

"I don't know." Ezra's voice was as flat as the headlights on the dark highway.

Anne stared thoughtfully out the windshield, following the path of the light beams. In the barrow pits she saw the red, glistening eyes of mule deer grazing the roadside. "Ezra, if the Lord is in it," she said, "I will go anywhere with you."

"Thanks," he said, and patted her on the leg.

"Just don't keep any secrets from me, okay?"

He nodded. But Anne was not guiltless, either. In the excitement and confusion of the night, she forgot to tell Ezra about seeing Austin Arbuckle in church.

CHAPTER EIGHTEEN

Tuesday morning and they were horseback again, men at play, pretending to work. Ezra and Jubal loped through the Riley badlands where slate-colored buttes stabbed at a cloud-dappled sky and sandstones balanced on gumbo pedestals. They rode the bay and brown to the back side of the ranch where the prairie rolled in great waves of sun-dried, bleached-white grasses.

"Look at all this feed," Jubal exclaimed as he pulled the bay to a halt on the tip of a rocky knoll. "I thought last year was the worst drought in Montana history."

"It was," Ezra said.

"But look at all this grass."

"We have been understocked ever since my Uncle Sam was killed," Ezra explained. He reached down and patted the lathered neck of the brown gelding. His hand came back sticky and wet with sweat and he brought it to his face. He loved the smell of horse sweat. It was salty, but sweet. The only thing better was a horse's springtime breath after chewing fresh, green grass.

"How many mother cows can this whole Riley place summer?" Jubal asked.

"Summer?" Ezra said. "I suppose six hundred pair."

"In Colorado ranchers are leasing grass at twenty dollars a month per pair. That's $7200 a month income from May through October. That's over $42,000 for six months."

"$43,200," Ezra said. He had played with all the figures from all the angles for a long time.

"Pretty good summer wages," Jubal said. "And I can get you the cows, all you have to do is watch them for six months, ship them back in the fall and I will even provide you a couple of horses like that brown to use."

Ezra smiled. "I thought you wanted me writing poetry and teaching Bible studies."

"You could do both," Jubal said.

"What about the word you gave me last night? *Leaving the land.*"

"It could be symbolic, brother. Maybe you are to leave it in your heart. You could have this whole ranch and still leave it by leaving it in His hands."

Ezra stepped off the brown to reset his saddle and stretch his legs. *Leaving the land.* The implication of the phrase reminded him of the nightmare of years before: he, Rick, and Jim horseback in the badlands, then separating; Ezra watching a coyote come close; the coyote speaking with the voice of Ezra's father.

He had not told Jubal about the dream.

"What you say about the ranch could be true," Ezra said. "But you forget one thing. I don't own the land. Most of this is Solomon's."

"Talk to him," Jubal said. "Lease it with an option to buy. In a couple years you could make enough to buy out Lacey and Diane and get them out of your hair."

Ezra swung back into the saddle. "Solomon doesn't listen to ideas unless they're his own," he said. "He doesn't want to part with land. It's his identity and it gives him enormous pleasure having one thing— grass—that everyone else, particularly Shorty Wilson, wants."

"It's a shame, all this grass going to waste. It would be better for the land if it were burned or grazed," Jubal said.

Ezra didn't answer; his eyes had caught a distant silver flash, sunlight reflecting off metal or glass. He reached back and pulled out his binoculars and trained them at the west.

"Spying again?" Jubal asked. "What do you see?"

"I think I see a miracle taking place," he said. He nudged the brown with his heels and the horse slid down the steep butte on his hocks, his front legs braced like a skier. They rode a half mile closer. Ezra dismounted, keeping his silhouette below the skyline, and refocused the binoculars. "It *is* a miracle," he said, and handed the glasses to Jubal.

"It's just a man fixing fence," Jubal said.

"No," Ezra said. "It's Austin Arbuckle working on Shorty Wilson's fence."

"We should ride down and say hello."

"I'm not in a howdy kind of mood," Ezra said.

"Now, brother," Jubal scolded. "Is that very Christian of you?"

"Probably not," Ezra said. "But I guess I have a suspicious nature."

"You need to work on that," Jubal said. "But as for now, it looks like he's driving on."

"Just as well," Ezra said.

"You are suspicious," Jubal laughed. "Maybe I will have to preach about presumptuous sins tonight."

"What are you going to preach on?" Ezra asked.

"Brother," Jubal smiled. "I never know the answer to that question until I get to the microphone."

"You're kidding. Pastor Tom holes up in his study all week long to prepare his messages."

"Pastor Jablonski has his way," Jubal said. "And I have mine. I pray and fast and try to listen to the Spirit. The Spirit tells me what to preach on and quickens the Scriptures to my memory."

"I wish Pastor Tom would do that," Ezra said.

"Pastor Tom doesn't know how," Jubal said. "Besides, he uses those long hours of study and marathon messages to hide his wounds from the people. Like most preachers, he doesn't want to display any weaknesses."

"He's as boring as watching mud dry," Ezra said.

Jubal laughed. "Is it the hippie or the cowboy in you that makes you so blasted independent?"

It was a good question and Ezra did not have an answer.

Jubal stroked his beard. He had been waiting for the right moment. "Last night I was offered the pastorate of your church," he announced.

"Our church?" Ezra said. "Pastor Tom hasn't even come up for reelection yet!"

"I know that. And that's what I told her."

"Her? Betty Lou Barber, right? She doesn't run the church, Jubal."

"She thinks she does."

"So what did you tell her?"

"I told her she didn't run the church," he said. "Of course, I said it very gently." His face was flushed with confidence. He had the Yellow Rock church if he wanted it, and he knew it.

They rode for another hour checking on Solomon's cows and calves. They put ten head of Wilson's cows back into his pasture. The Thoroughbreds took quickly to cow work; they were anxious to travel and eager to please. Jubal rode competently, but self-consciously, as if displaying his and his horse's talents. About 10:30 he declared he had to return to his motel room to study. They rode back quietly, the brown and the bay reeling in the miles like line on a fishing reel. After the horses were unsaddled and put away, Ezra walked Jay to his Suburban. "Guess I'll see you tonight," he said.

"I'll be there," Jubal said.

Ezra stopped at the Suburban's door. It was not easy for him to express his feelings to another man. "I just want to tell you," he said. "That, I, well, I really appreciate last night. Anne on the piano. Me and Dylan being prayed for."

Jubal slapped him on the shoulder. "Hey, brother, I'm just being obedient."

"Well, we appreciate it."

Jubal took off his hat and laid it carefully on the front seat. He brushed his curly brown hair back and looked at Ezra. His deep eyes held pain in their depths, like rocks at the bottom of a pool, but they glistened on the surface with the dancing light of the sun filtering through tree branches. He started to say something, but stopped. He got in the Suburban, then looked back at Ezra again. His face was soft and vulnerable and absent of sheen. "I'm glad you appreciate me," he said in an almost childish voice. Ezra could feel something grip him, like a small boy reaching for the shirt of his father, wanting to be picked up and held. Ezra nodded.

"I mean it," Jubal said. "All my life people have appreciated my music. I would rather they appreciate me." Then quickly, Jubal drove away.

Ezra stood alone in the yard for a minute. Jubal's words had been so sorrowful, so rich in their agony. *I'm glad you appreciate me.*

Ezra turned for the house. He checked the morning mail and the answering machine. Then in a sudden moment of sentimentality he dug out a photo album, sat at the table, and cracked it open. There was Uncle Sam, sitting in one of his several old Ford pickups, smiling devilishly. And Jim Mendenhall, larger than life, a comic sadness etched on his face. And Rick Benjamin mounted on his good rope horse, Ezra beside him on Gusto. Partners. He missed Rick in particular. Rick had always been there, willing to help, quick with encouragement, loyal to a fault. But Rick cared nothing for the matters of the soul. He wanted land, cattle, and to rodeo on weekends. After five years in Houston, his annual phone call was still a monologue about horses, the hills, cattle, and Yellow Rock, as if someday he could return and things would be the way he remembered them. The way they never were.

Rick would never be a Jubal Lee Walker, Ezra knew. He closed the album, gazed out the window and down the gravel road that led to the highway. But Jubal Lee would never be a Rick Benjamin, either.

"I am not going tonight," Darlene insisted, and she folded her arms across her chest and stared at herself in the mirror of her bedroom vanity.

"Look," said her husband. "If it's about Anne playing the piano—"

"It has nothing to do with Anne," Darlene snapped. "I like Anne. It has nothing to do with the piano. It has everything to do with that grandstanding Jubal Lee Walker and his conniving sidekick."

"You mean Ezra?" Pastor Tom asked. He hesitated while closing the knot on his tie and stood there like a man in a hangman's noose.

Darlene whirled around in the chair. "Yes, I mean Ezra Riley, your would-be newsletter editor. You see how chummy he is with this Walker. He brought him in, Tom, can't you see that? You would have to be blind not to notice. Maybe Betty Lou Barber encouraged him, I don't know, but I can guarantee you that Ezra Riley brought Jubal Lee Walker to this town for one reason: to split the church." It was the most she had said about anything in months and the outburst nearly exhausted her.

"Oh, Darlene," Tom said. "You're making a mountain out of a molehill. I talked to Ezra and Anne. They hadn't heard anything from Jubal Lee Walker in seventeen years."

"Like they're going to admit it," she said sarcastically.

"Darlene, you are now implying that the Rileys are liars, and I won't take that. They are good people. They are different than us, but I would never go so far as to accuse them of lying."

"I didn't mean to do that," she said defensively. She turned in the chair but did not look in the mirror.

Her husband came over and began rubbing her shoulders. "The people are going to get what they want and what they deserve," he said. "If Jubal Lee Walker somehow splits the church and we lose a confidence vote, what difference does it make? You are not happy here anyway. All you talk about is moving back to Pennsylvania."

Darlene choked down a sob. "I don't know if I want to go back," she said. "Maybe it's too soon. I don't care if we leave here or not, but I don't want to be run out on a rail by some Prince Charming who probably has women on the side."

"Darlene!"

"Well, it's probably true. What do we know about him? He called up out of the blue. He's talented and handsome and he seems to know something about horses which makes him very popular hereabouts. You should have checked on him more, Tom."

"Darlene, I'm repaying a debt."

"You don't owe this much, Tom."

He sighed, knowing it was true. They had been young, short of money, and down on their luck when they had walked into Pastor Franklin Walker's church years ago. Walker's denomination, doctrine, and beliefs were different from Tom's, but he had welcomed them and allowed Tom to try his hand at evangelizing. Tom had been a terrible failure. It still pained him thinking how Jubal's father had taken money from his own wallet to help them get to the next town. He owed Franklin Walker, but did he owe anything to Jubal? "Darlene," he said firmly. "You are coming tonight."

"Tom, please don't make me."

"Darlene, listen to me." Tom knelt beside her. "If Jubal Lee is not what you think he is, then you need to go for your own sake. You don't want to live with this bitterness in your heart. If he is what you say he is, then you need to come so you will be at my side to help pick up the pieces when all of this blows sky-high."

"Then you think it could, too?" she said. "You think it's all phony, all these theatrics with people falling over—I'm sure I saw him pushing them down, Tom. I'm sure I did."

He waved his hand gently to silence her. "I don't know if the demonstrations are real or not," he said. "I'm not worried about that right now. I'm not out to expose Jubal Lee Walker. My concern is for my people, for my sheep. I don't want anyone to get hurt."

"You need me, don't you?" Darlene said tearfully.

He put his arm around her. "I've always needed you," he said, and as he hugged his wife the pastor could not help but thank God for bringing Jubal Lee Walker to town. If it took a crisis to bring his wife back to life, and if Walker was that crisis, then the pastor was in Jubal Lee's debt.

Later that afternoon Ezra had to go to Yellow Rock to run errands. He drove across the Yellow Rock River, one of the last great undammed rivers in the world. It ran low and clear. The highway connected to Seventh Street, past the Crystal Pistol Bar and Restaurant, where Ezra's Uncle Sam had reigned as resident king, sage, and pundit. Ezra had not been in the Pistol for several years. He crossed the railroad tracks by the grain elevators, their steel noses pointed at a sky dotted with pigeons. He went to an auto parts store and got a new starter for his pickup. He could feel it tottering on its last legs and decided not to wait until it failed on the backside of Dead Man, seven or eight miles from home. The Car Quest clerks were overly polite to Ezra until one dared tease him about losing his job. The others watched apprehensively. Ezra laughed, breaking the icy tension in the air, and everyone was smiling when he left. He went to an office supply store for two large padded mailing envelopes for his manuscript—one to mail it with, one to include for return mail—and to the post office for postage. The manuscript was still in his office awaiting one last polishing, a cowlick or two to paste down on his only child before delivering it as a sacrifice to the gods of publication.

On Main Street he saw a new Dodge dual pickup with Nevada plates parked in front of the Coast to Coast store. Ezra was stopping for a red traffic light as the blonde buckaroo and the man with the splotchy face came out of the store. The blonde walked to the street side, fiddling in his pockets for the keys to unlock the driver's door. The older man waited for him on the curb, his arms filled with shopping bags. Then a third man came out of the store. Ezra felt him before he saw him. He had the cool, surly radiance of a dark and lean Doberman. A black hat was pulled low on his head, and a toothpick protruded from the side of his mouth. His face was pasty white beneath the shadow of his hat, evidence of being locked away from sunlight. Austin Arbuckle looked up and down the sidewalk cautiously, as if choosing who to see and who to be seen by, then walked to the dual pickup where he stood and chatted with the older man. Ezra could not help but be riveted by Austin's appearance. At one time he had been a friend, an older brother to Ezra and Austin's real brother, Cody. Through the years Austin slowly became a challenger and nemesis, and finally, an enemy. But he was always Austin Arbuckle, the grandson of Johnny Riley's surrogate father, the infamous Charley Arbuckle. That bonding of immortals forever linked Austin and Ezra.

The light turned green and the car behind Ezra honked its horn. Ezra popped the clutch and the truck jerked ahead, causing the blonde man to turn and look. As he drove through the intersection Ezra checked his rearview mirror. The blonde cowboy stood with his pickup door open, staring down the street in Ezra's direction. Austin was opening the other door. The two made a compatible and equal pair. Their evil seemed to balance the truck.

"Ezra, are you about ready? We need to leave for church," Anne called from the bathroom.

Ezra sat on the bed in his underwear, his dirty clothes at his feet. He had spent the last hour on his back in the garage putting the new starter in his pickup. He did not like mechanical jobs. He hated the grease falling into his eyes and hair and getting under his fingernails. Horse sweat was fragrant and natural, grease definitely was not.

Anne came into the room brushing her hair. "You are not even close to ready," she said.

"I just need a quick shower." He rose slowly, went to the bathroom and closed the door.

"Dylan wants to bring a friend tonight," Anne called after him.

"That's fine," he said. "Everyone should bring a friend."

"I invited Sally Johnson," Anne teased. "Who are you going to bring?"

"I don't know," Ezra said dryly through the closed door. "Thought I might invite Austin."

"You don't need to," Anne said. "He's already come."

Ezra opened the door and looked out at her with a stone face. "What did you say?"

"He was there last night," Anne said. "He came in late, sat in the back, stayed a few minutes, then left."

"Austin Arbuckle? You're kidding me, right?"

"No, I'm serious."

"Why didn't you tell me?" he scolded.

"I forgot about it until this morning," Anne said. "And by the time I remembered, you were already out riding with Jubal."

"Austin in church," he said. "I wonder what that means?"

"What do you think it means?" Anne said. "He's probably spiritually hungry like everybody else. Ezra, you need to get in the shower so we can go. I have to be there early and go over the music."

"You're sure it was Austin?"

"It was Austin. Hop in the shower."

"Any other surprises? Any phone calls from The Fort or from the sheriff?"

"There were a couple of calls right after I got home," she said. "But there was no one on the line."

"A couple?" Ezra asked.

"Yes. The phone rang several times and I answered and no one was there. About ten minutes later it happened again."

"No one said anything?"

"Someone hung up," Anne said. "I heard the click. Why? What are you thinking?" she demanded.

"Oh, nothing, just thinking."

"The phone calls are nothing, Ezra. We have a very handsome son in junior high, remember? It was probably a poor little lovestruck seventh grade girl who froze with fear when Dylan's mother answered the phone."

Ezra nodded and smiled weakly. "Yeah, that's probably all it was."

"Hop in the shower," Anne commanded. "I want to get to church. I have a feeling about tonight."

"What kind of feeling?"

"An excitement. Like something special is going to happen."

At five minutes to seven Betty Lou Barber was scurrying nervously about the church greeting newcomers, saying hello to friends from other churches, and basking in the excitement of the revival as if Jubal Lee Walker was her discovery and she had a part in his anointing. "Come in, come in," she rushed to some friends. She took them by the arm and led them to a pew. "This man is wonderful. He is so talented. He is going to be our new pastor, you know."

Anne sat on the piano bench watching Mrs. Barber with a detached amusement. *It's amazing,* she realized, *how different a church seems from the dais instead of the pew.* Pastor Tom and Darlene were seated in their normal pew by the front. They looked subdued as if attending their own hanging. At four minutes after seven Jubal Lee emerged from the study and strode to the microphone. His face glistened and his dark eyes sparkled. He strapped on his saxophone and mouthed the title of a song to Anne. Anne nodded her understanding.

Jubal's clear tenor sax split the air with a wailing rendition of "Joshua Fought the Battle of Jericho." He played through the song once, using the horn to call the people to their pews, then let his saxophone drop and sang in a loud, soulful voice:

> *You can talk about your King of Gideon,*
> *you can talk about your man, Saul,*
> *but there's none like good ol' Joshua*
> *at the battle of Jericho . . .*

Betty Lou Barber stood and began clapping her hands and the rest of the congregation followed. The revival was on. The music this evening was more forceful, more warlike than the night before. Jubal jumped from the saxophone, to guitar and vocals, to even sitting beside Anne and both playing the piano and singing. The crowd was not larger this evening, but it was more vocal. They almost shouted songs like "God's Got an Army," "The Song of Moses," "Mighty Warrior," and "When the Spirit of the Lord Moves on My Heart."

Jubal led the troops on a feverish climb up the mountain, then once they were on the peak, he pulled out his harmonica and did a sensitive, solo instrumental of "All Hail the Power of Jesus' Name."

From his front pew Ezra glanced around him. Half of the congregation stood with their eyes closed and their hands raised to the heavens. Including Dylan. Ezra's hands were clasped together at his belt. He loosened them and slowly brought his right arm as high as his chest, his palm open, and fingers extended. He was horribly self-conscious as if everyone had suddenly begun watching him. He looked around. No one was looking at all. He extended the arm and brought the hand shoulder high. It was a difficult task, his hand weighed heavily as if he were holding a five-gallon bucket of water. Finally, he decided not to think about himself, and the weight mysteriously went away.

"Brothers and sisters," Jubal said softly into the microphone. "We are gathered beneath the throne of praise. Please remain in an attitude of exalting the King." He paused and lowered his head in contemplation.

"I wanted to speak tonight," he continued, "on the power of God. But the Lord has changed my plans. He wants to demonstrate his power instead. I wanted to speak tonight from Mark sixteen and pray for those who need physical healing, but the Lord has whispered to me to speak from Romans thirteen. You may sit down if you wish, you may turn to your Bibles if you wish, but those of you who have the strength to stand as intercessors, please do so and keep your focus on the God of the heavens.

"Romans thirteen, verse one says: 'Let every soul be subject to the governing authorities. For there is no authority except from God, and the authorities that exist are appointed by God.'

"It goes on to say, brothers and sisters, you must not resist the authority of God or you will bring judgment on yourselves and that rulers are God's ministers onto us to do good.

"This is my third evening of having authority in this church, but it is an authority on loan to me, first from God, and second, from the pastor and board of this church. Tonight the Lord would have His local church authority honored. Would all of the board members please come forward."

Betty Lou Barber nearly pushed Armon from his pew. Four other men followed him reluctantly to the dais where they stood awkwardly as if waiting for a bus to another planet. There was a car salesman, a clothing store manager, a carpenter, a retired farmer, and Armon, a retired CPA. None of them were used to public attention.

Jubal looked over at Pastor Tom. "With your permission, Pastor," he said, and he reached into his jacket for a small bottle of oil, "I will anoint these men for service in this church."

Pastor Tom nodded. He did not know what else to do. Darlene was burning holes in the floor. To her, this was the ultimate insult. These men were her husband's elders, not Jubal Lee Walker's.

Jubal dabbed oil on the forehead of each man, then whispered to them: "please remain standing, gentlemen." The congregation watched him in anticipation. He did the unexpected. Stepping to the microphone he sang a cappella, his voice clearer and strong through two verses of "Amazing Grace." His talent was as masterful as ever. Without accompaniment he sounded not like a solo, but like a choir. The less stable would have sworn they heard angels or the chorus of a cloud of witnesses.

From where he stood Ezra heard several older women begin to cry softly, then another person began wailing in the back. He heard a soft "thump" when someone else hit the floor.

Jubal concluded the hymn and stood with his arms out as if holding the congregation in his embrace, then he turned to his left and farther extended an arm in invitation. His voice could have massaged the bristles from the back of a growling cur. "Pastor Jablonski," he said. "Would you and your wife please come forward."

CHAPTER NINETEEN

Aslice of tangerine moon hung in the western sky and pinpoints of stars punctuated the blackness. Ezra and Anne sat on the top of a haystack built of small square bales. A dim orange glow from the house tattled on Dylan, telling he was still up reading, traversing imaginary worlds with Walter Wangerin or Brian Jacques. The rest of the house was dark, a block of ebony set against the crushed purple of the night. Up and down the creek horned owls hooted on a party line and coyotes yapped gossip in the badlands. The night before Ezra and Anne were exhausted after Jubal's service and went straight to bed. This evening they were awake, wired by the activity of the past week and cruising on a second wind. Anne had suggested they go outside and drink in the crisp, clear air of the September evening. It was sweet and refreshing like bottled spring water.

Anne's head rested on Ezra's shoulder, and she pulled her windbreaker tight to keep warm. Like Ezra, she had few close friends. The young women she met in church were often single parents, or simply single, and eventually they married or found a better job and moved from Yellow Rock. She and Ezra had learned to be best friends to one another. "Are you thinking what I'm thinking?" she asked.

"I'm wondering what Jubal Lee prayed over Pastor Tom and Darlene," he said.

"I was, too," she said. "I couldn't hear him but I could see their faces. Whatever he said, it struck straight to the heart."

"Darlene acted liked she had been struck by lightning."

"Jubal did a good job with them," Anne said. "He talked with both of them for quite a while. It's been quite a week, hasn't it?"

"It was like this with Jubal when we were on the road. One madcap adventure after another."

"He doesn't talk about his wife and daughters much."

"It's probably hard on him being away."

"I suppose," Anne said.

A wispy cloud tried to cover the moon but was sliced to pieces by the sickle-bladed crescent moon. The fragments drifted away like orange life rafts on a black sea.

"Sometime I miss the hippie days," Ezra said. "Our literature and music meant something then. Everyone was reading Hesse, Watts, and *The Greening of America* and listening to Crosby, Stills, Nash, and Young."

"I don't miss it at all," Anne said.

"I miss the martial arts, too. I was so loose, strong, and quick. I loved the popping sound my gi sleeves made after throwing and retracting a punch."

"Are you having a middle age crisis, Ezra?"

"Does it sound like it?"

"Yes."

"Maybe I just want a little adventure."

"Do you want to leave the ranch and go on the road with Jubal?"

"I don't know," he said.

"I think he is still competing with you," Anne said.

"What?"

"Sure. Didn't you ever think he was? I was only around him for a couple hours in Lawrence while you were in jail, and I thought he radiated jealousy."

"He was probably mad because you weren't falling for his charms."

"Maybe," she said. She stared thoughtfully at the moon slice. "But I think he's competitive. He acts strange about those horses of his, too. They are like trophies to him. He doesn't love horses the same way you do."

"He was a horse trader," Ezra said. "A big-money one, but a horse trader, just the same. They learn to treat horses like objects, not friends."

Anne rubbed her hands as if she were nervous or cold. "Are you anxious about your job at The Fort?" she asked.

"No. I don't care if I ever go back."

"Can you tell me what Jubal's word was for you?"

"I can tell you part of it. The word itself was *leaving the land*. Just those three words. There is more to it than that. Jubal doesn't even know the rest. I will share it with you when I can."

Leaving the land. The phrase sent a chill through Anne that made her shiver.

Ezra felt her tremble. "Don't worry," he said. "The term is symbolic like the coyote dream of years ago."

"Have you ever had that dream again?"

"No, I hope I never do."

She squeezed his arm again and leaned into him for warmth. "I don't want to leave the ranch, Ezra."

"I know. I don't want to, either."

"But I'll go any place you want," she said. "Right now I want to go to bed because I'm getting cold, and I have to go to work in the morning." They held hands as they walked to the house. Ezra led because Anne was night-blind and he had always seen well in the dark, as if the darkness opened itself and revealed its secrets to him.

Anne fell asleep first, as she always did. Ezra lay awake until sleep finally caught him by surprise and pulled him down to its warm depths. He lay there for minutes, then was shaken by screams. The cries were desperate high-pitched wails and he ascended from his unconsciousness worrying for Dylan—the screams were somewhat like a child's—but then in his half-awakened state realized the cries were not of a person at all, but of an animal. They lasted only a few seconds but the echoes resounded in his mind. High-pitched, agonized screams as if animals were desperately trying to break through and communicate with a human. *They were horses,* he realized. What he heard was the sound of horses, not nickering or whinnying, but crying out in pain. He sat upright in bed, fully awake. He could still hear them. No. It was something else. Something similar to the sound, yet very different.

It was the phone ringing. By the third ring he was on his feet, scurrying to the living room.

"Hello?" he said.

There was no response but he could tell the line was open.

"Hello?" he repeated.

The phone clicked.

"Who was it?" Anne asked sleepily as he came to bed.

"Our seventh grade sweetheart is starting to call a little late," he said.

An hour later the phone rang again. Ezra heard it but chose to let it ring. On the fifth ring Anne rose and answered it.

"Hello?" she said. There was no answer but she could hear a person's breath on the other end. It was not the breathing of a twelve-year-old girl. She waited another instant, then reached down and unjacked the phone wire.

"No answer again?" Ezra asked her.

"It's not a girl calling for Dylan," she said.

Wednesday morning Jubal Lee pulled into the yard and backed up to the horse trailer he had left by the corrals. He jumped out of the Suburban and quickly hitched the catch over the ball and began raising the trailer jack.

"Going somewhere?" Ezra called out, walking from the house with a cup of warm Tang in his hand. Giving up coffee was harder than he had expected, and he was trying a variety of substitutes.

"I called the man I sold these horses to," Jubal explained. "He wants them delivered today." His voice and motions were rushed and his skin had the dull, jaundiced color of fatigue, caffeine, and stress. Dark circles were forming under his eyes.

"All the way to Canada?" Ezra asked.

"He's meeting me at Wolf Point," Jubal said, dragging two show halters out from under the Suburban's front seat. The vehicle was packed with tack, suitcases, books, loose clothing, and a sleeping bag.

"Want some company?" Ezra asked.

"Oh, it would just be a long boring ride, brother. I'm sorry I have to take this brown gelding away from you. He probably has you spoiled by now."

"I hate to see him go," Ezra admitted. He followed Jubal to the corral. The lead ropes dragged behind Jubal leaving two long trails, like snake tracks, in the dust.

"There's more where he came from and if the deal weren't already done, I'd give him to you," Jubal said over his shoulder. "But a deal is a deal."

Ezra followed in the wake of Jubal's cologne. It seemed unusually strong today, as if splashed on hastily. "Will you be back in time for tonight's service?" Ezra asked.

"No sweat, brother," Jubal said as he haltered the bay. "I'd never let the people down."

"It's a four-hour drive one-way," Ezra reminded him.

"That's why I'm rushing," Jubal said, and he pushed past Ezra leading the two Thoroughbreds.

"Good service last night," Ezra said. He wanted to ask Jubal what he had said to Pastor Tom and Darlene, what prayer had made the pastor's wife's legs quiver and had her suffocating tears in her handkerchief. But Jubal volunteered nothing.

"Sorry to be in such a rush," Jubal said. "If I travel alone, I can listen to praise tapes and get myself ready for this evening." He loaded the horses with a slap on each one's butt. "Have you given any more thought to my offer?" he asked.

"Anne and I have talked about it. We are willing to do whatever the Lord wants of us, but we have no leading. Everything around here is still up in the air."

"Don't let circumstances make your decision for you, brother," Jubal said. "It's either God's will or it isn't. I'm not offering you a paycheck, Ezra. I am offering you a ministry."

"I know. But it's a huge decision. Especially if we decide to leave the ranch."

"Remember," Jubal said, "no man owns anything. Not really. Everything already belongs to God. If you are too attached to the ranch, then it is probably time to give it up. There will always be other ranches." He jumped in the Suburban. "I gotta get going, brother," he said and waved a quick good-bye and roared down the lane. The dust hung in the air long after he was out of sight.

Ezra saddled Shiloh to ride on the Wilson fence line. As he led the sorrel from the barn his eyes fixed on the rifle scabbard and Jubal's warnings echoed in his mind. Carrying a rifle was foolish, he decided. He had never been the type to depend on weapons. He unfastened the scabbard and returned it to the tack room.

He pointed Shiloh in the direction of Austin's trailer house, taking a back route through the badlands on narrow deer trails that cut between boulders as large as Volkswagen buses and wound through plump cedar trees, their limbs heavy with fruitless berries and their evergreen musk hanging heavy in the cool morning air.

From the top of a moonscaped butte he focused his binoculars on a three-way corner of fence where the Riley land was intersected by Shorty Wilson's CRP and overgrazed summer pasture. One man on horseback was herding a couple hundred head of cattle out of the CRP toward an open gate aided by two neurotic blue heelers that had worried the cows into a stiff, bawling trot.

"So that's his game," Ezra said out loud as if talking to Shiloh. "Wilson's got Austin sneaking his cows onto CRP at night and moving them out in the morning." It was a dangerous plan, Ezra knew. The government regulations demanded no haying or grazing on conservation acreage for ten years and violators could be heavily fined.

Temptation struck Ezra in the chest like a fist. With one phone call to the county ASCS office he could have Wilson in water hot enough to scald a rock.

No. He shook his head like a dog shedding water, or a man casting out a thought. No, he wouldn't do it. *It wasn't the Christian thing to do.* If Ezra was to confront someone, it would be man-to-man. Not by a mysterious phone call. Not like some people.

As he watched Austin close the gate, he heard a single rifle shot to the north. It sounded like it came from Riley land. Ezra touched his spurs to Shiloh's side and galloped north following a well-used cow trail that paralleled the fence line. About half a mile later he came across the dual pickup with the Nevada plates parked on Wilson's side of the fence. He rode on slowly, staying to the sod where Shiloh's hooves would not be heard striking rock.

He peeked over each knoll cautiously, standing on tiptoes in the stirrups, only his hat and face breaking the skyline. He found them in another half a mile. The older man was kneeling beside the trophy antelope buck, holding its head up for the camera while the Nevada buckaroo took his picture with a Canon Sure-Shot. An arrow shaft protruded from behind the antelope's front leg. They were on Riley land.

"This will look good in the casino, huh, Clete?" he heard the older man say.

"He'll look good in the record books, too," the buckaroo answered.

"He looked better alive," Ezra said, approaching them on horseback.

The buckaroo whirled around. He had a face that could have backed a badger off fresh meat. "Who are you?" he growled.

"My name's Riley. And you are on Riley land."

"Oh, I don't think so," the older man said. "We are on Shorty Wilson's place."

Ezra pointed to the fence. "That's Wilson's place," he said.

The buckaroo never took his eyes off Ezra. The older man fiddled in his back pocket for a map. "I think this is BLM ground anyway," he said. "I'm pretty sure this is public land."

"No," Ezra said. "It is deeded ground. You are on private property."

"So what?" the blonde man snapped. "We shot the buck across the fence and it ran over here. You can't fault a man for retrieving his game."

Ezra rode a slow circle around the men and animal. Shiloh snorted at the scent of blood and the buckaroo pivoted on his boot heels, defining a small circle of his own, as he followed Ezra's every move as if the two of them were polarized by opposite currents.

"That's odd," Ezra said. "I don't see a blood trail. In fact, I don't see any tracks of this animal even coming from the direction of the fence."

"What are you saying?" the blonde man said. His voice was venomous.

"It's a warm day," the splotchy faced man said. "I sure would like to get this animal dressed out before it sours."

Ezra's eyes were on the buckaroo. "Let's not play games, gentlemen," he said. "You guys shot this buck on Riley property then you crossed the fence and stuck an arrow in the bullet wound." He saw the tendons tighten in the buckaroo's neck and his face turn pink.

"Now that's a rather serious accusation," the older man said.

"You should have thought of that before you did it. You used a soft-tipped bullet that never exited the body. You figured you could dig it out later when you skinned the buck. You used a quick, low-calibre shell, like a .22-.250, maybe smaller. I heard the shot. It didn't amount to much, just a loud pop. The rifle is probably behind that rock over there." Ezra nodded toward the Wilson fence.

"A real smart guy, aren't ya?" the buckaroo said, and he advanced toward the horse.

Ezra reached slowly down the right side of the saddle where his scabbard had been and touched only horsehair. He felt a quick surge of fear in knowing the rifle wasn't there, but he was still the mounted man, the man superior to the man on foot. He pulled the hand slowly back up and uncoiled his nylon lariat from his Oregon rope strap. In the right hands, a rope was an excellent weapon. A deadly weapon.

The older man saw the direction the confrontation was taking. "Now, boys," he said diplomatically. "Ain't no reason for things to get out of hand here. We're sorry to be causing you this inconvenience, Mr. Riley. What would it take to set things straight?" He reached for his checkbook.

"I don't want your money," Ezra said. He kept his eyes on the blonde buckaroo.

"Then how do we play this out?" the older man asked.

Ezra glanced quickly at the older man then back at the buckaroo. The blonde's hand was inching slowly down his left leg toward his boot top.

"You move that hand any closer to your knife," Ezra warned, "and I'm turning you two in to the game wardens for sure." The hand stopped.

"There's no reason to get the law involved," the older man said.

"I'm sure there isn't," Ezra said. "So here's how we play it out." He nodded at the older man. "You. Get the camera from your buddy and bring it to me."

The older man hesitated. He and Ezra locked eyes.

"Do we play this my way or not?" Ezra asked.

The man walked over, got the camera, and handed it to Ezra.

"Pull the arrow out of the wound," Ezra said. "And throw it over the fence." The older man did as he was told. The arrow pulled out easily.

"Okay, knife-boy," Ezra said to the blonde. "Cut out a circle of hide around the wound."

"You gotta be kidding," he snarled. He was a man accustomed to taking orders only from those he considered to be superiors. Men with more money, more power, the touch of death in their hands.

"I'm not kidding," Ezra said.

"Do it, Clete," the older man said. The splotches on his face were brightening under the warming sun and sweat stains were darkening his shirt. The buckaroo jutted his jaw angrily. He wanted to rush Ezra, pull him from the horse, hold the knife against his throat and listen to him beg.

But he knew he had to obey the older man, so he reached into his boot top, pulled out a knife with a five-inch blade and sliced a circle around the entrance hole of the wound. He turned and held the little piece of hide in his hand. "Give it to your partner," Ezra said. The Vegas buckaroo handed it to the older man.

Ezra cleared his throat. "Now the two of you stand together with your goat, I'm going to take your picture." Ezra backed Shiloh to a higher vantage spot. "Say cheese," he said. The men did not smile. Ezra took half a dozen pictures, rewound the film, pulled the canister out and put the film roll in his shirt pocket. "There are landmarks in the photo," he said. "There will be no question where the animal was." He rode to a nearby sandstone and placed the camera on the rock. "Bring me the piece of hide."

The older man advanced slowly and handed it to him. "So what's the purpose behind all this?" he asked. "Why don't you just take our money?"

"Any good lab will be able to tell that this hide had been penetrated by a bullet, not a broadhead arrow. The photo shows where you were, and it also shows there isn't any blood trail."

"Very crafty," the man said. "But what's the point? Are you turning us in?"

"I'd love to," Ezra said. "I would dearly love to. But I'm not that dumb. I turn you in, the next day I find my best saddle horse dead in the pasture with a bullet through his head."

"You still might," the blonde said.

"Shut up, Clete," Splotchy Face snapped.

"Yeah, shut up, Clete," Ezra said. "Here's the deal, boys. You can take the antelope and we will forget this little incident ever happened. But if you so much as frown at me during your stay in our fair county, the local game warden gets the piece of hide and the film."

"That's all?" the older man asked. "Why didn't you just let us pay you a trespass fee?"

"Because I want nothing to do with you," Ezra said. "Taking your money would tie me to Austin Arbuckle and Shorty Wilson."

"Well, aren't we finicky about our company," the blonde snarled. "I saw you drinking coffee with Jubal Lee Walker, didn't I?"

The older man took a step closer to Ezra. "What is your game with Walker, Mr. Riley? Whatever it is, I can assure you that we can take better care of you."

"Walker is just somebody I met years ago," Ezra said. "Now he happens to be preaching in my church."

The two men laughed. "Oh, I bet he is," the older one said. "I just bet he is."

Ezra spun Shiloh around; the whirling of the thirteen-hundred-pound horse threw rocks and dust toward Splotchy Face. "Gentlemen, this conversation is over. You have your antelope. I am sure you also have some very good reasons not to have the local law visiting you." He nodded at them and rode away. His back was straight and stiff and felt as big as a car hood. His muscles were tense as long as he was in their sight. Pride would not allow him to turn around and look, but fear told him he might take a bullet between the shoulder blades. As soon as he crested a hill and was out of their vision an enormous sigh escaped his chest, and Ezra nearly doubled-over in the saddle. He reached down and patted Shiloh on the neck. "I think we won that bluff," he told the sorrel. "But you stay in the barn tonight just in case."

CHAPTER TWENTY

When Ezra got back to the house, his answering machine was pulsating to a three-beat rhythm. He punched play.

The first said nothing. If it was the nighttime caller—the message was in the deliberate voicelessness.

The second caller spread dread into his bones. "Ezra, this is Cody. Lacey wanted me to call you. Said she thought you might listen to me. She's serious about selling the ranch but wants you to know that if you come up with a decent figure she will give you first crack at her share." Cody paused and Ezra knew he wanted to say something friendly, or at least civil, but nothing came to mind and the phone clicked. The voice of his former friend was hollow and echoing as if spoken through the barrel of a gun.

The third message came on: "Ezra, this is Janet out at The Fort. We have something here for you. Do you want to pick it up or should I mail it?"

Something at The Fort? Probably from the union representative, he thought, *maybe a date for a field hearing about my firing.* He punched The Fort's numbers and told Janet, the station director's secretary, that he would be right in. It was Wednesday, he could stop at The Fort while Solomon was getting groceries. Wednesday. Already? It had been a week since his suspension, and the memories of the corral panels splashing in the water tank were distant and vague as if happening in someone else's story.

Ezra went to Solomon's early and the old man was lying on a soiled couch reading the fine print in the Yellow Rock paper. He was seeing which bank was foreclosing on what parties. The house had not changed since Ezra's youth. Dust-coated arrowhead displays covered the walls and calendars were three and four deep on rusty nails.

"Let's go to town," Ezra said. "I have an errand to run."

Solomon half-rolled from the couch, caught himself before he fell, and rose stiffly to his knees. He glowered at Ezra with incendiary eyes and shuffled to where his farmer's cap hung from a deer antler. He hummed from deep within himself like a lion's growl or a rumble from the inside of a volcano.

Ezra stiffened. Solomon was angry, he realized, but Ezra hadn't a clue why. On light feet he moved around the old man and waited in the truck while his uncle double-locked the doors. Solomon had a fear of theft that normally amused Ezra—a thief would get lost in the house's clutter or leave such a deep trail in the dust he could be tracked to Canada—but nothing amused him today. Solomon was a ticking bomb.

"Any fights on the tube last night?" Ezra offered as Solomon climbed into the truck. The question was a diversion but Ezra did not expect it to work. Solomon's anger was a heat-seeking missile; once pointed toward an explosion it could follow the trickiest maneuver until it penetrated the enemy's heart.

"Naw," Solomon said gruffly. Ezra noticed his cap was not on straight. Another bad sign. Solomon's cap bill was like a rudder. If it wasn't pointed straight, he wasn't flying straight.

"Nothing on the tube, huh?"

"Naw," Solomon spat. "And if I wanted to do somethin' with the ranch I'd do it. You don't have to be sendin' no goldarn preacher up here to talk to me." The words blasted out and ricocheted and echoed in the pickup cab like bullets from a large-calibre handgun. Solomon's thin blue lips quivered with recoil, and his heaving chest percolated with anger.

"What are you talking about?" Ezra asked. Dread trickled down his spine like water through a rain gutter.

"That curly haired phony preacher that you sent up," Solomon half-shouted. "He wants to lease the place." His forehead glowed hot enough for frying eggs.

"I didn't send anyone up to you," Ezra answered adamantly. "I don't even know what you're talking about."

"Well, he was sure up here this mornin', waltzed in like he owned the place. The same phony shylock that's got the trailer parked at your place." Solomon continued with a string of vulgarities that would have melted tallow off a bull hide. Ezra was guilty by association. Ezra was guilty of manipulation and cowardice. Ezra was guilty, period.

Jubal Lee, Ezra thought, *what have you done to me now?*

Pastor Jablonski awakened that morning from a canyon-deep sleep where the pillows were boulders of goose-down, mourning doves cooed his name, and the soft gurgling of a bubbling stream sprayed the meadow-fresh air with charged ions. He awakened not knowing and not caring who he was nor where he was. He might as well have been an infant, innocent in slumber and blissfully ignorant upon awakening. In one night he had reclaimed the sleep stolen the past two years, and the only thing heavy on his heart this morning was hope, and the blankets he had pulled to his chest.

As awareness slowly came to him he realized it was Wednesday and duty told him to prepare for a day of Bible study for the night's teaching. Then he remembered Jubal Lee Walker. He did not have to teach, and rather than feel angry or threatened, Tom relaxed and a slow, wide smile spread across his face. He was relieved. His doubts about Walker were legion, but his concerns had been released the night before and his shoulders were wondrously light without the burden. He liked the people of his church, but if they wanted Jubal Lee Walker, that was all right with him. It would be God's will. He was aware of Betty Lou Barber's maneuverings. When he saw her take Jubal off to the side Monday night, he knew she was persuading him to stay, to throw his hat into the ring and be elected pastor once he and Darlene were dismissed.

He did not think it was fair but it did not matter. One way or another, the church would get the man they deserved. He knew his performance had been less than stellar. He and Darlene had chosen a hideout; as Butch Cassidy and the Sundance Kid had retreated to the infamous Hole-in-the-Wall, they had retreated to Yellow Rock. They had hoped for a small, caring church in a small, friendly town where their wounds could slowly heal as they ministered to people hungry for the Word of God. They wanted to nurture people and be nurtured in return, but they discovered within a few weeks that the honeymoon was over. The good, decent, down-to-earth churchgoing people who had voted unanimously in his favor were also capable of being demanding, insensitive, and cynical. He himself was not an emotional man, but the men of eastern Montana were frozen subsoil in comparison. They led stark, private lives battling a boom-and-bust western economy and temperatures that raced to both extremes of the thermometer driven by winds that relocated barn roofs and chilled bone marrow. The Yellow Rock River was muddier than he had imagined and the prairie so treeless he wondered if birds died of sunstroke. But he was of hardy Pennsylvania stock, Polish on his father's side, Dutch on his mother's. He could stay if Darlene showed any recovery at all—if the women in the church, particularly the opinion-forming Betty Lou, would embrace her.

The women in the church had been warm and welcoming at first. They cleaned their house, brought meals, invited Darlene to arts and crafts activities, and Darlene slowly responded. But then, as suddenly and as official as a clap of thunder, they deemed the recovery time over and demanded Darlene fulfill the obligations of a pastor's wife. *She* should be doing the ministering. *She* should be having the dinners. *She* should teach

Sunday school. *She* should be quietly at her husband's side for weddings, funerals, basketball games, and civic functions. Darlene fled to her two sanctuaries: the piano and the prescription sleeping pills from her Pennsylvania doctor. Both the piano and the drugs had turned on her: her music dried to a powder and blew away; the drugs sedated her into apathy, depression, and water retention. Her ankles became thick, her face sagged, and she stared at people as if they were ghouls rising from the dead to cut her heart from her breast. She was withering, a greenhouse flower in the desert where the few showers were likely coyotes marking their territory.

He reached across the bed to touch her. She was always there, covered by a white sheet—as the two girls had been—lying as cold and inanimate as a snowdrift. But he did not feel her, nor did he sense her weight balancing a bed that seemed unusually large. Tom slowly turned his head and discovered himself alone and the digital clock on her nightstand flashing 7:18. He had slept in. Darlene, he guessed, was downstairs making breakfast.

He showered, shaved, dressed, and went downstairs to a home conspicuously empty. Sunlight filtered in between the cracks of the curtains, but there was not even the aroma of coffee or bacon in the air. He entered the kitchen, eyeing it like an army general on a walk-through inspection, then passed on to the laundry room, back down the hallway, poked his head into the sewing room she never used, then back to the kitchen. He was not worried yet; he was only pleasantly confused, so he made a pot of coffee, burnt a piece of toast, and glanced through a copy of the Yellow Rock paper.

The table was littered with bread crumbs, and he was licking butter grease from his fingertips when Darlene walked in. She was wearing the pink and blue jogging suit he had given her last Christmas. It was crisp and bright from never having been worn.

"Where have you been?" he asked.

"I went for a long walk," she smiled. "Then I stopped at the church to pray."

He gave her the long, probing look that pastors' wives do not appreciate receiving from their husbands.

"I'm okay," she scolded him lightly. "But I sure have gained weight. You know, when I knelt at the altar this morning I felt like a sleeping bag stuffed with seat cushions."

"You're just a few pounds over," he said.

"Oh heavens," she declared. "And the angel Gabriel is just an average trumpet player. Would you like a real breakfast, or are you burning wheat to increase farm prices?"

Pastor Tom broke into a vacuous Cheshire cat smile. Was he in Wonderland? Would he disappear—be raptured?—and leave a dumbfounded smile hanging in the air? It was a miracle. He had always disputed miracles. Sometimes he wondered if Lazarus had really come back from the dead, or had it been a mysterious natural phenomenon? But no, Lazarus had returned from the land of the unliving. And he had brought Darlene back with him.

Ezra was glad to get Solomon out of the truck and sped away from the county market as if it were burning and he had matches in his hand. It did not take much to set Solomon off, an innocent remark sailing out of the blue could explode on the old man like a grenade in a bear's den. Even Anne once angered him with a simple observation about a fence line and he did not speak to her for a week. It took creative back trailing on Ezra's part to find her folly and explain it to her. The past July Dylan had accidently ignited Solomon and got his ears scorched for it. Dylan raced home with a whirlwind of profanity buzzing behind him, and the temperature on the Riley ranch dropped noticeably for the remainder of July. It took all of Anne's peacemaking abilities to keep Ezra from confronting his uncle.

"Don't do anything," she warned him. "He doesn't know how he hurts people and he's too old to change."

"The old cuss needs a good paddling," Ezra said to himself as he drove down Main Street. He could not tolerate anyone messing with his family whether it was Solomon or Austin Arbuckle. It was one thing to threaten him, but phone calls in the middle of the night involved his family, and the rage was burning white-hot in Ezra's soul and seeping out through his eyes.

He wasn't mad at Jubal Lee. In his confident, brash way Jubal had done what a lot of people had wanted to do: he went straight to the old man and asked him why he didn't do something with the place besides overworking and underpaying his nephew and letting the grass sit as bait for ground-vultures like Shorty Wilson.

Ezra told himself to cool down. He was thinking about Solomon; he was thinking about Austin; he was thinking about Jubal Lee; he was thinking about The Fort; he was thinking about strangers in the hills. He was thinking too much.

It didn't brighten his disposition any when he passed through the arched gates of The Fort. He knew if he met Frankforter in the hallway he would probably flatten Der Fuehrer with a dropkick to the chest. Ezra felt like a gasoline-drinking, fire-breathing dragon. If Frankforter so much as stuck his head out from his office, he would scorch his dome and singe his hair. He was being his father. The blood of Johnny Riley was boiling in his veins. Ezra was angry and frustrated and wanted to fight.

He sat in his pickup for five minutes taking deep breaths and remembering his favorite colors of sunsets. He knew he had to get control of himself. He was composed by the time he got to Janet's office. She met him with a smile. Ezra had been popular at The Fort. He was younger and better-looking than the other cowboys and had a cerebral air about him that suggested his reading went beyond Baxter Black, *The Agri-News,* and the auction bills posted on restaurant windows.

"How are you, Ezra?" she said cheerfully.

Ezra wore a smile like a mask. "I'm fine," he said. *Tally one more lie,* his conscience noted. He looked past her to the director's office. The door was open but the room was dark. "Has he come back from MARC?" he asked.

"Oh, yes," she said. "But then he took a week of annual leave. He won't be in until the Monday after next."

"Oh," Ezra said. "How about the union rep, has he been by?"

"He called a couple of days ago," Janet said. "He said he would wait until the director got back." She slid an envelope across the desk. "This came for you," she said. "But we had to open it to find out."

The 5-by-7 manila envelope was marked:

To the Cowboy by the Highway, U.S. Experiment Station, Yellow Rock, Montana.

Ezra tore it open and took out two enlarged photographs. One was of him alone on Shiloh next to a fence line. The other one was the same except for the attractive tourist lady standing on the highway side of the fence. *A week ago,* Ezra thought. Only a week, yet the two travelers and the cowboy on the horse were all strangers to him. He moved the photos to where Janet could look at them.

"Nice shots," she said. "Who's the lady?"

"Just some tourist," Ezra said. "They stopped me when I was riding fence and wanted to take my picture. They are from New York," he added, as if that explained their behavior.

Janet stared at the photos exactingly, the way grandmothers look at photos of their grandchildren. She finally brought her head up and locked her green, liquid eyes on Ezra. "We sure hope you come back to work out here," she said.

Ezra smiled. "It will probably take an act of Congress," he said.

As he drove back to the county market to get Solomon, he dug into the envelope and discovered a small handwritten note.

"Dear unknown cowboy," it said. "We very much appreciate your courtesy and would like to meet you again on one of our trips west. We hope you enjoy the photos. Sincerely, David and Amanda Silverstein."

The note was written on their publisher's letterhead. Binghampton House, New York, New York.

Ezra thought of this as a home for his precious child. He did not have to send his manuscript into the foul, dangerous streets of the unknown. Here were friends. It would be like sending Dylan to visit an aunt back East. He would send his manuscript to the Silversteins, and he would do it that day as soon as he got Solomon home.

The day had started terribly, he reasoned, but it was certain to get better now.

When Anne got home from work at 5:30 Ezra was not home, but Jubal Lee was by the corrals unhitching his horse trailer. He waved at her. Moments later, while she was changing clothes in the bedroom, a knock came at the door. Anne finished dressing quickly as she heard Dylan let Jubal in.

"Hey, little brother," Jubal said, "look what I brought you." He handed Dylan a small box.

"A Sony Walkman," Dylan said.

"I keep my promises, little brother. Now you can listen to my CD's."

Anne stepped from the bedroom and into the hallway. Jubal and Dylan had already moved to the kitchen. "You didn't have to do that," she said.

He shrugged. "I have to take care of my fans," he said.

"Mom, I'm going down to my room to listen to Jubal Lee's music," Dylan said and the sound of his footsteps followed him down the basement stairs.

"You really didn't need to do that," Anne said again.

"The boy is very talented," Jubal said. "It makes me happy to share some of my talent with him. A few years from now who knows what he will be giving me in return."

His tone was slightly patronizing, Anne thought, as if he somehow wanted this favor returned. "Well, thank you," she said. "He doesn't have a lot of the things his friends have but he is good not to complain about it." She went to the refrigerator and pulled out two covered dishes. "Would you like to stay for supper?" she asked.

"I better not," he said regretfully. "But thank you for asking. I went to Wolf Point and back today. I need to get to my room and take a long shower."

"I don't know where Ezra is—"

Jubal's eyes drilled her. He meant them to be soft but she felt them pin her to the kitchen wall. "Are you okay, Anne?" he asked. "You look a little tired."

She turned away purposefully—wishing Ezra would get home—and reached into the cupboard for three dinner plates. "Oh, it's nothing," she said. "We didn't sleep well. Somebody is calling the house, then hanging up. It happened twice last night around midnight."

"Ezra mentioned something to me about it yesterday," Jubal said. "He said it was some love-crazy girl."

"That's what we thought, but it's not."

"How do you know?" Jubal asked, his face etched with concern.

"I heard a man's breathing," Anne said. "Then I disconnected the phone." She was saying more than she wanted to, but it felt coaxed out of her, and it felt good to let it go.

"So, what do you think is going on?" Each of Jubal's questions led to an answer as if he stood at the end of a hallway holding an open door.

"I don't know," she said. "But I know what Ezra thinks. He thinks it's Austin Arbuckle." *That* was the name she wanted to say. *Austin Arbuckle.* Or was that the name he *wanted* her to say? In any case, it felt good to breathe it out and let it hang in the air like a foul vapor that could be deodorized.

"And do you think it is Austin?" Jubal asked.

Anne felt as if someone had taken her by the hand and was leading her on a narrow trail on a mountain ledge. She sighed so deeply her chest caved in and she nearly dropped the plates she was carrying to the table. He saw her trepidation and pulled her with his eyes into the kitchen chair opposite from him. She still had not answered his question.

"There is more to this than I know about, isn't there?" he said.

Anne's face was apprehensive.

Jubal's brown eyes softened. "If you don't want to talk about it—"

Anne instinctively looked around to make sure Dylan was not within earshot though she knew he was in his bedroom listening to music. She could hear Jubal's praise songs drifting up through the floor beneath her feet. She had a sin to confess and Jubal was a man of God, wasn't he? She cleared her throat and collected her courage. "There's something I should tell you," she said. "Last week when Ezra got fired he didn't tell me right away and I was mad at him for keeping things from me. During one of your services the Lord reminded me that Ezra wasn't the only one who kept secrets—" she suddenly paused as if feeling herself at the cliff's edge. Common sense told her not to take another step. Jubal's eyes coaxed her out into the air.

"I had a strange encounter with Austin about eight or nine years ago," she blurted. "It was a bitterly cold day, ground blizzards, wind chill of about eighty below. Ezra was out in the hills looking for his cows, and Dylan and I were in the trailer house alone. Dylan was only about three or four and he was napping when Austin knocked on the door. He told me he was out of gas. He played some real strange mind games with me—"

"Did he hurt you?"

"No, but I thought he was going to. I was scared to death. I even got a paring knife when he wasn't looking and hid it in my sleeve. I would have used it if I'd had to."

"So what did he do?"

"When Dylan woke up, Austin just up and left. He had plenty of gas."

"And you didn't tell Ezra because you knew he would slowly disassemble Austin until he could fit in a box of Cracker Jacks." Jubal's voice had an odd mixture of seriousness and humor, of envy and condemnation.

Anne nodded. "Either that," she said, "or Austin would hurt him. Austin's no wimp, Jubal. He was a bull rider and a barroom brawler."

"And that was the end of it?" Jubal asked.

"They did almost come to blows once. Austin become a cattle order buyer and bought our calves one year. He played a mind game on Ezra with his uncle Sam. I think Austin backed down."

"I have learned to trust a woman's intuition," Jubal said. "What is your gut feeling on this one?"

"I don't know," Anne said. "So much has happened this week. The phone calls might mean nothing at all. It could be kids at school. It could be anybody."

"Do you think Austin has a fixation?" Jubal asked.

"What do you mean?"

"An obsession of some sort. Maybe it's you. You're an attractive woman, and very unlike the local women. He was the county stud, if you know what I mean. Or he could be fixated on having backed down from Ezra once and is determined to salvage his pride."

Anne was feeling very uncomfortable. Jubal reached over and squeezed her hand. "Don't worry about it," he said. "There are spirits that can be bound in situations like these. We'll pray about it this evening."

She thanked him but she didn't feel any better.

Jubal rose to go, then turned back. "Speaking of Ezra not communicating, did he tell you about the job I offered him?"

Anne nodded. "It's very generous," she said. "But it is hard for me to imagine Ezra leaving the ranch."

Jubal's eyebrows collapsed together and a shaded light colored his eyes. "He didn't tell you about the word I gave him?"

"Sort of," she said. "But he's holding something back."

"Holding what back?" he asked.

"His interpretation, I guess."

"Oh, well, that's okay, sister. Words like these have to be confirmed by two or three witnesses," Jubal reassured her. "It is a language of types and shadows, of intrinsic and imposed means, of *logos* and *rhema*."

"I understand," she said.

He turned to leave again but stopped. He turned back slowly. "I am very sure of that word," he said. "I know it is from God."

"I'm sure it is," Anne said. "And whatever you said to Tom and Darlene certainly must have been, too."

"I don't make mistakes," Jubal said flatly. "There is just too much Holy Ghost in me for error." He excused himself. He needed a shower, he told her, and time to spend in the Word and prayer. She nodded and followed him to the door, but she was listening with only half an ear.

When he had gone she went back to the table and sat. She wondered why she felt so cold when she was alone with Jubal. It was like it was winter—as it had been with Austin—and she was in the house by herself with the doors and windows open and a ground blizzard from Alberta was raking the room with its fierce, frigid teeth and she was tethered to a chair, powerless to do anything but shiver.

CHAPTER TWENTY-ONE

Ezra was thinking about his life; what it was and what it wasn't. He was thinking about The Fort, Jubal's offer, money, the ranch, and busy little mindful things as they drove to town for the Wednesday night service. Then as he crested the high flat hill between the Riley Ranch and town he glimpsed a streak of color in his rearview mirror. He reached up and adjusted the mirror for a better look. "I need more than a box of sixty-four," he said.

"What?" Anne asked, as if awakened from sleep.

He nodded over his shoulder at the panorama lighting the sky behind them. "The sunset," he said. "I need more than a box of sixty-four colors to accurately describe this evening's sunset." The western horizon was so black it gleamed with a royal purple glow like the curtains Ezra remembered in his high school auditorium. Above the blackness a thin band of lavender and gold clouds lay like a slit eyelid. Draining from its corner was a slash of violent crimson, fuchsia, and magenta stain, as if the heavens were ripped and bleeding from the gash, spilling its colorful sorrow on the blue-black hills. Behind the black veil, over the lip of the divide, lay Louie and Scottie and Bull Creeks, where the horse-hunting Johnny Riley first met a pretty young divorcée, a squatter in an abandoned homesteader's shack. There, love was discovered that would later bring Ezra into the world.

"God is crying," Dylan said. His reflection in the rear window seemed imposed on the technicolor spectacle.

"What?" Anne asked. Something powerful and prophetic had spoken through the innocence of the child.

"It looks like a big eye," Dylan explained. "With blood and tears coming out. God is crying."

Anne turned to look at the sky. Ezra checked his mirror again. They each trembled involuntarily, unknowingly to the other, as the colors seeped below the horizon and the eye winked good-bye.

"I wonder what God is crying about?" Dylan asked quietly.

The mood in the sanctuary was heavy—stifled by indifference or blanketed with fatigue—but Betty Lou Barber was content. Her glazed eyes were turned inward in the narcissistic introspection common to successful manipulators. She was pleased with herself. Jubal Lee Walker had become her trophy and would have been as beautiful to her hanging lifeless on her living room wall as he was preaching, singing, and praying down the fire of heaven. She was certain it was only a matter of days before he officially claimed the pastorate, moved his family to Yellow Rock, and made their little church the most popular in town. She had already talked to Armon about starting a building fund. She envisioned a new structure on the outskirts of town, one holding four, maybe five hundred people. She did not know what Jubal had spoken to Pastor and Darlene the night before—she had asked but he would not tell her—but she was certain it was confirmation of his call and theirs, and theirs was certainly to return to Pennsylvania.

The only problem Betty Lou had not resolved was Ezra Riley. Jubal Lee seemed adamant that any plans include *him*. Why, she didn't know. It was one thing to include Anne, she was a pianist and guitarist, but what could Ezra do? He was a hard-luck, hard-scrabble cowboy, arrogant and independent. He had resisted all of Betty Lou's ingratiations. He seemed unmoved by either flattery or criticism. If anyone was going to be Jubal Lee's right-hand man, it should be Armon—had to be Armon. She would see to it.

At Jubal's request, the five board members were sitting near the front. He had explained to Betty Lou that it was time they learned to minister to the people themselves, and she had herded them to the second pew in the center, where they looked small and anxious, like youth group members scrutinized by adults. Ezra sat in front of them—again at Jubal's request—and the Jablonskis were in the section of pews to his right. Tom was relaxed and looked pounds lighter. Darlene had changed her hair and smiled to people as they entered.

The crowd was smaller than the previous nights. The curious had been fulfilled and stayed home to watch television. Sally Johnson came in late, slid into an empty pew in the back, and sat with her shoulders drawn together and her jacket on, as if coiled to spring at any second.

At 7:10 Jubal left the study and entered a sanctuary permeated with quiet anticipation. He did not bounce, flash ivory smiles or white torches from his eyes. He drug himself to the microphone, fumbling with his guitar strap. His suit needed pressing.

He never should have driven to Wolf Point and back, Ezra realized.

"You will have to forgive me tonight," Jubal said. "Being a vessel of God's fire night after night can leave a guy a little burned out. My flesh is slowly being mortified." He stared down at the floor for a long minute. "I want to do something different tonight," he said as he looked up. "I want to begin with a song that is not a praise song. It is a cowboy song by a truly great talent, a man named Ian Tyson. And I would like to dedicate it to my friend, Ezra Riley."

The corners of Ezra's eyes tightened. It was a slight reaction observed only by Anne who sat quietly at the piano. Someone dimmed the overhead lights and one direct beam from the ceiling was left to fall like a yellow shaft on the high-legged stool where Jubal sat.

"This is a song of travels and learning and the loneliness of friendship," Jubal said. Fatigue strained his voice but it still resounded clearly through the little church as plaintive and wrenching as a baby's cry:

The high soaring hawk
The dark awkward crow
The white gull alone on the
High rolling sea
Must make their way home
Best way that they know
No different for you and for me.
We will stay where the river runs through
The range and the sky buckskin and blue
We will ride to the end
On the wings of the wind
'Til we're home and our circle is through.

Jubal strummed the chorus again, his fingers punching the frets and his pick slicing the strings, then he softened and stared at Ezra. "Listen to the words, my friend," he said.

May the children read
May they understand what is of true value
So that the truth may be known
The glory of God and the dark side of man
For one day they must ride on alone.

Jubal continued the song and Ezra lowered his head. Others assumed he was embarrassed by the attention or was recalling memories of life on the road with his friend, but it was neither of these. Ezra felt a purifying tearing apart, like a jagged fork of lightning against a black sky. He knew Tyson's work well—he studied him as he had once studied Bob Dylan—and had the lyrics to this song committed to memory. The line "The glory of God and the dark side of man" was one of his favorites, and he wondered how Jubal had known that—was it coincidence or another display of his prophetic powers?

Jubal sang the song through one more time while Ezra explored the cave of his questionings. When Ezra surfaced, Jubal was finishing:

. . . for one day they must ride on alone.

An awkward silence fell on the people. They knew better than to clap. They were innocent voyeurs pulled unsuspectingly to a moment of intimacy so desperate it seemed criminal. Jubal Lee sat in the spotlight, his shadow traced across the floor until it streamed into the darkness. He looked very old and very young simultaneously. Ezra raised his head and their eyes met. Jubal's eyes were filled with longing expectations; solicitations for a nod, an embrace, a spoken gratitude. Ezra gave him a silence so deep and dark Jubal was afraid to enter it. He wallowed in the edges of Ezra's vision for a minute, like a child clumsily dog-paddling in a deep pool of a creek, then he pulled himself out and stood thin, white, and naked on the bank of Ezra's consciousness, exposed and vulnerable. He was small, waif-like and cold. *Let me in,* he seemed to be saying, but Ezra did not. Ezra's eyes were neither cold nor hard, they simply did not allow entry. Jubal shook his head, and Ezra imagined him flinging droplets of water, but the vision faded and Jubal was again on stage turning himself inside out, shedding one skin for another, changing roles. It was time to be spiritual, time to become the minstrel and psalmist. Time for the revival to begin.

Jubal led the congregation through four choruses untouched by magic or anointing. His work was mere performance, and his timing and sensitivity were out of kilter. Still, two people responded strongly to his singing: Betty Lou, whose ears were still tuned to the echos of her imagined successes, and Darlene, who timidly raised one hand while singing as someone who had just rediscovered her voice.

When the song portion of the service ended, Anne left the piano to sit with her husband. Jubal stood at the microphone for several minutes fumbling with the pages of his Bible as if his fingers were thumbs and the pages were a pool of glue. The delay became embarrassing until finally he looked out at the people, shrugged, and said simply: "I really do not know what to do this evening." He stepped back one step and rested his chin on a fist to contemplate the will of God. A silent but powerful hush rippled through the congregation as Darlene raised from her pew and walked to the microphone. She wore a navy blue suit rather than her usual dowdy knit dress, and the effect was slimming. Her hairstyle had changed making her seem like a different woman, even more so because of the smiling, assured countenance. "I am pretty new at this," she said. "But I know I have something I must share." At the sound of her voice, Jubal opened his eyes. She looked at him as if asking for permission to continue, he smiled, and left the stage, taking a seat by himself in a front pew.

"Most of you know me," Darlene said. "And you know how I have been for the past couple years. It is a terrible thing to lose a child, let alone lose two at once as we did. It is even worse to survive the accident that takes your children." Her eyes moistened with tears but her voice remained calm, steady, and determined.

"I have not been a very good pastor's wife the past two years. I am not justifying or defending myself, but you need to be where I have been before you judge me. It is a dark and lonely place. I had given up on God. I wanted nothing to do with Him. I wanted to die, and I must confess I went to bed every night thinking I should take all the pills at my bedside, not just the two the prescription called for."

Ezra glanced at Anne. She had a tear of empathy running down her cheek. Others in the congregation were humbled and respectful, too, with the exception of Betty Lou Barber, who had turned a stone-cold face to the wall and would not look toward the dais.

"I was born and raised in a church much like this one," Darlene continued. "My father was a board member and Sunday school teacher. He filled the pulpit on the Sundays the pastor was gone. It was a conservative, essentially nondenominational church. We sang hymns, preached from the Bible, and sponsored an evangelical outreach now and then. There wasn't any clapping or shouting. We were very *respectful*. I have never believed in modern-day miracles or 'words from the Lord.' Because of that background, and my own woundedness, the past few days have been very hard for me."

Jubal straightened in his pew. He knew where the pastor's wife was going. It would mean not only the salvation of this particular evening, but the redemption and validation of his ministry in Yellow Rock.

"Last night when Reverend Walker called me and Tom up to the front, I desperately did not want to come. If Tom had not been holding on to my hand, I would have run out the door. Frankly, I was beginning to think that Jubal Lee Walker was of the devil." Several nervous chuckles sounded in the audience, but quietness was still the rule.

"Most of you saw me up here shaking and crying. You know something happened, and I bet you are dying of curiosity." She smiled at the people then turned her head and looked at her husband. Tom sat quietly in his pew, one arm folded across his chest, his right hand on his face with an index finger above his lips and the thumb parallel to the jawline. He was shielding his mouth to disguise his quiet prayers of intercession.

"About six years ago," Darlene continued, "when the girls were about seven and nine we were living on the edge of town back in Grove City. It was a beautiful place with lots of wildlife, especially birds and deer. One day Caroline, she was our youngest, came running to the house with her hands cupped around something small and bright blue. I thought it was a ball of brightly colored cloth, but it was a bluebird. A male eastern bluebird. It had been injured somehow and she desperately wanted me to pray for it." She choked back a sob. Pastor Tom had lowered his head into one hand. He remained dignified and professional in his posture, but the overhead lights outlined a single tear path like liquid gold draining from his eyes.

"I couldn't tell my baby that I didn't believe in healing," Darlene said. "So I prayed for the bird but I was hoping it would just die from the shock of being handled so we could bury it in the backyard. When I was done praying, I told Caroline: 'Perhaps it is not God's will to heal the bird.'

"'Of course it is,' she said. 'God loves bluebirds. They are the birds of happiness.' She insisted on building a little nest for it in the backyard, where she fed it water with an eyedropper and bread crumbs with tweezers. I just knew that when the bird finally died it would break her heart."

She cleared her throat and collected herself. "The next Sunday morning as I was getting ready for church she ran into my bedroom and said: 'Mommy, the bluebird of happiness has flown,'" and I thought she meant the bird had died and I took her in my arms to console her, but she pushed me away, grabbed my hand, and began pulling me from the room. 'Come see, Mommy,' she insisted. 'Come see.'

"The bird was still in the backyard, trying to hop. Our older daughter Judith was safeguarding it from our cat. Caroline ran and picked it up, and said, 'Watch, Mommy,' and she tossed it into the air. Her eyes were so bright and hopeful. I knew the bird would fall, and I covered my mouth. But it fluttered its wings and stalled at the peak of the toss, then it flew. It was slow and awkward at first, but soon it was flying until it was gone from sight.

"'See, Mommy,' Caroline squealed. 'The bluebird of happiness can fly.'"

Darlene stepped back to compose herself for an instant, as if moving from the past to the present. "When Jubal Lee called Tom and me to the front last night, he told me that he had a word from the Lord for me. I must confess, I wanted to laugh in his face.

"He prayed for a minute then he asked me to raise my head and open my eyes and look into his face. I can still remember how dark and angry I was. I was daring him to say anything at all. I didn't care if it was from God or just a trick by Jubal Lee, I did not want to hear it.

"Then he took my hands and spread them out like little wings and said: 'Darlene, it is time for the bluebird of happiness to fly again.'"

She stepped back with her face in her hands. Anne reached across her pew for a box of tissues and took them to Darlene, who thanked her, wiped her face, and continued. "There are still a lot of things that have happened this week that I am not sure of. And I do not know what the Lord's plan is for Tom and me. But I do know one thing. The Lord spoke to me. The Lord spoke only what He could know." She trembled slightly at the microphone, having reached an end without an ending. She looked at Tom, then at Jubal Lee. "Thank you for your prayers," she finally whispered into the mike, then she rejoined her husband. He took both of her hands in his.

After several silent moments, Jubal returned to the dais. Ezra could tell that he was tempted to launch a new service, to renew the singing and follow with preaching. But he didn't. He did not even call people forward to be prayed for. He simply said quietly: "We cannot improve on what the Lord has done, let us simply go home now. Go home to be with your families and be thankful for the mercies of God."

With Jubal's pronouncement some people left immediately, some lingered at the altar, several went to talk to Tom and Darlene. Ezra looked around but Jubal was nowhere to be seen. Ezra was ready to go home. Four nights of revival had been uplifting to the spirit but wearisome to the flesh. He felt like he had spent a week digging ditches and was glad the service was over early.

He was also concerned for his son. When they got home Ezra walked Dylan to his bedroom. "Listen, son," he said. "If these services are tiring you out, I don't care if you stay home the next couple nights."

"I like church, Dad," Dylan said as he slipped out of his pants and pulled on a pajama top.

A canvasing of the bedroom walls told Ezra that he had not been in his son's room for a long time. The sports posters of Michael Jordan, Joe Montana, and Larry Bird had come down, replaced by colorful reproductions of Ferraris, Lamborghinis, and Porsches. "I really don't mind," Ezra said. "You don't have to go."

"I want to go," Dylan said. "I like the music."

Ezra smiled and tousled Dylan's fine brown hair. "Okay, son, I'm glad you like going," and he turned to leave the room.

"Dad?" Dylan said.

Ezra turned in the doorway, one hand on the doorknob, the other on the light switch. Dylan lay in bed with his covers pulled to his chest. His brown eyes sparkled with a deep curiosity.

"Were you really trained to kill people?" he asked. His curiosity about Jubal's comment at the Sunday lunch had been weighing heavily on his young mind.

Ezra was tempted to just say no, to say that Jubal sometimes exaggerated; instead, he pulled a folding chair from the boy's writing desk and sat down. "I was in the martial arts off and on," he explained. "I had one instructor in Nevada who thought the world was ending and America would be a chaotic wilderness. He taught us some rather extreme measures, but they were all defensive."

"Like what? What did he teach you?"

"It's not anything you want to hear about just before you go to sleep, Dylan."

"Dad," Dylan measured his sentence carefully. "Could you kill someone?"

"Do you mean am I physically capable or morally capable?"

"Both."

Ezra hesitated, stared at the floor, then met his son's waiting eyes. "Only if I was defending you or Mom," he said.

"Not if you were defending yourself?"

"Maybe. I don't know. When you are in those situations, you never know how you are going to react. You can't plan for it. Whatever type of person you are inside takes over as if the script is already written."

"Have you met people who have done it, you know, people who have killed people?"

"Besides soldiers in war?" Ezra asked.

"Yeah, besides that."

"A couple," Ezra said.

"They must not know anything about God," Dylan said.

"They are small people, son. They are small and evil. Remember, violence is never romantic no matter the cause. It is always disgusting and dehumanizing. Even when you win."

Dylan's eyes became mature and serious. "Violent people are small on the inside, aren't they, Dad?"

"That's right, Dylan."

"I want to be big on the inside, Dad," Dylan said. Ezra smiled, patted him on the chest, flicked the light switch off, and left the room.

Ezra went to bed content with one thing: to the best of his ability he was a good father. He wanted to be better, but he already knew he was far better than his own had been. His son would never lay alone in a bed desperate to talk, to ask, to explain himself as he had done. But the spark of self-righteousness he was entertaining died when he heard himself think: *It was the frustration with spoken communication that made me a writer.* Perhaps his father had been the way he was so Ezra could become the man he was.

His tired mind was entertaining that thought as he and Anne lay in bed.

"Dylan wants to be big inside," he said.

"What?"

"That's what he just told me. He wants to be a big person on the inside."

Anne's head relaxed on the pillow and a slow smile spread across her lips. It was Ezra's purpose to send her to sleep with a blessing, with happy thoughts of her son embracing her like warm arms. She was asleep in minutes.

When Ezra finally slept, exhaustion pushed him to the world of dreams:

He was a small boy, maybe ten, and the air was filled with dust, branding smoke, and the bawling of cattle. He was inside the wire pens on Dead Man. Outside the corral the pickups loaded with beer coolers and containers of food were backed up to the fence, and in the background sat old stock trucks with rickety stock racks and saddle horses tied to their railings. His father, Johnny Riley, stood over a large fire, the heat from the flames coaxing rivulets of sweat from his brow. He stood with his hands on his hips, a man in charge, watching the rest of the crew, waiting for the irons to heat. Uncle Willis was tightening the cinch on his rope horse and the old bay gulped air. His other uncles, Solomon, Rufus, Sam, Archie, and Joe, were filling vaccine guns, holding tally books, or pairing off in calf-wrestling teams. Rick Benjamin's father was joking with Diane. Austin and Dallas were stealing beers from the cooler while Pearl's head was turned. Charley Arbuckle stepped from the shadows of a gatepost, his lean gnarled body as weathered as a crooked cedar post, his big Stetson pulled down hard on his head, and his pants tucked into the stove tops of expensive handmade boots. He held a razor-sharp Case knife in his hand as he approached and thumped Ezra on the chest with a bony finger. "You're too skinny and weak to wrestle calves," he snarled. "Guess you have to carry the nut bucket for me." He thrust a coffee can half filled with water at Ezra. Charley turned and walked to the first calf stretched out on the ground. A red hot iron burned the hide to a crisp buckskin color and blue smoke rose in the air and hung there like a canopy. Charlie bent down on rickety knees, grabbed the calf's scrotum with his left hand and pulled it tight, then sliced the tip off with the silver-bladed knife. The sun glistened off the blade's polished edge. Charlie put the knife handle in his mouth and used both hands to pull the testicles out one at a time stretching thin white tendons like rubber bands before laying the knife edge to them. He plunked the detached testicles into the boy's coffee can and the water splashed in Ezra's face. The boy looked around him. Diane, Dallas, and Austin were wrestling calves, doing men's work, but Ezra was following old Charley like a pup behind a mean old dog, clinging to his tail like a shadow. One of his uncles shouted something at him. Something sarcastic and cruel that embedded in his little chest like an arrow. The sound of men laughing rang in his hear. His father just looked at him with a vague, helpless smile on his face and the laughter grew louder. They called him a sissy. The words did not hurt him, he had heard them all before. He was stung by only one thought: Why didn't his father protect him? Why did he allow him to be thrown to the wolves?

The laughing grew louder and rang in his ears. Then his uncles became the Las Vegas men, old Charley was Jubal, and the man standing at the branding fire with his hands on his hips was Tom Jablonski. "This is silly," Ezra heard himself say. "This is just a dream." But the laughter continued ringing and he looked to the horses for solace. They were pulling and straining against bit and bridle, their eyes white with fear, their mouths emitting a terrible high-pitched cry that rang in his ears and rang in his cars . . . *along with the laughter ringing in his ears.*

No, it was the phone ringing! Ezra rolled from the bed, leaving a trace of branding smoke clinging to the blankets and the laughter of the men curled in the rustling of bedsheets. He stumbled in the dark to the phone in the living room.

"Hello?" he said. He heard the line click on the other end and heard the bedsheets rustle again. Anne had been awakened. He felt violated by a weak bully, someone afraid to say what he had to say.

The phone rang again.

Ezra picked it up quickly. "Knock it off, wise guy," he said loudly into the receiver.

"Whoa," a voice said. "Merry Christmas! Are you an unhappy camper or what?"

"Rick? Rick Benjamin?" Ezra relaxed and took a seat in his reclining chair.

"You got it, Ez, and a Happy New Year, too."

Ezra's voice mellowed. "What's going on, Rick? Have you forgotten how to read a calendar? Your Christmas call is three months away."

"Hey, we don't have any seasons down here," said his former neighbor and riding partner. "It could be Christmas for as much as I know. What's going on in Yellow Rock?"

"Quite a bit, actually."

"That's what I'm hearing," Rick said.

"What have you heard?"

"I heard you took the deep six out at The Fort."

"It appears that way," Ezra said. It was soothing to hear Rick's friendly voice. He propped the footrest up on the La-Z-Boy.

"No more government bennies for you," Rick teased.

"Oh, and those benefits were wonderful," Ezra said. "All the red tape we could eat. What else are you hearing?"

"Oh, I'm told you are in tight with some flashy preacher."

"The rumors must be flying at The Buffalo Bar. What's your great source for all of this?"

"The wife's brother is in Yellow Rock, passing through from Rapid City. He finds The Buffalo a most hospitable place."

"So you know all the news," Ezra said.

"The rumor is you are leaving the ranch and going to Africa as a missionary."

"I leave next week," Ezra joked. "As soon as I get the sea legs installed on my horses."

"Is old Gusto still alive?" Rick asked.

"Yeah, so far."

"Guess you ain't leavin' the ranch, then. That old horse owns it, doesn't he?"

"I wish he did. So what's with the call, Rick? It's not like you to make more than one phone call a year. Are you getting more generous in your old age?"

"Just thought I better check on you. Lots of stories going around about you getting fired and getting in thick with this preacher and Austin being released from prison."

"What have you heard about Austin?" Ezra asked.

"Not much. He seems to be unusually quiet."

"The reason I barked at you when I answered the phone is that we have been getting some annoying calls. I think Austin might be behind them."

"Austin? Naw, I doubt it," Rick said. "He might send you a letter bomb or take a shot at you from half a mile away, but phone calls sound a little tame for an ex-con."

"Then it must have been you," Ezra joked.

"Not me. But I don't think Austin is the one to worry about if you think there's trouble in the wind."

"Oh, and from your vantage point in Houston, Texas, where do you think the wind is blowing from?"

"Many directions," Rick laughed. "Could be Lacey. Who knows, it could be your preacher friend calling you for money then chickening out. But if you get around to stirring pots be careful with Wilson's."

"Why should I? He's the source of many of my frustrations."

"The word is he's got Vegas connections, Ez. That's where his money is coming from."

"I think I've met them." He related the story about the antelope. He talked as quietly as he could, hoping Anne wouldn't hear.

"My brother-in-law mentioned those guys. They were in The Buffalo the other night. You kicked the wrong dogs, Ez. You should have just rode away and pretended you never saw a thing."

"Is that what you would have done?"

"Probably not," Rick laughed. "But it's what you should have done. There's already stories going around about those two."

"Like what?"

"The older guy owns a casino in Vegas. He's Mafia all the way to his hairline. The buckaroo is his bodyguard. The talk is he's a hit man."

"He looks like the type that would floss your teeth with an ice pick," Ezra said.

"Don't mess with them, Ez. I don't think either them or Austin have anything to do with the phone calls. That's probably just some silly girl calling Dylan. The older guy is Wilson's money line, he will probably be in your neighborhood every once in a while. You might want to get used to it. Don't do anything rash."

"You mean like unloading heifers in a dress store?"

"Let's not talk about that," Rick said. "No one down here knows I was in on that and I want to keep it that way."

"Don't worry, I'm not going to send the Mob after you."

"Be careful up there, Ez."

"Thanks, Rick. I appreciate the call. Say hello to Linda and the girls for me."

"Yeah, the same to Anne and Dylan."

"Well, until we meet on a high divide . . . "

"Adios, compadre." Ezra hung up and sat in the chair. He wasn't too worried about the Vegas men. Small towns had a way of spreading and inflating rumors, and if he needed leverage the chunk of hide and roll of film was safely stored away in his bunkhouse. A hit man and a casino owner. Ezra smiled. The two were probably just two-bit faro dealers.

Anne came out from the bedroom. "Ezra, what were you telling Rick about an antelope?"

"It's nothing," he said. "I just caught a couple guys trespassing."

"Then come to bed," she said and reached down and took his hand.

CHAPTER TWENTY-TWO

Ezra tossed restlessly until about 2 A.M., but then he awakened. He then tiptoed to the kitchen and took two muscle relaxants for his lower back spasms. When he awakened later, the bedroom door was closed. He was alone in bed, and shafts of sunlight were streaming through the bedroom window. The clock read 7:58. Ezra had slept in for the first time in years. Anne and Dylan had left for work and school.

He got up, showered, and ate a bowl of cereal. When he stepped outside, Shiloh nickered from the corral—Ezra had kept him in because of the Vegas hunters—and Cheyenne and Gusto whinnied from the creek pasture. He was late letting them in for grain and they wanted him to know it.

He heard Blondie bark as he poured grain in the horse troughs and assumed it was Jubal. He was wrong, Sheriff Bill Butler walked into the corral.

"Morning, Ezra," he said. His lean frame fit well in his light brown uniform. A thick leather belt encircled his waist with a black holster holding a Glock 9mm pistol.

"Morning, sheriff, what brings you out this way?" Ezra assumed it had to do with the antelope hunters, perhaps they had fabricated charges against him.

"Is there someplace we can talk?" Butler asked.

"We can go in the house, or if you want, we can sit on my bunkhouse steps."

"The steps are fine." Butler said. Long creases that looked like cat scratches lined his tanned face from his eyes to his jaw when he smiled.

Ezra put the grain buckets away and led the sheriff to the bunkhouse steps. They sat with their backs against large, twisted cedar posts decorated with deer skulls sun-bleached to the color of milk. The antler tines were long, smooth, and curved and reminded Butler of a Georgia O'Keefe art exhibit he had seen once in Santa Fe.

"Shorty Wilson called me this morning," Butler said. The morning sun filtering through the cottonwoods cast dancing shadows on his face and the sunlight lit his freshly shaven cheeks with a pink innocence.

"I suppose it's about that antelope," Ezra said wearily, still groggy from the relaxants.

Butler smiled. "You confess too quickly, Ezra. I don't know anything about an antelope."

Ezra scowled. "Then what's this about?"

"Wilson is accusing you of moving his cattle in on his CRP to get him in trouble with the Soil Conservation Service."

Ezra grunted sharply once. "That's baloney. I saw Austin moving cattle out of the CRP yesterday. My guess is he moves them in at night and takes them out again about dawn."

Butler tipped his hat back. His brow rippled with thought lines and his jaw joints popped before he spoke. "Wilson admits Austin has been taking them out the last couple mornings, but he says they have nothing to do with putting them in. He says they found the gate tossed back like someone had opened it."

"Cattle could have torn the gate down and drug it back when they came through."

"That's true."

"So you want to know where I was last night?"

"I figure you'll tell me."

"I was in church until nine. Went to bed at ten. Phone rang about ten-thirty, and I talked to Rick Benjamin until eleven. Then I went back to bed. I took a couple pills for my bad hip and slept in until almost eight."

Butler stared across the graveled yard at the white house where the old blonde dog was already seeking shade. "I knew your dad for many years," he said. "About as honest a guy that ever lived. But, he wouldn't have been above putting a sour neighbor's cattle in on his own CRP if he thought it was just and fair. But he would have admitted it if he was asked."

"I would, too," Ezra said. "And to tell you the truth, I thought about it. We have Wilson cattle in on us all the time, and he does nothing to keep the fences up or to control the weeds in his CRP. If he got in serious trouble with the government, it wouldn't break my heart. But I haven't been doing any riding at night."

"We're talking a huge fine if ASCS pushes it. Wilson is apt to get a little feisty if it comes to that."

"Let him. He can't prove I did something I didn't do. I did have a horse in the corral last night, but he was in there for his own protection."

"It's possible you are being framed," the sheriff said. "Got any idea who would want to do a thing like that?"

"Several. They all hang their hats on the Wilson place. There's Shorty himself. Mind you, I am not saying I did or did not turn those heifers into his store a few years back, but he's convinced I did. Then there's Austin Arbuckle. If you remember, you are the one who warned me about him. Then there's those two Vegas goons."

Butler reached over, plucked a dry stem of wheatgrass, and chewed on the end. "Cletus Pratt and Bernie Windsor?"

"I don't know their names," Ezra said. "But I caught them trespassing on our place yesterday."

"I hope you didn't stir any trouble with them."

"Just a little for flavoring."

"Pratt's a low-rent hood and delivery boy for guys like Windsor. He breaks fingers, makes the deliveries in dope deals, and has aspirations of being a real thug someday."

"And Windsor?"

"Owns a share in a Vegas casino and a car rental company. A Teflon hood. Nobody can get anything to stick to him, but he's plenty dirty."

"How come you know so much about these two?" Ezra asked.

"The parole officer saw them downtown with Arbuckle and ran a check on the plates. Pratt has a long list of arrests but no convictions. There's nothing on Windsor."

"Well, I don't know why they would want to frame me," Ezra said. "They're just taking the risk of getting Wilson in trouble. Same with Austin."

"It may be like you say, Wilson may have had Arbuckle putting them in there at night and someone else saw the cattle and turned him in. It's happened before. Wilson was turned in twice this spring."

Ezra yawned. He knew he should be more concerned but the warming sun was coaxing him to sleep like an overfed cat stretched out in the crook of a tree limb.

Butler noticed the fatigue. He could be sleepy, he knew, from having ridden all night. But guilty people seldom seemed so relaxed unless they were uncommonly arrogant. He didn't take Ezra for that. "Anything new about your job at The Fort?" he asked.

Ezra leaned back to stretch his legs. "Everything's on hold until the station director gets back. Then a union rep will come down from Helena for a hearing."

"You'll get the job back," Butler said. "That is if you want it." Two young magpies sailed in on glistening wings, settled near the dog dish, and hopped toward it with their necks pivoting and eyes shining like black diamonds. They each took one nugget of dry dog food and flew to a dead cottonwood where they cackled congratulations to one another. Blondie was now stretched out on her side sound asleep. Her left leg twitched.

"Your dog is dreaming," Butler said.

"That's all she can do anymore."

Butler gestured toward the corral at the silver-and-blue horse trailer. "I take it your preacher friend is still around," he said.

"Yeah. He'll be around for a few more days. Do you want to talk to him?"

"Oh, it's not important. How much do you suppose a trailer like that costs?"

"I don't know," Ezra said, folding his arms across his chest. "Twelve thousand maybe."

"I sure would like to have a trailer like that for my elk hunts."

They watched the magpies return one more time then Ezra said sleepily: "I give you my word, sheriff. I had nothing to do with turning Wilson's cows in on the CRP."

"Your word is good with me," Butler said, and he unhinged his long frame, stood, and stretched. "Mercy, the old joints could use some oiling." As he walked to his pickup, his back to Ezra, he raised one hand, more as a gesture of peace than to say good-bye.

Ezra leaned against the post for another twenty minutes floating in the rummy, chemical drowsiness. Finally he forced himself up, walked to the garage and came out dragging a posthole digger, tamping bar, and shovel. He decided to sweat the drugs out of his system by setting two big posts in the corral. The first half hour was drudgery but once his muscles warmed up and the sweat started flowing he enjoyed the workout—and the focus on the digging kept his mind off Shorty Wilson's accusations. By 11:30 he had both posts set and came in the house for a quick lunch. As always, he checked his answering machine. There were two messages. The first was from Jubal:

"Hey, brother. Let's get together for coffee today. This morning or this afternoon. Just leave a message here at the motel."

The second was a surprise. It was Jablonski:

"Ezra? This is Pastor Tom. It's 10:05 Thursday morning. Can I meet you for lunch today? Please give me a call."

Ezra dialed the motel. Jubal wasn't in so Ezra left a message for him to be at The Cattleman's at two. Then he called Pastor Tom's home. Darlene said Tom would meet him at McDonald's in half an hour. Could he make it? Ezra said he could. The pastor had never asked him to lunch before. He took a quick shower and drove to town.

McDonald's at noon was filled with high school students on break, and Ezra had to look through the laughing, teasing, smiling faces of youth and a forest of letterman's jackets before he found Pastor Tom in the back at a small plastic table.

"Ezra, sit down," Tom invited, gesturing to a bright red plastic chair. "How about a Big Mac? I have a weakness for the things."

"That's fine," Ezra said, wondering why anyone would choose McDonald's for a meeting site. Jablonski went to the counter and returned moments later with three Big Macs and two drinks.

"I always eat two," Jablonski said "Should I have ordered you another one?"

"No. One's enough."

"Well, let's bless it." Jablonski lowered his balding head and Ezra stared at it while he prayed. He couldn't help but feel self-conscious sitting at a table smaller than a tree stump blessing three Big Macs with a crowd of giggling teenagers around him. After a short prayer Tom unwrapped his first hamburger.

"So," the pastor said tentatively. "How do you think this situation with Jubal Lee is going to end?"

The question stopped Ezra just before his first bite. "How's it going to end? What do you mean?"

Jablonski tried to chew discreetly while he talked. "He has the people worked up now, but what do you think will happen when he leaves?"

"I don't know," Ezra said.

"He's been offered the pastorate, do you think he will take it?"

Ezra was surprised at the pastor's knowledge of the situation and his candor in expressing it.

Jablonski noticed his surprise. "I can read the Betty Lou Barbers of the world like a book," he explained. "A bad book, I might add. I know she has already tried to talk Walker into staying."

"What do you think Jubal should do?" Ezra asked, then he sipped slowly from his drink, awaiting Tom's reaction.

"I don't know," Jablonski said impartially. "That's up to him."

"Is it? It's your job we're talking about. How do you want it to turn out?"

Jablonski wiped his chin with a paper napkin and studied Ezra curiously. "It has nothing to do with what I want. I don't have a chance of being reelected," he said. "You know that."

"Do I? I think that's up to you, too."

Jablonski started on his second burger. "No, it's up to the voting membership. I couldn't get elected dogcatcher right now. No, no, I won't be around. But you will be, won't you? Or does Walker have other plans?"

"He's mentioned a thing or two," Ezra said cautiously.

"I thought so," Tom said. "That's why I want to give you this." He reached into his shirt pocket and pulled out a slip of paper.

"What's this?" Ezra asked.

"The phone number for Franklin Walker, Jubal's father. It took some doing but I tracked him down."

"Have you called him?"

"No. I thought about it. But I decided it wouldn't make any difference for me to call him."

"Then why did you bother to find his number?"

Jablonski leveled his gaze across the top of his half-eaten second Big Mac. "I just thought you might want it," he said.

"Has there been some kind of trouble?' Ezra asked.

Jablonski finished his burger and wadded the wrappers into a ball. "I got three phone calls yesterday from other pastors in town. It seems Betty Lou put together a ladies' tea Tuesday afternoon for the Yellow Rock Christian Women's Club. Walker was the guest speaker. At the end he prayed for them individually and half a dozen hit the floor. These are mostly good Baptist and Evangelical Free types. And a couple Lutherans. Only one or two charismatics in the bunch and they didn't drop. The word got back to their pastors, and those pastors are not very happy."

"I didn't know anything about that," Ezra said. "But, remember, Pastor, you are not charismatic or Pentecostal either, and neither is our church though Pastor Stephens was leaning that way before he left. We're not a bunch of holy rollers, yet we have allowed Jubal to minister freely. He probably feels he has a green light for the town."

"If he has operated without proper restraint then that is my fault," Tom continued. "Me and the board. And good ol' Betty Lou."

"The town will survive one Christian women's uprising," Ezra said.

"That was his second meeting," Tom said. "The first one was Monday afternoon with another group of women. Same sort of stuff."

"You don't think much of Jubal, do you?"

"I respect his abilities. I am thankful for his ministry. In my heart I believe I honestly want the best for him."

"But do you trust him?" Ezra asked.

Jablonski looked around as if wondering who might be listening, then wiped his mouth with a napkin. "I don't know," he said quietly. "The change in Darlene is the answer to a thousand prayers. I owe Jubal Lee Walker a debt. It has always amazed me how the Lord will honor boldness. Myself, I am not a particularly brave man. I like things structured, predictable. Walker will run right out on a limb and bounce on it with all his weight. It says something about faith. I guess."

"Until gravity intervenes."

"Gravity always does." Jablonski looked at his watch as if he had someplace important to be but didn't know where it was. "Let me tell you a story," he said. "Back in school I was an offensive lineman, a grunt that punched holes for heroes to run through. We had one little running back, a fireplug of a Cajun we called Bad Puppy. Best running back I ever saw. He was totally fearless and would have played in the NFL except he had a serious drinking problem. When he got drunk he picked fights with the biggest guys in the bars. He ate glass. He was crazy. He'd sober up with a mouthful of stitches and no memory of anything. He felt bad about it, but let him near a bar and he was in orbit all over again."

"And you think Jubal Lee is a spiritual Bad Puppy?"

Jablonski thought for a long moment. He was not going to make rash judgments. Finally he motioned at the piece of paper laying on the table near Ezra's hand. "Keep the phone number," he said.

Ezra folded the note and put it in the left front pocket of his western shirt. It lay heavily over his heart. His internal gyroscope told him everything was escalating. What he did not know was whether things were spinning out of control. "So how do you think things will end?" he asked the pastor.

Jablonski's words were firm and decisive, like water running off the high divides of the badlands. Good, flat words. Black and white. Right and wrong. "I will be overwhelmingly voted out at the business meeting. The people will vote Walker in. He will be a solid preacher for a couple months then he will begin traveling, fulfilling other commitments. The church will get mad but he will explain that traveling is his call, that he is a man with a large harvest field. He will ask the church to allow you to preach on the Sundays and Wednesdays when he is gone."

"I'm not a pastor," Ezra said.

"No, you're definitely not a pastor. But you are a communicator. You will do fine for the first few weeks. You might even be better than Jubal Lee Walker. If that happens, watch out."

"So you think it is a foregone conclusion that you are leaving?" Ezra asked.

"It's carved in stone," Jablonski said. "It might as well be the eleventh commandment." He looked out the window at the strip of pavement bordered by fast-food restaurants and motels that led to an entrance ramp to the eastbound lane of the Interstate. In his mind, he was already gone.

"If you leave, what will you do?"

"I am leaving the pastorate," Jablonski said.

"You're quitting?"

"That's right. I'm a relic, Ezra. My ministry days are over. If the modern church is going to place experience and emotion over scholarship, then it is time for me to find a new profession."

"Like what?"

"I don't know. I'm too old for my father's trade—stone masonry and concrete work. I am thinking about teaching. Maybe history."

"Why history?" Ezra asked.

"Because I'm history," Jablonski said.

"No," Ezra said adamantly. "Your ministry is not history. You simply need a change of attitude."

"Hmmm. Would you minister to the minister?" There was a subtle challenge in Jablonski's voice.

"I would if he would let me," Ezra said.

Jablonski stared out the window. A large diesel truck hauling a trailer load of concrete blocks on pallets chugged by, its smokestack belching blue clouds as the driver shifted gears and crawled up the Interstate entrance ramp. The truck turned and gained speed as it headed east.

Anne leaned against the tree on the grounds of the nursing home watching the contrail of a jet fade into a bleached September sky. It was an unusually warm day for the season, and the weatherman was predicting thunderstorms for the evening.

Sally Johnson walked from the employees' lounge with a cigarette in one hand and a Styrofoam cup filled with coffee in the other. She lowered herself athletically to the grass. "So," she said to Anne, "are you going to ask me how I liked church last night?"

"How did you?" Anne said.

"I liked that preacher's wife, Donna May, is that her name?"

"Darlene."

"Whatever." She exhaled a cloud of smoke that Anne prayed would drift the other way. "Anyway, I like her. She's a good head who has paid a terrible price."

"Yes, she has," Anne said. "And what did you think of Jubal Lee Walker."

Sally held up her Styrofoam cup. "See this?" she said. "My second husband and I honeymooned on Martha's Vineyard. We rented a car, packed a lunch, and stopped at a little store and bought the most expensive bottle of wine they had. We hiked up a beach for an hour to a secluded cove. No one but us and the gulls. I laid a tablecloth out on the sand and we ate cold fried chicken and potato salad. Then we opened the bottle of wine. Only thing was, we had no glasses, just a couple of used Styrofoam cups the salad had come in. I rinsed them out the best I could but that three hundred dollar wine still tasted like potato salad." She stopped abruptly as if the point was obvious and stared at the sky and smoked.

"What is the moral to your story?" Anne asked.

Sally never looked down. Her eyes were riveted on a blueness that was paling to white. "Simple," she said. "It doesn't make any difference how good the wine is if the cup is dirty."

The Cattleman's Cafe was quiet when Ezra walked in. He found Jubal sitting in a back booth with a pot of coffee on the table.

"Hey, brother, how's it going?" Jubal chirped. He looked tired and wired. His eyes were wide, as if propped open with toothpicks, and the muscles around them twitched nervously. The waitress called to them from the counter but Ezra politely waved her off.

Neither said anything for a moment. Finally Jubal commented: "You look a little tired, Ezra."

"Have you looked in a mirror?" Ezra asked.

"It's the caffeine, brother. People are always inviting me out for coffee, or they invite me to their house and serve coffee. I swear, you need a cast-iron gut to be a minister."

"Pretty powerful service last night," Ezra said.

"Yeah, the Lord is good, brother," Jubal said, lapping up the compliment like a puppy at a milk bowl.

Ezra measured his words. "Pastor Tom appreciates your word for his wife."

"That's good," Jubal said, then he thought for a moment. "You've seen him recently?" he asked.

"I just had lunch with him," Ezra said.

"Oh, and how is he doing?" he asked defensively.

"He's a little concerned about a couple of meetings you held earlier this week. He's gotten a few irate calls from the ministers of other churches."

"The hirelings always yelp when someone else feeds their sheep," Jubal said.

"Well, it's no big deal. Pastor Tom doesn't expect to be around much longer."

"Is that right?"

"That's what he says. What do you think, Jubal? Has the Lord shown you if Pastor Tom is going to be voted out?"

"I don't believe in voting, brother, you know that. If your pastor is meant to go, he will know."

"Destiny?"

"God's will."

"But you don't know the plan?"

"No, of course not. Why all the questions about it?"

"I'm just curious about your opinion," Ezra said. "So what's going on? You wanted to see me about something?"

"I want to know if you are coming with me."

"Where?"

"You know, in the ministry. Come with me for a week. We will go to Sheridan, Jackson Hole, and Cody. It will give you a taste for the life."

"I don't know," Ezra said. "Life is plenty hectic around here. I will probably have a hearing next week about my job."

"So? You don't like that job anyway, brother."

"There's other things."

"Like what?"

"Well, first of all you stirred things up with my uncle—"

"Man, I was just trying to help you out," Jubal snapped. His eyebrows were raised in a gesture of innocence.

"No problem," Ezra said. "Actually, I would like to get away from Solomon for a week."

"Then let's go."

"There's other things. We've been getting some odd phone calls. Someone calling in the middle of the night, then hanging up."

"Just some prankster."

"Yeah, probably, but I had a little run-in with those Vegas boys."

"You what?" Jubal paled at the mention of them, and his puppy eyes became dark and hard.

Ezra let him simmer for a second before explaining. "They killed that trophy antelope buck with a rifle on Riley land. Then they stuck an arrow in the wound for the photo. I caught them."

Jubal blew softly on his coffee. "You should have just let things drop, man. Why can't you let things drop?"

"It was a matter of principle."

Jubal stared down at the table. His skin was the almost colorless shade of buckskin with the grainy texture of shoe leather. "Those boys don't have principles," he said quietly.

"I don't think they are going to bother me," Ezra said. "I didn't turn them in but they know I can anytime I want to."

"I think you should get out of town for a week," Jubal said. "Bring Anne and Dylan with you if you have to."

"That's just part of it," Ezra continued. "I had a visit from the sheriff this morning. It seems Shorty Wilson is blaming me for putting his cattle in on his CRP."

"You're getting set up, man. You have been messing with the wrong crowd. You need to let things cool down for a while."

"Why would the Vegas boys take a chance of getting Shorty in serious trouble?"

"Who knows?" Jubal said. "They don't think things out. Or maybe they want him in trouble. He probably has his own debts, brother."

"In any case, I think I'd better stick around."

Jubal's voice became as flat as the tabletop. "You're planning on staying on the ranch, aren't you?"

"I don't know. Maybe."

"Why stay?" Jubal implored. "I know the ranch pulls on your heart, brother, but you are just setting yourself up for a big-time heartbreak. Your sisters are going to give you grief, Solomon isn't going to help, and in the end the place will be owned by lawyers and the government."

"That could happen."

"It's likely to happen. Plus the town is dead spiritually. Yellow Rock is the driest place I have ever been in. We can find you a little place with some acreage outside Sheridan. You can bring your horses. We will minister as a team with Sheridan as the hub. Gillette, Rapid City, Billings, they are all just a quick drive away."

Ezra pushed his hat back and leaned into the corner of the booth. "So the point of all this is you think that I need to go with you to develop my spiritual leadership?"

"That's right. Don't forget the word I gave you. *Leaving the land.*"

"Well, if you are seeing so much," Ezra said, "tell me who is turning the cattle in on Wilson's CRP and who is calling our house in the middle of the night."

"I don't know," Jubal said. "I only see what the Lord wants to show me."

Ezra stared at him thoughtfully.

"You have your own suspicions, don't you?" Jubal asked.

"I do."

"This might be touchy ground," Jubal said, "but has Anne shared her story with you?"

Ezra stiffened and sat up. "What story?"

"About Austin."

"What about Austin? You mean seeing him in church?"

"No. She told me this happened a long time ago. He stopped by one winter day while the two of you were living in the trailer house."

"What happened?" There was an angry urgency is Ezra's voice.

"Nothing, except some mind games on Austin's part. He had her pretty rattled, though."

"She never told me."

"She knew what you would do, Ezra. She knew you would go hunting him, and there would be some sort of trouble."

Ezra stared down at the flat, brown, polished tabletop. Its surface seemed to slide forward into the future. "There just may be," he said. He rose from the booth.

"Where are you going?" Jubal asked.

"Home."

"No, you're not. You're going to look for Austin. Doggone it, I'm sorry, Ezra. I never should have said anything."

Ezra turned to leave. Jubal reached out and grabbed him by the arm. "Let it drop," he said. "It's history and nothing happened."

"Something is happening now," Ezra said. "Somebody is calling our house in the middle of the night and someone is trying to get me in trouble with the law."

"Don't do it, man. Just chill."

Ezra pulled away from his grasp and raised both hands with the palms up and fingers spread. "Hey, it's cool," he said. "I'll see you in church tonight."

Ezra left the cafe propelled by his own storm. People noted his urgency and wondered. Jubal watched him go and was tempted to follow. But he didn't and considered himself wise for resisting the temptation.

zra's knuckles whitened as he grasped the steering wheel and drove from The Cattleman's Cafe. His fury was as focused as a train racing downhill through a tunnel. He remembered there was a horse sale at the stockyards. Before going to prison, Austin Arbuckle had worked at the auction, making five dollars a head riding saddle horses through the sales ring. *Austin needs money more than ever,* Ezra thought.

In the recesses of his mind a small voice warned him to calm down and reason with himself. It was a feeble voice, like a coyote pup whimpering in the badlands, but it was drowned out by the Irish temper that boiled in his bloodstream, crying with the fury of a lynch mob for justice and masculine satisfaction.

A mile from the stockyards, near the entrance of the Pioneer Memorial Museum, Ezra saw the flashing lights of a patrol car in his mirror. He angrily pulled over, expecting a city policeman, a lecture, and a traffic citation, but it was Sheriff Butler who approached his pickup. Ezra stayed in his truck, gripping the steering wheel, and quivering with unbridled emotion.

"Afternoon, Ezra," Butler said. "Driving a little fast aren't we?"

"Yeah," Ezra confessed. "I'm trying to get to the stockyards before the horse sale is over." His speech was quick and choppy.

"No sense killing yourself on the way," Butler said. "Are you in the market for a new horse?"

"I'm always in the market for a good horse."

Butler patted the side of Ezra's door. "Well, I'll let you continue on your way," he said. "But slow down."

"Thanks, sheriff."

"Oh, Ezra," Butler said. "One more thing." He reached inside his jacket and pulled out a 5-by-7-inch manila envelope. "There's something here I want you to look at."

Ezra took the envelope, muttered another thank you, but continued staring ahead. Butler appraised him for a moment, deciding whether to question him further or to let him go and see how things turned out. One thing he knew, Ezra was not racing to the stockyards to buy a horse. He would let things go, he decided, and the sheriff walked back to his car.

When the patrol car turned back to town Ezra flipped the unopened envelope onto the dashboard and sped from the museum parking lot toward the sale barn. The contact with Butler had helped cool his anger, but Ezra was still determined to confront Austin.

The sale had just ended; trucks and trailers were being loaded with purchases and a steady stream of spectators filed from the parking lot. In front of the sale arena ranchers in small groups talked about the weather, cattle prices, and horseflesh. They wore clean western shirts, their best hats, and tooled leather belts with their names inscribed on the back. Their tanned faces were freshly shaven and they talked with the relaxed energy of men hungry for socialization. In the pens, professional traders haltered horses for the next auction on their circuit. They were men with quick, predatory eyes, expensive boots, and soft hands. Several had their accomplices, pretty young blonde women in tight pants, helping them lead horses subdued by the tranquilizer phenylbutazone to horse trailers with Minnesota and Wisconsin license plates.

Ezra parked near the brand inspector's office. The groups of visiting ranchers glanced at him, detecting the urgency and tension in Ezra's body.

Jim Mendenhall stepped from the auction office. Since Sam Riley's death, heavy drinking had bloated his belly and face and flushed his cheeks with the unnatural chemical glow of a polluted bloodstream. A gray felt hat with a dark sweat stain circumscribing the brim was pulled low on his head, and his spurs tinkled as he walked across the graveled parking lot to his truck.

Ezra cut him off. "Jim," he called out.

Mendenhall turned and a slow curiosity rose in his blood-stained hazel eyes. "Hey, Ezra," he said quietly.

"I'm looking for Austin," Ezra said. "Have you seen him?"

Mendenhall could feel the heat radiating from Ezra's arms and shoulders, the hardness in the eyes, and the tension in hands half-formed into fists. "You sure you wanna find him?" he drawled.

"I'm sure," Ezra said.

"He's over under the shed," Mendenhall said, nodding his large, flushed head toward the pens nearest the sale arena, the ones sheltered from the weather by six-foot plank walls, roof, and catwalk.

"Thanks," Ezra said, and he spun on his boot heels toward the pens, dogged by the curiosity of the onlooking ranchers. Mendenhall watched him go. A part of him wanted to follow for the entertainment, another part wanted to stop Ezra, or at least warn him that Austin was not alone, but the sum of his various parts could not overrule the pull of The Buffalo Bar. Mendenhall shrugged his big shoulders and got in his truck. *Fights were always disappointing anyway*, he told himself. *A lot of talk and some huffing and puffing but little action.* Not since Johnny Riley died had there been a real fighter in the country.

It was dark and cool under the shed. The lowering afternoon sun filtered in through the rafters, casting a webwork of shadows on joists, rafters, and corral poles. Pens of young horses milled nervously as Ezra walked by. They smelled his anger as a thick, foul stench and saw it illuminate the darkness and leave a trail of embers in his wake. Ezra saw Austin from fifty feet, recognizing the tapered back in the new white shirt bending over a saddle.

"Arbuckle," Ezra said as he approached.

Austin rose from the hips and pivoted around slowly. Sunlight fell on a face that seemed whiter, flatter, and colder than Ezra had remembered. He had the countenance of a snow-covered prairie with a white lacework of old scars from bull rides and bar fights etched on his pale skin. His nose had been crushed and was spread from cheekbone to cheekbone, his brows protruded like prairie dog mounds above the little dark holes that were his eyes. A glimmer of recognition lit his pupils.

"Hi, Ezra," he said.

Ezra walked into the pen and closed the gate behind him. Racks of hay lined both sides of the stall, and the cement floor was matted with straw that had been yellow and crisp that morning but was now soiled by manure and urine and tamped by hooves. Austin seemed shorter and thinner, as if prison had dried his soul and pulled it inward, collapsing his frame and muscle. "We have some things to settle, Austin," Ezra said.

Arbuckle did not say a word. His face deadened with the fatalism of a man who had been cornered in cellblocks and exercise yards. He accepted the situation with a grim apathy.

Ezra stopped at the borders of Arbuckle's undefined personal space, close enough to threaten, not so close as to force a quick, defensive action on Austin's part. Behind him he could hear boots on gravel as several cowboys, sensing the possibility of a fight, rushed to the shed wall to peer over the top plank.

Ezra glowed with an intense, malevolent confidence. "What's the game?" he asked.

"What are you talking about, Ezra?" Arbuckle asked. His voice was as flat and edged as a prison-made knife.

"The calls in the night, the cattle being turned in on the CRP and me getting the blame. That's what I'm talking about." Ezra's voice rose by a matter of degrees with each word, like a thermometer touched by a lit match.

"I never accused you of putting those cattle in," Austin said. "Wilson did."

"Don't con me, Austin. The CRP game belongs to you and Wilson. I never put those cows in there."

"Neither did we," Austin said.

Ezra took one step closer. Arbuckle did not flinch, stiffen, or back up. He stood his ground with the quiet deliberation of a man talking to his postman, reviewing the mail and weather. Sometimes one got good news in the mail, most of the time it was bad. Arbuckle's face was a road map of bad deliveries and poor decisions.

"What about the calls?" Ezra demanded. "Calls in the night and no one on the line."

A flicker of embarrassment softened Austin's eyes. "I called a couple times," he said.

"A couple times? How about six or seven times?"

"No. Twice. That's all."

"What happened in the trailer house," Ezra said. "A winter day about seven years ago? What happened then, Austin, between you and my wife?" Ezra's senses were heightening. The smells of dust, horse manure, and urine, the odor of diesel engines, the echoes of footsteps on the catwalk above him, the thoughts dancing like little lights in his opponent's eyes; everything was clearer, sharper and amplified.

Ezra saw the energy coil in Arbuckle's arms and shoulders, making each limb seem alive like a snake, then spread through the chest and into the legs. Ezra sensed the flow but did not respond to it. He had expected it earlier, had entered the pen prepared for its outburst. His stance begged Arbuckle to strike first knowing his training was precedented on self-defense, and his argument in court, if necessary, would be the same.

Austin checked himself. He saw Ezra poised to counter an attack, knew that he was provoking it, using Anne as the ultimate offense, and realized that in a clash of pride, even should he win, a return to lockup would be his reward. If there was going to be a first punch, Austin decided, he would not be the one to throw it. "The deal in the trailer," he said. "That was a long time ago. A whole different lifetime. And I'm sorry about it."

Austin's attempt at an apology fell on deaf ears. "If you mess with me or my family," Ezra said, "it will not be a game. It won't be a pushing contest or an ego trip. If you mess with my family, I will put a serious hurt on you. Do you understand?"

"I think we have a basic misunderstanding here," Austin said.

"There is no misunderstanding," Ezra said. His right hand was cocked and pulsated with eagerness as if a small and angry animal, a badger or wolverine, lived in his fist and was demanding release. His mind screamed at him to initiate the action, then he saw Austin's eyes dart to Ezra's right and heard the metallic rattle of a gate being slowly opened. He heard a voice behind him say: "Is this a private party, Arbuckle, or is it an open house?" Ezra turned to see the Vegas cowboy, Cletus Pratt, enter the pen. For an instant he thought about attacking first, sending a boot heel deep into Pratt's kidney area while his side was exposed and begging attention. But he stopped, his mind changed by a nonverbal warning, a radiance of an unspoken thought from Austin: *Don't do it!*

"It's a personal affair," Austin said as Pratt stepped closer. "Ezra and I go back a long ways. This is just a family discussion."

Pratt moved closer. His blue eyes were cool with death and a toothpick jutted cockily from his lips. He got face-to-face with Ezra. "You been dealin' the cards lately," he taunted. "Now let's play the hand."

Ezra stood firmly, holding the blonde's stare. His anger had not allowed him to see peripherally; to consider all possibilities. His spat with Austin seemed childish compared to the grim viciousness he saw in Pratt. Fighting was not a matter of pride to Cletus Pratt, it was business.

Ezra was in danger and knew it. Physically he was capable of challenging, perhaps besting Pratt, but mentally and spiritually he had left the shelter of his nature and training. He was literally in the criminal's pen, in a game where they called the shots and made the rules. Ezra's skills were dependent on honor and justice, on defending the weak and championing the outnumbered. He had made it a contest of pride and Pratt had turned it to a display of meanness. Ezra could feel his confidence waning and his skills receding. The instincts of his training had left him and would not return until the vanity was repelled and the battle was only for survival. With Pratt, he realized, they might not return in time. He could pay for the folly of his anger in an instant, with one knife blade in the side, a knee to the groin, or a head butt between the eyes, and once he was down, Pratt had the coldhearted viciousness to end it.

The Vegas cowboy reached up and pinched Ezra's cheek. Ezra smelled bourbon on his breath and saw the glaze of cocaine on his eyes.

"I wouldn't do that," Ezra said, but his voice was forced and unconvincing. Ezra had met a demon he hadn't the authority to repel. His best hope was for Pratt to remember the photos and antelope hide, but he didn't dare mention it himself. To threaten legal action would be tattling and showing a weakness that Pratt would quickly exploit. He had to somehow maintain the man's respect, which was hard when he stood gripping Ezra's cheek. Each stood waiting for action from the other.

But Austin made the move. Slowly, he reached up and pulled Pratt's hand off Ezra's face. Pratt did not resist, but he did not back off either.

Austin spoke to him criminal to criminal. "Let's cool this," he said. "Things are likely to get bad. No one here needs the attention of the law. Let's let things drop, okay?"

Pratt cursed Austin while keeping his gaze locked on Ezra. "I don't care if you get sent back to the pen," he said.

Austin stepped closer so his voice could not be heard outside the stall. "Clete," he whispered. "You might take Ezra, but you won't take him easy. Before you finish the law will be here. You got too much to lose, man. You're holdin', remember? You got a trunkful. You got one, maybe two concealed. Ezra's got the chunk of antelope hide. No way you can come out of this as the winner. You'll do time for this one, and there just ain't that much satisfaction in it."

Realization and reasoning slowly worked their way past the chemicals that fueled Cletus Pratt's dark nature. He released his grip, took one step back—his eyes on Ezra like the dual barrels of a shotgun—and raised one eyebrow. "Next time," he told Ezra. "Next time, my turf, my play." He turned and left the stall with an angry bounce and swagger in his step. As he passed, the heads of the curious cowboys peering over the top plank disappeared like pumpkins falling from a wagonbox.

Ezra slowly released a deep breath and his eyes followed Pratt down the concrete alleyway. The beast of foolish pride still growled within him. He had been surprised by Pratt, then humiliated, and now the foe had mockingly turned his back and walked away. Ezra considered calling after him, taking the battle to the alleyway and finishing matters once and for all.

Arbuckle saw Ezra's calculating stare. "Don't do it," he said.

"What?" Ezra asked.

"Whatever crazy idea you are entertaining."

Ezra turned back to Arbuckle. Austin had helped him, yet as far as he knew, if it were not for Austin the situation would never have developed. Arbuckle was still his opponent. "Our business isn't finished," he said.

"No," Austin said, shaking his head. "I don't suppose it is."

When unreleased, Ezra's anger always turned inward, where it manifested itself in cruel, self-destructive depression. The voices of pessimism chanted in his soul, the colors left the sunsets, and his life seemed a fruitless web of defeat and confusion. He would never own the land; he would never be published; he could not please God nor provide for his family. In his despair he heard the echoing taunts of Charley Arbuckle, his uncles, his sisters, and he was reduced from manhood to the basest form of adolescence. He was a tortured child staked and chained by circumstances and expectations, his eyes pecked at by crows, his flesh bit by hordes of fire ants. He was not a man. He was a boy. A boy with no protection.

As Ezra drove away from the stockyards he felt locked in a torrent of emotions. He had felt justified in confronting Austin, his fires stoked by self-righteousness, but now he felt beaten and humiliated. A hero would have whipped the two of them to the admiring applause of the onlooking cowboys; a godly man would have been an example of selfless meekness and moral courage. But he had been neither and nothing was settled. There was no accounting for the phone calls, the cattle turned into the CRP, the trophy antelope laying dead on the range. At best, his war with Austin Arbuckle had stalled. At worst, he had foolishly ventured alone into a den of snakes with no one to stand at his side. Who would watch his backside if Arbuckle and Pratt decided to settle matters far from witnesses and civil law? Rick Benjamin was gone. Jubal Lee Walker was spiritually above the battle. Uncle Sam was dead. Where was his father? Where was the last true fighting man of Yellow Rock? Johnny Riley lay in his grave, his bones eleven years cold. Ezra needed a partner, a protector, then ironically he understood that what he lacked was a shepherd. A pastor. His battle was a spiritual one—true, he had taken it to the arena of flesh—but it was still spiritual in origin. Jubal had warned him, yet, Jubal's moralizings rang hollow. The man Ezra missed was Tom Jablonski, the former offensive lineman, the protector of quarterbacks and blocker on running plays. But where was Tom: hidden in his study creating sermons no one listened to.

Ezra needed someone to talk to. His world was unraveling. In the past nine days he had lost his job, reunited with Jubal, was taken to new spiritual heights, accused of a felony, threatened by hoodlums, shamed by a nemesis, offered new opportunities that meant leaving the ranch, and had been the recipient of Solomon's ire. On top of all of it, Jubal Lee had spoken a word to him that was monstrous in its implications, and yet through his ministry to Darlene Jablonski, Jubal had proven himself capable of being a vessel of God. But was he solid enough as a person to deserve Ezra's trust? Was he a man to follow and serve? Ezra didn't know.

Ezra was certain of only one thing: he was confused.

As he drove home he flipped on the radio to battle the voices clamoring in his mind. He did not expect to hear Pastor Tom's voice and didn't recognize it at first because he had listened to his program only twice before. Tom's program was preceded by leaden, sentimental music, an early warning to most listeners hurrying home from work to quickly change stations. His messages were always the tailings of his Sunday sermons, clumps of iron ore dumped in the mine cars of anecdotes. No one listened to him, Ezra was certain of that, but the church felt compelled to sponsor the programs.

"Greetings, this is Pastor Tom Jablonski of the Yellow Rock Community Believers' Church . . . " Ezra reached to turn the radio off. He did not want to hear Tom Jablonski. He did not want to hear Jubal Lee Walker. He did not want to hear anything.

"I am speaking to you live today," Pastor Tom announced, "instead of on tape." Ezra hesitated. Pastor Tom always prepared his radio shows a week in advance.

"I would like to confess to the residents of Yellow Rock that I have been a prideful and stubborn man. Somehow I thought that my messages would be a light to the community and provide answers to deep questions. I was wrong.

"I do this radio program from the best of motives. I care about people. But I also do it for the worst reasons. I am scared of people. I am afraid of you. I want to touch you indirectly. I am insecure about meeting you on the street or in your home. I want to meet you here, on the airwaves, where I can give you the gospel, as I know it, but I cannot give you me. And you cannot reciprocate. You can turn me off—and many of you have—but you cannot talk back. I want to give you that opportunity. In the next few days I invite you to call me at 421-5949 and let me know what you think of my messages."

Ezra's jaw dropped. The unthinkable was occurring. Pastor Jablonski was asking for criticism.

"I don't know how much longer I will be in Yellow Rock," Jablonski continued. "But should I leave, I want to leave as a person, not as a faceless voice spouting platitudes."

He is saying good-bye to the town, Ezra realized.

"So call me at church or call me at home. Call me anytime you want. If you have hated my messages and found them self-righteous and boring, let me know. I want to be real with you."

The program ended. *No, Tom Jablonski had ended. It was not a tape,* Ezra reminded himself, *it was a man.* There was a minute of dead air before the radio announcer realized the format change and hastily plugged in music.

Anne was home when Ezra walked in. "Did you hear Pastor's radio program?" she asked.

Ezra nodded. "I did." His shirt was wet from nervous perspiration and smelled of the sale barn. He ripped it open, the western snaps popping like firecrackers, rolled it in a ball, and tossed it at a pile of laundry accumulating next to the washing machine.

"Ezra, what's wrong?" Anne asked.

"My life," he said angrily.

She approached him tentatively, her eyes brimming with concern but her mind flinching against an outburst. "Tell me," she said.

"You tell me," he said. "You tell me about Austin Arbuckle and an incident in the trailer house that happened seven years ago."

Her face ashened. "Jubal told you."

"Yes, Jubal told me. And you are the one always saying that I have trouble communicating."

"Ezra, if I had told you—"

"If you had told me, what? I would have gone after Austin? You're right, I would have. Better to do it then than seven years later."

"Oh, no. You went after him today, didn't you?"

"Yes. And it wasn't just about you," Ezra snapped. "Someone is turning Wilson's cows in on his CRP and blaming me. Someone is phoning this house a couple times a night and hanging up."

"Did Austin admit anything?"

"He says he called a couple times. He insists he and Wilson have nothing to do with the cows—" He stopped himself. Anne only knew about Pratt and Windsor by overhearing his conversation with Rick Benjamin. He decided not to tell her anything more.

She slumped to a chair in the utility room. "Do you want to stay home tonight?" she asked.

"I don't know what I want," Ezra said. "So far today I have had run ins with the sheriff, Pastor Tom, Jubal, and Austin. It seems like the gates to hell have been thrown open and demons have been sicced on me like a bunch of blue heelers. And I feel like someone is orchestrating it, making it happen."

"I am supposed to go to church," Anne said. "Jubal is expecting me to play the piano. But I will stay home with you if you want me to."

Ezra looked at her, looked around the room, looked at the jackets hanging on the wall, and grabbed a worn denim shirt and pulled it on. "I will be in the bunkhouse for a while," he said. "I want you to go to church whether I do or not. You need to be at the piano."

"Dylan stayed in town with a friend," Anne said. "If you decide to come, I will honk before I leave."

Ezra buttoned the shirt as he walked across the yard to his office. He walked in, flipped on a light, and sat in his chair, his eyes resting on the piles of old church bulletins that contained the notes for his book.

Leaving the land, he thought. *Leaving the land.*

CHAPTER TWENTY-FOUR

At a quarter after six Anne grabbed her Bible, got in her car, and honked her horn. A dim light shone through Ezra's office window but he did not come out. She let the car idle and entered the bunkhouse. His old Kaypro was on, its green cursor blinking like the eye of a digital cat, but Ezra was not there. She got back in her car and left for church.

Horseback on a high mesa east of the house, Ezra watched the dust billow behind Anne's car as she drove from the yard. He tickled Shiloh with spur rowels, and they slid down a gumbo hill, crossed a dry creek that cut a twisted wound through a brushy coulee, and trotted uphill to a larger flat—one that stretched in all directions farther than bullets could carry. It was a hiding spot for antelope, a dancing ground for sage grouse, and where his cows calved in the springtime. He sat alone on the flat, a small, dark spot in a sea of cured grasses, watching the slate-colored sky, wishing God would write a message for him on its blackboard surface. He saw the shadows lengthen, watched the scintillating light on cottonwood leaves that jittered in the casual evening breeze in the autumnal creek bottom below him. He thought of leaving this. He imagined his best days, the mornings spent horseback riding on newborn calves, their mothers standing by stiff-legged and big-bagged, maternal concern carved on their broad faces. He thought of evenings riding home, his muscles aching with a sweet soreness, the flying of nighthawks in the air, doe deer dancing daintily from the meadows, their fawns be-bopping after them. He thought of stepping down stiffly to open wire gates, feeling his shoulder press against cedar, watching the light rays race down barbed wire like currents of electricity. He thought of remounting, feeling his horse brace for the discomfort, his leg lifting over the cantle, his foot searching for the stirrup as a pup nuzzles for a teat. He thought of the bad things. Finding newborn calves eaten alive by coyotes, spraddled cows on their backs in washouts, their sad, brown eyes a light to be extinguished; he thought of droughts and prairie dogs, Canada Thistle and fierce winter storms. He thought of Solomon and his selfish eccentricities and his sisters and their sometimes sentimental, sometimes cruelly pragmatic mood swings.

He considered his back, stiffening with the pain of having heaved thousands of hay bales and sacks of feed. He thought of eastern legislators, California-bred environmentalists, fuzzy-hugging animal rights activists, and belligerent, demanding sportsmen. He thought of Shorty Wilson, Austin Arbuckle, and the boys from Vegas.

He looked again at the gray, slate-colored sky. What was land that it would have such a pull on a person, and what were people that they were so bound to the familiar, or so bound and determined to escape it? What was God that He seemed so invisible, so inaudible to most, so present, so relational with others?

Who was he who professed Christ but provoked confrontations? He had behaved wrongly at the stockyards, and it whittled an agony into his heart. What was his life, his call, his destiny? Did other men even concern themselves with those questions, or was he cursed with the wonderings of a poet and mystic? If he had to be a cowboy and a writer, why could he not be content to be a cowboy poet, costuming himself in the sentimental and entertaining banquet crowds with slapstick and self-aggrandizement? If he were to be religious, why could he not content himself with a simple, legalistic Christianity that placed little value on either experience or emotion? Those churches abounded, and they would all welcome him they were so starved for a masculine presence. Was he doomed forever to a hard-scrabble poverty, sweating to make ends meet while his best years trickled away like water? Would he ever be successful as a writer?

He chuckled lightly to himself and was pleased to hear his own voice. There was no demand in America for cowboy mystics.

Should one leave the land willingly, or stand and fight for it, knowing the banker, lawyer, or politician might rip it from your heart at your weakest hour, leaving you penniless and dispirited?

And what did God require of him? What did *leaving the land* mean?

He had many, many questions and stared hard at the gray slate of sky, but he was not Daniel in the court of a foreign king, and no hand materialized to write answers upon its ethereal board. It was not God's purpose to talk to him, it was God's purpose to have Ezra talk, to battle his natural independence with a gesture of submission. He dismounted, a lone cowboy silhouetted on a high, grassy ridge as the sun set in the western sky. He bent his knees to the ivory grasses and spoke aloud to his creator. Ezra apologized for his action at the stockyards, he prayed blessings upon Austin. He thanked God for Jubal Lee and Pastor Tom. He blessed his sisters and uncle. When his heart was prayed out, he stood, gripped the saddle horn with both hands, and stared at the last glow of light in the west. He was alone but not lonely; individual but not unanswerable; assertive but not arrogant. He was a horse broken to bit and bridle, the saddle marks on his shoulders caused by the rubbing of a rugged, wooden cross. By facing his greatest fears and greatest loves, by acknowledging both his weaknesses and strengths, Ezra Riley was becoming what his Lord required of him. Usable.

At 7:20 Jubal peered out from the pastor's study. There were some thirty people anxiously waiting in the pews, less than ever, but he expected this. He would explain it away with the biblical illustrations of a remnant. Jubal was not concerned with numbers. He wanted to see one person and one person only: Ezra Riley. Anne said she did not know where he was or whether he was coming. He could not wait any longer and was turning the doorknob when Betty Lou Barber rose from her pew and walked to the microphone. The sound of her throat clearing amplified through the building drawing all eyes to front and center.

"Attention, everybody, attention. I know we are late getting started but I am sure that is because Reverend Walker is in the study getting a special word for tonight's service. Now we have all been blessed by Reverend Walker's ministry. This is the fifth night that he has preached in this church and not once has he taken an offering. Now that is very generous on his part, and very rare—" she waited for a chuckle from the crowd "—but we have all been so blessed by Reverend Walker that I think it is time that we bless him in return." On cue, Armon and the other board members rose, went to the back of the church, and came forward with the offering plates.

Jubal smiled and closed the door. *Thank God for Betty Lou,* he thought. She had bought him more time, time for Ezra to arrive. Besides, he could certainly use the money.

By 7:30 Ezra had unsaddled Shiloh, tossed him a flake of hay, and was walking from the corrals to the house. The wind was stirring and a squall-line of black clouds lipped the western horizon. He entered the house, washed his hands, splashed water on his face, and stared at himself in the mirror, wondering if he would go to church or not. He might as well go, he decided, but had to change shirts again. The old denim shirt had frayed cuffs, holes in the elbows, and a sprinkle of oil stains across the front. He pulled it off and aimed it at the laundry pile where his other shirt lay on a mountain of dirty sheets, pillowcases, socks, and towels. When he saw it he remembered the piece of paper Pastor Jablonski had given him. The number scribbled on it would be undecipherable if washed. He bent down and pulled the paper out and looked at the number. He was curious to know where in Minnesota Jubal's father was living. He thumbed through the front pages of the phone book looking at the map with the area codes. Minnesota had three area codes but 517 was not one of them. The number for southern Minnesota was 507. Pastor Tom must have made a mistake. On a whim he glanced at the surrounding states and quickly noticed 517 in central Michigan. *Why not?* he thought. He punched the number Jablonski had given him.

A man answered after the third ring. Ezra recognized the silver baritone immediately though the voice had graveled with age. "Hello?" the man said as if calling out to a congregation of one.

"Pastor Walker?"

"Yes, it is, sir."

"Pastor Walker, I'm sure you don't remember me, I talked to you once seventeen years ago in a city park in Kansas."

"In Manhattan," Pastor Walker said.

Ezra was surprised. "Yes. In Manhattan, my name is—"

"Don't tell me, don't tell me," Walker said. "Let me guess. Uh, oh my, it has been a long time. No, wait. Ezra. Ezra Riley."

"Yes, that's right. How did you remember?"

Walker laughed. "I practiced for years rolling my *r's* to make them sound just right. It's quite an art, you know. After I met you that day, I fell in love with your name. Ez-rrrr-aaa, Rrrrr-iley. It made for great practice. I said your name every day for months before I decided my conscientious elocution was an exercise in vanity. What can I do for you, Mr. Riley?"

Ezra paused, not knowing what to say. "How long have you been in Michigan?" he asked.

"Two years, son. We've been here two years and seven months."

"Were you in Minnesota for a while?"

"No. Minnesota is one state I have never pastored in. Why do you ask?"

"Oh, no reason," Ezra said. "I, uh, was wanting to get a hold of your son, Jubal Lee. I heard he might be in Minnesota." It pained him to lie, but he was certain the truth would be more hurtful.

"Oh, he could be, but I doubt it. Jubal likes the West. He's somewhere where there are horses and ranches, I'm sure of that."

"You don't know where Jubal is?"

A sadness entered the man's voice. "No, I haven't heard from Jubal for almost a year now. Haven't heard from him since the divorce."

"The what?"

"The divorce."

"Yours?" Ezra asked.

The man hooted a quick laugh. "No, no. Millie and I have been married for forty-one years, God bless her. I meant Jubal's."

"Jubal's divorced?"

"I'm afraid so, it's a pity, too. Shelley is a wonderful girl and of course, those granddaughters of mine, Shannon and Sarah, they're just beautiful. I don't suppose we will get to see them much now, though."

"They are still in Colorado?" Ezra asked.

"Yes, in Trinidad. But there is some pretty bad blood between Shelley's folks and Jubal. Unfortunately it spills over on me and Millie."

"I'm sorry to hear that," Ezra said. "So you don't know where Jubal is or what he is doing?"

"Oh, I'm sure he is playing music, he might even be preaching if he found someone to license him, or maybe he doesn't care about credentials anymore."

Ezra was tiring of his own dishonesty. "Mr. Walker, ah, Reverend Walker, I mean. I just want you to know that I have thought many times of the conversation you and I had in the park long ago."

"That's good, son. Has it born any fruit?"

"I came to the Lord five years ago," Ezra said.

"That's wonderful, just wonderful. I bet you have been wanting to share that news with Jubal and didn't know how to reach him."

"Well, yes,—"

"I'm sorry I can't help you, Mr. Riley. I haven't heard a word from my son since that business about the fire."

"The fire?"

"Oh, I guess you wouldn't know, would you? It happened this past spring, just as the divorce was being finalized. Jubal and Shelley had eight horses in a barn at her father's place. The barn burned down. Every one of those horses died."

"That's terrible."

"It must have broken his heart, coming on the heels of the divorce and all, because we haven't heard from him since."

"I'm very sorry, Reverend Walker."

"Oh, now, life goes on, Ezra Riley. God is still on His throne and as long as He is I will pray for my son."

"So will I."

"Please do. Well, I must go now, Ezra Riley. It was very nice to hear from you. I prayed for you often. I had hopes for you the moment we met."

"Thank you for believing in me," Ezra said.

"I hope you find my son," the father said. "You were good for him seventeen years ago, and you would be good for him now. Good-bye, Ezra Riley."

Ezra slumped against the wall. The receiver dangled from his hand until the phone emitted a loud, obnoxious buzzing that rattled him from his thoughts.

Jubal Lee's music was forced and uninspired though still highly skilled and professional. Only Anne seemed to consciously notice the dark shadow covering the melodies and the edge in Jubal's voice, but in spite of the striving of a few, the congregation did not respond as before. Fewer people stood, fewer hands were lifted, and the music drew no one to the altar.

After five worship choruses, Jubal motioned for Anne to stop and she stepped from the piano to a pew. Pastor Tom and Darlene were in their familiar position, sitting politely as if waiting for a train or bus. There was a detached peacefulness to their countenances like prisoners who had accepted their sentences.

Jubal searched the room again for Ezra. He was not there. No matter, he decided, he would preach the word the Lord had given him whether his intended audience was present or not.

"It has been a pleasure and a privilege to be here the past five evenings," he said. "And I regretfully mention that my time in Yellow Rock will be finished tomorrow night. It has been a memorable time and I hope to return soon."

Very soon, he thought, depending on the actions of the church board.

"Please turn with me to the Gospel of Matthew." There was the rustling of pages, like the wind stirring dry leaves across bleached grasses.

"The call of the traveling evangelist is unique," Jubal said. "My life is the highway I am the fire of God. My purpose is to stir things up, to kindle and ignite. My role would be different if I were a pastor. I would be rooted, patiently determined to slowly plant, cultivate, and nurture.

"There is a special purpose for the traveling prophetic voice. I am not lost within the forest of familiarity that surrounds the hometown pastor. Please turn to the end of chapter thirteen in the book of Matthew."

He read to them verses fifty-three through fifty-eight, a description of Jesus being unable to minister in his hometown of Nazareth.

"'A prophet is not without honor except in his own country and in his own house,'" he read, quoting the words of Jesus. "Our Lord experienced the limitations placed upon him by his hometown.

"I tell you the truth," Jubal proclaimed. "If Ezra Riley, who is not able to be here with us this evening, was at this moment raising the dead on Main Street of Yellow Rock, the townspeople would not accept him or the miracle. 'Who is this man?' they would say. 'Is he not the rancher's son?'"

Anne tensed. Although it appeared innocent, she resented Jubal using Ezra as an example.

It did not bother Betty Lou Barber. She could not imagine Ezra doing miracles, but she barked a loud amen anyway like a trained seal hungry for a reward.

Jubal continued: "The book of Matthew also says, at the end of chapter ten, that he who receives a prophet in the name of a prophet shall receive a prophet's reward." He pulled the microphone from its stand, coiled the cord, and paced the edge of the dais. "Where is the reward of the prophet in the hometown? There is none. That is why the Old and New Testament prophets were a wandering bunch. They were driven from one town to another by angry people. John the Baptist was itinerant. Jesus said that the Son of Man had no place to lay His head." He paused and looked out at the people as if he were throwing a wide loop, casting a large net, ready to pull them in.

During the silence Betty Lou barked again. Her amen sounded like a cough.

"There comes a time," he said dramatically, "when the true child of God must leave his native land. He must leave it or be driven from it."

Anne's face flushed with anger. For a moment she thought of getting up and leaving, but she knew she shouldn't. She needed to stay and hear what Jubal had to say.

"There is a time," Jubal repeated, "when the man of God must leave the land." His eyes fell pointedly upon Anne.

She did not flinch. She held his gaze as a child might hold a wasp in a bottle.

Jubal returned to his pacing. "Imagine what works some of you might do if you were to leave Yellow Rock. Imagine what miracles might be wrought at your hand if you stepped out in faith, going forth two by two, and leaving behind the comforts of your home, your toys, and your neighbors."

He was unusually dapper tonight, Anne realized. His attire the past couple evenings had been more casual, his mood more friendly and relaxed. This night he wore a western suit she had not seen before, black with small sequins embroidered above the yokes. It gave him a stiff, formal bearing.

"If you feel that you cannot leave your native land literally," Jubal continued, "then you must do so symbolically. You must wash the dust of provincialism from your feet. You must break away from the mind-set, the limitations, the prejudices, and the familiarities of the small town. You must be willing to die to self and be a fool for Christ.

"This very moment, all across the town of Yellow Rock, men and women laugh at religion; they rebel against the commandments of God like spoiled children; they mock the Almighty as if He were but an old man, tottering on His last legs. Can the hometown Christian be a witness to the pagans? Or does it take the boldness of a stranger to stand and proclaim the truth?"

A hush fell on the sanctuary. Even Anne, who had felt trespassed upon and manipulated, sensed the conviction of his words. She resented Jubal for his pointed remarks at Ezra, but she could not deny there was a semblance of truth in his message.

"I am a wanderer," he concluded. "I am a man of no reputation. I am jeered and laughed at. But I am free. I am a dead man who strives only to die further."

Anne looked over at Tom and Darlene. She could not read them. They sat solidly, like statues, or people frozen in time. They were either deep in thought or merely spacing out. Anne did not know which it was. She looked at the people around her. They, too, were passive and unmoved. Jubal's challenge was beyond them. It floated over their heads like a child's balloon. *What would Ezra have thought?* she wondered.

"The final thought I would leave you with is this," Jubal said. "If you are rewarded for receiving a prophet, are you punished for not receiving one? If you are rewarded for receiving a righteous man, are you punished for ignoring a righteous man? If it is spoken unto you by a prophet, as it was voiced by Abraham to Sodom, to leave the native city, will you leave the land? Or will you be as Lot's wife and turn to look back?"

He put the microphone back in the stand, walked to a bank of switches on the far wall, and turned off all of the lights except for the one that illuminated the large wooden cross at the front of the church behind the baptismal. The people sat for several minutes looking at the cross, the symbol of suffering and love, the intersection of humanity and divinity, wondering if Jubal Lee would come back to the dais. They felt helpless without an official closure of the service. After fifteen minutes Pastor Tom walked over and turned on the lights. Jubal Lee was nowhere to be seen.

At 9:20 the phone rang at the Riley ranch. Ezra rose from the kitchen table where he had been reading his Bible and answered it. There was no one on the other end. He placed the receiver back in its cradle and stared out the living room window at a night darker than the depths of a coal mine. Sheet lightning flashed in the sky. Wind, cured grass, and a dry electrical storm. It was a night for fires. In the blackness the highway did not exist without headlights to trace its route and there were no headlights. Anne would be home soon, he knew. Dylan was staying overnight in town. The phone rang again and a slight smile played on his lips. He picked it up, expecting no one. No one was there. He put it down again. He looked straight ahead into the window and could see his own dim reflection. He saw the tingle of excitement that lit his face when he remembered the envelope the sheriff had given him. In his anger and confusion he had forgotten all about it.

Ezra jogged from the house to his pickup. The wind was cool with a trace of moisture riding its back. He felt along the dashboard until he found the crisp stiffness of the envelope and jogged back to the house.

He opened it beneath the light in the kitchen. It was a single photograph. At first he could not make it out. It was a black-and-white illustration of meaningless patterns in the dirt. Then slowly it came into focus and he realized what he was looking at. He put the photo back in the envelope and wrote Anne a hasty message. He went to the utility room and pulled on his boots, spurs, hat, and strapped on his old, weathered chaps. He took a yellow slicker from a hook and folded it under his arm. He walked blindly to the corral. Shiloh was surprised to see him. Ezra did not turn on any electrical lights as he caught and saddled his horse. He did it by feel, by the familiarity of practiced repetition. Anne was just leaving the church as Ezra swung into the saddle. Shiloh acted confused and discomforted as they left the corral. The horse subtly tried to veer back to the house, but Ezra pointed him northward, and Shiloh pushed on. Ezra could not see the horse he sat upon. He lifted his hands and held them in front of his face. They were invisible. The world was lit only by brief flashes of lightning, sound, and the clip-clop of Shiloh's tentative hooves and the hooting of voyeuristic owls.

CHAPTER TWENTY-FIVE

Anne could not understand it. As she drove down the lane there was not a light burning anywhere on the ranch. The house, garage, bunkhouse, and barn were all dark. She remembered Ezra's experience in the trap and was terrorized by the idea that he was not home, that he was somewhere in the hills. But where? She did not know. The night was dark and windy, and she was night-blind.

The wind banged the house door open, and she struggled to close it as she groped for the porch light. The switch was on but the light wasn't. The bulb was either burnt out, or the electricity was off. She felt her way through the utility room, calling Ezra, and stepping over shoes and boots. She found a hallway switch. Nothing. The power was out. The dark stillness in the house was shattered by the ringing of the phone. She stumbled through the kitchen to the living room, knocking phone books and notepads to the floor as she felt along the desk for the receiver. She had it by the fourth ring.

"Hello," she said breathlessly.

The silence was ominous. She slammed the phone down hard. "Listen to that, you creep," she said. Anne moved carefully back to the utility room and rummaged in a closet for a flashlight. The first one she found was dead. The second was dim but strong enough for her to return to the kitchen to find the candles she had stored away for power outages. She lit three candles and used their light to call the Rural Electric Cooperative. Yes, the lineman's wife told her, a line had blown down somewhere north of town. She assured Anne that her husband was on his way. But they lived twenty-seven miles east of town and it would be a while before he got there. *Where was Ezra?* Holding a candle in her hand she returned to the coatrack in the utility room and took inventory. Ezra's spurs and chaps were gone—so were his boots, hat, and slicker. Sadly she realized she did not know if he had ever come home. The weather had been nice earlier, he may have ridden too far only to have to return in the wind and dark. His horse could have fallen in a hole. She cursed him. With all the love in her heart she cursed her husband for his stubborn independence.

He could be anywhere in the hills with a broken leg, or worse, and she was helpless. She tiptoed carefully downstairs to her sewing room. She kept a good flashlight there, one hidden from Ezra and Dylan, who were always misplacing them. Her candle illuminated the freezer as she passed it and for a moment she thought she saw a flash of light outside. *No, she told herself, it had to be the reflection of the candle against the shiny freezer door.* When she reached the tiny sewing room, she heard a knocking above her. Was someone at the door? *No,* she told herself. It was the nameplate she had tole-painted and hung above the door. It always rattled in the wind. As her hand found her hidden flashlight, she heard the front door open and slam closed and felt steps on the floor above her. Someone was in the house. Whoever it was had stopped just inside the door. Ezra wouldn't do that, she told herself. Ezra would know the power was off and would feel his way through the room. And he would call out to her by name. The person took one more step, the weight on the ceiling above her seemed monstrous to Anne. *Who was it?* she wondered. *Jubal? Austin?* She was in a small basement room of a pitch-dark house. There was no phone in the basement though Dylan had often asked for one. *Was there a gun anywhere in the basement?* She didn't think so. Anne hated having guns in the house. She had no idea where her husband was or what had happened to him. Suddenly the sickest of fears hit Anne in the stomach. Ezra had provoked Austin. The hoodlums from Vegas were friends of Austin. *What if they had done something to Ezra? What if they had returned for her?* She heard one more slow, tentative step. A voice cried out: "Hello." It was a man's voice. A voice she had never heard before.

It was a monumental task Ezra had set before himself, and when Shiloh tried to curve homeward he was tempted to let the horse have its head and abandon the plan. But he made himself push on, trusting Shiloh to see what he couldn't. Ezra could see nothing at all except when sheet lightning illuminated the sky and outlined the trees, hills, rocks, and the arrow of pure deep blackness, like a spilled river of ink, that was the well-worn cow trail Shiloh was following. Once the horse realized the rider's determination it settled into a cautious, plodding pace that slowly put a long stretch of loneliness between them and the house.

Ezra had no real plan. Even the photograph did not provide a definite clue stating this was the night to risk injury or death prodding about sightless in the storm-swept badlands. He had one hunch: the phone calls were made to determine he was home by the person responsible for Wilson's cows being in the CRP.

His pickup would have been far more comfortable, but the night was too dark for Ezra to approach the Wilson ranch without headlights. Besides, he knew his adversary was horseback so the game should be finished on equal terms, one rider against another. But was his adversary crazy enough to be out on a night like this? Ezra had heard cow camp tales about cowboys riding in pitch-black electrical storms; tales of horses falling in holes, and the most dreaded fear: lightning. One cowboy was found miles from his dead horse, wandering the hills, unsure of his own name; another had survived the electrical charge but broke both arms, a leg, three ribs, and his jaw from the violent contraction of his muscles throwing him violently into rocks. And then there were Ezra's own uncles, Willis, Rufus, and Archie, all electrocuted by lightning fixing a fence line that had been torn down by Ezra's wrongdoing. *Was this to be the payback? Would he be lightning struck for the sins of his youth?* He was now closer to Wilson's CRP than he was to home. He decided to go on.

Ezra felt the fence line that he could not see. The wires rubbed against the left legging of his chaps causing him to flinch and rein Shiloh away. But the cow trail ran alongside the fence line and the horse veered back knowing it was easier and safer to walk in the trail. Ezra swung his left leg up and over the saddle horn and rode sidesaddle. It was better to take the chance of being tossed off if Shiloh spooked than to remain tense riding next to invisible barbed wires. The lightning continued flashing, illuminating the hills with a sterile, colorless casting that reminded Ezra of the dark lights and strobe of his hippie days, of a drug den in San Francisco and the menacing face of a biker with a knife in his hand.

The main thrust of the storm passed and the winds slowly waned. The sky lightened in the south and a tip of moon, and a few stars poked out of the clouds above him. But the electrical activity remained intense, and a ragged fork of horizontal lightning lit the western sky and for a second the night seemed as bright as day. Ahead of him Ezra glimpsed two gates: the one between the Riley land and the CRP and the one between Wilson's grazing pasture and the CRP. He also saw thick, dark squares that he knew were Wilson's Angus cows. It had taken him an hour and a half to ride four miles but he was where he wanted to be. He pulled Shiloh to a stop and dismounted. He could not see the gates now so he walked down the trail, leading his horse, his left hand extended at shoulder height feeling the posts. He knew when he felt two posts together, linked by a single strand of smooth wire, that he was at the gate. He stopped there, breathed a quick prayer of protection, then threw the gate open and waited. For legal purposes he decided not to enter Wilson's land until he knew cattle were being moved into the CRP. He guessed they'd be moved in early to give the cattle more time to graze but the rider was probably waiting for the storm to subside. He could come anytime, Ezra knew, or it could be hours.

Anne remembered that Ezra had given Dylan a rifle for Christmas. An old lever-action .25-.20 he had purchased at a farm auction. Anne had resisted allowing Dylan to keep the rifle in his room but Ezra had told the boy it was okay, providing the gun was never loaded and the ammunition was stored outside the house. An empty rifle, Anne decided, was better than no rifle at all.

She moved slowly down the short hallway from her sewing room to Dylan's bedroom cupping her hand over the flashlight. She was thankful Dylan had stayed with a friend as she entered his room. The little rifle leaned in a corner next to Dylan's writing desk. As she reached for it she heard steps above her, and the man called out "Hello" again. She clutched the gun, but in pulling it to her, the barrel caught the cord to Dylan's desk lamp, and it crashed heavily to the floor, shattering the light bulb. Anne's heart jumped and she froze, her ears straining to hear. The man had heard her. She heard his steps move through the utility room to the basement stairs. Each step he took down the stairs reverberated through the basement. She flicked her flashlight off and stepped into the hallway, the rifle in her hands. She saw light bounce off the freezer, then saw a ball of whiteness approaching. The man had a flashlight, too.

"Hello," he said. "Anyone down here?"

It would only be seconds before he saw her and she had nowhere to run or hide.

"I have a gun," Anne said. "Who are you?"

The light moved down the hallway floor, crawled up a wall, and moved horizontally. Suddenly it blinded Anne as it bathed her in a pale yellow-white light.

"Mrs. Riley?" the voice asked.

"Yes," Anne said, holding the rifle crooked in her right arm and shielding her eyes with her left hand.

The light disappeared with the click of his flashlight turning off.

"I'm Sheriff Butler," the man said. "Please put your rifle down."

Anne sighed, then hesitated. "How do I know you are the sheriff?"

His light flashed on again and he turned its beam on the silver badge above his left pocket.

Anne sighed deeply this time and leaned the rifle against the wall. "You had me scared to death," she said.

"I'm sorry," he said. "I saw all your vehicles were here but no one answered when I called. Then I looked in and saw candles burning on the table."

"I'm home alone," Anne said. "The power was off when I got here."

"Where's Ezra?" Butler asked.

"I have no idea. He wasn't here when I left for church at 6:30. I don't know if he ever came back or not. He's horseback somewhere."

"In this storm? It's totally dark outside."

"I know," Anne said. "I'm afraid he could be hurt."

"Let's go back upstairs," Butler said. "Can you follow my light?"

"I have a flashlight," Anne said.

Anne followed Butler up the stairs to the utility room. He flashed his light across the wall of coats and hats.

"Ezra's chaps and spurs are gone," she told him.

"You didn't find a note or anything?"

"No." Anne led the way back to the kitchen. The candles were still burning on the table casting dim, dancing shadows on the walls as they flickered. Butler ran his light across the table. No notes. "Does your answering machine have a memo feature?" he asked.

"Yes," Anne said. "But he never uses it." Anne stepped into the living room and flashed her light on the desk. There were no memos and no messages on the machine.

"What's on the floor?" Butler asked.

Anne reached down to pick up the phone books and note pads she had accidently knocked off the desk earlier. She lay the notepad on the kitchen table and turned it to the first page. There Ezra had scrawled with a felt tip pen: *Anne, I'm going horseback to the CRP. Don't worry if I'm late. Ez. 3.*

"Ez, three," Butler said. "Do you ever call him Ez?"

"No, a few of his friends do."

"What's Ez. 3 mean?"

"His Bible was on the floor, too," Anne said. "It must mean Ezekiel, chapter three."

"Is that relevant to anything?" Butler asked.

"I don't know." Anne stared down at the note for a moment, then she looked back to the tall, lean man whose strong features were made harsh by the light and shadows of the candles. "Sheriff," she asked. "Why are you out here?"

"I gave Ezra something earlier today. I wanted to talk to him about it. It was a photograph in a manila envelope."

Anne cast her light on the floor beneath the desk. "There it is," she said. She reached down, picked it up, looked at it curiously, and handed it to the sheriff. "What is it?" she asked. "What does it mean?"

"Judging by the note," the sheriff said, "I would venture to guess that Ezra knows who's turning Wilson's cattle in on the CRP."

"And he's out there to catch him." The refrigerator suddenly hummed loudly and Anne jumped. Down the hall the lights in the utility room came on.

"Power's back," Butler said.

"I'm so glad," Anne said. She noticed that Butler appeared kinder in the light. She blew the candles out, then looked up at the sheriff. "What's the big deal about this CRP anyway?" she asked. "Why would someone be trying to get Ezra in trouble with Wilson, and how much trouble can it be?"

"For multiple violations Wilson could lose all of his CRP payments and have to pay back all that he's received. In his case we're talking thousands and thousands of dollars. We believe Wilson is in partnership with people in Las Vegas. If he loses that money, so do they."

"But who's framing Ezra?"

"Only Ezra knows," the sheriff said. "And he may not know for sure."

Ezra stood next to his horse for almost an hour, rubbing his neck, letting him graze when he wanted, watching the sheet lightning move to the north, and grimacing when the vertical lightning stabbed at the earth. *Lightning strikes the planet one hundred times a second,* he remembered. *More people die from lightning, often from the return stroke ascending back to the cloud, than from any other natural phenomenon. Thirty percent of people struck by lightning die, the others suffer a variety of injuries, most commonly heart and brain conditions.* These facts came back to him from helping Dylan with a seventh grade science project. Ezra was certain of one thing: if lightning did not strike him in the hills, it would when he got home. Anne would be furious.

Shiloh's head raised and his ears pricked. Ezra could feel a nicker gathering in the horse's throat and he pinched Shiloh's nostrils to cut off his air. "Sorry, boy," he whispered, "But we have to be quiet." There was movement in the darkness. Thick, heavy black objects bobbed in the purple backdrop. Cattle were moving. A faint whistle came through the air. A man's whistle. Ezra reached for his saddle horn, pulled himself into the saddle, and unfastened his lariat. He had chosen not to bring a firearm. If he needed a weapon, he would depend on his rope.

The gate between Wilson's pastures was only a hundred yards away but Ezra could not see it. He knew its location by memory and kept his eyes trained on that spot. He heard muffled hoofbeats of a horse at a slow gallop. He heard the beats stop. Lightning flashed above him and for an instant a dark horse and a man opening the gate were outlined in a colorless fluorescence. He could not recognize the horse or the rider. Ezra made himself be patient, he needed to wait until all the cattle had been moved in, then he would ride in slowly, quietly, hoping to surprise the man when he returned to the gate.

Wilson's cattle were practically trained and moved easily to the gate. When lightning flashed, the heads on the black baldies—the Angus with Hereford breeding—shone, and they seemed bodiless, their white faces glowing in the light like floating Jack-o'-lanterns. Ezra could feel the movement of the cows and hear the occasional tenor bellow from a calf, the sound of hungry jaws on dry grass as the cattle moved onto the Conservation Reserve Program. He heard again the whistling of a man urging the herd through the open wire gate.

Ezra touched Shiloh's side lightly with his spurs, and the horse stepped tentatively forward. He had only to ease a hundred yards down the fence line to confront his antagonist. The unknown rider pushed the last few through the gate. Ezra saw the swirl of darkness that was his horse chousing the stragglers. The man was now through the gate and fifty yards deep into the CRP. Ezra was the same distance from the gate. The night was still dark, the sky heavy with clouds, and Ezra wished he had brought a flashlight. How easy it would have been to have hid near the gate, then flashed the light on the man when he dismounted. But he had left the flashlight on the shelf in the calving shed.

He could barely see the motion of the horse turning back to the gate. But Ezra was there now. He had the gate blocked. It would only be a few more steps, a few more seconds.

The lightning that split the sky seemed to cast its pale shimmer only on Ezra and the hills behind him. It blinded him for an instant, but in that same second, he was illuminated, like a statue outlined in a fluorescent silver paint. He felt the stranger stop his horse. He heard the action of the horse pivoting on its hind legs, he detected the beat of galloping hooves, the rustle of cows scattering in the grass.

The stranger had seen him and was galloping away. Ezra dug his spurs into Shiloh and the race was on.

CHAPTER TWENTY-SIX

The pasture was one section, a mile long by a mile wide. Seventy years before it had been homesteaded by Finnish emigrants. They had not "proved up" and it became open range for several years and was considered a "trail section," a strategic piece of ground used for trailing horses, cattle, and sheep from the open prairies of the north to the railroad stockyards in Yellow Rock. In the late twenties it was purchased for back taxes by a sheep man, but after the drought of the thirties it was idle again until purchased by the CBC wagon boss, Charles Arbuckle.

It stayed in the Arbuckle family for fifty years until purchased by Edison Benjamin for his son, Rick, in the 1980s, along with fifteen other sections of Arbuckle land. Drought, high interest rates, and a crash in the cattle and wheat markets forced young Benjamin out of business in 1984, and the section, along with the remainder of the Arbuckle and Benjamin places, was sold to Shorty Wilson.

Wilson plowed the hardpan sod and planted wheat in the fall of '84. Then after three years he placed the section and another three thousand acres of sod-busted land in the government's Conservation Reserve Program.

The six hundred forty acres was now the setting for a game of blind man's bluff played on horseback. Ezra trotted Shiloh westward, stopping every minute to listen, careful to avoid the Angus cattle that suddenly appeared in his path like big black boulders. The pasture was bordered to the south by a two-lane blacktopped highway, to the west by a graveled county road, to the north by the Wilson grazing pasture, and to the east by Riley land. There were only three gates leading out of the CRP. Ezra had entered through the one coming in from the Riley land on the east, the unknown rider had pushed the cattle through the gate to the north, and a western gate opened to the highway. The rider, Ezra guessed, would race for the western gate or hide in the darkness and sneak back to the gate he had come through. But which?

The old Arbuckle place, where Austin now lived in a small trailer house, was a mile up the creek to the north. If the rider was Austin, or possibly the Vegas cowboy, he would come back to the north gate, unless there was a vehicle parked near the highway. In that case he would go west.

The sky was continuing to lighten but the night was still dark and pierced by both vertical and horizontal lightning flashes. One particularly bright flash briefly illuminated the ground for a hundred yards before him, and Ezra saw yellow heads of dry grass but no washouts, holes, or obstacles. But farther on, he caught a brief sparkle, like the twinkling of a large eye, that he assumed was a reflection off a saddle's silver concho or a silver-inlaid bit. The rider had started west but had now changed course to the southeastern corner. He planned on hiding there, thinking Ezra would race to the highway gate, then double back. Ezra reined Shiloh southward. There was no gate in the southeast corner of the fence and if the cowboy hid there he was cornered unless he had fencing pliers and cut the wires.

Ezra pulled Shiloh to a stop and thought about his situation. If the man sat quietly in the corner, he would hear Ezra's approach, and if he was armed, Ezra could be shot from the saddle. If Ezra approached too slowly, so as not to be heard, the rider might himself tiptoe away and Ezra would flounder in the dark searching for someone who wasn't there.

His best chance was to take the offensive and hope the man was not packing a weapon. Ezra knew the terrain, the other rider might not. He would gallop to the corner, raring his speed by the visibility given him by the lightning and flush the rider out, forcing him to surrender or into a full-out race across the CRP. If it became a race, the lead horse was in the most danger and would create a trail through the cattle and other obstacles for Shiloh to follow. Ezra reined his sorrel farther to the south, traveling at a slow trot until the horse stopped stiffly when it sensed the fence. Ezra wheeled Shiloh to the east and pointed the horse toward the fence corner. He looked at the skies. Having feared lightning all night, he now prayed for one good flash, one quick illumination to tell him if the rider was in the corner or not.

It came. A sweep of sheet lightning ripped the sky, followed by a vertical strike that hit somewhere so close it made the earth shake and the fence line sparkle with electricity. The following contraction of air produced a rumbling thunder that sounded like two freight trains loaded with coal crashing head on. Shiloh spooked sideways away from the fence, then stood, trembling. As the horse jumped, the world was lit briefly by a pale yellow light that displayed a ghostly figure, transfixed in the electric blue of the night. He was there, a man on a horse, and then he was gone. As the thunder died Ezra heard the faint sound of galloping hooves and he spurred Shiloh to follow. The sorrel leaped obediently into the darkness, his powerful hindquarters pushing earth behind him, his front legs stretched out, claiming new ground. Shiloh sensed the other horse, knew it was running from him, and pursued the horse like a greyhound after a fox. Ezra bent forward in the saddle, his right hand holding his lariat and saddle horn, the left holding the bridle reins and a tangle of Shiloh's mane. He had to rely on his horse's surefootedness and common sense. The darkness rushed by in ink-coated waves that glimmered with imaginings. Ezra tried closing his eyes and riding within his own darkness, briefly awash in sound and feel until he opened his eyes again and saw the same inky blackness, the night a cavern of darkness punctuated by brief exclamation points of lightning.

He was gaining on the rider. He could hear the hooves, could sense movement ahead, could feel Shiloh's neck arch and his ears point. He saw sparks, shooting out like little fireworks, when the horse's shod hooves struck rock. The rider was going up a small, rounded hill, a rocky island in the sea of CRP grass. He was but sixty feet ahead, twice the length of Ezra's rope, three times the distance Ezra needed to accurately throw a loop. It never occurred to Ezra to yell out for the man to stop. The man was not going to stop, the stakes were too high—the game now played was beyond the borders of sportsmanship.

Ezra saw another burst of sparks as his opponent crested the hill. It was two hundred yards to the gate, but unless the sky flashed with brilliance, neither man would see the fence or gate immediately. The rider would have to slow down or risk charging his horse into four tight strands of barbed wire. Shiloh charged up the little hill, his own shod hooves striking rock and leaving a trail of glistening spark. Lightning struck again, and the air crackled with electrical tension.

As Shiloh flew over the hill he collided with a wall—a cow searching for salt sage had stepped aside when the first rider came by then stepped forward again, and Shiloh slammed into her side, throwing Ezra airborne into the night as the horse and black cow went down in a crash of bodies and tangle of hooves. An instant before impact, Ezra's training told him to duck his shoulder and roll. He hit heavily on his right side, the air rushing from his lungs, and rolled several times before coming to a stop. He heard a thrashing near him, knew it was Shiloh and the cow floundering to find their feet, and tried to roll further but his body did not respond. For an instant he was paralyzed by the shock of the impact, his instinct commanded actions his muscles could not obey. Then ahead of him, somewhere near the gate, he saw a small glow and he wondered if he was even conscious. He lifted his head. *Was it headlights or a flashlight?* He heard Shiloh struggle to his feet and shake himself. He heard the cow grunt, get to her feet, and limp away. The glow was growing. He heard a familiar growing roar and a faint crackling. He sensed Shiloh's apprehension.

Fire.

Fanned by the northern winds, long fingers of flame were reaching across the pasture, licking and crackling at the dry grass and bearing down quickly upon them. Ezra jumped to his feet and stabbed into the darkness to catch Shiloh's reins just as the horse was about to bolt.

The fire stretched like a jagged hand, growing ravenously, the smoke curling upwards, visible only where the clouds parted to reveal open sky. The race was over, the rider was gone, and Ezra turned his attention to the immediate threat. In the instant of circling his horse and reaching for the stirrup he wondered how the fire had started. *A lightning strike? Sparks from the horse's hooves? Or had the rider stopped and deliberately started the fire himself?*

He swung into the saddle, his right shoulder aching, and trotted Shiloh toward the gate that lay open to Riley land. When he reached it, he turned and looked back. The fire might be blamed on him, he knew that, but he would not run. Fires were meant to be fought. He rode a short distance to a barren gumbo mound, dismounted, stripped his latigo free, and pulled the saddle and blankets off. He unbridled Shiloh and patted the horse on the neck. Relieved of tack, the horse stood confused for a moment. Ezra slapped him on the shoulder. "Get out of here," he shouted. "Go home." The horse turned and trotted off into the darkness.

The flames were now a long orange line dancing southward. Ezra pulled off his spurs and chaps, grabbed the thinner of the two saddle blankets, and ran toward the fire.

Moments after the sheriff left the Riley house the phone rang. It was Solomon.

"I see an orange glow to the north," he said. "I think there's a fire up there. Where's Ezra?"

Anne did not answer the question because she did not know. "Where is the fire?" she asked.

"I'd guess it's on Wilson's CRP," Solomon said.

Anne hung up then punched the numbers for the Rural Fire Department, misdialing twice because she was thinking about Ezra. *Where is he?*

As if satisfied, the storm ceased after the fire began. The big, roiling cirrocumulus clouds sailed eastward, a dark and flashing armada of vengeance, leaving no spray of rain in their wake.

Using his sore arm and shoulder, Ezra beat the fire with the saddle blanket. The dry grass burned quickly in two tiers as flames jumped from the crowns of standing wheatgrass and smoldered in the old grass that matted the prairie floor. Fighting the fire by hand by himself was futile, but Ezra fought it furiously. He was not concerned about the fire's damage—fire was nature's cleanser and Wilson's CRP and Solomon's undergrazed pastures would both benefit from the cleansing—but he was angered by its source. The fire did not seem natural. It was a wildfire born of bad intentions, as if the fire itself was evil, and he was determined to resist it symbolically. Around him cattle stirred clumsily ahead of the fire and to the north he saw headlights racing down the gravel road from the direction of Austin's trailer. To the west other vehicles were stopping on the highway. It would only be a matter of minutes, Ezra knew, before he had help. Neighbor would phone neighbor, the Rural Fire Department would be activated, and hopefully someone would call for equipment, a bulldozer, or motor grader to blade a fire line.

His efforts on the line were futile. Where he succeeded, the fickle winds changed and the fire advanced in new directions. It had spread westward first, defining an orange line from the Riley property almost to the highway, but the breezes altered and it was now racing to the south and east toward undergrazed Riley land lush with old grass and a forest of sagebrush. The sagebrush, Ezra knew, would erupt like Roman candles, burn hotter than kerosene, and scar bare faces if approached.

Ezra had to run to stay with it but the fire still beat him to the Riley fence. Sweat rolled from his brow, and his face felt baked by the heat. When Austin arrived the CRP section was already burned to black ash and the cattle had torn down the fence and scattered onto Riley ground except for a few that stood stupidly on the burnt ground, their hooves scorched, and their dull eyes watering from smoke.

The air sparked and crackled as the tall silver sage erupted in flame. Austin parked his pickup on a dry creek bed and ran to the fire with a flapper in his hand, a fire-fighting tool resembling a huge fly swatter. Ezra crawled through the scorched fence wires to work beside him, neither saying anything to the other, the two of them working feverishly in an oven of flames. Smoke from the sagebrush rose thick and black in the air. By the time other neighbors and the Rural Fire Department had arrived, the fire was half a mile down the Riley creekbottom, was angling up grassy coulees, and was licking the crowns of sod-crested buttes. The people were only shadows working in the darkness of the night and smoke and the light of the flames, and Ezra seldom knew who he was working beside. His shoulder and armed ached, his throat was dry and hoarse, and his eyes were red and swollen. Men alone would never stop the fire. It could burn to Solomon's house, or beyond it, to Ezra's. It could reach the horse pasture and pin Cheyenne and Gusto against a fence.

"We need equipment," he yelled into the dark. Someone had to make a phone call but Ezra did not want to leave the fire. He moved through the firefighters, looking for a fire department truck with a radio.

"Call in for a blade," he told a truck driver.

"Who do you want me to get?" the man asked casually.

"I don't care," Ezra yelled. "Just get some heavy equipment out here fast."

Anne had arrived moments before and recognized Ezra's voice. "Ezra!" she shouted. "Where are you?"

He came to her through the smoke, his hat pulled low on his head, his torn and dirty horse blanket hanging from a limp arm.

"Are you all right?" she asked. "Where's your horse?"

Ezra continued whipping at flames. "I'm fine," he said. "I turned Shiloh loose. I want you to go to the highway and wait for the equipment that is coming. You will need to lead them in, they won't know the roads."

"You don't want me to stay and help fight the fire?"

"No, I'd rather you make sure the blade gets here without taking a wrong road. Where did you park the pickup?"

Anne pointed to the other side of the creek. "Over there," she said.

"Anne, the fire is almost there already," Ezra said.

"Oh, no," Anne moaned. "I'll get it." She left Ezra and ran into the darkness, trying to beat the flames. She tripped and fell, and rose to see the bouncing headlights of a fire department water truck flashing in her face. The driver was wandering through the thick brush looking for a place to cross the creek. Anne pointed frantically to her left, guessing where the crossing was, then ran to the truck. The fire was inches from her rear tires as she drove away.

Soon three water trucks were on the front line trying to slow the fire's progress while men on foot chased little blazes up grassy coulees. Ezra looked to the east and saw a long black mound, like a black elephant standing in the dark, tipped by an orange and yellow glow. The fire had reached the Watkins' flat and was advancing across a ridge that was inaccessible by vehicle. He grabbed a fire flapper from a passing water truck, tossed his blackened saddle blanket away, and began jogging toward the high, grassy flat.

He felt someone jogging beside him. He heard the breathing, the sound of boots on grass and ground, the whisking of dry grass against pant legs, before he saw the shadowy form. The two of them reached the plateau in unison and speechlessly began fighting fire. They raced from one hot spot to another, letting the fire burn where the fuel was sparse, and fighting it fiercely where the black sagebrush and tall needlegrass was thick. Below him Ezra caught glimpses of the main fire working southward down the creek, its fiery head interrupted by gouges of darkness that was the success of a water truck's crew.

When it seemed the ridge fire was unstoppable, the wind suddenly stopped and a surprising drizzle of rain began to fall. The droplets sizzled as they hit the thick, black ash of the earth and the hottest flames began to dim. The two men worked quickly to smother the fire line, kicking burning sagebrush trunks and cow manure patties back into the charred burn as they swatted at the weakening flames. The drizzle seemed to fall from a cloudless sky—in fact, it fell from one small cloud, almost imperceptible through the layers of smoke—and lasted only minutes. But in that brief shower the fire on the plateau was defeated, and after half an hour mopping up around its edges, the two men moved simultaneously to the plateau edge to watch the main fire below.

The fire still moved south, its advance orange and red against the black chalkboard of the sage-covered bottom, but the line was being broken, erased where a D-8 Caterpillar was gouging a deep fire line. Ezra could barely hear the strain of its diesel engine and the clanking of its metal tracks.

"The dozer is doing its job," the man beside him said. Ezra turned to the craggy outline of Austin Arbuckle silhouetted against a starry sky. The storm was now gone, the clouds had vanished and the air was calm.

"Yeah, it is," Ezra said.

"Good thing," Austin said. "We never would have stopped it otherwise. How much do you think it burned?"

The charred area lay on the ground like one big, black patch on a dark quilt. "It got all your CRP," Ezra said. "And a mile of our creekbottoms, and who knows how many little coulees. I'd guess it at twelve, maybe fifteen hundred acres."

"Fires always look bigger at night," Austin said. There was a relaxed familiarity in his voice. Less than twelve hours ago the two had been at the edge of throwing fists, but that was a different time, a different place.

Ezra sighed and nodded toward the northwest. "My saddle is down there somewhere," he said. "I hope it survived."

"You rode to the fire?" Austin asked.

"No, I was already out here when it started."

The silence was almost audible. Ezra knew what Austin was thinking.

Austin pondered the risks in his question first, then asked: "What were you doing out here on horseback in the dark?"

"Trying to catch the bad guy," Ezra said, and he knelt on his haunches to relieve the ache in his legs and back. Below him the last hot spots of the fire were slowly being extinguished and they flickered out like bulbs burning out on a Christmas display.

"Did you catch him?" Austin asked.

"No," Ezra said. "But he may have caught himself." He rose and stretched. It was well past one in the morning—Ezra had no idea of the actual time—but the work was far from over. He would need to guard the fire all night, watching for hot spots, kicking smoking embers, and shoveling smoldering manure back into the burn.

"Bad guys do get caught," Austin surmised.

Below them the fire was all but out. Bouncing headlights marked the trail where neighbors were going home. Austin turned to Ezra. "If you want to go home and get some sleep I'll babysit this ridge," he said.

Ezra was not going anywhere until his conscience was clear. "Austin, about that incident this afternoon at the sales barn, I want to apologize. I was way out of line."

"No you weren't," Austin said. "I had it coming. It was just six or seven years late."

"No. I was wrong. I was jumping to conclusions. I thought you were purposely harassing me and my family. Especially after Anne said she saw you in the back pew of our church. I guess I never thought you might be there for your own reasons."

"Five years in the pen can change a man's way of thinking," Austin said. He stared out into the night as if it represented all the darkness within the world. "If there're answers out there, I want to know about them," he said.

"There're answers," Ezra said. "Come on, let's patrol our fire line." They walked off together, side-by-side, the long fire flappers in their hands, two figures silhouetted against a star-pricked sky, walking a long black ridge, arresting sparks and smothering embers, walking guard on what had once been a fire.

CHAPTER TWENTY-SEVEN

The morning dawned bright and cool with a slight blue haze hanging over the treetops in the creek. Anne awakened alone. She knew Ezra would stay on the fire line, but she had hoped he might come home before she left for work. She stepped from the bedroom to the bathroom tentatively, like a doe testing the scent of the air before coming to water. There was something in the air, a scent almost as discernible as the smoke that still lingered outside, dimming the morning light and painting the sun a fluorescent orange. She took a few minutes to read her Bible—Ezekiel, chapter three—was it coincidence she had been reading all week the verses Ezra had mentioned in his note? She finished dressing for work. There was something in the air, but it wasn't ominous. It felt more like destiny, though she would not have used that word. She would have said *conclusion*. It was not that things were fated, but that they occurred by design with a beginning and an end. And something was coming to an end.

Austin's pickup pulled into the yard minutes after Anne left. Ezra got out, unloaded his saddle—which had been untouched by the fire—and Austin drove off.

Ezra was exhausted, dirty, and sore. He reeked of smoke, and his right shoulder throbbed. He tossed his chaps and spurs on the front steps and packed his saddle and bridle to the tack room. He was worried about Shiloh but saw he had found his way back to Gusto and Cheyenne. He poured a bucket of feed in the horses' trough, went to the house, made a phone call, then soaked in a hot tub of water.

He made himself a breakfast of toast and eggs, sorted through the morning mail.

He remembered a neighbor's comment while fighting fire on the fence line: "This wire will have lost its temper," he had said. Intrigued, Ezra looked up "temper" in the dictionary and was surprised to see the word had so many meanings. He had considered it negatively, the volatility of Riley blood boiling before spewing. His dictionary showed seventeen meanings and all but the first three were positive. He wrote a few of the definitions down on the backside of the manila envelope the sheriff had left him.

He was finishing chapter three of Ezekiel—reading it from Anne's Bible—when the sheriff's patrol car pulled into the yard. He watched Butler get out with a piece of paper in his hand. Ezra met him at the door. He knew what was coming, how it was to be handled, and what was to be said as if everything was scripted, destined to happen according to a precise plan.

"Mornin'," Butler said. "I take it the fire is all under control."

Ezra nodded. "Austin and I babysat it all night," he said.

"Hmm, interesting bedfellows," Butler said.

"Very interesting," Ezra said. "And enlightening."

Butler's clear blue-gray eyes turned downcast. "I hate to do this," he said. "But I have a warrant for your arrest."

"For what?" There was no surprise in Ezra's tone, just dry words released into the air as if for someone else's benefit.

"For starting the fire last night," Butler said. There was a jesting twinkle in his blue eyes.

"I never started that fire," Ezra said loudly.

"Maybe not, but Wilson filed the charges early this morning."

"So I'm going to jail?" Ezra asked.

"I'm afraid so, but you should be able to make bail later this afternoon."

Ezra grabbed his hat and walked to the car. He stood waiting at the back passenger door where the backseat was separated from the front by steel mesh.

"You can ride in the front," Butler said.

Ezra nodded and opened the front door. He sat next to a 12-gauge Remington pump shotgun. Hunting maps were strewn across the dashboard.

At the jail Ezra changed into a pair of sandals and orange khaki pajamas with PRISONER stenciled across the back. The office was quiet, and no one paid any attention when Butler ignored the usual paperwork and procedures. The sheriff did hand Ezra the phone. "I suppose you want to call a lawyer," he said.

Ezra took the phone and dialed. "No," he said. "I want to call my pastor." He made the call.

Butler took a heavy ring of keys off a hook. "What size cell do you want?" he asked.

"The biggest you have," Ezra said. "I'm claustrophobic."

"I have just the one. We actually have three different sizes. The largest one has an intercom. I can hear the prisoners but they can't hear me. It also has camera surveillance." He escorted Ezra to a 15-by-17-foot cell. The Yellow Rock sheriff and police offices were combined in one building with jail cells in the basement and top floor of a three story structure that also served as the county courthouse. Ezra was put in a cell by himself on the third floor. Down the block were several other prisoners, a bad-check artist, a drunk driver who had resisted arrest, and a petty burglar. At the end of the block was a thick hook set in the ceiling above a trap door in the floor now welded shut. It was the gallows area, last used in 1942.

The more dangerous offenders were kept in the smaller basement cells encased by solid three-eighths-inch steel plating. They measured only ten feet by twelve and would have driven Ezra mad.

Ezra's cell held four iron-framed cots welded to the walls. The bedding consisted of a thin mattress encased in plastic, two sheets, and an army-style wool blanket. A stainless steel commode and sink sat in one back corner. A lightbulb in the ceiling was encased in steel mesh and secured by a heavy padlock. A small steel plate, welded to the walls like the bunks, served as a desk. It resembled a heavy-duty TV tray.

Ezra looked at the tray. "I even have a place to do my writing," he said.

"You'll have a lot to write about," Butler joked.

Ezra winced when the barred door closed behind him and the key turned in the lock. He listened to the sheriff's footsteps retreat down the hall, then Ezra stretched out on one of the lower cots. It felt good to lie down. He remembered his other jailing in Lawrence, Kansas, and how afraid and claustrophobic he had been. In contrast, he felt secure this time. A cell was a restful place after the frenzy of his past ten days.

He was almost dozing when Butler brought Pastor Tom to the cell. He left the pastor outside the cell, staring through the door.

"Gracious, Ezra," Jablonski said. "What is this all about? This must be some terrible mistake."

"Thanks for coming, Pastor," Ezra said, rising from the cot.

"What do you want me to do?" Pastor Tom asked. "Get you a lawyer? Call Anne?" His sincerity was touching, and Ezra knew this was the true Jablonski, the servant, the offensive lineman running interference or stepping back to protect his passer. Jablonski was a genuinely humble man, one suited not primarily for leadership but for delegating authority and implementing programs.

"No," Ezra said. "I need you to do something more important than that. I need you to find Jubal Lee Walker. Tell him I am in jail and that it is very important that I talk to him."

Jablonski was both disappointed and confused. "Jubal Lee? But, shouldn't I get you a lawyer first? The sheriff said you were in on an arson charge. That's serious, Ezra."

"I only need to see Jubal," Ezra said.

"But, does Anne know?"

"No. Not yet."

"Do you want me to tell her?"

"No, I will be out by this afternoon. In fact, I plan on being in church tonight."

"You do?"

"Certainly," Ezra said. "The fat lady hasn't sung yet, Pastor Tom."

"What do you mean?" There was more to this than the pastor understood. He had made jail calls before but none like this.

Ezra stepped up to the bars and held them lightly in his hands. "Let me ask you something, Pastor. The power that comes upon Jubal Lee Walker, is it of God, or are we being deceived?"

Jablonski spoke with conviction, as if uttering his last words from the gallows. "I think it is the power of God," he admitted.

"Do you have any reason to doubt the word he gave Darlene?"

Jablonski shook his head. "No," he said. "It was definitely of God."

"But the message and the messenger do not always appear to line up."

"I've noticed."

"Can God speak true words through the ungodly?"

"The gifts of God are irrevocable," Tom said. "I don't really understand that, but that's what the Bible says."

"If the gift cannot be removed, then surely God can withhold the blessing upon the gift."

"I suppose," Tom said. "Or he can simply remove the messenger."

"Yes," Ezra said thoughtfully. "That would be an option."

"Uh, Ezra," Tom said slowly. "This is a very strange conversation. You are in jail. Shouldn't we be doing something about that?'

"We are," Ezra said.

"You want me to find Jubal Lee."

"Yes. Tell him I need him."

"Ezra, can I ask you one thing? This probably doesn't seem like the time or the place, but am I a bad preacher?"

"The worst I have ever heard," Ezra said with a smile. "But that doesn't mean you are a poor pastor."

"And you want me to find Jubal Lee." Tom said.

"He will probably be at The Cattleman's Cafe. The second booth from the back."

At first Ezra waited tensely for Jubal's arrival, but the tension finally wore him out, exhaustion set in, and he dozed heavily. He dreamed it was hunting season and he was patrolling the ranch for trespassers. Near Dead Man Creek he stopped a man in a pickup. The man was from out of town and did not realize it was private property. Ezra mentioned he had driven past a "No Hunting" sign. He had not seen it, the man said smugly. Ezra was gracious. He said that it was okay, he would not file charges. The man boldly asked if he could continue hunting. Ezra looked at him incredulously and the man's face turned red with anger. He demanded to hunt. Ezra heard a voice within himself say: *Do not tolerate trespassers.* The man knew Ezra's thoughts and threw back his head to laugh. From his lips came the tortured scream of a horse.

Ezra came awake to a loud metallic clanging, the sound of the jail-block door opening. He rose from the bed and watched Sheriff Butler and Jubal Lee Walker come down the cool, dark hallway. Jubal was wearing a white western shirt yoked with the oranges and reds of a sunset, black Wranglers, a silver-belly Stetson, and deep concern on his face. His black, leather-bound Bible was in his left hand.

"Can you let me in the cell?" Jubal asked the sheriff.

Butler nodded and opened the door. Jubal Lee walked in and the door was locked behind him. "Thirty minutes," Butler said.

"So, I visit you in jail again," Jubal said. His smile was wry but friendly, as if trying to make light of a bad situation.

"The last time you brought a tall blonde," Ezra said. "And I married her."

Jubal laughed. "I'm glad you are keeping your sense of humor. So what's going on? Pastor Jablonski said something about arson?"

"That's right. What do you know about arson, Jubal Lee?"

Jubal looked dumbfounded. "What do you mean? It's a serious charge, I suppose. That's all I know."

"It's a very serious charge," Ezra said. He leaned against his cot, his arms folded across his chest. He had to be gentle but very firm. He was like a baseball pitcher on the mound. He had only three pitches to throw and was behind in the count. He needed a strikeout. "The way I see it," Ezra said, "there are two types of arson. The physical type, where someone burns another person's structure down, and the spiritual type, where someone starts a wildfire that destroys another man's spiritual structure."

Jubal's brows narrowed. "What are you talking about?" he asked.

"Where have you been keeping the horse?" Ezra asked. A hardball, straight down the middle. Strike one.

"What horse?"

"That good brown gelding you so graciously let me ride."

"Hey, man, you know. That horse went to Canada with the bay." Jubal's friendly compassion was replaced by a slick confidence and a dark defensiveness coiled at the base of his spine that began crawling upward, one vertebra at a time.

"Is the horse in Canada?" Ezra asked quietly. He was composed, exhausted, saddened. Tempered. A curve ball at the knees. Strike two.

"What's this all about?" Jubal demanded. "Did you hurt your head last night or what? You're acting crazy."

Ezra reached under the mattress and pulled out the envelope the sheriff had given him the day before. He opened it and handed the photograph to Jubal. "Tell me what this is," he said. The last pitch, high and inside, close to the heart. Strike three.

Jubal looked at it, turning it one way, then another. "Heck if I know, brother."

"Look carefully. You will see the very clear imprint of a horse track. A horse with a bar shoe."

"Yeah, so?"

"The brown gelding was correctively shod. You said you did the work yourself. It was a bar shoe."

"Man, there's lots of bar shoes around," Jubal said, handing the photograph back. "And what difference does it make?"

As far as Ezra was concerned, Jubal had swung and missed three times. He was out but he was refusing to step away from the plate. "This photo is of a bar shoe on a racing plate," Ezra said. "There aren't many of those shoes in this country. That's the type of shoe you would find on a race horse or a polo pony. I have one shod horse. Shiloh wears rimmed shoes with heels. The funny thing is, Austin tells me that Wilson doesn't have a shod horse on the place. He thinks it's too expensive to take care of a horse's feet."

Jubal walked to the door. "Man, you are out of it. I came here to help you, man, but you've gone over the edge. I'll come back when your head clears." He rattled the door. "Sheriff," he yelled. "Sheriff!"

"This is the second time a bar shoe has been your undoing," Ezra said. "Should we talk about the barn fire in Trinidad?"

Jubal wheeled around, his eyes blazing. "What do you know about that?" he said angrily. The deep, dark force had risen to the surface and his face snarled like an enraged dog on the end of a short chain.

Ezra steeled himself. He did not like doing what he was about to do, but it was time for the truth. Mercy could wait. "I know that eight horses died in a suspicious fire that destroyed your father-in-law's log barn." he said.

"So?" Jubal asked calmly.

"But those were not your father-in-law's horses, were they? They were canners you bought through a sales ring and substituted in the middle of the night. You stole the other horses."

Jubal's slick veneer was peeling like layers of onion skin, revealing a vicious self-righteousness. "Those were my horses," he snapped.

"The papers were in your name and Shelley's," Ezra said. "And you were afraid you were going to lose them in the divorce proceedings."

"How do you know all this?" Jubal asked. "I never told you about the divorce."

"No, you didn't tell me, did you?" Ezra said. "You acted like you were still married."

"I am still married," Jubal shouted. "In the eyes of God Shelley and I are still married. God is opposed to divorce."

"Did you stay long enough to hear the horses scream, Jubal? What does it sound like? It's awakened me twice this week, once just moments ago. It doesn't sound human, does it? It sounds like an animal impersonating a child, an animal desperate to be human, desperate to learn the language so as to cry for help. You know what it sounds like? It sounds like an angel having its wings ripped out by demons."

Jubal turned and looked away, a heavy, lacquered glazed deadened his eyes. He was entombed in denial, he was a rock, he could not be touched. When he turned and finally looked at Ezra, there was a primitive savagery where the glaze had been. He retreated to the darkest jungle of his soul, where night cries cannot be named, and beckoned for something bestial and wicked to take command.

Ezra stood, stretched, and eased himself into a corner of the cell where he leaned with his back against the bars. It was a conditioned move, the training from earlier years telling him to protect his backside. "You bought eight head of canners in a sales ring somewhere," he said again, driving the truth home. "One night when no one was home you pulled up to your father-in-law's barn and switched horses. Then you set the barn on fire. All the insurance investigator found were eight charred carcasses, he couldn't even tell what colors the horses had been. And thirty-two hooves with shoes. Racing plates. You got everything right except for the bar shoe. There wasn't one and Shelley's father knew the brown gelding should have had a bar shoe."

Jubal took a step toward Ezra. His face was not that of a friend, a preacher, or even the rebellious child of the highway. He was someone Ezra had never seen before. "Man, you are a good writer," he said sarcastically. "You have one heck of an imagination. But that's all it is, man.

Imagination. The insurance company settled up with Shelley's dad. The case is closed, man."

"Maybe," Ezra said. "But that's the way it went down, isn't it? You have been selling the horses one or two at a time to finance your lifestyle."

Jubal turned back to the door. "Sheriff," he shouted.

"Do you really want the sheriff?" Ezra asked.

Jubal turned around and pointed his finger. "You were supposed to be my friend, man. Now you are concocting some crazy story just to save your butt. The next thing you'll be saying is that I started that fire last night."

"You did," Ezra said.

Jubal threw his hands in the air. "See?" he exclaimed, as if petitioning the heavens.

"Actually," Ezra said, "I only *think* you started the fire last night. It may have been lightning. It might have been the sparks from your horse's shoes. Or maybe you stopped at the gate and threw a match in the grass. Why don't you tell me?"

"You're crazy, man!"

"*Man?* You have been calling me *man* for the last ten minutes. What happened to *brother?* You are talking now like you talked on the road seventeen years ago. Why aren't you using the religious term, *brother?*"

Jubal pointed the finger again. "Back off, man. You don't know where you're coming from. I didn't set any fires, man. The only fires I set are holy fires. I am a vessel of God. I set holy fires, man, holy fires."

Jubal's anger was rooted in the absolute conviction of his own innocence. He had thoroughly deceived himself, Ezra realized.

"Let's talk about those holy fires," Ezra said. "I have no doubt that you are gifted and musically, you are a genius. But you learned nothing from the hippie days. You still want to be high all the time. Back then it was pot and acid, now it's the anointing of God. You think it's yours to use as you choose."

Jubal's face was raspberry red and his eyebrows arched and knotted like twisted worms. "Man, don't talk to me about anointing. What do you know? You were rotting away in a little dead-end church until I arrived."

"Much of this does confuse me," Ezra said. "I spent years studying the occult and psychic powers. Since my conversion to the Lord I have learned a little about the gifts of the Holy Spirit. You seem to operate in those gifts, and yet, your life is such a lie. I can only imagine that God loves you very much, Jubal. He gave you great gifts when you were just a child and your heart was pure, and now He is hesitant to take them away.

He is giving you a last chance to repent, but if you don't you will have crossed the line."

"You are a small-minded, small-town person, Ezra. I have ministered in the biggest cities with the biggest names. I have started ministries in a half-dozen towns and you think you know about my gifts, about my calling. You don't know anything."

"I know you are gifted, but you make mistakes. You don't know when the anointing leaves and the human flesh takes over."

"I don't make mistakes," Jubal said calmly.

Jubal's fury was so cold it seemed inhuman and beyond reason or mercy. Ezra braced himself for what he had thought was unlikely: a physical attack.

"I am so full of the Holy Spirit that the anointing never leaves me," Jubal declared. He stepped closer. His eyes held a deep hatred. "My word for Darlene," he said. "That was a true word, wasn't it?"

"I think it was," Ezra admitted.

"The word I gave you: *Leaving the land.* That is a true word, too, Ezra. But you won't listen, will you? You are meant to serve with me but you are too carnal. You won't leave your ranch, you won't leave Yellow Rock, and look where it got you." His right arm swept the small cell, his left hand held his Bible tight against his chest. "You are defying God," Jubal proclaimed. "Is *leaving the land* a true word or not?"

"The word is true," Ezra said. "But the spirit you have used to enforce it is false."

"What are you talking about now?" he mocked.

"Phone calls in the middle of the night, the cattle getting turned into Wilson's CRP, telling me old news about Austin and Anne. You manipulated events to make me leave Yellow Rock."

"Phone calls? Man, what *are* you talking about? Austin made the phone calls."

"Austin made two phone calls," Ezra said. "He told me so last night. The first one was to tell me he was home from prison, but he chickened out and hung up. The second time he called to warn me about you after coming to the church out of pure curiosity. You can't con a con, Jubal. But he changed his mind and hung up when I answered. When you saw that the calls were getting to me, you started making them."

Jubal rattled the door again. "Sheriff," he yelled. "I'm in here with a crazy man."

Ezra glanced up at the television camera and intercom. Jubal had not noticed them. He knew the sheriff was seeing and hearing everything. But he needed to keep Jubal talking.

"How many horses did you ride at the Bucking Horse Sale?" Ezra asked.

Jubal turned around and laughed. "What? What in the world are you talking about?"

"How many?"

"Twelve. You know. You were there."

"You rode nine," Ezra said. "You and Austin both rode nine. Austin and I agree on that. We spent a long night together last night."

"So? That was seventeen years ago, man."

"Your life is an exaggeration that has turned into a lie," Ezra said. "This is a simple town. People will accept just about anybody, even outlaws, as long as they don't claim to be something they are not. Your life is one of pretension. The more people are around you the more wary they become. Dogs don't wag their tails when you walk down the street, Jubal."

His eyes turned white with anger, the veins throbbed in his neck and his forehead glowed red like a cheap skillet on a hot stove. "You are a tool of Satan," he said. "You are trying to destroy my ministry, my work for God. You are the one who is deceived, Ezra Riley. You are arrogant and independent, you won't submit to godly authority."

"Let's talk about submission," Ezra said. "You call yourself *Reverend*. Who ordained you? Let me see your credentials."

"Papers mean nothing, man. You know that."

"Perhaps. But a lack of papers can mean something. It can mean you are a loose cannon. Whom do you report to? Where is your accountability for Jubal Lee Ministries?"

"I have a board of directors, man. I was going to put you on it. I have people in five towns that support me. You are the only one who is not hearing the call. You are the one who has the submission problem."

"Why is it so important to you that I join you?" Ezra asked. "Seventeen years ago you latched onto me like you were a lost puppy. Now after all this time you show up again, talking about destiny and God's will? What's it all about, Jubal?"

"It is God's will," Jubal said. "We are meant to be a team. I gave you a word from God but you won't listen to it."

"I listened," Ezra said. "In fact, the Lord gave me that very same phrase, *leaving the land*, last Sunday morning during Pastor Tom's message."

"Then you know it's true. You know you are supposed to leave the ranch." Jubal's eyes widened with a gloating pleasure. He had been confirmed.

Ezra smiled. "*Leaving the Land* is the title for the book I have written. The Lord gave me the title and your word confirmed it. I mailed the manuscript to a publisher three days ago."

"A book title," Jubal laughed. "You think the word I gave you is a book title?"

"That's all it is. I got my own word from the Lord while reading the Bible and praying last night. Ezekiel, chapter three. It says I am to stay and be a witness to my own people."

"You aren't a prophet," Jubal shouted. "I am. The Lord gives me words. I hear from God."

"Just because you hear from God doesn't mean you are close to Him."

"I hear from Him. I gave you a true word."

"You confirmed a book title for me, nothing more."

"You are nuts," Jubal said. "And you think I *need* you? You have it all backward, Ezra. You need *me*."

"No. Seventeen years ago you needed me for my street smarts, my instinct for survival. You still need that," Ezra said. "That's why you are obsessed with thoughts of destiny. You have talent, but no character. You want me to be your conscience because deep down inside you know you are out of control."

Jubal's stare became white hot, it radiated through the air as surely as the purity of God had in his preachings. But it was not the same.

"You talk about destiny because you are insecure," Ezra said. "You have convinced yourself that greatness can come your way in spite of your laziness and lack of integrity. Your father was right when I talked to him years ago. Your talent has become your undoing."

Jubal threw his Bible down, it hit the slick floor and slid into the hallway. Both of his hands knotted into fists.

"You chose me as some sort of pseudo-father figure," Ezra said. "But you need to be responsible for your own actions. You need to forgive your father."

"Don't talk about my father," Jubal shouted. "Don't bring him into this. He never did anything for me. He was always too busy preaching, too busy doing God's work. What do you know about being a preacher's kid? What do you know about being dragged from town to town, from school to school, from church to church? You had it all. You had a ranch and horses, and you left it, but you got to come back to it. I never had anything to leave. I never had anything to come back to. Don't tell me what my father was like because you don't know."

"You're playing a blame game, just like when we were hippies," Ezra said. "There are a lot of things I could blame my father for but I wasn't such a great son, either. You think you are blameless because you had a bad childhood. I think it's time you grew up."

Jubal's open hand flashed out and slapped Ezra across the face.

Ezra's cheek reddened but he remained calm. He was restrained not by a biblical admonition but by his morning's reading of the dictionary. He was tempered. "I talked to your father last night," Ezra said calmly. "He loves you and is praying for you."

Jubal slapped him again, then stepped back and assumed a fighting stance. "Let's spar," he said.

"What?" Ezra said curiously. Jubal never ceased to amaze him.

"Let's spar. Your karate against my tae kwan do. Let's do it, man." His words were cold and jagged like icicles hanging from his heart and lips.

A closure happened in Ezra's heart and hope died. The game was long over but Jubal refused to relent. "I'm not fighting you," Ezra said.

"We're not fighting," Jubal said. "Fighting wouldn't be Christian. We're sparring. Come on, man, let's do it." He bounced lightly on the balls of his feet, his arms up and fists clenched.

Ezra stared at him and shook his head in resignation. "You need help, Jubal. Confess to the fires. Confession is good for the soul."

The kick rose from Jubal's hip and struck Ezra in his sore shoulder, throwing him back against the jail bars. He winced in pain and faced his attacker, his arms at his side. "I'm not fighting you," Ezra said again.

"I'm confessing to nothing," Jubal said, and he kicked again.

Ezra blocked the kick with a front rising block, spun Jubal to the far corner and jumped away. Jubal wheeled around, his fists ready to strike, his right leg cocked to kick.

Ezra raised his hand. "Hold it," he said firmly. Jubal stopped in his tracks and lowered his leg. Ezra reached down and felt under the mattress of his cot. His hand came back with a key. As Jubal's mouth dropped in surprise, Ezra turned to the cell door, reached through the bars and unlocked it, opened the door, stepped through, then slammed it close, leaving Jubal locked alone in the cell.

"What's going on?" Jubal said. He suddenly seemed very small and young. His hands dropped. Ezra looked at him and saw the teenager who had stepped from the car in the desert of Nevada, his fear masked behind a false arrogance, his mind and heart confused by the world he lived in and the world that lived within him.

"There were never any arson charges against me," Ezra said, nodding up at the small camera and intercom speaker. "I called the sheriff this morning and arranged this to see if you would confess. The insurance investigator is still after you, Jubal. He will get you in time."

"You can't keep me in here," Jubal said. "There are no charges against me. This is entrapment."

"One last time, Jubal," Ezra said. "Do you want to talk about the fires?"

"Go to hell," Jubal said.

Ezra looked at him with a deep pity.

"Let me out of here or I will sue you, the sheriff, and this whole lousy county."

There was nothing more to be said. Sometimes those who reject the truth are those who have heard it the most, have handled and tasted it, have become so familiar with it that it loses all value and is easily traded for anything that glitters. And even glass glitters like a diamond when it is surrounded by darkness. Ezra stepped over and picked up Jubal's Bible. He placed the key in it. "I have a book I want you to read," Ezra said and he slid the Bible through the bars.

Jubal glared at him. "You have defied a man of God," he said.

Ezra shook his head sadly. "You know, Jubal, if you are ever to have a ministry again it will be a prison ministry. From the inside." Ezra turned and walked away, listening to his own steps on the cold corridor floor. He stopped at the jailblock door and looked down through the bars of the cells.

"You have defied destiny," he heard Jubal shout.

Ezra did not answer. He did not believe it. Only God, not destiny, could be defied. He sadly realized he might never see Jay Walker again.

CHAPTER TWENTY-EIGHT

The sanctuary of the Yellow Rock Community Believers' Church was quiet and dimly lit by the light above the rugged wooden cross over the baptismal. Pastor Tom Jablonski and Ezra Riley sat alone in the front pew. Pastor Tom turned his head to look at the congregation that had come for what was to be the last night of the Jubal Lee Walker revival. Only church regulars were in attendance. There were no guests.

Betty Lou Barber sat with her husband in the back pew. She could not understand what had happened. She had been gassing her car that afternoon at the mini-mart when she saw Jubal Lee leave his motel in his fully loaded silver and blue Suburban, pulling his matching enclosed horse trailer with *Jubal Lee Ministries* scripted on its side. He drove past her up the Interstate entrance ramp and headed west. Her mouth dropped. The man of fire was leaving. The fuel of God was gone. All her hopes, dreams, and plans for the church were sailing away. Her gas tank overflowed and gasoline splashed on her dress and shoes, staining them with a sickly-colored, foul-smelling residue.

Pastor Tom turned to Ezra. He knew about the incident in the jail cell, but he did not know Jubal Lee had left town. He thought that Jubal might show, that he would either stage his own justification or sincerely ask for forgiveness. Pastor Tom was a man of mercy. He held no ill feeling toward Walker. He wanted to see him healed and restored to ministry. "It's 7:10," he said. "What are we going to do?"

Ezra was stone-faced. "I'm going to introduce a guest speaker," he said. He rose, asked Darlene to go to the piano and Anne to take a stool prepared for her and her guitar.

"Five nights ago I was up here before you," he said, "to introduce a guest speaker. We certainly had an interesting week, didn't we? I don't believe any of us will ever be the same after our visit from Jubal Lee Walker.

"In the past week I have learned a lot about the power of God and the importance of freedom in praise and worship. I have also learned about accountability and commitment. I believe the main thing I have learned is that it is far safer to follow a man with character and few gifts, than a man with many gifts and no character. A man with character might obtain gifts. A gifted man will not necessarily learn to develop character.

"This evening I introduce a new speaker. A surprise speaker. He is a man of character, and a man with his own giftedness. I present to you, from Yellow Rock, Montana, Pastor Tom Jablonski."

Ezra extended his hand to Pastor Tom who sat stunned in his pew. A polite hand clapping from the congregation brought him to his feet and he stood embarrassed beside Ezra.

"This is indeed a new speaker," Ezra said, "because I present to you Pastor Tom Jablonski . . . without notes or sermon outlines." Ezra smiled, moved the microphone toward Pastor Tom, and sat down.

The pastor stood for several minutes staring at the red carpet on the sanctuary floor. His eyes moistened and his hands fidgeted at his side. He seemed soft and vulnerable when he finally looked out at his flock, yet he also looked like a bigger man.

"I don't know what to do without notes," he said nervously.

"Speak from your heart," Armon Barber shouted out.

Jablonski smiled weakly and nodded his head. "When Darlene and I came here two years ago," he began, "neither of us could speak from our hearts because they were too broken. We were probably in no shape to try to minister to anyone. I might have done okay if I had ministered out of my weakness, but I tried to minister from my strength. And I thought my strength was scholarship.

"I love you people. I wanted to touch you with the gospel, but I was afraid to touch you with my humanity. I tried sermon outlines and radio programs and newsletters, instead of just sitting down, having coffee, and sharing a prayer.

"Darlene and I are better people now. We learned a lot this week and much of it was upsetting to me and to my rigid beliefs. But I want you to know one thing: I thank God for Jubal Lee Walker, and I am glad the Lord brought him to this town."

The silence in the church was deep and respectful.

"I don't know what the future holds," Jablonski concluded, "but I want to tell all of you that it has been an honor to be your pastor." He stood awkwardly for a moment, like a man balancing himself in a small boat, then he stepped off the dais and returned to his pew.

Nobody said or did anything for a couple of minutes. Ezra could see tears glistening off both Anne's and Darlene's cheeks. Darlene left the piano and sat beside her husband. Ezra smiled at his wife. He was always telling her she cried too easily. She smiled back and cried some more. For another minute or two Ezra sat and he wondered what Jubal Lee would do in this situation. For with all of his faults, in the right environment and when in the right attitude, Jubal had truly known how to grasp the Lord's garment and beg His will. Jubal would wait and pray, Ezra decided. So he waited. In a few minutes he heard steps coming down the aisle and Ezra looked up to see Armon Barber standing at the microphone.

"I'm the president of the board of directors, I suppose," Armon said. "And I don't think we should wait for the annual meeting two weeks from now to make a decision on our pastor. Everyone who is on the church roll is here tonight. That's better attendance than we ever get for the meeting itself. I move that we give Pastor Tom our vote of confidence by a unanimous raising of our hands." He lifted his right hand in the air. All across the sanctuary hands slowly lifted until the final one, Betty Lou's, was in the air.

"Well, I guess that makes it official," Armon said. "I'll turn this back to our new preacher."

Tom Jablonski walked strongly back to the dais. His eyes were moist but his cheeks were dry. He did not seem surprised or humbled. He seemed fulfilled, as if he had just awakened from a bad dream and discovered that the sun was still shining, that birds still sang, that there was hope for tomorrow. "I want you to know," he said, and paused for effect. "That I can't sing. And I can't play the saxophone."

The room burst with a healthy, healing laughter.

"And I won't preach from outlines and notes again," he promised.

"Praise God!" someone shouted from the back.

Ezra Riley smiled, then laughed with the others, but in his mind he saw a long, lonesome stretch of highway and a silver and blue vehicle speeding toward a blazing red horizon. In the vessel was all the talent and charisma that any one man could ever hope for, and pursuing it, like a hound of heaven, was the certain destiny of judgment.

"God bless you, Jubal," Ezra said softly.

EPILOGUE

In the fall's soft rustling of the ivory grasses he heard the voice of God. Ezra Riley lay with his face turned to a pale canopy of October sky. The shadow of a single cumulus cloud lit upon him briefly, then whispered by, wavering over the land like a large butterfly wing. If its passing was ominous, he did not notice. It only cooled him momentarily as he relaxed in the lap of the soil.

Ezra felt nourished by the earth, rooted to origin and destiny by having his flesh upon its brown skin. He was a lover of the land and felt loved in return. He was not pantheistic in his passion, he was simply an earth person, as others are people of other elements, of sky and water. Perhaps even fire. He wondered who the fire people were. Rock stars? Satanists? Arsonists?

His other love, a horse, stood nearby, its head low and ears splayed, one hind leg bent in the posture of repose. Split leather reins trailed from the bridle's grazing bit across the blue gamma and slender wheatgrass to Ezra's hand. He held them loosely. Horses also represented the soil to Ezra. They walked the earth, slept on the earth, ate from the earth, fertilized the earth. He had heard theories that some men born of the prairie became wonderful sea captains, the waves of rolling grasses and endless sky graduating to waves of salt water and limitless horizons. He did not feel that way. The sea scared him. He needed something to put his feet on. He liked foundations, the feel of the substance in a world increasingly turbulent.

He reclined on a small crown of sod on the back side of the Riley ranch. The crown was an oasis of dry, waving grass in a fire-scorched desert of charred soil dotted with the sooted, bare stems of sagebrush. He was on the divide, where decisions were made, where the water ran one way or the other. The next day he would return to work at the Fort Kellogg Range and Livestock Experiment Station. *Or would he?* In New York, his manuscript was being read at Binghampton House by David and Amanda Silverstein. They had dropped him a short note, thanking him for sending it, saying they liked the title, telling him they would be in touch.

He watched the sky slowly dapple itself with puffy cumulus clouds. He felt a breeze skitter through the grasses and tickle his neck. He wondered to himself about his friend, Jubal Lee Walker. *Why was he the way he was? How could one born with such a sensitive soul turn so twisted? Why had God brought him to Yellow Rock?* Ezra did more than wonder about it. He agonized over it. *How could a man born from good stock, endowed with special gifts, authentically used by the Spirit of God, and so knowledgeable of Scripture become so deluded and dangerous? Was there a message for him in this experience with Jubal?* He had to know.

In the soft rustling of the ivory grasses he heard the voice of God.

The voice did not come from the heavens, it whistled softly through the dry stems, then up from the bottom reaches of his own soul. It was not audible, yet it was heard. It did not answer his questions, yet, it told him everything he needed to know.

"It could have been you, Ezra Riley," the voice said.

ABOUT THE AUTHOR

John L. Moore is an award-winning writer whose articles and short stories have been published in *The New York Times Magazine, Reader's Digest,* and many other publications. He received the Critic's Choice for Fiction Award from *Christianity Today* for *The Breaking of Ezra Riley* when it was first released in 1990.

His first novel from Thomas Nelson was *Bitter Roots. Leaving the Land* is a sequel to *The Breaking of Ezra Riley,* which we republished in 1994.

John lives with his wife, Debra, and their two children on a ranch near Miles City, Montana.